W9-COX-768

"I am choosing you to become mistress to the Sheikh."

He made it sound so...*mechanical.* "Is there a new vacancy, then?" Sienna questioned acidly. "Or will I be sharing the post?"

Hashim was so used to complete compliance—to grateful and eager acceptance from adoring women—that for a moment he was taken aback by her flippant attitude. "I do not think you realize the honor I am affording you," he said icily.

"No, I probably don't," said Sienna gravely. "Perhaps you could tell me a little more about what this exciting position entails?"

"You will have an open charge account." His black eyes flicked disparagingly over her jeans and stained T-shirt. "And in future you will buy clothes that please you, and please your Sheikh. I should like to see you in silks and satins from now on."

"How delightfully simple you make it sound," Sienna murmured. "Anything else?"

Introducing a brand-new miniseries

This is romance on the red carpet...

FOR LOVE OR MONEY is the ultimate reading experience for the reader who loves Harlequin Presents®, and who also has a taste for tales of wealth and celebrity and the accompanying gossip and scandal!

Look out for special covers
and
these upcoming titles:

Coming in October 2005:
His One-Night Mistress
by Sandra Field #2494

Coming in November 2005:
Sale or Return Bride
by Sarah Morgan #2500

Sharon Kendrick

EXPOSED: THE SHEIKH'S MISTRESS

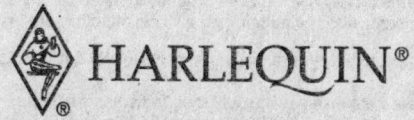

HARLEQUIN®

TORONTO • NEW YORK • LONDON
AMSTERDAM • PARIS • SYDNEY • HAMBURG
STOCKHOLM • ATHENS • TOKYO • MILAN • MADRID
PRAGUE • WARSAW • BUDAPEST • AUCKLAND

With special thanks to Paul McLaughlin, editor of Kroll's Report on Fraud—and a pretty mean writer himself!

ISBN 0-373-12488-0

EXPOSED: THE SHEIKH'S MISTRESS

First North American Publication 2005.

CHAPTER ONE

IF ONLY there had been some kind of warning…storm clouds gathering on the horizon, perhaps, or a sudden chill wind which iced your skin. Like an omen. But the day was sunny and golden with not an omen in sight, and 'if only' were the two most useless words in the language—Sienna knew that more than anyone.

And even if she had known—what could she have done that would have made things different? Nothing. She was as powerless as a leaf torn from its branch by a cruel autumn wind.

Yet her mood was light as she slipped into the back entrance of the Brooke Hotel, via the garden. The ivy-covered walkway was her favourite way into the building, for when you stood in the secret courtyard it was difficult to believe that you were right in the centre of London—with the hubbub and bustle of the busy streets only a stone's throw away.

Here the sounds of the city were muted and softened by the tall, waving branches of trees which acted as a haven for all kinds of birds. Bees buzzed drowsily around the flowers and little ladybirds landed on your bare flesh and sometimes nipped it if you weren't looking. These days she was essentially a city girl, but this place reminded her of a country childhood which seemed another world away.

Sienna loved the Brooke. It was where she had fled to. Where she had been promoted. Where she had made the slightly scary decision to go freelance—but the hotel still provided the bulk of her work. As an events organiser, she organised weddings, birthday parties, book launches and bar mitzvahs—and her name was becoming well-known on the busy London social circuit. From fairly humble and untrained beginnings, she had certainly landed on her feet.

And if she ever stopped to think how she'd got here... Well, that was the whole point—she didn't ever think about it. Thinking never got you anywhere. It took you to all kinds of dark and disturbing places and in the end it changed precisely nothing. In life you just had to learn from your mistakes. To get through the bad times in the hope that there would be some good ones waiting round the corner. And there were. Of course there were.

Today, the dark onyx reception desk was massed with startling orange Bird of Paradise flowers mixed in with black irises and red lilies. It was a dramatic look, and not one favoured by shrinking violets—but then those kind of people didn't tend to stay here.

Money and power and a hungry desire for something 'different' were the driving forces behind the screamingly influential clientele of the Brooke. Film-stars. Entrepreneurs. Royalty. Anyone who was anyone.

They all flocked to the converted eighteenth-century mansion where there was never an empty room. Where, as a client, you paid through the nose for luxury and discretion.

Sienna rode up in the penthouse elevator. She was meeting a Mr Altair, and before she met a client she always allowed herself a little daydream about just what kind of party they would want. A themed affair, perhaps? Like the time she had decked out a marquee to recreate a French circus—and had only just managed to persuade the trapeze artist not to flounce off in a huff because he hadn't had star billing!

Or the time she had crammed a ballroom with a thousand red roses for one of the most over-the-top engagement parties she had ever had a hand in.

Sienna smiled. Her job required that she had the organisational skills of an army general—combined with the smooth tongue of a career diplomat.

As the lift doors slid open, the door to the penthouse was opened by a tall, olive-skinned man. Some sixth sense should have told her then—but why would it? With his black eyes and the expensive suit which didn't *quite* disguise the gun in his breast pocket the man looked like any other foreign 'minder'. Which she supposed was the modern word for bodyguard—and she came across plenty of those in this line of work.

'Hello.' She smiled. 'My name is Sienna Baker and I have an appointment with Mr Altair.'

A flicker of something she couldn't quite put her

finger on passed over his impassive features, but he merely nodded and pushed the door to the apartment open. He stood by to let her pass but did not follow her inside, and as the door clicked shut behind her Sienna felt inexplicably apprehensive. As if she was closed in. Trapped. Though agoraphobia would be the last thing she should be suffering from in a room of these dimensions.

She looked around her, her senses swamped by the sudden crowding of different sensations which began to jostle for supremacy in her mind.

For a moment she was dazzled by the sheer impact of the light which spilled in from the enormous windows, and she screwed her eyes up in confusion as the faintest trace of a disturbingly familiar scent began to drift towards her. The exotic smell both tantalised her and began to make her stomach twist painfully, and she couldn't work out why.

And then she saw the man standing completely still with his back to her, silhouetted against the London skyline—tall and dark and lean and proud, as if he had been carved from some black and unforgiving rock—and Sienna felt the blood drain from her face as he moved, like a statue coming to life.

She sucked in a breath of disbelief as her eyes flickered over him, her mind screaming out its protest as she began to register every detail about him. The slick black hair with the faint wave to it. The broad shoulders and the long legs. The arrogant and autocratic stance. Oh, please, no. Please. No. But now the scent which pervaded the suite became more understandable—and wasn't smell supposed to be the most evocative of all the senses?

Did she whimper or make a sound? Was that why he had begun to turn around? And now the breath caught in her throat as she began to issue a silent and heartfelt prayer. She prayed like she hadn't done for a long, long time, since she had been begging some mysterious presence to take the pain away. If no one had been listening then, then let them be listening now.

Don't let it be him. Oh, please don't let it be him. But her heart plummeted like a stone as he turned to face her.

Hashim surveyed her with cold and glittering black eyes, acknowledging the heavy stab of desire in his loins with a grim kind of pleasure, remembering the splayed abandon of her legs the last time he had seen her, and the aching only increased.

He had long denied himself this moment because he had told himself that he could, but in the end desire had proved irresistible. Hashim despised the weakness which made him want her, yet he embraced it, too. And he intended to savour every moment of it. This woman who had deceived him would pay, and she would pay with her body!

He let the narrowed ebony gleam of his eyes linger on her figure, to see if time had marred its perfection, but it was as firm and as lushly slim as a prized young

Saluki—the silky-sleek hunting dogs much favoured by the tribes of his native land.

It was hard to pin down what made her quite so desirable—for hers was not a fashionable look. She was too petite and curvy for modern tastes, yet her body was to die for. And if you added to that the ingredients of innocence and sensuality...

Innocence!

Hashim's mouth hardened as he thought of what a sham appearances could be.

He let his gaze drift upwards, to her face. How white her skin was, he observed with impartial interest—and how contrasting the deep rose of her lips. Ah, those lips! One of the very first things he had noticed about her had been her natural pout, which some women spent thousands of dollars at plastic surgeons trying to recreate.

Now those same lips trembled under his scrutiny, and he longed to crush their petal softness beneath the hard, seeking warmth of his own. But that would have to wait...and the waiting would only increase his eventual pleasure.

'Sienna,' he murmured as the warm throb of blood beat between his legs.

The way he said it took her back to somewhere which was out of bounds, and her heart buckled with pain as she stared at the man she had once believed herself to be in love with.

He was both ugly and beautiful, his face unique—defined by hard contours and the ravages of warfare.

An exotic, foreign face. The cruel beak of a nose and harsh slash of his mouth only added to his allure, and those clever black eyes could make a woman feel as if he was slowly stripping her bare...

Seeing him again was a moment she had lived out in her mind over and over again—though not much lately, it was true. But wasn't it simply human nature to wonder how she would react if ever she saw him again? As time had passed she had convinced herself that the sobbing wreck of her early days had been replaced by a confident woman who would give him a cool smile and say, *Hashim! Well, long time no see!*

How wrong she had been. How very wrong and how very *stupid*. As if any woman could look at a man like that without wanting to melt into a helpless puddle of longing at his feet. But the longing was eclipsed by another emotion, and that was wariness...or was it *fear*? What the hell was he doing here?

'Hashim,' she whispered, like someone waking from a long dream. 'Is it really you?'

'It really is.' His hard eyes mocked her, enjoying her discomfiture in a way he had not enjoyed anything for a long time. 'You seem surprised, Sienna.'

'Surprise implies something pleasant,' she said shakily.

He arched heavy black brows in sardonic query. 'And this is not?'

'Of course it's not!' Nervously, she flicked her tongue over her lips to moisten them, and then wished she hadn't, for his black eyes were drawn to the movement as a snake to the charmer's pipe. 'I'm shocked—like anyone would be.'

'I disagree—a lot of women might be delighted to see a man who had once featured in their lives, but I guess it's different in your case.'

Her eyes pleaded with him to stop, but he did not, and his hard mouth twisted into a cruel imitation of a smile.

'I expect your past is always coming back to unsettle you in all kinds of ways—but you have only yourself to blame, my dear. If you didn't keep so many unsavoury secrets, then you might be able to sleep a little easier.' He allowed his eyes to linger on the exquisite swell of her breasts and the swift shaft of desire became blunted with the memory of betrayal. His mouth hardened. 'Though I can't imagine any man letting *you* sleep easy at night.' Except maybe him. The mad, duped fool who had protected her and respected her. Who had cherished her as if she had been a delicate and priceless piece of porcelain.

And then seen her crushed into smithereens before his eyes.

But he was a fool no more...that day had gone...never to return.

Sienna wanted to tell him not to stare at her that way, but she knew if she did that then he would do it all the more. He was not a man to be thwarted or dictated to, and in his hard black eyes was the glitter of danger. She swallowed, terrified to ask the question because of what the answer might be. Until she told herself that this was just some horrible, unfortunate coincidence—it had to be…

Or was it? Suddenly she wasn't so sure. Did anything ever happen completely by chance?

'What are you doing here, Hashim?'

He thought how easily his name came to her lips. How little she realised the honour accorded to her by being able to speak it so freely where most women would dip their eyes in deference! Even the sophisticated women in his life—and there had been many—had always been slightly in awe of his power and position. He stared at her, and the anticipation of what he was about to do made his blood sing with pleasure. 'You know very well why I am here,' he reprimanded silkily.

For a second her world was suspended in a moment of disbelief as she was frozen by the stark sensual intent in his eyes. And it was as if just that one sizzling look had begun something which her unresisting body was powerless to stop. She shook her head, trying to stop the stealthy and hated shiver of desire. 'No, I don't.'

'Shame on you, Sienna—is this how you always react when you are booked in to have a business meeting? You are being paid to organise a party for me—remember?'

His soft, mocking words made her throat close over with fear and she swallowed it down. There was no way she could have any kind of meeting with him—business or otherwise. He must know that!

'No!' she said, as calmly as she could. But as she shook her head the heavy weight of her piled-up hair wobbled, as if itching to cascade down her back. 'That's not what I meant, and you know it!' She looked around her with slight desperation, as if any minute now she would suddenly wake up and discover that the whole incident had been some ghastly nightmare. 'I'm supposed to be meeting a Mr Altair! Not you.'

He gave a cold smile. 'But "Mr Altair" *is* me, Sienna. Didn't you realise?' His smile grew even colder, even though the undulating movement of her hair made him ache to unpin it and set it free. Free to tumble onto the warm nakedness of his chest. And his belly...

'Altair is one of my many aliases,' he drawled. 'Surely I used it when I knew you?'

'No,' she whispered. 'No, you didn't.'

'Ah. So much changes with the passage of time, does it not, Sienna? What else has changed, I wonder?'

She felt like a woman who had woken up in an alien place, where all the rules of survival had changed, and she knew that she had to take control—not just of herself but of the situation, too. She was no longer a young girl, besotted and completely fixated by a man who was light-years away from her in terms of experience. The wrong man, she reminded herself painfully.

With an effort, she gave him a smile. A rueful, grown-up smile. 'Look, Hashim, I presume that now you've seen me you've changed your mind. We aren't going to be able to do this—you know we aren't.'

His eyes glittered with provocation. 'To what... precisely...do you refer? What aren't we going to be able to *do*, Sienna?'

She didn't rise to the sexual taunt. If she kept it on a business level then she might be safe—but if she allowed the discussion to stray into the personal or— even worse—the past, then she really was in danger.

'But what are you doing here?' she questioned, still with the last vague hope that things were not what they seemed. 'When you always stay at the Granchester?'

'Maybe I find that the memories there are too tainted,' he mocked. 'Or maybe I find that I just can't resist the attractions on offer here...' Once again he let his eyes linger with insolent hunger on the swell of her magnificent breasts. 'Your...reputation in the capital is growing, Sienna,' he added silkily.

She didn't suppose he was alluding to her backlog of satisfied clients. It was not a compliment at all, but a thinly veiled insult, implying...implying... Oh, she knew damn well what he was implying! Feeling as though her lungs had been scorched, she sucked in a breath to steady herself. 'But presumably you're not expecting me to work with you,' she said quietly.

He gave a heady, husky laugh of anticipation. 'For an employee you sure as hell make a lot of presumptions. It could get you into a lot of trouble if you're not careful.'

She had forgotten what a curious mixture he was, of the ancient and the modern, the forward-thinking and the ludicrously old-fashioned. He was one of the most intelligent men she had ever met—so why the hell was he deliberately misunderstanding her reservations? 'Oh, Hashim—don't be so...dense!'

'Dense?' He tilted his chin imperiously and his eyes narrowed into glittering ebony shards. 'You dare to address *me*—a *sheikh*—in such a way?'

In the past he had never pulled rank—but then he hadn't needed to. She hadn't cared about his position—hadn't even known about it to start with. And by the time she did it hadn't mattered. Or at least she'd thought it hadn't—but that was yet another indication of just how out of her depth she had been. Because of course it had.

It had mattered a lot.

CHAPTER TWO

SHE should never have met him, of course, for theirs were two such different paths in life—destined never to cross. But country girls sometimes went to live in big cities and became receptionists in super-smart hotels—the kind of places where you bumped into real-live sheikhs when you were on your way to work. Just like a fairy tale. And sometimes the fairy tale came true—but what it was easy to forget was that there was always a dark side to the story.

Sienna had gone to London for the usual reasons—and then some more. In the midst of crisis she had needed money and a solution. And after that... Well, after that she had needed to forget. And, as well as offering her anonymity, the big city had also offered her the opportunity to work her way up the ladder in the hotel industry—and to live rent-free in one of the most expensive parts of London. A perk which had made up for the long and unsociable hours.

The first time she had seen Hashim, Sienna had been on her way to the hotel for a late shift. It had been a beautiful day, and she'd been enjoying the sunshine.

She'd been wearing nothing out of the ordinary—a floaty kind of summer dress—but her hair had been down and she'd walked with the unconscious vigour of youth. In her daydream she'd barely noticed the slight commotion of people milling around the dark-windowed limousine of the world-renowned Granchester Hotel.

And then she had seen the figure emerging from the car. He'd been tall, with a natural autocratic poise, dressed in a coolly pale suit which had made the dark olive of his skin look so silken. It had gleamed soft gold and contrasted with the hard ebony glitter of his eyes.

For a split-second as they'd looked at one another it had been like something out of one of the old-fashioned films she'd always been a sucker for. As if she had been waiting all her life to see just that man looking at her in just that intent and interested way. His eyes had narrowed as a bodyguard had shot an arm out in front of her, bringing her to a halt.

'What do you think you're doing?' she had protested, and the man had smiled a hard kind of smile, and then said something in a husky tongue which was foreign to her.

'Let her pass,' he clipped out, as if he was translating the command for her benefit, and the bodyguard grunted and moved aside. Sienna inclined her head.

'Thank you.' She walked off down the road, somehow aware that the black eyes watched her, burning into her back, branding her with their strange exotic power.

And then, a few weeks later, he came into the hotel and Sienna just froze.

He looked…she swallowed…he looked so vibrant…so *different*—as if someone had plucked a bright and very exotic bloom and placed it in a vase of white flowers. She could see people in the foyer giving him sly little glances, and others—women— giving not so shy ones. And his two bodyguards— ever-present in the background, solid as a brick wall and silently sending out messages to *keep away*.

Experience had made Sienna wary of men, and so her unexpected reaction to this one took her by surprise. When desire had never really touched you it was a bit earth-shattering when it did. 'Um, um…' She could feel her cheeks growing pink. How unprofessional! 'I mean, good morning, sir.'

Hashim's eyes narrowed with interest. It was the girl with the green eyes and the body! And what a body!

Carelessly, he flicked his hand to indicate that the bodyguards should remain where they were, and he moved forward to the desk himself, fully aware of the impact he was making as he stared down into her face. 'Hello again,' he said softly.

His accent was silky, rich and deep, and the tiny blush which had begun deepened to heat her cheeks. Her heart thumping in her chest as if it had just discovered how to beat, Sienna jabbed her finger at the booking diary. 'Can I…can I help you, sir?'

The side of him which had been indulged from the

cradle wanted to lower his head and whisper that, yes, she could spend the afternoon in bed with him—but her innocent blush meant that he had unconsciously moved her into a category of women with whom it was not acceptable to flirt outrageously.

'I am meeting one of your guests here for lunch,' he said instead.

'And the guest's name, sir?' she questioned, looking down at her booking list and wishing she could stop blushing.

He gave it, and saw her eyes widen—for the politician he was meeting was well known, and Hashim knew very well the potency of power and connections. He had lived with them all his life.

'He's waiting at the table, sir. I'll take you in to join him.'

She stood up to show him the way, and he enjoyed following her into the restaurant, so that he could watch her unobserved.

She was not tall, but he liked that—for he believed that a woman should look up to a man—and although her hips were narrow, her bottom was as curved as her breasts, and designed to be cupped by the warmth of a man's hand.

But it was her green eyes, shaped like almonds, and the pinkness of her cheeks and the rose pout of her lips which stayed in his mind. During lunch he gestured for one of his guards to approach, lowering his head to give an instruction in his native tongue, and the guard was dispatched to the reception desk to acquire her phone number.

But Sienna refused to give it. What a cheek—sending his henchman! And in a way it just confirmed her rather jaundiced view of men. She wished she could go on her break right then, but it wasn't for ages, and when he came out of the restaurant she was still sitting there.

She looked straight through him, as if he wasn't there—something which had never happened to him before. But he was too intrigued to be outraged, and some alien emotion directed his steps towards her.

'You wouldn't give me your phone number,' he mused.

'You didn't ask me.'

'And was that such an unforgivable sin?' he teased.

She turned her head away, unsure how to cope with him, this powerfully built and exotic man who was making her feel things she wasn't used to feeling.

'What is your name?' he asked, without warning, and she turned back to find herself imprisoned in the blazing ebony spotlight of his eyes.

'Sienna,' she whispered, as if he had sucked the word clean out of her, without her permission.

'Sienna,' he repeated softly, and nodded. 'So, are you going to have dinner with me, Sienna?'

Somewhere in the recess of her mind was the thought that staff *definitely* weren't supposed to fraternise with the guests—until she remembered that he wasn't actually a guest. And even further back was another thought—that she was rather good at getting out of her depth. 'I'm not sure.'

'Why not?' he questioned softly.

'Because I don't even know your name.'

'Ah! Did not one of your finest poets once ask: "What's in a name?"' His black eyes narrowed. 'My name is Sheikh Hashim Al Aswad.'

Sheikh? *Sheikh?* Something in his eyes made her stare at him, aghast. 'You're not really a sheikh, are you?'

'I'm afraid I am,' he replied gravely.

Sienna stared up at him. Now his dark looks and foreign air and the unmistakable aura of authority made sense. 'But what on earth would I wear?'

And he laughed. 'It doesn't matter,' he said truthfully. 'You are so young and so beautiful that you would look wonderful in anything.' Or nothing, of course.

That night he took her to a restaurant which overlooked the silver snake of the river which wound its way through the city. The stars outside seemed close enough to touch. And the evening felt magical enough for Sienna to feel that she could.

She had thought she might feel awkward and out of her depth, but instead she was so—*excited*, and determined to enjoy every second of it. Even the simple little cotton dress she chose seemed okay, because her thick dark hair reached almost to her waist, and she wore it loose and saw the narrow-eyed look of approval he gave and knew she'd got it just right.

It felt like an old-fashioned date was supposed to feel. Hashim ignored the fact that there were two armed bodyguards seated a few tables away, and more outside. This felt different, and he wasn't quite sure why. Because she seemed so transparently innocent?

'So tell me about yourself,' he instructed.

Sienna hesitated, wondering where to begin. Was this true lives or true confessions? She had once done something she didn't feel too great about—but that one-off act didn't define her as a person, surely? She'd probably never see him again after tonight—so why let him in on a secret which might ruin the evening?

She thought about what a man born to a sheikhdom would most like to hear. Well, she couldn't compete on a material front, that was for sure! She leaned forward and clasped her hands on the starched linen tablecloth, and tried to paint a picture of a very different life.

'I grew up in a little village. You know—a proper English village, with lambs gambolling around the meadows in the springtime and cherry blossom on the trees.'

'And in summer?'

'It rained!' She wriggled her shoulders. 'Well, actually, it didn't—it just seems to now, whenever I go back. But maybe that's because I'm an adult now. When I was little the sun always seemed to be shining and golden.' She stared into his face, thinking that she had never seen eyes quite so black. 'I suppose that most people's childhoods are like that. We view them through rose-tinted glasses.'

He thought not. Certainly his own had been nothing like that, but he would not describe it, nor compare the two. He would not have dreamed of expressing his own thoughts about growing up. Privacy was second nature to him and always had been—drilled into him from the very beginning. Instead, he picked up on the wisftfulness in her voice. 'If it was so idyllic, then why did you leave?'

Sienna fiddled with her napkin. 'Birds need to fly the nest.'

'Indeed they do.' His eyes narrowed. 'And is life outside the nest all you dreamed it would be?'

Sienna hesitated. It could be scary. It gave you opportunities, and they could be scarier still. 'Well, you gain freedom, of course—but you lose stability. I guess that's what life is like, though—gains and losses—hopefully it all balances out in the end.'

'You have a very wise head on such young shoulders,' he said gravely.

'You're making fun of me.'

'No.' He shook his head and gave a gentle smile. 'No, I am not. I find your attitude quite charming, if you must know. How old *are* you, by the way?'

Would he think her too young? *Too young for what, Sienna?* 'Nearly twenty.'

But he smiled. 'Only nearly?' he teased.

'Now you,' she said. 'What on earth do sheikhs *do*?'

His mouth twitched. She really *was* irresistible. 'Sometimes I ask myself the very same question. Mainly, they rule a country, and that involves much fighting and the quest for power—but they also oversee oil exports, which is why I am here.' *And they are surrounded by a wealth that most people couldn't begin to comprehend.* Especially not her.

Sienna crumbled a piece of unwanted bread. 'So where's home?'

For a moment he said nothing, and then gave an odd kind of smile. 'Qudamah is my home—but I come from a race of nomadic people.' His black eyes glittered. 'We do not settle easily.'

If she had been older she would have recognised that he was defining boundaries—but as it was his romantic words simply fired up her already over-working imagination.

Later, in the darkened limousine, his hard thigh brushed against hers and Sienna could hardly breathe. But there was no kiss, merely the request—no, the *demand* that he see her again.

It all happened so fast—Hashim's life slipped into a different timescale and he found himself experiencing something which was unknown to him: a tumult of feelings which he was too seasoned and too cynical to call love. Yet his ancestors had been poets and sages, as well as warriors, and he was prepared to acknowledge that somehow Sienna touched a part of him which had before gone neglected. It was as if her innocence and her beauty had begun a slow melt of something he had not known was frozen.

Maybe it was his heart.

She trembled when he kissed her, and he could feel the tension of both eagerness and fear when he took her in his arms. It seemed unbelievable—given her age and her liberal Western upbringing—but something told him that his instinct was correct.

One evening his eyes burned into her as he stared down into her flushed face. 'You are innocent of men?' he demanded.

'Yes,' she admitted in a low voice, wondering if that admission would drive him away from her. 'Yes, I am.'

'Innocent virgin,' he moaned as he kissed her. '*My* innocent virgin.'

Of course that changed everything. The knowledge of her purity filled him with delight, but there was also the certainty that he now bore a heavy responsibility towards her. For a man whose life had been burdened with responsibility, it was another he could have done without—and yet he found himself embracing it.

He saw her whenever he could, wondering if the frequency of their meetings would remove some of the magic, but the magic remained. He had spent his life avoiding any kind of commitment, yet now he saw that as a deficiency, not a blessing.

He took her to discreet restaurants and she showed

him the hidden, secret places of the city. She made him feel alive. Never before had sex been denied him, but this was a self-imposed restraint, and he discovered that doing without something you really wanted could be unbearably erotic.

And yet her innocence made her suitable. Eminently suitable. Of course many bridges must first be crossed, and the first of those would be to introduce her to his family. But without pressure on either side. On neutral territory.

'How would you like to accompany me to a wedding, sweet Sienna?' he asked her one afternoon, looping his arms around her waist.

Sienna looked up into his black eyes. 'Whose? Where? When?'

'My cousin's,' he murmured. 'In the South of France, next month. My mother and sisters will be there.' He glittered a smile at her. 'Will you come as my guest?'

Sienna knew that this was important. A statement. An indication that things were getting serious. She gave him a slow smile of delight. 'I'd love to,' she said simply.

Hashim spoke to one of his aides. 'Will you arrange it, please?'

'But, Your Highness, you are quite sure?'

Hashim frowned. He would not be dictated to! The history of his country was studded with examples of sheikhs who had taken commoners as wives...

But a couple of days later there was a rap on the

door when he was working in his study, and Hashim looked up to see the Arctic dark eyes of his equerry, who was carrying what looked like a glossy magazine between his fingers, as if it was contaminated.

'Yes, what is it, Abdul-Aziz?' he demanded imperiously. 'I am going out shortly.'

His equerry's face was grim. 'Before you do, Your Highness, there is something I must draw your attention to.'

For the umpteenth time, Sienna raked her hands back through her hair—fizzing over with a mixture of excitement and nerves.

Hashim was sending a car for her and they were having dinner at the Granchester Hotel, where he was staying.

She was still reeling from his invitation to the family wedding—so excited at the prospect of going public with him that she hadn't had time to worry about what she was going to say to his mother.

She would just be herself, without artifice or airs, for that was who Hashim liked her to be. She gave herself a little shiver of excitement as she walked up the imposing marble stairs of the Granchester Hotel.

But Hashim was not there to greet her, and neither were any of his staff. Not even the hatchet-faced Abdul-Aziz. Instead, she got a message delivered with a rather knowing look from the receptionist as she was directed up to his suite.

It isn't the way you think it is! Sienna wanted to

say to her. *Hashim has never treated me with anything but respect!* But as she rode up in the private lift which led to the penthouse she wondered why he had changed the pattern of their meetings.

Hashim opened the door himself, and Sienna was taken aback when she saw him—for she had never seen him dressed like this before. Tonight he looked exactly as she had imagined a sheikh *would* look.

Gone were the immaculate hand-made suits he usually favoured—which contrasted with his exotic looks and made him such a tantalising combination of East and West. Instead he was wearing a pair of filmy silk trousers in a deep claret colour, with a silky top in the same material. The rich hue made the most of his exotic colouring, and Sienna felt the roof of her mouth dry—for he was barefoot and the shirt was open, and through it she could see his olive hair-roughened chest, darkened with contours of muscle and sinew.

She had never been confronted quite so vividly by his overt masculinity before, and her heart gave a startled little leap as she found herself wondering if he was actually wearing any underwear at all.

But it was more than his state of undress which unsettled her—for his eyes looked *dangerous* tonight. Steely and brittle. Like jet. Something stopped her from hurling herself into his arms in the breathless way which always made him laugh—and she wasn't sure whether it was excitement or fear. But why on earth would she be frightened?

'You look beautiful tonight, Sienna,' he said deliberately.

Were nerves getting the better of her, or was there an odd undertone to his voice? 'Thank you. I—' But her words were lost beneath the hard, heady pressure of his mouth, for he had pulled her into his arms without warning and had begun to kiss her in a way which took her breath away. 'Hashim!' she gasped.

Her mouth opened up beneath his and it was enough to ignite all the fire and the fury which had been smouldering away inside him. He kissed her until she was melting and aching and moaning beneath his seasoned touch, and only then did he lift his head and glitter a hard, bright question down at her.

'Hashim…what?' he questioned huskily, moving his mouth to her throat to trace a featherlight kiss along its silken path.

It would be madness to protest that he had never kissed her like this before—not when she had spent hours wondering why.

'Oh-oh-oh!' She shuddered as he lightly drifted his hand over her breast.

A grim, silent smile of triumph curved his hard lips as his fingertips returned to whisper over their pert lushness. 'Oh, what, Sienna?' came the silken query. 'Is that good?'

'Oh! *Oh!*' she gasped. 'So good!'

A tiny pulse flickered in the centre of one tensed olive cheek. 'Tell me what it is you want,' he grated.

Instinct took over from reservation and sent the

words spilling out of their own accord. 'That,' she sighed, as his fingers brushed fleetingly against the aching mounds of her breasts. 'That's what I want!'

He cupped the magnificent swell in his hand and rubbed a slow and deliberate circle with his thumb. 'Like *this*, you mean?'

She nodded as pleasure constricted her throat into a tight, dry band.

'I can't hear you, Sienna,' he urged softly.

'Yes,' she moaned. 'Yes! Just like that. Oh, Hashim…'

How he had misjudged her! Oh, yes! He could feel her responsive body pressing close to his, and knew that if he put his hand up her skirt she would not stop him. How far would she let him go in public? Would she let him unzip himself and plunge right in? Probably.

'You want that I should make love to you by the lift?' he demanded hotly.

In some dim recess of her mind she was aware that he sounded almost…*harsh*…*disapproving*… But maybe that was because he had been holding back for so long. Didn't they say that men had difficulty controlling their sexual hunger? Sienna drew back and swallowed breathlessly, lifting the palm of her hand to touch his rugged face, but it looked oddly cold and forbidding. Obviously he was holding himself tightly in check and she must not make him wait any longer—he had played the gentleman to her heart's content. It was time.

'Let's go to bed,' she whispered daringly.

His mouth hardened. 'Yes,' agreed Hashim, in an odd kind of voice. 'Why don't we?'

Without warning he shut the door with an echoing slam, then picked her up and carried her towards a vast double bed which was covered with a lavish embroidered gold coverlet.

'Fit for a king!' Sienna murmured with delight, but there was no answering smile in his eyes as he put her down on it.

'Only a sheikh this time, I'm afraid,' he responded tonelessly. 'Are you disappointed?'

She wanted to ask him if something was wrong, but by then he had come to lie down beside her and her last reservations melted away.

'Now, then,' he said decisively, and began to unbutton her dress, a pure feral smile of hunger emphasising the deep lines around his mouth. 'Ah…' He sucked in a slow breath of pleasure as her breasts were revealed to him, spilling lushly pale from the pink lace which confined them. 'So firm. So tight. So taut. Like two rich, ripe fruits. Beautiful. So very, very beautiful. You have the most beautiful breasts that I have ever seen, Sienna. What a lucky man I am.'

Something in his words unsettled her—but any slight anxiety she experienced was allayed with the expert motion of his fingertips, and Sienna closed her eyes.

'Yes,' he murmured approvingly. 'Lie back and enjoy it.'

Oh, but he was so thoughtful. Beneath that steely exterior he cared for her own pleasure first and foremost. She felt him unclip her bra and give a shuddering sigh. Her eyelashes fluttered open and she surprised a look of almost...*reluctance*...on his face. But then he lowered his head towards her and she could feel the approaching warmth of his breath.

'Hashim...' She swallowed. She wasn't sure that he'd heard her. 'Hashim,' she said again, almost desperately this time, for more than anything she wanted him to kiss her, to whisper sweet words to accompany these erotic gestures.

'Shh,' he instructed silkily, for he knew from experience that conversation could break the mood and concentration. He knew what he wanted and he was going to allow nothing—*nothing*—to stop him from achieving it.

Sienna squirmed on the cold coverlet and the expert movement of his hands made her need for reassurance vanish. Her breasts had never felt like this before. As if they had swollen to twice their normal size and were prickling with excitement—the blood coursing through them so that the slightest touch sent shafts of pure pleasure spiralling through her. She squealed as his tongue licked against the sensitised flesh.

'You are very responsive for one so...*innocent*,' he observed against her puckered nipple.

Another shaft of pleasure so acute that it bordered

on pain shot through her, and she was aware of an empty, echoing longing, just crying out to be filled. 'A-am I?'

'Yes, you are. And now you will be more responsive still….'

Sienna's breath caught in her throat, for his hand was moving downwards now, inching towards the heated clamour—the very heart of where she most wanted to be touched—and Sienna silently prayed that he wouldn't stop.

'I won't,' he said roughly, and she realised that she must have spoken the words out loud.

'Hashim,' she whispered, letting her lips rest against the soft furnace of his skin. 'Hashim, I love you.'

For a moment he stilled, then shook his head very slightly, silencing her with his expert caress. He touched her molten and responsive heat with such delicate skill until she gasped in disbelief—like someone frantically seeking something only not quite sure what. Restlessly, her head moved from side to side as she stumbled towards a place of promise so beautiful that she was certain it could not really exist.

But it did. Oh, it did. She found it and fell into it, sobbing out her fulfilment, scarcely aware of Hashim pulling away from her. But, as reason and sanity began to seep back in, she realised that he was getting off the bed and moving away.

Over to the other side of the room and as far away from her as possible!

She blinked as she struggled to catch her breath. 'Hashim?' she croaked in confusion. 'Is anything wrong?'

'Wrong?' He paused before answering her question, sucking in a deep breath as he sought—successfully—to bring his desire under control, to be replaced with the slow simmer of rage. 'I think that we're through with playing games, don't you?'

Sienna sat up on the bed, aware that her clothing was in disarray, feeling somehow cheapened as she stared into the forbidding mask of his face. A Hashim she'd never seen before, and one she barely recognised. 'Why are you behaving like this?' she questioned in bewilderment. 'Don't you…don't you want to make love to me? Properly?'

'You think I would deign to contaminate myself by *entering* you?' he questioned insultingly. 'You who have fooled me!'

'I don't have a clue what you're talking about!' But some self-protective instinct made her begin to button her dress with trembling fingers.

'The sweet little virgin!' he ground out furiously. 'Like hell you are! Sweet little virgins don't take their clothes off and pose for pornographic photos!'

And then it all became horribly, horribly clear. That calendar. Those twelve photos. Oh, those wretched, wretched photos.

Sienna flinched and let out a shuddering sigh. 'You've seen them?'

Had there perhaps been some insane part of him

which had been hoping that it was all a mistake—that she had a secret identical sister waiting in the wings, perhaps? Because, if so, that futile thought was banished by the look of guilt on her face.

His hopes and dreams for what might have been now crumbled before his eyes like desert dust as he realised his mistake. He had believed her to be the woman he *wanted* her to be, not the woman she really was. He had been sucked in by her beauty and her air of innocence. Oh, what a fool he had been!

'Yes, I've seen them!' he grated, remembering that he had been about to introduce her to his family! That he had actually been entertaining thoughts of her as a future bride. Fool!

'Hashim—please—it isn't how it looks,' she said desperately.

She had agreed to do the calendar as a one-off to get her mother the operation she'd needed. Her mother had been crippled with pain and facing ruin, and the badly needed operation had been expensive. It had been an unconventional way to get the money, yes—but the only way which had been open to her at the time. And surely if Hashim realised how *desperate* she had felt. How *hopeless* her mother's predicament…

'Please, Hashim…I can explain—'

'What? How you came to be rubbing your breasts and simulating *orgasm*?' he cut in brutally, but despite his disgust he nevertheless felt the hard leap of desire. For even though their existence destroyed any future between them, he was not hypocritical enough to deny that they were magnificent photographs. 'You think that there is any acceptable explanation for *that*?' he snapped.

'It isn't—'

But his rage was such that he barely heard her. 'On the head of my camel you are a magnificent actress—I commend you for that! You have succeeded in fooling me. And you have lied to me,' he added bitterly, remembering the way she had told him that she was a virgin—and that she *loved* him.

'I did not lie to you! I just...' She looked at him and shrugged her shoulders helplessly. 'Couldn't think of the right time to tell you.'

'But there would never have been a right time! In my culture, such conduct from the consort to the Sheikh would be utterly repellent—surely you must have known that?'

Sienna stared at him. Of course she had. Was that another reason why she had buried it away? As if by doing that she could pretend it had never happened? So that she wouldn't have to face the repercussions of her actions? Could carry on living in her little fantasy world with Hashim—untouched by the past and untroubled by the future? But had she ever imagined that the outcome would be any different from this? That there would be some magical, fairy-tale solution despite what she'd done?

No. Hashim would never forgive her.

The reality of seeing the contempt in his black eyes

was almost too much to bear, and Sienna stood up and picked up her shoes, her hair falling down over her face, concealing her pain from him.

But she paused by the door, lifting her gaze to his, unable to suppress the tiny flicker of hope which stubbornly refused to die.

'Is that it, then, Hashim? Is it…over?'

'Over?' His mouth hardened, for he wanted to wound her. To hurt her as she had hurt him. To destroy her dreams as she had destroyed his. 'I think you forget yourself. Did you ever expect that it would be anything other than a very temporary diversion?' he questioned imperiously. 'For I am the Sheikh and you are but a commoner.' His made his final thrust. 'A true commoner.'

CHAPTER THREE

How painful the past could be.

But as the mists of memory cleared, and Sienna looked into Hashim's steely black eyes, the pain came flooding back as if the years in between had never happened.

She remembered the way she had stumbled from his suite that evening, the tears beginning to slip from beneath her eyelids. Somehow she had made it home and howled into her pillow like a wounded animal. She had never known that it was possible to cry that much. Or to hurt that much. To be revolted by the thought of food and want only to sleep—but sleep had never seemed to come, and when it had, it mocked her with images of the dark face she had grown to love so much.

For the first and only time in her life she had understood the meaning of the word heartbreak—and she never wanted to experience it again.

It had taken her countless months to put her life back on track, to rejoin the human race. But a lot had changed since then—and most importantly *she* had changed. She was no longer the innocent young girl who didn't have a clue about life or how to handle men.

Just keep telling yourself that, she thought, with

more than a hint of desperation as she met his glittering stare.

'You're remembering the last time we saw each other,' he observed, an odd kind of note in his voice.

Had her face given her away? Maybe he had read in it her vulnerability and her anguish. 'How could I not?' she questioned, trying to keep her voice from shaking. 'I only have to look at you and it all comes flooding back.'

He stared at her and his black eyes were as hard as jet. Did she imagine that it was any different for him? He felt the hard leap of desire. 'So it does,' he agreed softly.

'Maybe we should try a joint counselling session,' she suggested, trying to keep it light. 'You know— like people who want to stop smoking.'

How flippant she sounded, he thought—and how cynical. Were those traits that she had kept cleverly hidden from him? And why not? Had she not been a woman adept in the art of concealment? 'But maybe I'm not ready to stop,' he said deliberately.

Sienna felt an odd kind of lump in her throat, and something both seductive and yet infinitely threatening hovered unseen and unspoken in the air. Now her voice did tremble. 'And wh—what's that supposed to mean?'

'Well, at least for you it was a…how shall I put this?' A cruel kind of smile lifted the corners of his lips. 'A satisfying encounter.'

His implication was very plain and very insulting, but it wasn't even true—or at least not in the way that mattered. Maybe in one sense it had been satisfying—on a purely physical level, yes—but on an emotional one it had been as barren as one of the deserts in his homeland. Fulfilment without tenderness was never satisfying for a woman, and it had left her empty—as if he'd ripped out an essential part of her and carried it off with him. 'Is that how you would describe it?' she questioned bleakly.

'Wouldn't you?' he mocked.

'Not really, no.' She looked into the cold black eyes and knew that he would never understand in a million years—nor even want to try. Why would he? Sienna shook her head, hoping to drive away some of the sadness. 'Anyway, what's the point in discussing it? Things have moved on.'

His face remained impassive, but inside he felt the flicker of anger mixed into a potent cocktail with sexual hunger and anticipation. She had fooled him once, but never again! Did she really think for a moment that now that he had her in his sights he was about to let her go? Did she not realise what he wanted? That he had come here to achieve just this?

But, like the expert hunter he was, he knew that there were many ways to play with your quarry. Had she too regretted the abrupt end to that meeting? Perhaps for her as well as for him there had been bitter regrets that their lovemaking had not been complete?

'Yes, things have moved on,' he agreed. 'But they seem to have brought us back to the same place. I am here and you are here—so just what do you think we ought to do about it?'

He took a step closer to her. He was close enough now for her to study him properly, so that she could see how much he had changed—though none of the fundamentals had. He was still the most breathtakingly masculine man she had ever laid eyes on. As if he had stepped from another age and another time. His own particular scent drifted up her nostrils—a vital, spicy scent that spoke of raw virility and reached out to the most feminine side of her.

Briefly, Sienna closed her eyes in helpless recognition, and when she opened them again it was to see the warm ebony fire in his. She could feel herself drawn to him. Like a child who had been left outside in the cold for too long. He promised the certainty of warmth. Of comfort. And security.

She wasn't aware that he had moved again, but he must have done—please God it hadn't been her— because suddenly she was in his arms, her senses not giving her time to question her sanity as he bent his head to graze his lips across hers.

It was electric. Like fire. Ice. All extremes which could shock the system to its very core—that was Hashim's kiss. It awakened in her something which had lain dormant, sleeping since the last time she had been in his arms. Back then she had—in her naivety—imagined that all kisses would press the button to instant sensual combustion, but in the interim she had discovered how way off the mark she had been.

His expert lips were both hard and soft, seeking yet

commanding—and they tasted sweeter than the richest honey. Her own opened beneath them, to taste the warmth, to feel the seductive slide of his tongue into the moist interior of her mouth, and she gasped, buckled, so that his arms caught her against him, imprisoning her in an iron-hard grip which made her melt against him.

A great wave of longing swept through her. Physical—oh, yes—but something else besides. Something which was infinitely more powerful and far more dangerous. As if Hashim alone could fill some emotional space which seemed ever-constant inside her.

For countless seconds she felt the rush of blood and the clamour of response—the warm, primitive throb of blood as it centred and pooled at a place which made her ache. She felt one of his hands reach down to cup her buttock, and silently she begged him to move his fingers round, to delve into that secret place once more.

He seemed to read her thoughts—for he laughed as he moved his hand, teasingly drifting his fingers across her aching mound. She moaned in sweet response. He murmured something in a tongue which was foreign to her, but the mocking and triumphant tone of his words spilled over her heated senses like icy water and Sienna froze in disbelief.

What the hell was she doing?

With a wrenching effort she tore herself away, staring at him wide-eyed. Her breathing was ragged and her pulse was racing like a piston as she struggled to calm herself, smoothing down her dress frantically. Her face was on fire, and so, too—surely—was her heart. 'What the hell do you think you're doing?'

His smile was arrogant, though his eyes were cold. 'Exactly what you wanted me to do.'

'No!'

'Yes. You are hungry for me,' he taunted. 'I could do it to you right now and you would not stop me.'

Too angry and uncaring to think of the consequences, Sienna raised her hand as if to strike him, but he reacted instantly—quicker and more deadly than a cobra as he caught her wrist in his hand.

'You dare to strike the Sheikh?' he thundered.

'You dare to foist yourself on me?'

'Foist?' Giving a cruel laugh, he dropped her hand. He had demonstrated his superior speed and dexterity—she would not be fool enough to try that again. 'I can think of many different words to describe a woman grinding her hips against a man in silent plea to have him enter her—but foist is not one which springs to mind.'

She felt the flush of mortification. 'You...you...'

'Oh, spare me your empty insults, Sienna. They count for absolutely nothing when we both know that what I say is true. You want me,' he stated flatly.

'Don't flatter yourself!'

'Ah! Denial is such a powerful force, is it not?' he mused. 'Especially in women.'

As well as weaving subtle mazes with his clever words, was he telling the truth? Did she want him still? Maybe physically, yes. But emotionally—never!

'Just because you know which buttons to press, and all the ways to seduce a woman—'

'Now you are flattering *me*,' he interposed cruelly.

'It doesn't mean she necessarily *wants you*,' she stormed. 'It just means that her body is reacting as it has been conditioned to do by nature—there's a world of difference.'

'And do you turn on so easily for all men?'

'You're disgusting!'

'You have grown fiery,' he observed, noticing that she had chosen not to answer the question—though his arrogant pride would not allow him to believe that she would melt for another man in quite the way she did for him. 'Very fiery. Yes. I like that in a woman.'

'But I'm not looking for your approval. I have grown up, Hashim—I'm no longer the docile young girl who thought you were the greatest thing since sliced bread!'

It was both the right thing and the wrong thing to say, for while it burst the strangely seductive bubble of thwarted desire, it reminded him of her lying and cheating and duplicity.

'Yes, so docile,' he hissed like a rattlesnake. 'So young and so *innocent*! Like hell you were.'

She stared at the stark condemnation which was sparking from his eyes. He had judged her, and found her wanting. And, damn him, he was right—she *was* still wanting. Wanting him. 'Oh, Hashim, I was innocent in so many ways,' she said, her voice sad now. 'Why don't we forget the whole thing? Let me just walk out of this door right now and out of your life for ever.'

Was she mad? Did she not recognise his intent, nor realise that when he desired something it was always his for the taking? His mouth hardened. No, of course she hadn't recognised it—how could she when she had never seen it before? Her experience with him had been bizarre—and unique. Five years ago he had found himself bewitched by her and he had tempered his usual autocratic wishes—except that it had seemed to happen without any conscious effort on his part.

Now let her see the real Hashim! Who treated women as they liked to be treated! If you were cold and disdainful it seemed to make them want you more—never was a woman more giving in the bedroom than to a man who had treated her with contempt.

'I think you forget yourself,' he said icily. 'I have hired your services and therefore you will behave as such. You will show me respect and listen to my wishes.'

'*Respect?*' she echoed. 'Are you out of your mind?'

'Yes, respect,' he ground out. 'That is if you know the meaning of the word.'

Sienna blinked as a tremor of fear ran through her. Surely he didn't think…didn't think… She drew in a deep breath. Appeal to his sense of reason, she told herself. He is a powerful and successful man, and surely he will understand that it would be folly to extend this torturous interview for a second longer than necessary.

'Hashim,' she said quietly. 'You can't honestly expect me to organise a party for you.'

'Why not?'

'Because…because there's too much history between us!'

'Now you flatter *yourself*,' he bit back. 'A few shared outings does not qualify as history. Nor does the fact that you opened your legs for me.' He saw her face drain of all colour, but he pressed on ruthlessly. 'But it is your reputation that has excited my interest.' He paused deliberately. 'Your reputation is admirable, Sienna—at least in a purely professional sense. Your work is highly regarded and I want you to organise a party for me.'

'*Want* or demand?' she questioned.

'The interpretation is yours.'

'And if I refuse?' she questioned quietly.

'Don't go there,' he warned softly.

'I have nothing to lose by turning you down.' And everything to gain. Like her sanity.

'You don't think so? On what grounds? And could you cope with the consequences of your action?'

Sienna wrinkled her nose. 'Consequences?'

'Sure. I would inform the manager here of my extreme *displeasure* that you had reneged on an agreement. How would you explain it to him? Do tell, for it fascinates me.' The black eyes challenged her.

Appeal to him. Ask him nicely. And even though

the words threatened to choke her, she got them out. 'I'm hoping it won't come to that, Hashim.'

But he carried on as if she hadn't spoken. 'Would you explain that I'd once felt you climax beneath my fingers? I'm sure he'd be *very* interested to hear that—it might even turn him on—but do you think it qualifies you to refuse my request?'

'Don't be so disgusting!'

'That's twice you've used that word,' he mused. 'You think sexuality is disgusting? How you surprise me—since your own must have earned you a great deal.' Had she blown all the money? he wondered. And why in hell hadn't she capitalised more? Used that amazing body to make herself a small fortune? Become rich by exploiting her fabulous breasts, instead of fixing up other people's parties?

Sienna tried one last time. 'You are right—my reputation *is* good *and* well-established. So much so that I can afford to turn you down!'

'People will hear—for I will make sure of it. And they will wonder and ask you why. What will you say to them? Will you lie, Sienna? Stupid question—of course you will!'

She shook her head. 'I could say that we dated a couple of years ago—I could…pretend.' She stumbled on her ironic use of the word. 'Pretend that I would find it too painful to work for you.'

'And you will look foolish.'

'I can live with that.'

'You may not have the luxury of making that decision.' A look of determination hardened his eyes to jet. 'Either you work for me or your career is over. That much you can believe.'

There was a pause. 'This is *London*—in the twenty-first century,' she told him, her voice rising in disbelief. 'Not some desert kingdom where your word is law! You may be a rich and powerful man, but in the end you're just a client. Same as any other,' she finished defiantly.

Her spirit and resistance was making his hunger grow—did she not realise that either? 'You can stand there and attempt to argue with me all day, but it will make no difference in the end. For I mean what I say, Sienna—if you do not accept this commission, then I will ruin you.'

'*Ruin* me?' Her laugh was high, and slightly hysterical. 'Even if you could—' Something was beginning to tell her that his threat was not an idle one. 'Even if you could—why would you?'

'Because you are like a dark stain in my memory,' he breathed. 'An encounter I should never have had, but which I cannot close the book on until it has been brought to its rightful conclusion.'

The meaning of his words was beginning to sink in, but Sienna didn't quite believe it—didn't dare believe it. She could hear the deafening pound of her heartbeat. 'And what conclusion is that?'

There was a pause, and he captured her eyes in mocking taunt. 'You only have to say the word, Sienna, and we can have an action replay. We can put an end to the business we started five years ago.' Deliberately he stroked his palm down the muscular flank of his thigh and his eyes became narrowed, opaque. 'Like right now, if you like.'

His heartless words tore into her and Sienna recoiled from the blatant sexuality which shimmered from him like a halo. 'Are you suggesting…suggesting that I go to *bed* with you?'

'I'm not particularly fussy about the venue,' he drawled, and nodded his dark head in the direction of a sumptuous scarlet velvet *chaise-longue*. 'That might provide a stimulating setting, don't you think? Ever done it on one of those?'

The question made her feel cheap, but presumably that had been his intention. 'You have to be out of your mind,' she breathed.

'My mind has nothing to do with it,' he said silkily. 'So what do you say, Sienna—are going to risk all you've worked for going up in smoke, or are you going to do the sensible thing and accept the commission?'

Sensible? She suspected that jumping off a high cliff would have been more sensible, but Sienna cared desperately about the career she had worked so hard for. Her job relied almost entirely on word-of-mouth recommendations, and even if she fudged the real reasons for her reluctance to work for Hashim it would reflect badly on her. Very badly. People might start to think she had issues…that she was difficult to work with…

Did she have a choice?

No.

But if she was to be forced into a corner by his

autocratic will, then it was vital that she stopped behaving like a victim. Was she going to let him think that she was scared of him? Cowed by him? Unable to resist his sensual lure?

Never!

She nodded, drawing in a deep breath to give her courage. 'Very well. Since you give me little choice I will accept your commission. Satisfied?'

Hashim felt the stirring of excitement and anticipation. So he had won the first battle. A battle he had not been expecting—but when he stopped to think about it would instant capitulation have pleased him? No. Nothing in life felt so good as something which you had to fight for. 'Oh, no, Sienna—not at all satisfied. But I intend to be. Believe me when I tell you that.'

She could hear the sultry note of desire which had deepened his voice and decided to ignore it. Act professionally, she reminded herself.

'Right,' she said coolly. 'Let's talk business—'

'Alas!'

He cut her short with an imperious wave of his hand, though he didn't look or sound in the least bit regretful.

'It cannot be now,' he murmured. 'For I have another appointment.'

Sienna stared at him, knowing that he could have broken any darned appointment he wanted but was choosing not to.

'So I will meet with you tomorrow to discuss the

details of my…*requirements*. Over dinner, of course,' he finished silkily.

She opened her mouth to say that she didn't do dinner with clients—except that would not have been true. Of course she did. She could not refuse him—he knew it and she knew it. Never in her life had she felt so helpless—like a fish with a great big hook in its mouth, just about to be reeled in by a heartless man who would like to gobble her up for breakfast.

'Very well. Dinner tomorrow it is. But you can wipe that triumphant smile off your face right now, Hashim—because the party is *all* you are getting and I mean that. There's no *way* I'm going to sleep with you!'

He said nothing, but gave a mocking smile, lifting a thick brown envelope from the ornate table beside the door and handing it to her. 'You may want to look at this,' he said.

Something in his eyes told her that this was nothing to do with the party, and her heart began to pound. She realised the contents at the exact moment she asked the question. 'What is it?'

'Oh, just an old calendar,' he drawled. 'You may recognise it.'

CHAPTER FOUR

SIENNA took the envelope downstairs to an empty office, then pulled out the calendar and stared at it dully. She hadn't seen it for a long, long time, and she was scarcely able to recognise herself in the sexy and provocative poses. She guessed that by today's standards it was pretty tame—but even so, nothing could disguise the earthy sensuality of the pictures.

They had flown her out to the Caribbean and dressed her in a variety of clothes—well, that wasn't strictly true, for the garments had all been designed to reveal rather than conceal, and they had all left her breasts on show. But that had been the whole point.

A filmy kaftan soaked with water. The bottom half of a low-slung bikini. A glittery thong. Sienna closed her eyes, but was unable to block out the vivid, Technicolor images.

She remembered her initial feeling of panic when they had told her what they wanted her to do. It had taken two rum punches before she had been able to lie face down in the sand and smoulder at the camera for the first of the shots.

And Sienna would never forget the moment she'd seen a Polaroid of her pouting glossy self, with sand-sprinkled skin and messy hair, and dark, peeking nipples. How she had given a little gasp of disbelief and been slightly repulsed by the glinting approval in the eyes of the art director.

Even now she could squirm at how naïve she had been. And even now the photos still had the power to shock her. With trembling fingers she shoved the calendar into her briefcase and let herself out of the hotel, taking in great gulps of hot and sticky summer air.

She spent a restless night, and the following day there was a constant dull ache at her temples. When she walked through the hotel foyer dressed for dinner she felt as if she was going to her own execution.

'Cheer up!' said the night porter. 'It might never happen! Going somewhere special, are you?'

Serena gave a wan smile. 'I'm having dinner with one of the guests in the Rainbow Room.'

'Lucky you!'

Sienna gave a hollow laugh. 'Yes, lucky me!' she echoed wryly. 'Still, at least it's beautifully air-conditioned up there. The temperature outside is claustrophobic.'

'Tell me about it!' said the porter.

Overnight a heatwave seemed to have descended on the capital, with all the force and stifling nature of a heavy fire blanket dropped down to envelop the city. The streets outside the cool hotel had been curiously airless, and Sienna's throat felt as tight as if she were still out in them.

As she rode up in the lift she stared at herself in the tinted mirror. The cool linen dress she wore still looked fresh, and the apricot hue of the glass gave her face a healthy-looking glow which completely belied the way she was feeling inside. But she was not going to let that overwhelm her. And she was not going to let him intimidate her.

The nude photos were part of her past. She couldn't change that, and neither could she rewrite her brief and confusing relationship with Hashim. But she had learned along the way, and that was the whole point of experience—good *or* bad.

Those had been pivotal events in her life which had made her into the cool and confident professional she was today. The change hadn't been easy, or instant, and she was not going to throw it all away because Hashim wanted to exact some kind of erotic payback for what had happened all those years ago. Or rather, what had *not* happened.

He despised her—he had made that perfectly clear—even though his body still wanted her. And on some level she still wanted him, too. But she would not allow herself to be picked up and used like some kind of convenience—to be tossed away at the earliest opportunity. And she would not repeat the mistakes of yesterday.

If he said things to rile or provoke her she would not rise to them. They could not have a scene if she didn't react to him. If he attempted to taunt her then she would just give him a cool and glacial smile. She would remain brisk, crisp and polite—in short, she would be utterly professional, and he would be unable to find fault with her.

Surprisingly, he was already at the table. She was a little early, and had expected him to be late, but, no, there he was. Waiting. Making the rest of the room shrink into insignificance. At a shadowed corner table sat two of the ever-present bodyguards.

Sienna walked towards him, looking for some kind of acknowledgement—a nod of his dark head in greeting—but there was nothing. Just those black eyes trained on her like twin barrels of a hunter's gun.

His hard, lean body was completely still, but his stance was tense, the powerful limbs coiled like a lion before pouncing. He seemed completely oblivious to the covert glances of the other diners in the room. To the almost tangible air of excitement among the normally celebrity-jaded waiters.

Hashim watched her approach, helpless and yet furious with himself for being unable to suppress the instant leap of lust he felt, for he had trained himself to control his desires. To be master of his wants and needs—not servant to them. A man who could control his sexual hunger was all-powerful, for sex made men weak. And his control had never failed him. How else could he have so ruthlessly given Sienna pleasure and then denied himself the relief of his own body? And bitterly regretted it ever since!

Yet on one level she remained a mystery to him. He had known women more beautiful than her—so what was the secret of her particular allure? The seductive sway of her hips? The too-big eyes which looked like those of a startled deer? Or just the fact that he had never had her when other men had? That he had paid homage to her virginity only to have its falseness revealed to him in the most humiliating way of all.

He let his eyes rove over the breasts themselves—so proud and magnificent and full. Yet she was hiding her most marketable asset beneath that rather unremarkable linen dress. His lips curled. How he hated linen—surely the most unflattering material a woman could wear, with its coarse feel and its tendency to crumple. And surely it was a little late in the day for such unwelcome modesty?

Yet the very *familiarity* of seeing her again was taking him into the unknown realms of fantasy. The past was a place he did not revisit. At least never before now. His restless and nomadic nature saw no point to it. For him there was not the comfort—nor the danger—of long-standing friendships. His destiny was to stand alone.

Then why are you breaking your own rules? taunted a small voice in his head.

He did not rise to greet her when she got to the table, and, interestingly, this small lack of courtesy wounded her. Could he not just have pretended—gone through the motions of normality?

'Hello, Hashim,' she said, as calmly as possible.

'Sienna.' Not a flicker of emotion crossed over the diamond-hard features. 'Please sit down.'

'Thank you.' She glanced up at the waiter, who pulled her chair out, and then there was nowhere else to look other than into the enigmatic black eyes. Their dark light swept over her, and she felt a moment of sheer physical weakness until she remembered her vow of earlier. Professionalism. 'So.' She flicked him a quick smile. 'Where shall we begin?'

'So quick to do business?' he murmured.

'One should always strive for professionalism,' she answered coolly.

'Ironically, that is what Abdul-Aziz always says.'

Sienna remembered the aide who had seemed to so dislike her. 'And is he here with you now?'

Hashim shook his head. Hot-headedly, he had blamed his aide for showing him the calendar, even though he had only been doing his job. But for a while the Sheikh had seen him as a bearer of bad tidings—and he was as superstitious as the next Qudamah man. So he had sent him home, and in a way the split had been necessary—for the older man had begun to see himself in a role which was not befitting a royal aide. He had begun to love the fatherless Hashim as a son. And Hashim had no need of extra love.

'Abdul-Aziz was posted back to Qudamah,' he said. 'He is married now, with a son of his own.'

'*Married?*'

'Yes.' And then, because this exchange seemed almost too *cosy*, too familiar, he allowed his eyes to drift over her face. 'Aren't you going to thank me for the calendar?' he questioned deliberately.

She had wondered when he would get around to mentioning it, and she had practised her response until she had it word-perfect. 'No, I'm not. And if you continue to talk about it then I will walk out of here right now.'

He gave a faint smile. 'Then I guess we'd better get the ordering out of the way.'

She glanced down at the menu, which was like a blur though she knew it backwards. 'I'd like the Dover Sole, please. Grilled, no sauce. With a side salad.'

'The choice of a woman on a diet,' he observed.

'Not at all. A woman who is careful about what she eats, that's all.'

'Careful?' His black eyes glittered. 'How very curious. Not a word I would have associated with you.'

She leaned forward. Big mistake—for now she was in full range of his subtle, spicy scent, and it crept over her like sensual fingers. She sat right back again. 'Why don't we clear something up before we go any further? You don't know me. Maybe you never did—but you certainly don't now. So you aren't qualified to make any judgments about me. Understand?'

The waiter reappeared as Hashim glittered her a look which said *Aren't I?* Sienna watched as he gave the order quickly, almost impatiently—like someone who had spent much of his life eating in expensive restaurants and was bored by them. She guessed he had.

And now take charge, she told herself. Behave like you would with any other new client. She reached into her handbag and pulled out a notebook. He eyed it with distaste.

'Is that really necessary?' he questioned acidly.

'I'm afraid so. You wouldn't be very happy if I forgot everything you told me, would you? And so far you haven't told me anything.'

'But you look like you're interviewing me—and we're in a restaurant!'

'Well, you chose it.'

'I know I did—but would you have agreed to dine in my suite if I had asked you?'

'Not a snowball's chance in hell.' She looked at him, daring him to defy her. 'Presumably you wanted me to be a captive audience?'

Hashim's eyes narrowed as he considered her quickfire responses. Smart. And sassy. No matter how good an actress she was, she couldn't play smart unless she really *was* smart. 'Captive?' he mused. 'Yes, perhaps I did.' He imagined her tied to his bed with black satin ribbons, wearing nothing but scarlet underwear and a pair of matching high heels, and he felt the heavy stab of an erection.

'So, is it going to be a big party?' Sienna asked, cutting into his erotic thoughts.

'Party?' With a distracted movement of his shoulders Hashim brought himself back to the subject in hand with an effort. 'No. Very small. A private dinner party for ten.'

'And the guest list?'

'One of my assistants will organise that side of it. I am afraid that most of my guests will refuse to deal with a stranger.'

Defensively, Sienna picked up her water glass. 'In that case I'm surprised I'll be any use at all.'

'But that is where you are wrong. You will be responsible for the event itself,' he said. 'I'd like you to organise the music—I thought perhaps a string quartet. And the lighting—I like lots of candles, by the way. And the wine and the food—of which there must be an interesting and imaginative vegetarian selection. The mood of the evening will be down to you, Sienna. Everything you need you must ask for, and it will be supplied.'

How effortless everything was when you were rich! You snapped your fingers and got what you wanted. Sienna allowed herself a small smile. Well, not quite *everything*. He couldn't have *her*.

'And what kind of ambience do you want?' she questioned. 'Is there any particular reason why you're giving this party?'

There was one brief moment of hesitation. 'As a thank-you,' he said smoothly, running the tip of one finger reflectively along the soft linen of his napkin. 'For some of the many people in England who have done me favours.'

Bizarrely, Sienna found herself wondering if that

included sexual favours—but since his dark, lean looks were attracting all kinds of predatory glances maybe it wasn't such a bizarre thought after all. 'Have you thought which of the hotel's function rooms you'd like? There are several.' She looked at him expectantly. 'Or do you just want to me to choose?'

He stared at her. 'But that is the whole point, Sienna,' he said softly. 'I don't want it held here—or indeed in any hotel. A hotel is too impersonal for the needs of this particular event. I want you to find me a house.'

Sienna looked up from her pad and met the dark steel of his eyes. 'What kind of house?'

'A fine country house—with gardens and a view— a very *English* house. It should have at least ten bedrooms, so that my guests can stay overnight should they so desire it. There should be a lake which will magnify the light of the moon and double the number of stars. Somewhere that symbolises everything which is beautiful about your country. Can you do that for me, Sienna?'

The poetry of his words momentarily threw her, as did that fleeting, dreamy look which had softened his hard face, and she swallowed. 'How long have I got?'

'A month.'

'A *month*? That isn't long. Certainly not to find the kind of house you're looking for.'

'Are you saying you can't do it?'

'Oh, I can do it,' she said. 'But you might have trouble getting your guests there if they've only got four weeks. Important people have busy diaries—especially the kind of people I imagine you'll be inviting.'

He gave a low laugh. 'Please do not concern yourself on that score. They will attend,' he said softly. 'If I so wish it.'

'By royal command?' she mocked, resting her wrist against her water glass and enjoying the sudden cool sensation. 'Tell me—just out of interest—have you spent your whole life getting exactly what you want?'

'Material things, yes. That is, I imagine, what you meant?'

'It wasn't, actually.'

'No?' He studied the dark shadows beneath her eyes. Was he responsible for those? Or had some lover shared her bed last night—making use of her body and denying her sleep? He found himself unprepared for the dark jealousy which twisted his gut, and his voice hardened. 'Money is the preoccupation of most women,' he said harshly. 'Surely not even you would deny that?'

How cynical he sounded. Sienna felt a wave of something like regret wash over her—for she had only helped to convince him that women would do all kinds of things for money. She wished the food would arrive, so that she could eat it and go. Yet wasn't there a tiny part of her which was revelling in the opportunity to be this close to him again? To feast her eyes on a man she had once loved to distraction— and told him so.

Briefly she closed her eyes as she remembered whispering it to him, on that last, terrible evening. And the way he had just ignored her trembling statement.

Try and obliterate the past, she told herself, but she stared down at the food on her plate without really seeing it.

'You aren't really hungry at all, are you, Sienna?' he said, his silken voice weaving its way into her troubled thoughts.

He breathed her name in a way she remembered him once breathing it in passion, putting the emphasis on the last syllable and holding it in his mouth as if it were a mouthful of fine wine.

'Not really, no.' He was looking at her in a way which was making whispers of longing tiptoe over her flesh—and she had to snap out of it.

She needed to protect herself against his enchantment, and she found herself wondering how other women coped. Surely she couldn't be the only woman he bewitched with his curiously old-fashioned air of mastery and chauvinism? And women weren't *supposed* to be bewitched by qualities such as those. They were supposed to look for tolerance and compassion—not simply the desire to be swept off their feet by a flashing-eyed Alpha man.

She laid her fork down and pushed her plate away. 'Well, since we've tied up the business side of things, and neither of us looks as if we're about to tuck into the food, then you'll forgive me if I take my leave—'

'No.' The word was emphatic. 'I will not. You aren't going anywhere because I haven't finished with you. Not yet.'

Did he mean to make her sound disposable? she wondered. Like something he could just crumple up and throw away? And suddenly it wasn't easy not to be intimidated, to take charge and be calm and un-flappable—all the things she had learnt to do in order to survive and succeed.

Maybe this was one conversation she couldn't get out of having, and maybe it was a waste of time to try. Like having a tooth pulled—wasn't that ravaging moment of pain worth it just for the blessed relief you felt afterwards?

'Well, fire away, Hashim,' she said, using her last bit of bravado. 'And get whatever it is you want to say off your chest.'

He traced a thoughtful forefinger along the edge of his lips. 'I simply cannot understand why you chose obscurity,' he said.

She stared at him. 'Excuse me?'

He gestured towards her, as if he was about to in-troduce her to someone at a party. 'Oh, there is no doubt that you have become successful—'

'Why, thank you,' she said drily.

'But only in a purely *relative* sense.' His gaze was very steady. 'It puzzles me that you have stayed working in hotels.'

'Lots of girls do.'

'But lots of girls do not look the way you do.'

'Hashim, *please*—'

'You could have earned a fortune by capitalising on your body, and yet you chose this. So tell me...' His question hung on the air and Sienna waited breathlessly. When it came out it was disguised with the silken cloak of civility, but the look of disgust which hardened the ebony eyes told its own story. 'Why did you never pursue your career in topless modelling?'

CHAPTER FIVE

WHY did you never pursue your career in topless modelling?

With Hashim's critical question ringing in her ears, Sienna felt like someone who had put a piece of expensive lingerie away in a drawer, only to pull it out and discover that it had become faded and moth-eaten. He made her feel cheap. Tawdry. Something she hadn't felt for a long, long time, and she glanced around them, as if the other diners might have overheard.

'You worry that people might be listening?' A cruel smile curved his lips. 'So you have not boasted of your days working in *glamour*?' The word dripped with contempt. 'You are concerned about what others think, perhaps? I cannot believe *that*, Sienna—for why reveal your body if you are afraid of people finding out about it? Why allow men to feast their eyes on your nakedness if you then act coy about it?'

'I'm surprised you bother asking me questions to which you obviously have all the answers,' she said quietly. 'Or rather, you have *decided* you know the answers. You think I am a certain kind of woman—so why don't we just leave it at that?'

'Because I am…curious.'

Yes, of course he was. He was fascinated in the same way that people couldn't help themselves looking at a roadside crash—they didn't want to be part of it, but something compelled them to watch. 'Why do you think I didn't pursue it, Hashim?'

He shrugged. 'Because I suspect you saw that in the end it would work against you. Would spoil your greatest ambition of all.'

'And what ambition would that be?' she asked faintly.

The tip of his forefinger rested thoughtfully against the dark shadow of his jaw. 'I think that you saw the seamy side of the industry, as girls who expose themselves often do. You anticipated that real dangers existed—and so you decided to work in the real world instead. An honest though a much harder living. But I suspect that you found it even harder than you imagined, and so you looked for an escape—an easier way—easier even than taking your clothes off.'

Sienna flinched. 'Go on,' she said, in a pinched kind of voice.

'You realised that you had an extraordinary gift which few are given. The gift of beauty.' His voice became cold as he recalled how he had fallen for the oldest trick in the book. 'Sirens had it, and lured sailors to their death. Men are driven mad by beauty. And you decided to use it as women have used their youth and their looks since the beginning of time. As a bargaining tool.'

Sienna swallowed, willing herself to float out from

her body—to hover suspended in the air above them, looking down at this horrible little scene to hear the words of vitriol which were spitting from his lips.

'With you, presumably?'

He shrugged. 'With me, yes—or with anyone else who happened to fit the bill at the time. I do not flatter myself that I would not have been moved aside if somebody even richer than I had stepped into the frame. You wanted a wealthy benefactor and for that you decided to play the Cinderella role. You chose a humble job as a receptionist, where your beauty stood out like…' He frowned, as if he was trying to remember something, the ebony brows knitting together, and then his face cleared. 'Ah, yes! Like a diamond in the rough,' he said softly. 'Hoping and praying and plotting that someone would sweep in and take you away from all that.

'And I must say that you were very good,' he continued, eyeing her thoughtfully. 'Even I was taken in by your deceit. You really did come over as an innocent and unspoilt girl. In a way, I suppose I should commend you for your acting ability!'

'Your English is quite perfect, Hashim,' she said unsteadily.

'I know it is,' he agreed arrogantly. 'I had an English tutor as a young child, and I am as fluent in your language as I am in my own. But why do you change the subject, Sienna?'

'Why do you think?' She felt as she imagined battered wives might feel. That after a while the punches no longer seemed to hurt. Insult someone enough and eventually the slurs would simply run off their skin like water. Let him rant and have his poisonous say, and then it would be over.

He narrowed his eyes at her. 'And still you do not contradict me?'

'What's the point? You are the worst kind of bigot—for you do not open your mind to the possibility that you might be wrong. You have made your mind up that something is so—and therefore it must be. I'm a topless model without any morals, and now it seems I'm an old-fashioned gold-digger to boot! Nothing will change the way you view me—so why should I even bother trying?'

'Because you have no defence against what I say!' he accused.

'We aren't in a court of law!'

'No, but that is where you might have ended up!' he declared hotly. 'In the end you *did* make the right choice—even though you have had to work hard for a living. But the women who continue along that path so often end up compromised. Next time—or the time after that—the photos that you agreed to do would not have been so tasteful. You would have got older, and as your youth faded you would have become more desperate. Soon you would have accepted less and less for more and more. And one day you might have ended up fully naked on some garage mechanic's wall in one of those explicit shots—'

'You *bastard*!' she hissed.

'But that is where you are wrong, Sienna. Your barb does not offend me because it is untrue—my birth was completely legitimate. Whereas what I say to you *is* true. The facts are indisputable.'

Sienna lifted a hand to the waiter who had begun to hover anxiously on the periphery of her vision. 'A glass of red wine, please.'

'Yes, madam.'

'You did not storm off,' he observed. 'As I suspected you might.'

Sienna shook her head. Her legs would not have carried her anywhere. She took the wine from the waiter and drank a large mouthful. Gradually its warmth and vitality began to seep through veins which felt as though they had been injected with ice.

'Why does it bother you so?' she questioned. 'Haven't you had girlfriends with questionable pasts before?'

'Of course I have. But they did not pretend to be something they weren't.'

There had been women who had made no secret of their hunger for his body and his money. And there had been actresses, too—of course there had—including one who had starred in a film which had broken the mould at the time. Some of the critics had called it soft porn. But none of that had mattered—they had just been cheap flings. What he'd seen had been what he'd got, and he had accepted that.

With Sienna it had been different—or at least he'd thought it had. They had been much more serious about each other. And when the sordid truth had been revealed to him he had felt outraged. It had made him question himself—he who had never had to question anything.

To a man impervious to self-doubt it had been a hard lesson to learn—that his judgement was not infallible—but ultimately it had made him stronger. And if there had still been one small fragment of his character which had believed in the fantasy of the perfect woman, then she had banished it for ever. He would never make that mistake again.

'What if…?' Sienna hesitated, feeling as if she was fighting for more than just her self-respect. She couldn't bear it when he looked at her that way—with such cold condemnation written in his eyes. 'What if you could understand my reasons for having done the photos?'

'Greed is never difficult to understand!'

'You have to understand that it wasn't like that—it really wasn't! I needed the money urgently.' She sucked in a breath and it felt like hot fire scorching down her throat. Would he believe her? 'To pay for an operation for my mother.'

There was a pause, and then he said, 'Bravo!' He gave a small silent handclap and then looked around, an expression of mock amazement on his face. 'But what has happened to the violins?' he taunted sarcastically. 'I can't hear them. Are there hordes of orphans at the door, too—waiting for you to put food in their mouths?'

'It's true, I tell you—it's true!' She wanted to stand up and rush round and drum her fists against his chest. To shout and to rail against him despite all that she'd vowed. But she couldn't—was that another reason why he had chosen the restaurant? To protect himself from an emotional scene? To enable him to insult her as much as he liked, knowing that she wouldn't be able to fight back?

'Whether you choose to believe me or not is up to you—but I'm not lying to you. Why don't you have one of your henchmen run a check on me?'

His eyes narrowed. 'What kind of operation? Cosmetic surgery, perhaps? Was she once as beautiful as you, Sienna, and could not accept that time was bleeding her of her beauty?'

Oh, how he must despise her! *Don't rise to it. Fight your corner with pride and with dignity.* Sienna bit her lip as she remembered her mother's pain and—nearly as bad—her worry. 'It certainly wasn't vanity, but neither was it a matter of life or death. Though maybe in a way it was. She needed a hip replacement—she runs a riding school, you see. Without the operation she faced disablement and the closure of her beloved business.'

Sienna looked down and realised that her hands were shaking, but that was nothing compared to the unsteady racing of her heart. She looked again, and this time there was appeal in her green eyes. *Just believe me!* they said. And never had a sense of injustice burned so strong.

'She was at her wits' end, Hashim, and so was I. So I took the easy way out—I admit that. I had once been told that I could make a lot of money—that I wasn't tall enough for the catwalk but that my face and figure could make my fortune. I wasn't at all interested at the time, but I remembered it when I needed to. And I did it. A one-off which I never repeated nor ever would.' She stared at him, braving that dark-eyed look of censure. 'And that's the truth. I swear it.'

There was silence for a moment while he brooded on what she had told him. An interesting development—if it was true. And if it was then perhaps it made her actions slightly less contemptible. But did it actually change anything? Make him forgive her for what she had done?

Never!

In the world Hashim inhabited women were modest and demure, and it was unimaginable to think of them posing naked for money and men's pleasure. He closed his mind as he pictured the calendar as clearly as if someone had just put it down on the table in front of him. Because they weren't just nude shots— no matter how 'artistic' the photographer had tried to make them. She looked…she looked… He felt an involuntary shudder run through his big body and the pooling of lust in his groin.

She looked as if she was begging the viewer to drive himself between her silken thighs!

And no matter what had motivated her it didn't change the fact that she had posed for the erotic shots.

But neither did it change the fact that he wanted her—and he would not rest until he had lost himself in that exquisite body. And only when he had done that, could he cast her aside and forget her.

He was calm again when he spoke. 'And your mother—she approved of your actions? Condoned them, perhaps?'

'Of course she didn't! She didn't know. Not until afterwards.' Sienna shrugged and stared down at the fish congealing on her plate. She wanted to say that she had regretted it bitterly ever since—but that wouldn't be true. She had been glad to help her mother—the only bitterness she had felt was against Hashim, and the way he had made her feel about herself. But even that could not seem to rid her of her longing for him.

Stupid, hopeless longing. How was it possible for this man to deride her, to criticise and pour scorn on her, and yet she was still drawn to that dark, lean body, wanted to see those black eyes soften with passion once more? 'So that's it. Subject closed.' She lifted her eyes and met his stare with a steady gaze. 'So now you know—can we please just forget about this whole farce? You can't possibly want me to work for you—not really. Get someone else to arrange your wretched party for you.'

The corners of his mouth lifted upwards in a cruel imitation of a smile. She still did not get it! Oh, foolish, foolish woman. 'On the contrary, Sienna,' he said softly. 'I do not want anyone else. It is you I want and you that I shall have.'

And Sienna began to tremble.

CHAPTER SIX

A MONTH was no time at all—but in a way Sienna was glad that Hashim had demanded such an outrageously short time to arrange his party. If it had dragged on over weeks, then what kind of state might she have found herself in?

As it was, she had her work cut out to find a venue—and there certainly wasn't time to think about his thinly veiled threat, or the sensual way he had looked at her.

Determinedly, she put him out of her mind and holed herself up in her tiny office at her home in Kennington and rang round, using every contact she'd ever made until at last she struck lucky. She could have the use of Bolland House, set in a hundred acres in the glorious Hampshire countryside. She had driven down to see it and had pronounced it perfect.

She had found a local acclaimed chef who cooked using fresh organic produce sourced from nearby farms. She had chosen flowers, and was bussing in her favourite sommelier—though she had warned him that some of the guests might not be drinking alcohol and asked him to provide a wide selection of soft drinks which were rather more exciting than orange juice!

In fact everything was now in place...and with just three days to go it felt a bit as she imagined the atmosphere in one of the giant space stations just before they sent a rocket into flight—the tension of the countdown was almost unbearable. Especially in this heat.

'I'm making coffee!' called a voice from the kitchen. 'Do you want some?'

'Love some!' Sienna called back, and sat back in her chair and sighed. It was funny how circumstances could change out of all recognition in such a short time. Up until that meeting with Hashim, Sienna had been utterly contented. She had her little terraced house in Kennington, which she had bought as a neglected and nearly derelict wreck. She had spent every spare minute doing it up—stripping the walls, sanding the paintwork and painting it in light colours, filling it with mirrors to make it seem bigger and brighter. She had saved up to have a new bathroom and kitchen put in and had painted the front door in a deep, dark blue.

When the house had been habitable, she had taken in a lodger to help with the mortgage—Kat, who was now in her last year of studying languages at a nearby university. And only then had Sienna given herself the luxury of turning her attention to the garden and the challenge of making something pretty out of the small square of ground which had looked like a builders' yard.

'Coffee's ready!' called Kat.

'Coming!'

Sienna got up and went through to the kitchen, where Kat was just putting the cafetière and mugs onto a pretty spotted tray, her red hair falling over her shoulders. She looked up as Sienna came in and smiled. 'Shall we drink it in the garden?'

'That would be lovely,' said Sienna, but she could hear the flatness in her own voice as she went out into the sunshine.

She felt like an outsider to the rest of the world. Usually she revelled in pride and pleasure at the small oasis she had created in the middle of the city, but not today. She could see the sunlight dappling through the honeysuckle, but she couldn't seem to smell the fragrant blooms, nor appreciate its simple beauty. Hashim's reappearance in her life seemed to have sucked the vibrancy out of everything except the memory of his dark and cruel face, and his hard, virile body.

She took the coffee that Kat poured for her and stared into the cup as gloomily as someone with a fear of heights being told to do a high dive.

'Are you going to tell me what's wrong?' said Kat.

Sienna looked up. Her teeth gritted into the bright, cheery smile which she had become rather good at perfecting. 'Oh, just work. You know. It's frantic at the moment.'

'You don't usually complain,' observed Kat, her eyes narrowing. 'You're usually glad when it's like that.'

'Well, it's hot, too. Isn't it?' Sienna wiped her damp brow with a jokey and exaggerated gesture—because how could she tell Kat what was troubling her, and *what* could she tell her?

Oh, I had a fling with a sheikh until he discovered that I'd done some topless photos, and then he…he…

Little beads of sweat studded her forehead and she wiped them away with an angry hand. How awful it sounded when pared down to the basic facts.

She wouldn't tell Kat. Because if she told Kat about Hashim then that would give him an identity which would live on for ever. Kat would want to know all about him—who wouldn't? No, she wouldn't tell anyone. She would do what he wanted her to do and then hopefully he would leave her alone.

Hopefully?

That was part of the trouble, too. He had forced her into this corner and yet a part of her wanted to impress him. To engineer the most wonderful dinner party for him and dazzle him—leaving him with an altogether better memory of her than he currently had.

And wasn't there another part of her—a stubborn and stupid and romantic one—which wished that she could just go back and rewrite history?

Sometimes she started thinking about how it might have been if she'd never done those photos—but then she made herself stop. Thinking like that was a pretty pointless exercise. If she hadn't been able to come up with the money quickly then her mother's life would have collapsed around her—and how could she have lived with *that*?

And even if he hadn't found out it would never have been anything more than a fling—for how could it have been? What had she been imagining—that he'd buy her a whopping great ring and marry her, take her back to Qudamah as the Sheikh's wife? Sienna took a mouthful of too-hot coffee and winced.

'Steady,' warned Kat, only half jokingly.

'Oh, listen—there's that wretched phone again!' Sienna leapt to her feet and gave her housemate an expression which said sorry. But in truth she was glad to get away—to keep herself busy instead of fending off Kat's concerned questions.

'Posh Parties,' she said as she picked the phone up, and then gripped onto it with whitening knuckles.

'Hello, Sienna,' Hashim said softly.

He had the kind of voice which made your skin shiver in spite of yourself, and Sienna closed her eyes in despair. She hadn't spoken to him since that night in the restaurant, and sometimes she had half imagined that she'd dreamt the whole thing up.

But life was rarely as kind as that.

'Hello, Hashim,' she said calmly.

Most people might have asked if it was convenient to talk, but not him.

'It is done?' he questioned, watching as a blonde on the other side of the foyer crossed one slim, silk-stockinged leg over another and slanted him a smile.

'Everything is arranged,' she said mechanically. 'You got my photos of the venue?'

'Yes.'

'And you are happy with the menu plans?'

'Perfectly happy.'

'Drinks seven-thirty to eight, dinner at eight-thirty.' She hesitated. 'Obviously I will be down there earlier, to oversee everything—but do you...do you want me to stay until the end?'

'Most assuredly I do,' he said smoothly, and unseen a slow smile of anticipation curved the cruel line of his mouth. 'And you will dress to party, Sienna. I want you to blend in. Or stand out,' he added mockingly, a jerk of longing arousing him as he imagined her baring her white and perfect breasts. And she would. Oh, she would.... 'The choice is yours.'

She opened her mouth to tell him that she didn't need advice on what to wear—until she realised that antagonising him would get her nowhere. Grit your teeth and bear it, and it will soon all be over.

'I shall look forward to it,' she said crisply.

Hashim's smile became hard-edged. He could see the blonde sliding her tongue wetly over her lips but he turned away. He had never been turned on by the very obvious—and besides, his thoughts were given over to one seduction alone.

'Let's hope it lives up to our expectations,' he murmured, and his black eyes dilated, like a cat's. 'I'll see you on Saturday.' Abruptly he terminated the connection, before the sultry throb of desire could be transmuted to his voice. Because he wanted her to be relaxed, her guard down.

Sienna replaced the phone and stood staring at it for long, countless moments. After Saturday it would all be over.

And suddenly she couldn't wait.

Clunking up the grand drive in her battered old car, Sienna arrived at Bolland Hall just after teatime and let herself in.

'Hello!' she called, but there was no response. She walked through the arched hallway into the dining room and saw the table laid for dinner. She was unable to resist a smile of satisfaction. It was perfect.

Beside Georgian silver and priceless crystal, crisp damask napkins were folded into pristine rectangles and tall candles were ready to be lit.

Everything was as it should be.

There was a stunning floral centrepiece. Fragrant flowers of pink and ivory, dotted with the occasional yellow rose—chosen especially because they were the Sheikh's colours. The colours his jockeys wore. The colour of the Qudamah flag—pink and cream, with a tiny splash of gold in one corner. She breathed in their scent appreciatively.

Similar arrangements of flowers were dotted around the place, and Sienna made her way through the silent house, briefly wondering where all the staff had disappeared to—but they were probably having a well-earned break, since they had clearly been busy.

In the vast kitchen, berry-dark and luscious individual summer puddings lay cooling in the fridge, along with marinades and champagne. Crisp meringues sat snowy-light on a tray next to a bunch of perfect grapes and a dish of white peaches. Several bottles of claret had already been decorked, ready to be carefully poured into the eighteenth-century crystal decanters.

Sienna smiled again. Let Sheikh Hashim Al Aswad try to find any fault with her arrangements!

She heard the crunch of gravel on the drive and wondered if the staff were back. She glanced at her watch. Probably. But as she glanced out of the window she saw a low and screamingly expensive black sports car drawing to a halt. Well, if that was one of the staff then she needed to switch career—and sharpish!

She clip-clopped her way into the hall as the doorbell rang and pulled open the door, her face and her body freezing as she saw Hashim himself standing there, a lazy smile touching the corners of his lips.

Sienna swallowed. She had somehow expected to see him clad in an impeccable dinner jacket, with black tie and snowy white shirt, and dark, tapered trousers which would make his legs look endless. The Western style he seemed to favour the majority of the time.

But he was not. Tonight he was dressed in clothes which heralded far more exotic climes...in fine silk the colour of a pomegranate which clung faintly to hard muscle and lean sinew. It provided the perfect backdrop for his rich black hair and golden-dark skin, but it reminded her of another time—a bitterly erotic one. She felt shame and desire and regret bubbling up inside her, but most of all she felt longing—felt it with an intensity which took her breath away.

Please don't let it show, she prayed silently.

Hashim saw the play of conflicting emotions which crossed her features, and an emotion which was almost alien to him caught him in its silken snare.

Excitement.

'Hello, Sienna.'

'Hashim!' she said softly, in a tone he couldn't quite work out. 'You're…you're early.'

She stood bathed in the soft yet fierce light of the setting sun and he thought that he had never seen her look more beautiful—that thick, shiny hair caught up and woven with glittering clips, making him aware that her neck was classically long and swan-like.

Her dress was made of some light, delicate fabric, layer upon gossamer layer of it, in swirls of rose which made him think of the petals of her mouth. The dress was modest by anyone's standards, even his— and yet he was struck, not for the first time, by how the hint of a body could inflame the senses far more than if it was on show.

As if his senses needed any inflaming!

But he kept his face calmly impassive. This had, after all, been a long time in coming—and he was a master at keeping his feelings hidden. He must not strike until he was certain…

'Aren't you going to invite me in?' he queried mockingly.

She knew she should tell him that it was not her place to invite *him* in—that this was his party, and his money paying for it—but all those thoughts just flew straight out of her mind. For his proximity was making her head spin. She shrank back as he passed by her—as if that could make her immune to the raw virility which seemed to radiate from him. But nothing could make her immune to him.

The black eyes were studying her face as a fox's might just before it devoured a chicken—whole—and a smile was playing around his lips. A smile that made her feel hot and prickly and distinctly…*odd*.

'Do…do you want a drink?' she questioned. 'Or to have a look around—check things out?'

'No.'

She wished he wouldn't stare at her that way, and yet she never wanted him to stop doing it. Pull yourself together, Sienna, she told herself. Remember who he is.

'I'm afraid that the staff have gone off on an extended break,' she said, trying for something light, something to dispel the atmosphere which was fraught and heavy—building into something she didn't recognise nor even want to acknowledge.

And maybe that was why she relaxed and didn't

see it coming. But even if she had would she honestly have been able to stop it? Or *wanted* to stop it?

Because Hashim suddenly pulled her into his arms without warning and anchored her firmly against the full length of his body. His smile hardened.

Don't, she told herself weakly as she felt the musculature and the power. Fight him.

But she did not fight him. She trembled.

And Hashim briefly closed his eyes as one arm encircled the slender column of her waist, sighing with soft triumph as he felt the instinctive flowering of her breasts crushed to his chest. What he had desired for so long would soon be his. It was going to be easier than he had even dared anticipate.

He tilted her chin with the tip of his finger, his black eyes glittering with an inner fire, and she smouldered beneath his scorching gaze. 'Who cares about the staff?' he drawled, and his lips began to move towards her as if a magnetic force compelled them to.

'But—'

'Shh.' His lips grazed hers, touchpaper-sure. 'There are a thousand things I wish to do and show to you, and we must waste not a second.'

Time froze. Her heart seemed to thump out a million beats in those few seconds. His face swam before her, shifting in and out of focus, and she drifted her eyes over it greedily, drinking in the hard, flat planes, the thin, jagged line which ran down the side of his cheek and scarred it.

But most of all it was the mouth which tempted

her—the voluptuous cushion of the lower lip contrasting so markedly with the cruel hard line of the upper one. She could see the gleam of his white teeth and the soft pink of his tongue. It was as if all the time in between had never happened, as if nothing existed nor ever had except for what was here and what was now. In this room, in his arms, in the heightened and fragile atmosphere, with the unsteadiness of their breathing and the scent of the flowers.

'Hashim,' she whispered, but she never knew what it was she intended to say, for his eyes had hardened in tune with his body and he bent his head to blot out the world.

CHAPTER SEVEN

A KISS could be a question and an answer. It could take or give. But Hashim's kiss robbed Sienna of everything except her own helpless response to it. Somewhere at the back of her mind a thousand voices screamed out their protest, but she silenced them as ruthlessly as if they had been her enemies. Instead, she opened her mouth beneath the hard, seeking warmth of his lips. And was lost.

Hashim gave a low laugh of delight at the ease with which she pressed her lips so eagerly against his—it grew in the back of his throat and came out like the small groan of a playful lion cub.

'Oh, yes,' he murmured into her mouth, and she murmured back, something muffled and incoherent— the mindless sound women sometimes made when they were ready for sex.

But Hashim was careful, and although he felt his heart pounding, desire hardening him with its exquisite torturous heat, he knew that this seduction must be a cold-blooded one. One wrong move and she might flee from his arms. One incautious word and all would be lost.

He knew which buttons to press—for his experience of women was encyclopaedic. He knew when to cajole and when to demand. When to lead and when to follow. But with Sienna it was different. She had stated her resistance to just this act, and while her body might be responding at the moment the mind could be a powerful deterrent. Particularly in a woman's case.

It was, he realised, as he drifted his mouth away from her neck and began to kiss softly at the line of her jaw, the very first time in his life that he'd had to actually *seduce* a woman. Normally he had to fight them off. Vaguely he remembered something he had read when schooling himself in the art of love, as royal males of Qudamah did when they reached the age of fifteen. That when a woman was uncertain, you must take it slowly. Very slowly. You must make her believe that you do not have love in mind until it is too late for her to stop. And women did not so easily reach that place of no return as men did.

His mouth was featherlight—provoking and enticing—and Sienna's head fell back. '*Hashim,*' she breathed, and all her hopes and longings were focused on that one little word.

He leapt on the spark of assent and sought to fan the fire with sweet words of his own. 'What is it, sweet Sienna? Sweet, sweet Sienna,' he whispered. His lips touched the base of her throat, teasing it with the tip of his tongue—an erotic and neglected area, or so he had been told—and her little moan told him that his information had been correct. At the same time he began to stroke his fingers down the curve of her hips, taking great care to avoid the obviously erogenous zones. 'That pleases you?'

She felt the pulsing of her blood, felt the words spill from her mouth as if she had no control over them. 'Oh, yes!' she gasped. 'Yes!'

Unseen, he smiled, now risking the flat of his hand lightly skating over her bottom, and in silent answer to the unspoken progression of his movements he felt her squirm against him. The smile disappeared as he let it skate right back again, to cup the pert globe with possessive fingers. Of course she was responsive! Was he forgetting what kind of woman she was? But he dampened his anger down, for it made him harden even more. And it was not his wish to just rip her panties off and drive into her. He would make her eat her defiant words of the other day in the most delicious way possible.

And she would beg him to do it to her!

He teased her and excited her, drifting his fingertips along her thighs, skittering them over the hungry fork of her, but, like a man spoilt for choice at a feast, he deliberately stayed away from her breasts. His mouth hardened. Those he was saving until last.

'Hashim!' she gasped in wonder, as he tiptoed sensation all over her skin, ignited it where he touched, leading her down a path so unbearably sweet that she could scarcely believe this was happening.

His mind worked more quickly than his fingers. If he sought out the classic place of seduction—a bed— then it might allow time for reality to snap into focus and break the spell. He felt himself grow taut, tense, tight, hard as he realised that it was going to have to be here. *Here!* Like a schoolboy with no place to go—but the thought of that, too, excited him. Making do was not something he had ever encountered before, and as always the novel had an intoxicating power all of its own.

When he touched her leg she made no objection. He could feel her impatience and he rewarded it with the slow slide of his hand beneath the filmy layers of her delicate dress, circling the cool satin of her inner thigh to the sound of a tiny moan made at the back of her throat.

'You like that?'

What could she say? Especially as his fingertips were now skating over the moist silk of her panties. Her skin was blazing, her heart was thundering, and warmth and longing overwhelmed her. For only Hashim could make her feel this way—this alive— this wonderful. Like one of those statues brought to life at the end of a play, able to live properly at last. 'Y-yes.' She shuddered. 'You know I do.'

'Then hold me, Sienna,' he urged. 'Hold me.' And as her hands fluttered up to catch hold of the broad bank of his shoulders he gave a grim kind of smile. That was not exactly what he had meant, but for now it would have to do.

Exulting in the freedom of actually touching him again, Sienna was aware that the tips of her fingers were pressing into the fine silk which covered the infinitely finer silk of the skin beneath. Her nails began to scrabble cat-like against the slippery material, as if she wanted to rip it from his body, and he gave a low laugh of delight.

'Ah, yes,' he murmured appreciatively. 'Much better! I see that time has done nothing but hone your appetites.'

His words should have warned her, or stopped her, or cautioned her, but she was in a golden fog of wanting as he began to touch her with a slow, expert caress, and too bewitched to stop him, wanting more, far more.

He pushed aside the damp fabric of her knickers and touched her intimately, where her heat seared against him, and he felt the warmth of her and now he, too, groaned.

'Hashim!' she cried out, startled by sensation—like someone who had jumped out of a parachute after a long absence and forgotten just how mind-blowing it could be. And it had been such a long time...

'You like that?' he teased.

The word was wrenched from her. 'Y-yes.'

'What else do you like?'

'You know,' she breathed. He seemed to know *everything*.

Amid the clamour of his senses he had one last thought of clarity. That the bodyguards stationed at the end of the drive and on the outskirts of the surrounding farmland could not completely guarantee his privacy. Rogue photographers from the hated press might be hiding in the undergrowth—and what a story this would be!

Sheikh caught in flagrante with employee!

Ruthlessly, he continued to move his fingers against her, until, glancing down, he could see that she was lost. Her eyes were smoky and she trembled like a leaf. Was she as receptive as this with every man? he wondered grimly, unprepared for the poisonous snake of jealousy which coiled around his heart. His black eyes scanned the hallway and the dim, dark corridor which ran from the far end of it. Along there they would be unseen.

He felt her stir restlessly and kissed her again, for he knew that a kiss held more power than anything else. That women could be made to fall in love under the spell of a kiss—for they read into it all their secret desires and needs. He felt an infinitesimal moment of hesitation before she melted right into him, and he knew then that her capitulation was certain.

He picked her up in his arms and carried her towards the cool flagstones and the muted colours of a long, silken rug which softened it, lying her down on top of it. Sienna's eyes fluttered open as if she had suddenly just come out of a coma and realised where she was.

'What are you doing?'

There was a strange kind of startlement on her face which almost moved him—until he reminded himself that disingenuous questions like *that* one were sometimes asked out of habit more than necessity. Had she learnt somewhere along the line that men were turned on by innocence? But he would play along with the game if it eased her conscience.

'What do you think I'm doing?' he said softly, as he lay down beside her—*he*, the *Sheikh*, lying on the floor with a woman. 'I am fulfilling my wildest dream and fantasy.'

And hers, too.

'Really?' she questioned tentatively.

'But of course,' he said smoothly, taking her into his arms, knowing that his embrace would dispel any lingering doubts. 'I want you, Sienna. My beautiful Sienna. Indeed, I have never stopped wanting you. Did you not know that?'

She shook her head, her mind a whirl of confusing thoughts. 'But you—'

'Shh.'

His face was close to hers, his breath warm on her face, and all she wanted was for him to kiss her again. She felt the ground hard beneath her back, and the hard body pressing against hers, and fleetingly she wondered how and why she had allowed this to happen. But it was only very fleeting, and suddenly it didn't matter. She couldn't stop. She didn't want to stop.

Once—a long time ago—Hashim had given her a taste of passion and it had branded and spoiled her for ever. The men who had tried to get close to her subsequently had had an impossible act to follow, even if they hadn't been aware of it at the time. And might not this single act help her to exorcise a ghost which was all too real, to move on and break free of his enchantment?

She licked at her dry lips. 'We do not have very long. Wh-what about the staff? The…the guests?' she managed.

Hashim stilled, his eyes narrowing. If there had been any tiny vestige of guilt at his cold-blooded seduction then she had banished it with her words. She knew *exactly* what she was doing. She was sexually hungry, as he was, and probably almost as experienced. Well, then—let her see who was the most magnificent lover of all her conquests!

For he too had been enchanted by the sense of nearly. Of something unfinished and incomplete. In his anger—with himself as well as with her—he had sent her packing before he had properly had his fill of her, and that sense of aching and burning frustration had never quite gone away. Well, now it would—and it would be gone for ever.

'We have long enough,' he said, and the stark note of hunger made his voice sound hollow—as if it came from a long way away—and for a moment he scarcely recognised it as his own.

And hunger made his hands tremble, made his need to join with her overwhelm him with a desire which banished all his carefully conceived plans. Forgotten was his long-nursed wish to feast upon the magnificent breasts which she had displayed for all the world to see. Instead—unbelievably and inexplicably—he found that he didn't want to wait. No—*couldn't* wait.

With a groan, he rucked up her skirt and found himself ripping off the delicate panties. She made no protest, her legs parting for him instantly. His robes were not encumbered by belts or buttons or zips. He could slither off the light silk of his trousers with ease until he was free at last, sliding on the necessary protection with the impatient fumbling of a schoolboy. And then he was touching and nudging against her with a restrained and magnificent power. At last! Such sweet torture, this moment of expectation, but a torture to be treasured and savoured until he could bear it no longer.

'Now,' he whispered—not a question but an emphatic statement, and in answer her lips pressed into his shoulder, opening against him, closing around his flesh. He could feel the wet of her tongue and the sharp graze of her teeth and could contain himself no longer. He drove hard into her.

There was one moment before he realised, a split-second as he worked out what was happening but by then it was too late. He saw the screwing up of her eyes, the way her little white teeth bit down on her bottom lip, and then he knew. By the mountains and the rivers!

'Sienna!' The word was torn from his lips even while her body became taut, like a bow stretched around him, before the arrow of his desire pierced through to the very heart of her. 'Sienna!' he said again, but this time it was on a note of wonder.

'Oh,' she breathed, the word a little feather which drifted away as the pain became transmuted into a growing and indescribable wave of pleasure and he began to move inside her.

He had planned his own release with little concern for hers—not like the first time—but now it was different. Now it was a virtuoso performance. Never had he taken so much care with a woman as he thrust all the way inside her—but then, never had the weight of such responsibility lain so heavy on his shoulders.

He found himself being gentle with her—an odd and unfamiliar kind of gentleness which made what was taking place seem to do so in slow motion, like a film viewed through a gauzy lens.

'Ah, Sienna.' And her name came out on a long, shuddering sigh.

He was slow for as long as he needed to be, and then a little faster. He held back for as long as he needed to, and then he drove in again, harder and then harder still. He teased her when she breathlessly began to beg for more, relentlessly retreating to take her further along the inexorable path, and just when he thought that he could withstand no more of this exquisite self-control he felt her begin to convulse around him.

Her cries split the air, her legs splaying and her back arching as her sweat-sheened face fell back, and she was calling his name in wonder and in disbelief.

And then—oh, sweet, sweet desire—then he let go himself, in an orgasm which rocked his world on its axis—which took him completely out of his body. It was a slow drift back to earth, and he fought it every bit of the way.

It had been the most mind-blowing sex of his entire life—but that should not have surprised him, not really.

After all, he had been waiting for this for a long, long time.

CHAPTER EIGHT

THROUGH the soft darkness Sienna became aware of her heart as it beat within her, strong and loud and steady. And then she became aware of another beat and another heart—so close to hers that it almost felt as if it was inside her. She felt warm and complete— as if she had been made whole at last—the slight aching deep inside her a glorious physical reminder of what had seemed like a perfect dream.

Opening her eyes, she took in the scene with something approaching disbelief. It had not been a dream. She was lying on a carpet in a dim, cool corridor in Hashim's arms, her dress around her hips, and he was staring down at her. Impossible to read what was in those glittering black eyes, but his question gave her some idea.

'Why didn't you tell me?' he asked quietly, his voice as deadly as the silent snakes which glided around the foothills of Qudamah's mountains.

'Tell you what?' she teased.

'Do not play games with me! You are a *virgin*!'

She heard the accusation in his voice and the pink bubble of contentment began to dissolve. 'I was,' she corrected.

He shook his dark head. 'I cannot believe it!'

'I'm afraid you have incontrovertible evidence, Hashim.'

'But…how?'

At any other time his incredulity would have been almost laughable, but now…now it just hurt. 'Surely you don't need me to tell you that?' she questioned quietly.

His mouth tightened. He was still reeling from this one incredible piece of knowledge which had rocked his world just as surely as his orgasm had. For the fact of her innocence had blown all his preconceptions out of the water. And it had done something else, too….

From the start his instinct about her had been that she was innocent, but the existence of the calendar had convinced him that her innocence had been a sham. But if *that* instinct had been correct then what about the other ones which had crowded in on him at the time? The ones which had left him muddled and confused making him wonder if he had found in her something which he had not thought possible?

And hadn't he been glad to abandon those feelings by seizing on her questionable past with something like relief? As if he found it easier to live in a state of cynicism rather than one of hope and longing, like other men.

He shook his head again, dazed and angry, too. 'It should not have been like that.'

She wanted to tell him that it had been perfect, but something in his attitude was puzzling her. He was acting as if something *shameful* had just taken place—rather than the something wonderful it had been. She stared up at him. 'What was wrong with it?'

'Wrong?' A frown creased his brow as he studied her face, rather as a scientist might intently bend over a test tube. 'Nothing was *wrong* with it.' How could she fail to understand? 'But it would never have happened if I had known. Why did you not tell me, Sienna?'

Because she hadn't been thinking of anything except the touch of his lips and the hard, strong embrace of his lean body. She had found it impossible to stop something she had wanted for so long—even though she had denied wanting it. Had told herself that it was wrong to want it.

'We weren't having much of a conversation at the time,' she said, aware that her voice sounded flippant.

'Your first time should not be with a casual lover on the floor of an anonymous house,' he said, and his deep voice was tinged with regret. 'Your virginity is a gift which you have clearly treasured, as every woman should. You should have saved it for a man you love. Who loves you.'

And with those sad words he smashed all her foolish hopes and dreams. He made her feel as if she had offered him fresh flowers at dawn—still wet with the morning dew—and he had taken them and carelessly tossed them into the gutter, to be ground underfoot into dust and crushed petals.

He seemed so far away, even though he was right next to her. A moment ago he had been kissing her over and over again, but he was not kissing her now. The hands which had wrought such sweet magic were not touching her now. It was done. Finished. And Sienna felt the dull ache of dawning realization, which eclipsed the deeper aching in her newly awakened body.

She had allowed…no, she had been a more than willing participant in *allowing* herself to be brought here. To lie with him on this hard stone floor and to…to… She would not use the words 'make love', for it had not been that. It had been nothing to do with love. He had just told her so.

So why were erotic and tender images still jostling for position in her mind? The way she had called out his name in breathless wonder. The way her body had shivered its pleasure, and the way that pleasure had grown and surged and taken her into a place where the senses reigned supreme. And she had stupidly allowed herself to believe that for him it meant more than simply pleasure. That his whispered words of encouragement and pleasure had been voicing some deeper emotion than mere desire—a longing more precious than lust. But in that she had been totally wrong.

Sienna swallowed, forcing the memories away, for they would soon bring nothing but pain. It was too late for regret, but not too late for pride. 'Well, there's no point in having a post mortem, is there?' she said, hearing the false brightness in her tone.

He was silent for a moment, and then his eyes imprisoned her—searching and seeking to know. 'Why has there been nobody else?' he demanded.

It was a question she had asked herself many times—and, oh, how it would feed his monstrous ego if she told him what she suspected was the truth: that he was the only man she had ever remotely imagined making love to. Men had tried, but they had failed. Or was it she who had failed—to abandon foolish hope and try to make the best of an ordinary life?

'You make it sound like a fault on my part that there hasn't been,' she said bitterly.

His eyes narrowed. 'What happened between us that last time. The way I behaved. Did that put you off men?'

'In a way.' But not the way *he* meant.

'You should have told me,' he said, and now his voice was angry. 'Back then you should have told me. But now—*now* when you are older and more independent, a true woman at last—you should have said something!'

'Would you have believed me?'

Another silence.

'Would you?' she persisted.

'No,' he said eventually. 'I guess I wouldn't have.' He felt like a man who had been swimming towards a familiar shore only to discover that he was headed for a strange land of which he knew nothing. None of it made any sense to him. How could it? She? Of all people? A *virgin*?

'Because you'd already made your mind up about what kind of woman I was. The photos proved that I must be some sort of slapper!'

Hashim's eyes narrowed, his English for once deserting him. 'Slapper?'

'The kind of woman who will just sleep with anyone. You didn't look further than skin-deep, did you, Hashim? You just made a judgement about me. But people are a lot more than they appear to be on the surface. Not cardboard cut-outs but living and breathing flesh and blood, with flaws and strengths all their own! Don't you realise that?' she finished.

'I'm afraid that my position sets me apart,' he told her coolly, seeking a familiar refuge behind the invisible barrier of his royal status. 'I do not have the luxury of the time to dig deep beneath the surface.'

'Or the inclination to even try?' she challenged.

'Maybe not,' he admitted, for it was impossible not to answer that lancing question in her green eyes.

Sienna nodded, forcing herself to voice the bitter truth. She had allowed passion to cloud her vision, but now that passion had passed it was achingly clear. 'You see women as commodities,' she whispered. 'To be used for passing pleasure but little else, other than maybe one day motherhood.' And she felt a stupid great yearning as she realised that Hashim would never put her in *that* category. Not in a million years. A woman who had allowed herself to be photographed in that way, a woman who had fallen oh-so-easily into his arms, was merely a woman to be discarded. And the aching sense of longing for something she could never have washed over her in a bitter tide.

He could feel her retreating from him—not just mentally, but physically, too, and that reawakened the desire which had been obscured by his startling discovery. He was used to calling the shots, and by rights *he* should have been the one to distance himself from her now. Or not.

'Ah, Sienna,' he murmured, and reached out his hand to cradle her face. 'What is done is done. Is it not a little late in the day for words of recrimination?'

Involuntarily Sienna trembled—for the touch of his skin was soft and warm and exquisite to behold. It had the power to lure her back into that place of unimaginable pleasure. But at what cost? She shook his hand away and sat up.

'Yes, you're right, it is. I should have said all this before.'

'But you could not!' he breathed triumphantly. 'For you were as much in thrall to me as I to you! What just happened between us was as inevitable as the passing of night through to day. I knew that.'

'Well, we're all entitled to make mistakes,' she said woodenly. 'And anyway, we're wasting time, sitting around here talking. Your guests will be arriving very soon and I suggest that we both of us try to tidy up.' She reached up her hand to feel the bird's nest mess of her hair, wondering how the hell she was going to tame it down.

She was surprised that he wasn't leaping around fretting. He hadn't once mentioned the no-show of the staff. Or the fact that his guests would be upon them shortly. And then something else occurred to her—dripping into her thoughts like slow poison—something which in its way was almost as bad as what she had just let happen. She could feel the heavy plummeting of her heart as everything clicked into disturbingly sharp focus.

Oh, no.

How could she have been so *stupid*?

Slowly, she turned her head to stare at him. 'But there aren't going to be any guests—are there, Hashim?'

He met the accusation in her eyes but he did not flinch from it. 'No.'

'There were never going to be any guests, were there?'

'No.'

She geared herself up for the next blow, knowing the answer to her question before she asked it. 'And the staff? The staff I so carefully vetted and booked but who didn't bother to show?'

'I allowed them to prepare for the dinner, so that your suspicions would not be alerted, and then I cancelled them.'

'You cancelled them,' she said slowly, feeling sickened by the sheer cold-bloodedness of his plan. 'Just like that?'

He shrugged. 'It was not difficult. I paid them in full.'

'*You paid them in full?*' she repeated, her voice shaking, haunted by the thought that she had followed suit. Fallen into line and done exactly what Hashim had wanted. What he had planned. He had lured her into a sensual trap which she had embraced with all the enthusiasm of the convert. She felt the hot sting of hurt but she would not allow it to be converted to tears. She would *not* cry in front of him.

'You snapped your fingers and everybody jumped, I expect. You and your damned money and your damned power,' she whispered. He had tricked her into organising a party just so that he could seduce her—how low could a man sink? And how could she have let him? How *could* she? The true extent of his deception brought fire into her voice.

'You think you can just pick people up and use them, move them around like pawns and then throw them off the board when you've finished with them?' she raged.

Hashim listened, waiting patiently for the storm to pass. Let her rage be spent, and then afterwards let her see sense. Realise that what had passed between them had been magnificent and that to let it go would be a waste of the highest order. Why, he could take her upstairs to one of the magnificent bedrooms, where they could continue to take their pleasure. Her anger would soon be forgotten after a night in his arms!

'Sienna—'

'No!' she said fiercely, pushing away from him and scrambling to her feet. She had seen the brief darkening of his eyes, and she might be new to this game but she knew exactly what it meant. And did she trust herself around him? No, she did not. Her spirit might be fighting all the way, but around Hashim her flesh was as weak as it could be.

She moved as far away from him as possible. There was no dignified way of adjusting her dress and her panties, but she did her damnedest, raking her fingers back through the hair which had tumbled in untidy tendrils all down the side of her long neck.

And at least she had the enjoyment of seeing *Hashim* get to his feet and begin to rearrange his clothing, his face now tight with obvious displeasure and a simmering kind of anger. Or was it merely frustration?

She walked out into the hall, all the warmth and comfort and pleasure evaporating from her body like raindrops on a scorching pavement. And then she caught a glimpse of herself in the mirror and recoiled at the sight of her flushed cheeks and mussed hair— the definite look of someone who had been rolling around the place.

How could she? Oh, how *could* she?

She picked up her handbag and a silken voice stopped her in her tracks.

'Where do you think you are going?' he questioned softly.

Composing her face, she turned round, and suddenly she didn't care *what* he tried to threaten her with. Just let him try. Nothing could be worse than what she had just allowed to happen, despite all her supposedly good intentions. 'Home,' she said crisply. 'Where else?'

'You could come home with me.'

Sienna almost choked. 'I'd rather spend the night in a lions' cage! And anyway—I wouldn't call a luxury hotel suite a *home*! It isn't yours, it's anonymous—just like this place. There's nothing of you there, Hashim. A luxurious room with no soul. And that's your life. Empty.'

For a moment a dark shadow passed across his heart. She dared to say this to him? To accuse him of an empty life? He, who had palaces and oil fields and people scattered all over the world who were eager to do his bidding? No woman had ever dared say such a thing to him. She was daring to look at him and speak to him as no woman ever had before…almost as his *equal*. Again he felt the sensation of being on unfamiliar territory, and his mouth hardened in anger.

'I forbid you to go!'

'Well, you can't. You don't own me. You don't even employ me any more. I've done what you asked and now I'm leaving.'

His eyes narrowed as he glanced around the carved

wooden interior of the airy hall. 'And what of this house and your obligation to it?' he demanded.

'It's not my concern. Not any more. *You* sort it out! Here!' And she flung the keys at him.

He caught them one-handed, realising that she meant exactly what she said. She was leaving! Walking out on him even though she had been sobbing out his name only moments before. And suddenly he was filled with a reluctant kind of admiration which only renewed the subtle throbbing of desire. 'Has anyone ever told you how beautiful you look when you're angry?' he questioned softly.

'Fortunately, most people have a more original line than that!'

'But it is not finished yet, Sienna,' he said evenly. 'I tell you that quite unequivocably. You have but tasted the pleasures I can give you, and soon you will be greedy for more.'

'Oh, but you're wrong. So wrong.' She stared at him. 'After all, we're even now. I deceived you, and now you've paid me back by deceiving me. We can call it quits. I just want to forget you and your fake party. In fact, I want to forget all about you.'

He shook his head and his mouth curved into a cruel smile. 'You still don't understand, do you, Sienna? Those are not *my* wishes—and the Sheikh always has *his* wishes fulfilled.'

He wasn't listening to a word she said! Frustratedly, she turned away, and his dark laughter was still ringing in her ears as she slammed her way out of the front door, running down to where her beaten-up little wreck of a car was parked beside his smooth, dark sports model. And if she needed some concrete evidence of the insurmountable differences in their lives she had only to look at their two contrasting cars.

It's over, she told herself fiercely.

So why did she look up into the driver's mirror to see his tall dark figure, the silken pomegranate robes whispered by the breeze to caress that hard, honed body which had made such sweet and unforgettable love to her?

She turned the key in the ignition with an angry jerk. It was over.

CHAPTER NINE

HASHIM rang her. Repeatedly. Sienna kept the phone on 'divert', but once she picked it up without checking and heard his voice, and quietly terminated the connection with a trembling hand.

He sent her a cheque—such a grossly inflated cheque that the businesswoman side of her momentarily weakened, until she allowed her righteous fury to put it in an envelope and send it back to him. She supposed she could have torn it up—but returning it might help to get the message through loud and clear.

He even tried flowers—and for some reason those riled her more than anything. How *dared* he think he could buy her off with a bunch of flowers?

'They're lovely,' Kat said wistfully, sniffing at the lily-of-the-valley and freesia and roses.

'Have them—they're yours!' And Sienna unceremoniously dumped the monster bouquet into her bemused lodger's arms.

Her work, which had previously fulfilled her, suddenly seemed a chore, and her life felt like a punctured balloon, coloured grey. Kat had taken to asking if she was sickening for something, and Sienna knew that she really was going to have to snap out of it. She had a business to run and she couldn't divert her phone for ever. And Hashim seemed to have got the message at last, since he had left her alone for nearly a week.

She was sitting in her minuscule office, trying to concentrate on an engagement party which seemed to mock her with its celebration of love, when the telephone on her desk rang. Tiny hairs on the back of her neck began to prickle as she heard a disturbingly familiar dark, silken voice, and she wavered for a second. She could hang up, of course—or she could have the courage to tell him to leave her alone. And she couldn't keep running away for ever.

'What can I do for you, Hashim?' she questioned coolly.

'Why have you failed to cash my cheque?' he demanded.

'Because I don't want your money!'

'Ah, Sienna,' he purred, like a trainee lion cub. 'Don't you realise that resistance turns a man on?'

Especially a man who wasn't used to being resisted. 'That isn't why I'm doing it,' came her icy reply.

He knew that. As a ploy it would have failed, because he would have seen through it. As a genuine wish it excited him. Greatly. 'I want to see you,' he said softly.

Images of his dark mocking eyes swam into her unwilling memory. 'Well, you can't.'

Did she not realise that he could hear her breathless note of hesitation—and the reluctant longing which matched his own? His voice dipped into a mocking caress as he felt the hot, hard jerk of desire. 'Then say it like you mean it.'

Sienna closed her eyes, but that only made it worse. Now the images were of a hard body entering hers with almost heartbreaking sweetness. 'There's no point,' she said wildly.

'On the contrary. There is every point. I have a proposition to put to you.'

'A proposition?' Suspicion crept into her voice. 'Planning another fictitious party, are you?'

He gave a low laugh. 'Now, that's an idea! Meet me and I'll tell you all about it.'

'Have you listened to a word I've been saying? I don't want your phone calls or your flowers, and I certainly don't want to *see* you, Hashim!'

'Yes, you do,' he murmured. 'You know that and I know that. You are unsettled and so am I. Why keep fighting it? Your work will suffer, for a start.'

And he was right, damn him! She had almost more work than she could reasonably cope with, and—ironically—no inclination to do it. It had taken every bit of concentration she had to prevent herself from sitting staring into space and thinking about the dark Sheikh, trying to school herself away from wanting him, but in reality... Oh, the reality was so different.

'If I meet you, will you promise to leave me alone?'

He gave a wry smile. How had she managed to get

so far with such an appalling sense of logic? 'If that is what you desire,' he said carefully.

Desire. What a dangerous and provocative word that was. Sienna clenched her fist as she felt the empty little tug of her heart. 'Name a time and place.'

'Now.'

'Now?'

'I am very close to your house. I will be waiting.'

'You *are* joking!'

'What's the matter, Sienna?' he mocked. 'Are you never spontaneous?'

She was wearing her oldest jeans and a T-shirt which one of the football team had given her at college. There was a rip at the hem and a stain on it which she thought might be *crème de menthe*, but she wasn't entirely sure. She glanced in the mirror at her unwashed hair, which was caught back in a ponytail. Maybe if he saw her like this—the real, basic Sienna—then he would get the message.

'Okay,' she said slowly. 'I'll meet you.'

'Five minutes,' he clipped, and hung up.

Pausing only to brush her teeth, telling herself that she would have done the same no matter who she was meeting, she slid on a pair of old flip-flops and let herself out of the house, wondering where he was waiting.

She didn't have to wonder for very long. A shiny limousine with tinted windows was parked at the end of the road—presumably because the road was so narrow it could go no further. In front of it and just to the rear were two leather-clad outriders on powerful motorbikes. It was like a scene straight out of a film, and Sienna could see a couple of curtains twitching as she walked towards it.

My neighbours will never look at me in quite the same way she thought, as a chauffeur stepped out of the driver's seat and opened the door for her.

Telling herself that she could hardly be rude to Hashim's employee, she had no choice but to slide into the soft-cushioned luxury of the back seat. It took a few seconds for her eyes to become accustomed to the dim light, but she could see Hashim sprawled negligently on the back seat, watching her.

Today he was wearing Western clothes—not a shimmer of soft silk in sight. An immaculately cut dark suit, with a snowy shirt and a tie which gleamed dully in the reduced light. Sienna could feel her heart begin to pound.

'Nice of you to get out of the car yourself,' she said.

'I was thinking of your reputation.'

'Liar.'

He laughed. 'Your assessment of me is wholly and completely wrong, Sienna—my honesty has at times been described as almost brutal.'

Brutal. Yes. There *was* a brutal side to his nature. And yet it contrasted with the extraordinary gentleness he had displayed when she had lain so helplessly in his arms. She felt the drying of her lips, and as if he had read her thoughts he leaned forward and touched his mouth to hers in a barely-there kiss which started her senses sizzling.

'Don't,' she said weakly.

The same cold skill and calculation which made him a world-class poker player made him kiss her for long enough to hear her sigh, and then he stopped and leaned back against the seat to study her. He pressed a button by his side and said something she did not understand. The car began its powerful acceleration.

'Where are we going?' she questioned, in alarm.

'Just driving around—we will draw less attention to ourselves that way—this car tends to attract sightseers.'

'Why don't you travel in something less ostentatious, then?' she questioned acidly.

'Because I cannot,' he said simply. 'It needs to be bullet-proof.'

And—perhaps for the very first time—Sienna allowed herself to see the downside of his life. Hadn't there been part of her which had somehow thought that the bodyguards which accompanied him were simply for show? As some kind of indicator of his power and lofty position? She had never actually stopped to think that someone might want to *shoot* him, and now that she had she found her stomach twisting over in anxiety.

'Now, let us both be honest,' he said quietly. 'Can you do that?'

'You don't take any notice of me when I am.'

But he shook his head. 'No, Sienna—I am talking about *real* honesty. I do not mean that you should say what you feel you *ought* to say, but what is truly in your heart.'

'Then I'm at a disadvantage—for *you* don't have a heart!'

He paused, for it was not the first time this accusation had been flung at him. 'Have you thought of me?'

She opened her mouth to say no—but something in his eyes stopped her. 'Yes.'

He nodded his head. 'And for me it is the same. I have thought of little else. The way you felt in my arms. You haunt me, Sienna—for I cannot forget the great gift which you gave to me.'

'Which you took, you mean,' she corrected him quietly. 'You set me up and seduced me—as you had intended to do right from the start.'

'Yes,' he said bitterly. 'Of that I am guilty—I robbed you of your greatest virtue. But I would not have done it had I known that you were innocent, and that innocence has changed everything.' He paused, studying the lush fullness of her mouth, and when he spoke his voice was almost reflective. 'What passed between us was not enough—not for me, nor for you. You were beautiful and responsive, but your initiation into the pleasures of the body should not be limited to a single session on a cold floor, our bodies not even naked.'

She was glad then for the dim light, for she began

to blush and he saw. His eyes narrowed and she wondered if he was remembering—as she was—that very first blush such a long time ago. 'It's over,' she said, aware of how lacking in conviction her words sounded. Was that because she didn't *want* it to be over?

He thought how strange it was that a woman could still blush with innocence, even when that innocence was gone. 'Ah, but that is where you are wrong,' he whispered. 'It is not over. Indeed, that was only the beginning.'

Sienna blinked, because suddenly the picture had shifted, changed focus. Was he asking her to be his *girlfriend*? 'What are you saying?' she whispered.

'You came to me untutored—a beautiful novice,' he said huskily. 'And yet, in a way, it was as new for me as it was for you.' His black eyes glittered. 'You see, I had never had a virgin before.'

He made himself sound like a jockey who had attempted a higher than usual jump, and his matter-of-fact words fractured the tiny flicker of hope which had begun to spark into life. But maybe that was a blessing, because the very word 'virgin' was charged with emotion—and emotion could, she realized, be character-changing in every sense of the word. It could make you weak when you most needed to be strong. 'Am I supposed to be flattered by this remarkable statement?'

'Yes,' he said simply. 'For I am admitting to you that I found the experience profoundly moving.'

As an admission it bordered on the arrogant, and if it had been anyone else then Sienna might have said so. But something stopped her. Maybe it was the look in his eyes. As if he had lifted away a veil and allowed her to see a whisper of contrition. And the unexpected glimpse of this gave him the fleeting shimmer of vulnerability, reminding her that deep down he was just a man—that all the rest was just packaging.

'Go on,' she said steadily. 'I'm intrigued.'

'I want to teach you everything there is to know about the art of love.' His smile was edged with hunger. There was the briefest of pauses before he spoke again. 'I want you to become my mistress,' he said softly.

Sienna stilled. *'What?'*

'I am choosing you to become mistress to the Sheikh.'

He made it sound so…*mechanical.* 'Is there a new vacancy, then?' she questioned acidly. 'Or will I be sharing the post?'

Hashim was so used to complete compliance—to grateful and eager acceptance from adoring women— that for a moment he was taken aback by her flippant attitude. 'I do not think you realise the honour I am affording you,' he said icily.

'No, I probably don't,' said Sienna gravely. 'Perhaps you could tell me a little more about what this exciting position entails?'

Because no one ever made fun of him Hashim did

not recognise the mocking tone in her voice. He had never had to persuade or to entice a lover before, and such coercion did not come naturally to him.

'You will have an open charge account.' His black eyes flicked disparagingly over her jeans and stained T-shirt. 'And in future you will buy clothes that please you and please your Sheikh.'

'Do you have any particular requests?' Sienna questioned meekly. 'Favourite colours? That kind of thing?'

Hashim's eyes narrowed suspiciously. Was she agreeing without further argument? Damn the woman—why did she keep coming out and surprising him? 'Obviously what you are wearing today is thoroughly unsuitable.'

'Obviously,' she agreed steadily.

'I should like to see you in silks and satins from now on,' he said coolly. 'And velvets and lace. Nothing *man-made*.' He shuddered. 'You should dress to please me, for when I am pleased then it follows that you shall be, too.'

'How delightfully simple you make it sound,' Sienna murmured. 'Anything else?'

His black eyes gleamed with anticipation as he imagined clothing her in delicate underclothes—and then ripping them off! 'As you know, I spend the majority of my time in Qudamah, but I frequently travel to the major cities to conduct business on behalf of my country, and when I do I wish for you to fly out to join me. I will send my private jet for you,' he promised silkily.

She ignored the airborne carrot he dangled. 'But what about my job?' she questioned seriously.

'Your job?'

'Or rather, my career,' she corrected. 'I've built it up from scratch and worked hard—I can't just abandon it to flit off to all the corners of the globe on a whim.'

Hashim gave her an impatient look. 'Your job will no longer be necessary. You will have all the money you need. You can give it up.'

Give it up? Sienna could not hold her feelings in any more. Did he have no idea how real people lived their lives? She supposed that he didn't. 'I'm not doing any such thing!' she declared. 'I take pride in my work, Hashim. I have a number of big contracts in the pipeline.'

'Sub-contract them.'

'No, I will not.'

'Sienna, you are stretching my patience!'

'And you're stretching mine! Do you imagine for a moment that I can be bought?'

There was a moment of silence. 'Everyone can be bought—you of all people should know that.'

'Are you still on about those wretched photographs? Can't you just let it go?' She stared at him and then reached for the door. 'I won't be insulted by you any more. And I don't have to be. You've had your pound of flesh, Hashim—just be satisfied with that.'

Suddenly he found himself wishing that he could bite the words back. 'Sienna. Don't go.' He caught her arm and began to caress it with his fingers. 'Please.'

She closed her eyes, her inner turmoil lulled by the touch of his hand, recognising that his plea was an unfamiliar one. She had made her stand and demonstrated her independence and her pride—but nothing could change the effect he had always had on her, and still did. The melting way he made her feel inside whenever he touched her. The way his very presence made her feel so *alive*. If she took that out of the equation there would be nothing to consider, but it was far too powerful to disregard.

She opened her eyes again. 'It's not all about what *you* want, is it, Hashim? It's about what I want, too.'

He had been almost certain that she was—incredibly!—going to turn him down, and it was Hashim's turn to be surprised. Was she playing games with him? 'You mean you are giving consideration to my proposal?'

'Of course I am. A woman would have to be pretty stupid not to, wouldn't she? It isn't every day that she is offered a chance to play the starring role in Cinderella!'

But, inexplicably, his triumph was now tempered by a fleeting sense of disappointment—for it now appeared that she was going to give in, and he had been enjoying doing battle with her. 'So you will agree?'

'Only if you agree to my terms.'

'*Your* terms?' he repeated, outraged.

'But of course. Why should it all go your way?'

Because it always had done—all his life! 'Name them,' he snapped.

'Well, you can forget the idea of a charge card, for a start—I don't want it, thank you all the same. I don't earn a fortune, but what I do has been honestly come by—and I usually manage to scrub up well enough without the benefit of costly clothes. And I will only fly to see you if it is convenient. To me.' Because soon it would be over, and when it was she would need her livelihood just the same as she always had. 'I will continue with my life as normal—if you want to see me then you will have to fit in around me.'

'But what you ask of me is outrageous!' he protested.

She shrugged. 'Then forget the whole idea. In fact,' she added truthfully, 'that would be much better for me in the long-term.'

'But in the short-term you do not want to forget it,' he murmured, pulling her into his arms. 'Right now your body is screaming out for me. You know that I am growing hard even now, just as you are wet with wanting. Aren't you?'

'Hashim, you're…you're…' But her words were forgotten, for he had put his hands underneath her T-shirt to cup the aching mounds of her breasts.

'No bra?' he questioned shakily, torn between excitement and disapproval as he felt their velvet weight against his palms.

'I never wear one when I'm working at home. Oh!' She gasped as he bent his mouth to one hardened nipple and began to suckle it. His hand was skimming the narrow indentation of her waist, which led down to an unforgiving waistband. And now his hand had moved to the fork of her thighs, and he was touching her through the denim…touching her and touching her. 'Hashim, wh—what do you think you're doing?'

'Guess.'

'But…but we're in the car.'

'The driver can't see. Do you want me to stop?'

She squirmed with pleasure beneath his touch. Not yet. Just a couple of minutes more and then she would stop him. 'We can't actually *do* anything if I'm wearing jeans, can we?' she asked breathlessly.

'Can't we?' He laughed, skating a featherlight fingertip over the most intimate part of her.

How could she feel this way? As though he was touching her flesh instead of the thick material of her jeans. 'Hashim—'

'Shh. Let go,' he urged, excited now as he watched her. 'Just let go.'

And to her eternal shame she did just that. Forgot the fact that she was writhing around in the back of a car in the middle of heaven only knew where. Forgot that she might have salvaged a little pride by returning his cheque and refusing his calls. She just went right along with the demands of her body, allowing herself to be carried along by the sweet and irresistible torrent.

'Oh!' She half sobbed as he increased the movement of his finger.

'Yes,' he murmured. 'You are so close, Sienna. So beautifully close. Let me watch you as I give you pleasure. Let me see you orgasm in your blue jeans.'

And then that feeling was upon her again—that out-of-this-world, flying-to-paradise feeling was sweeping her up and away, orchestrated by the relentless and expert caress of his fingers. And suddenly she had begun to cry out—little cries of astounded pleasure—until the fierce pressure of his mouth blocked out the sound and her body shattered into a million beautiful pieces.

For countless seconds she felt the spasms of her body shuddering to a slow halt, the sticky warmth of contentment. She was aware of Hashim stroking away the hair from her sweat-sheened brow.

'How can that have happened?' she whispered, half to herself. 'How?'

Unseen, he smiled. How little she knew—and how much he had to show her! He lifted her chin so that he could stare down at her with black eyes which mocked and lanced. 'Ah, Sienna,' he said softly. 'Do you see how much you have to learn?'

Lying curled in his arms in the aftermath of her orgasm, she was at her most vulnerable. 'Perhaps I do,' she agreed drowsily.

Maybe when you first gave your heart to someone it was difficult to claw it back again. With Hashim there had always been a sense of something left uncompleted—hadn't he said so himself? Maybe this really was the answer. If she saw more of him then mightn't it diminish some of the magic which surrounded him? Which made her see him as she failed to see other men?

'So you will agree to be my mistress?'

She turned her face up to his and opened her eyes very wide. 'Only on a strictly informal basis.'

'And will you come back to my hotel now and let me give you dinner?'

And, presumably, bed. But that was what a mistress *should* do—and who was she to complain if it meant that Hashim would make love to her?

'I'll need to go home and get showered first.'

He gave a slow smile of anticipation. 'We'll have a bath together,' he said. And he would send out those disgusting clothes of hers to be laundered.

CHAPTER TEN

Six months later

'You are late,' Hashim said coldly, as Sienna walked into the hotel bedroom.

'Only a little.'

'I have been waiting,' he said ominously, 'for over an hour.'

'Sorry, darling.' Sienna slipped off the soft green cashmere coat she had allowed him to buy her for Christmas, its emerald *faux* fur collar gleaming in the pale winter sunshine. It was the *only* thing she had allowed him to buy—and then only because it was Christmas. Even though—as she had teasingly pointed out—he didn't actually *celebrate* Christmas.

'But *you* do!' he had growled.

In a way, it frustrated him that she had steadfastly refused to be showered with the gifts which he thought were her due—but then, he didn't have a monopoly on frustration. She had discovered early on that it went hand-in-hand with the pleasures of being a mistress.

It was such an unreal existence.

So many of their meetings were conducted in secret—behind the closed doors of hotel rooms—while they lost themselves in each other's arms. Sometimes they would slip out to a discreet restaurant for a meal—though always shadowed by the ever-present bodyguards.

It was easier in Paris or some of the Spanish cities—which afforded more anonymity—but being abroad only increased Sienna's sense of unreality. The certainty that this relationship could not last, and her fear of when it would end. Whether it would be less painful if it happened sooner rather than later.

It was as though what they had between them was so fragile that any kind of analysis might shatter it. And it wasn't even something she could talk to her girlfriends about—and certainly not her mother. When you had an ordinary relationship—were having those ordinary fears about where it was headed—then friendly advice was yours for the taking.

But being a mistress was an indeterminate occupation, frowned on by society in general—both his *and* hers. For it flew in the face of the family values which most people believed in, deep down.

Only in her case she was not strictly a mistress. Hashim didn't have a wife waiting at home. Instead he had a country—which was far more demanding.

She turned to watch him as he pressed a button on the wall and the heavy drapes slid silently to a close, blocking out the daylight and enclosing them in their own private world.

Hand provocatively placed on her hip, Sienna raised her eyebrows as he turned round. 'You complain that I've kept you waiting, and yet you haven't even kissed me hello yet!'

Exasperated and turned on, he pulled her into his arms and kissed her. 'Hello.'

'And hello to you, too.'

He rubbed his forehead against hers. 'How you love to make me angry, Sienna.'

'No, I don't,' she said seriously. 'It's just that you work yourself up into a complete state when I don't do exactly what you say.'

'But you never do what I say.'

'Ask me something—anything—and I will!'

He took her face between his hands and looked down at her. 'Will you kiss me again, my non-compliant and informal little mistress?'

She lifted her lips to his, winding her arms around his neck, giving a little yelp of pleasure as their mouths collided in a kiss which this time was much more than a greeting. It was a hard, hungry and frustrated kiss. She hadn't seen him in nearly a month, and he wasn't supposed to be here for another fortnight.

But he had sandwiched in an extra trip to London on the way back from the States and called her at the last minute. Sienna had decided not to play games for the sake of it and had agreed to change her diary around. And bought a new set of underwear.

In between the frantic unzipping and unbuttoning of their clothes there were fractured bursts of conversation.

'I've missed you,' he groaned.

'Good.'

He reached down and slid off first one high-heeled shoe and then the other, caressing a silk-clad ankle on the way. 'You're supposed to tell me that you missed me, too.'

'That…oh!' She shivered as he rippled his fingers up over a stocking-top and circled the satin flesh above it. 'That is what I would call fishing for a compliment.' She gulped.

His hand halted. 'So you didn't?'

'You've only been gone a month.'

'Only?' he questioned ominously.

She reached down and guided his hand back again. 'Yes, yes, yes—I've missed you. I've thought about you constantly and dreamt of this moment! Is that better?'

'Much better,' he murmured. 'If it is true.'

Oh, yes, it was true, she thought as he carried her over to the bed and put her down in the centre of it. She had missed him more than he would ever know and more than she would ever tell him. She might have been a novice when she started her affair with Hashim—but she was growing to learn the rules. And the number one rule seemed to be always keep something back.

She had recognised early on that her Sheikh was a natural hunter—and that like all hunters he enjoyed the thrill of the chase. He was never more passionate than when she didn't leap into line. It wasn't the hardest psychology in the world to work out that a man for whom the world jumped would be fascinated by someone who didn't.

And for Sienna it was less about game-playing than protecting herself. Stopping herself falling deeper in love with a man who could never reciprocate the emotion. But holding back love wasn't as easy as playing hard to get. Love was like sunlight outside the dark of a barn—there were always cracks and crevices for it to come flooding inside.

She pushed the thoughts away as he took off her dress, her bra and her panties—though he left her stockings and suspender belt on. Lying back against the cushions, she watched as he removed his clothes, peeling off his suit and shirt and skimming off his silken underwear until he was formidably and powerfully naked.

Sometimes she touched herself while he undressed, as he had taught her to—rubbing at her breasts or teasing him with the tantalising stroke of a finger between her legs. Sometimes he even liked to watch her bring herself to orgasm—but today she could see a tight tension in his muscular body, and she frowned and did not tease him.

When he came to lie beside her she noticed the dark shadows beneath his eyes and lifted a finger to touch them. 'You're tired,' she observed softly.

'Then make me untired.'

'Is there such a word as untired?'

'There is now.' He closed his eyes as she licked

with her tongue from nipple to belly and then beyond, to where he was unbearably hard. 'Ah, Sienna,' he groaned. 'Where the hell did you learn to do that?'

'You taught me, Hashim,' she murmured, before taking him slowly into her mouth. 'Remember? You taught me everything.'

Afterwards he thought that he had taught her perhaps too well... She was like a whore in the bedroom—as a woman should be. She was everything he had ever dreamed of—and more. And one day another man would benefit from his tutition—perhaps sooner than either of them had anticipated. Another man would see her head bobbing up and down on his lap, her mouth working sweet spells while she took him to paradise and back. His lips twisted as a sting of pain caught him unawares, but then fatigue wrapped him in its gritty arms and he slept.

When he awoke it was to see Sienna lying propped on one elbow watching him, her hair spilling down all over the rosy flush of her breasts, and in that hazy moment between sleep and waking he gave an instinctive smile—for this was the place in which he most liked to find himself.

She thought that he looked like a lion who had temporarily sated his huge appetite. A fleeting look of contentment before the relentless and ruthless search for sustenance once more. He drove himself, she had realized, more than most men would even be capable of doing. And, whilst he had a huge capacity for hard work and long hours, she had never seen that weary tinge to his smile before.

She touched his lips with a gentle finger. 'So, is it jet-lag?'

'Maybe.' He kissed the finger. She was so easy. So perceptive. Sometimes it was hard not to tell her the things on his mind, but he rarely gave voice to his innermost thoughts. For a ruler it was preferable to keep your own counsel, but sometimes—in the aftermath of making love to Sienna—he found himself wanting to offload his problems, as other men apparently did. He wondered what had changed, and when it had happened.

Something had crept up on him unawares. Maybe it was like the shadow on your jaw. You didn't notice it—and it wasn't until your chin was grazed with the dark rasp of stubble that you remembered it was well on its way to becoming a beard.

Sienna brushed away a lock of the dark hair which had tumbled onto his forehead. Against the white sheets his body looked so golden and erotically dark—like a rich oil painting brought into vibrant and glowing life before her eyes. 'You don't usually suffer from jet-lag,' she observed quietly.

'No.'

There was silence for a moment, and Sienna knew that she could do one of two things: she could get up and go into the plush kitchen of the hotel suite and make them both a cup of the iced jasmine tea he so loved and which she had learned to love, too. She could put on soft and soothing music and run him a deep, deep bath and then join him in it. And later they would make love again. And again. That was what a mistress would and should do.

Or she could venture onto the always precarious path of finding out just what was going on in that clever, quick mind of his. Six months ago she wouldn't have dreamed of contemplating it—but hadn't Hashim been softer of late? Didn't the enigmatic and formidable side of his nature sometimes seem less dominant, so that sometimes he seemed much more *accessible*?

'So, do you want to tell me what's wrong, or do you want me to run away and do womanly things?'

'Like what?'

'Oh, you know…tea, a bath, music.'

A smile edged the hardness away from his mouth. 'No, don't go. Stay here. You've just done the most important thing a woman can do for a man.'

There was another silence, and Sienna tried hard not to read too much into his words. Just because he had sounded uncharacteristically tender it did not mean anything. He was basically applauding her rapidly improving skills as a lover and thus his own skills as an expert tutor—that was all. Or he was being slightly more affectionate because they hadn't seen each other for a few weeks. There were any number of reasons.

But the shadows were still beneath his eyes; the weariness still outlined his mouth. She thought about what he had taught her, and about her refusal to just jump when he snapped his fingers. Hashim respected that, she knew. What he would not countenance was fear or timidity.

'Are you going to tell me what's wrong?'

He shifted position a little, so that he was lying gazing into the huge green glitter of her almond-shaped eyes. The breasts he had once been so obsessed with now seemed just a part of the beautiful whole of her, but still their pert rosiness reminded him of how she had used them, how that could never be undone—at least not for him.

'Just tired. It's nothing,' he murmured—which was true, though only part of the story. There was growing opposition in Qudamah to his Western lifestyle—a demand from some factions that he settle down and embrace completely the culture of his ancestors. There had been views expressed that his trips abroad should be curtailed, with all his energies focused on his homeland.

And didn't Sienna herself exemplify everything that the more traditional elements in his country loathed about the West? Hadn't Abdul-Aziz increasingly been hinting that the liaison was damaging his credibility? That things would blow up if some resolution were not reached? And Hashim knew what that resolution should be.

'It's nothing,' he repeated firmly.

Sienna did her best not to let her face crumple with disappointment. She had asked him and he had closed up—she could tell from the shuttering of his face. Well, that was up to him. It had been her choice to ask and his not to tell her. Asking was one thing, and perfectly acceptable. Prying was something completely different.

She took his words at face value, as he clearly wanted her to. 'So, when did you last have a holiday?'

'A holiday?' he questioned, as surprised by the choice of topic as by her sudden change of subject.

She laughed, pleased to have perplexed him. 'Yes, a holiday. That's the thing that most people do when they're tired and they want to relax.'

He screwed up his eyes. 'I don't remember,' he said.

'No recent bucket and spade job in Spain?' she teased.

'Bucket and spade job?' He frowned.

'Have you never built sandcastles, Hashim?' she questioned.

He laughed. 'Sand is not a big deal in Qudamah—not with so much of it around. We tend to escape from it rather than build our leisure time around it,' he added drily.

'I'd never thought of that.' She snuggled up to him. 'So what kind of holidays did you have when you were a child?'

He frowned. 'You don't really want to know.'

Which meant he didn't really want to tell her. But a woman could not exist on sex alone, no matter what her status. 'Oh, yes, I do!' she said firmly.

And Hashim found himself smiling as he allowed himself a rare dip into nostalgia. How long ago a childhood could seem, and yet how astonishingly clear the memories if you opened the floodgates on them. 'My male kin and I used to take our falcons up into the forests, where we trained them to kill.'

'Nice!'

Idly, he circled the pad of his finger around one of her nipples, feeling it instantly point and peak, and he felt the heavy stir of desire returning. 'There we learned to be men,' he said dreamily.

'No women?'

'Not one.'

'But what about your mother? Didn't she want to go along?'

He remembered the very first trip, being torn from his mother's arms. He had been just five years old and had cried his eyes out. How remorselessly the others had teased him! And his father had told him that the painful separation was all part of the process of learning to be a man. He could imagine what a Western psychologist would say about *that*!

'Females were not part of the endeavour,' he said thoughtfully. 'Their place was at the Palace.'

'And didn't they mind?'

He hesitated. 'My mother *did* mind, as it happens,' he admitted. 'And she made vocal her concerns. It caused a great deal of conflict between her and my father—but she was determined that the women of Qudamah should make some of the changes which women over the world were initiating at the time. Nothing like burning their bras, of course,' he added hastily.

Sienna laughed. 'Well, no.'

'But through her efforts the women of Qudamah were gradually granted small freedoms.'

'Such as?'

He shrugged. 'Oh, they were allowed to walk in the capital unaccompanied by a man—though many still prefer not to.' He saw her face. 'To you this probably means nothing—a woman who has grown up with personal freedom and takes it for granted probably cannot comprehend that in my country it was a kind of revolution.'

'She sounds like an amazing woman,' she said.

'She is.' The words *I should like you to meet her* hung unsaid on the air. For, no matter how true they were, how could he possibly utter them in the circumstances?

Sienna was quiet for a moment. She had heard the deliberate omission and she wouldn't have been human if it hadn't hurt her. What a different world he painted, and how his words emphasised the huge gulf between their cultures. If she had never understood his extreme reaction to her calendar shoot she certainly did now. If it was considered a mighty advance for a woman to go out on her own, then how must the baring of her breasts for an erotic calendar have seemed to a man of such a traditional upbringing?

But if ever she succumbed to the hopeless temptation of thinking *what if*—then all she had to do was remind herself of the insurmountable differences which had always been there and always would. No matter what they did—it was *doomed*.

And Sienna had realised something else, too—Hashim might have been bordering on the brink of love all those years ago, but his feelings—and hers—had been nothing but a violent rush of emotion which had nothing to do with their real lives. Even now nothing had really changed. Their brief time together was spent in a vacuum.

He saw the clouds which had shadowed her eyes, but he did not enquire what had caused them. He had a pretty good idea, and some things were best left unspoken. Why go out and find hurt when it waited like a shadowy figure just around the corner? Instead, he touched her cheek. 'And when did *you* last have a holiday?'

'Last year. I went to Australia to visit an old schoolfriend. She's settled down there—married an Aussie.' The spark of an idea began to form in her mind. 'Wouldn't it be lovely to have a break together, Hashim?' She looked around at the lavish yet soulless bedroom. 'Somewhere that wasn't in a hotel?'

He played along with her fantasy as she had played along with so many of his. 'And where would we go?'

Sienna put her head to one side and considered. 'I guess we'd stay in England. Travelling abroad would be too much hassle, and you travel too much anyway.

It would be somewhere you could be completely incognito—completely free.'

'Does such a place exist?' he mocked.

Sienna nodded. 'I know of a beautiful old converted farmhouse—it's right in the middle of nowhere. I hired it once for a rock star's fortieth birthday and everyone was raving on about it.'

'But where would my bodyguards stay?'

'There's a cottage in the grounds. Not too far and yet far enough…'

Her voice tailed off and he read the erotic promise in her eyes. An unbearable temptation crept over him. Something was going to have to give in his life soon, and he knew that it was going to be his relationship with Sienna. But before it did…

Couldn't he have the briefest taste of what it was like to be 'normal'? Just an ordinary man taking a holiday with a woman who excited and calmed and provoked and stimulated him in dizzying succession? Someone who was part of his past and now his present, but could never be part of his future…

'Can you arrange it?' he questioned suddenly.

Sienna blinked. 'You're serious?'

'Yes.' He did a quick calculation in his head. 'I can manage next weekend, if that fits in with your job?'

She was too excited to notice the faint sarcasm in his voice. Or to question whether two weekends on the trot was not pushing their luck.

She nodded. 'Well, yes—of course I can. If we can

get it. It's quite short notice—but it should be fine. I mean—who in their right mind wants to holiday in the English countryside in the middle of February?'

'Well, I do.'

They looked at one another and Sienna started giggling.

'So do I.'

CHAPTER ELEVEN

THERE was a huge fireplace, an ancient-looking kitchen, and a bed in the main upstairs room which looked exactly as it must have done a century before.

The bodyguards were settled in the cottage by the main gate, with a widescreen TV and the promise of a huge, no-questions-asked bonus, and Sienna and Hashim were finally on their own.

'It is like stepping back in time,' Hashim murmured, his black eyes fascinated as he glanced around him. 'And it's freezing.'

'Yes, it is.' She turned to him. 'Can you light a fire?'

His smile touched on the arrogant. 'Naturally.'

'Well, then—over to you. I'm going to make us something to eat.'

But he shook his head. If they were playing honeymoon—which he rather imagined that they were—then there was something far more pressing than food or fuel on the agenda. 'You want to eat food?' he murmured. 'Or to eat me?'

'You are outrageous!' she protested, but only half-heartedly, for his hands had slithered underneath her sweater and were making her nipples grow very hard indeed. 'We…we ought to draw the curtains,' she said breathlessly.

She went and yanked across the faded chintz and he came up behind her, skimming his hands down over her hips. 'Mmm. I am pleased to see that you are wearing a skirt.'

'Because my Sheikh does not like jeans,' she said demurely, and closed her eyes as she felt him reach beneath it to graze his fingers over her searing heat.

'You are ready,' he observed, on a slight note of surprise.

'I've been ready for hours,' she admitted, hopping and almost stumbling in her eagerness to help him take off her panties.

'So have I,' he admitted huskily.

They only made it as far as the big, old-fashioned sprung sofa, where Hashim kicked off his trousers and then pulled her down onto his lap, guiding her slowly over his aching shaft before plunging deep inside her.

'Oh!' she moaned, as he filled her completely, moving her up and down until she thought that she could bear it no longer. Almost before she could believe it to be happening she felt herself begin to dissolve.

And Hashim felt it, too—shatteringly and simultaneously—and as her body began to convulse out its pleasure so did his follow, in almost complete harmony. And in those few last seconds before the power of it temporarily obliterated consciousness their eyes met, locked and held.

'Sienna!' he gasped as she began to shudder around him, and her name seemed to be torn from his soul.

'Hashim!' she breathed brokenly, her fingers digging into the rich silk of his skin. *If only I could tell you how much I love you.*

For a while they stayed just like that, Sienna still astride him, gazing down and stroking her hand along the rugged outline of his jaw.

'What are you thinking?' he questioned softly.

That what should never have happened had done so. That the falling in love was complete. That it was too late to stop herself and protect herself. And it had happened just at the time when she suspected it was all coming to an end.

'You should never ask a woman something like that after making love to her.'

Not when she's vulnerable enough to tell you something you won't want to hear. She shivered a little as the flush of passion on her skin began to fade.

'Better get that fire going,' she said lightly, and climbed off him.

Escaping into the kitchen while he built the fire, she made soup from organic vegetables and served it with chunky wholemeal bread, and cheese which had come straight from the nearby farm. They quenched their thirst with elderflower water and then drank scented tea, sitting on a furry rug in front of the gradually roaring fire.

'Do you like that?' she asked.

'Perfect,' he said, but there was a sudden heaviness in his heart.

They watched a video of Sienna's favourite film—an old musical which soon had her sniffing like a hay-fever sufferer.

'You're crying!' he accused.

'No, I'm not—it's just a corny old film,' she said crossly.

'Come here,' he said.

And, even though it made her heart ache, she went.

They spent their time doing simple things. Wrapping up warm before walking over the crunchy morning frost which hardly had time to melt before a setting crimson sun turned the fields into fire every afternoon.

His bodyguards seemed quite content to be doing their own thing, and there wasn't a peep out of his phone. Once they even ventured into the small local pub for lunch, and if anyone wondered why there was a big, dark car sitting gleaming in the car park, no-body bothered asking.

The real world seemed such a long way away, and part of Sienna fervently wished it could stay that way. If it weren't for his position they could live a life like this all the time. He was right—she *had* always taken her freedom for granted—and never had she cher-ished it more than during this weekend.

She watched him relax. Saw the dark shadows melt away from beneath his eyes and the tiny, fan-like creases at the corners of his black eyes ironed out as if by magic.

And for Hashim it was a provocative glimpse of a life he could never really know. He had not felt as unencumbered as this since those long-ago days of falconing in the mountains of Qudamah.

'Ah, Sienna,' he said on their last morning, when they sat eating pancakes for breakfast. 'Don't you wish that life could always be this simple?'

She smiled, knowing full well that there was no point in coming out with a stock phrase like: It *could* be like this. Because it couldn't.

She put the lid back on the golden syrup. 'Do you want to listen to the radio?'

Hashim frowned. 'What for?'

'Well, Qudamah seems to have been in the news a lot lately.'

Funny how you could look for an opportunity to say something and then find, when it came, that you wished you didn't have to. He gazed down at the clear amber of the delicate tea. 'There is going to be an election very soon—and elections always demand a lot of my time.' He looked at her. 'I am going to have to fly back tomorrow.'

Sienna nodded. 'I know you are.'

He drew in a deep breath. 'And I'm not sure when I'll be back.'

She felt the tendril of long-held fear finally wrapping itself around her heart. 'I know that, too.' Don't make him have to say it. Accept what is inevitable.

Make it easy on yourself. 'Hashim, it's okay. You don't have to say it. I know it's over.'

He didn't deny it, but the dark eyes which he lifted to her face were troubled. 'I do not wish this, Sienna—but increasingly I recognise that my place is in my homeland, not here.' He gave a restless little movement of his shoulders. 'There are obligations I now need to fulfil. And I don't want to tie you down to a relationship which can never go anywhere. Or to make you a promise I am unable to keep. If this fades into failed intentions and meetings which never happen then all that we will have left to remember is bitterness.' His voice grew hard. 'And I cannot face that. Not for a second time. Not when…'

The words were there in his mouth, just begging to be said. But words could be dishonest—even if you meant them. They could open up all kinds of unrealistic expectations. If he tried to explain how much she had come to mean to him then would that not tie her to him anyway—no matter how much he tried not to let it? What if she started seeing them as star-crossed lovers instead of just getting on with her life?

She saw the discomfiture on his face and jumped in to rescue the situation—or rather to rescue herself. She had had more with him than any woman could have hoped to have, and she would ensure that he remembered her with dignity.

'It's been wonderful. Gorgeous. It was a fine affair,' she said softly. 'But now it's over.'

His eyes narrowed. He had expected…what? That

she might at least shed a tear for him! Or that her face might indicate some feelings of dejection! His pride was hurt, yet his pain came from deeper feelings than pride. He pushed them away with an instinct borne out of self-protection. 'You seem almost pleased about it,' he observed coolly.

'Oh, Hashim,' she said impatiently. 'Of course I'm not *pleased* about it—but I recognise that it has to be, so what's the alternative?'

Women had begged him before—many times. They had shed tears and clung to him. Hadn't there been a selfish side which had thought that Sienna might do the same? For if she behaved like all the others, then wouldn't that make it easier for him to walk away from her without another thought?

But there had never been another relationship like this one, he recognised. Nor ever would be again. His destiny would not allow it—for his flings and his freedom must now be curtailed. The luxurious but weighty doors of his royal prison were waiting to clang shut on him, and if he took himself down the path of useless and indulgent analysis then what good would it do him? Or her?

'Come here,' he said simply, and opened his arms.

Sienna didn't need to be told that this was the last time. It was written in his eyes and spoken in every lingering kiss and caress. His hands and his fingers seemed as though they were discovering her for the first time, and yet bidding her farewell as they did so.

'Oh, Hashim,' she said, in a choked kind of voice.

'Let us lie once more in that old bed,' he whispered, and she nodded.

He carried her up the rickety staircase towards the room they had shared, bending his head so as not to knock it on one of the dark beams, and put her down as carefully as if she had been a cherished and delicate piece of filagree.

Their undressing was slow and silent, and as she sank back into feather pillows his dark body moved over hers. She thought about how many couples had lain in this bed, like this. How many children had been conceived—maybe even born here? Ghostly generations of long-ago lovers joined them—wordlessly entering the indefinable space between past and present. For at what point did the present become the past?

Their climax would bring an end to it all, and the sex would become just a memory. As would the rest. She trembled as Hashim thrust into her with a hunger and a poignancy which made hot salt tears slide from beneath her eyelids.

'Ah, Sienna. Don't cry,' he said afterwards, wiping the tracks away with his finger.

They lay there for a while without sleeping, and then Sienna stirred. Be the first to make a move, she told herself. Don't put yourself in the position of being the deserted one.

'I'd better go and pack up the kitchen.'

He tightened his hold on her waist. 'I can have one of the guards come over and do it.'

But she shook her head and prised his fingers away as if she was removing a clam from the side of a rock. 'No, Hashim—that will defeat the object of our ordinary weekend. I'll go and chuck all the leftover food away—you can wash the dishes.'

He was torn between outrage and humour. 'Yes, Sienna,' he murmured, but his heart was heavy.

They were quiet in the car on the drive back, even though the driver was firmly locked away behind soundproof glass. It had begun to rain, and through the tinted windows she could see droplets battering against the glass, as if the heavens themselves were sobbing.

It was only when they were approaching South Kensington that he laid one dark hand on hers.

'You will come back to the hotel with me?'

'No.'

He asked for no explanation; but then he had known what her answer would be. 'Sienna?'

She turned her head back to face him and her green eyes were sombre, but there was a soft dignity about her which took his breath away. He thought about how often in the past he had been able to persuade her to do something against her will just by the sheer power of the sexual chemistry which existed between them, but he recognised now that nothing he could do would change her mind. Not this time.

Something had changed. In her. In him. In them both. For not only would she refuse to succumb to him, he would no longer make an attempt to have her bend to his will. Somewhere along the way they had become equals, and for Hashim it was a bittersweet awakening. An awareness that it had come at the wrong time—but could it have ever been the right time?

Not with Sienna, no.

He bent down to the Qudamah-crested dispatch box which accompanied him everywhere and pulled out a slim leather box. He held it out towards her but she shook her head, the thick dark hair flying like a storm.

'No, Hashim!' She would not be paid off—have him bid her farewell with the expensive baubles she had previously refused to accept. 'Whatever it is, I don't want it. I don't want your diamonds or your emeralds, thank you very much! I told you a long time ago that I could not and would not be bought, and I meant it!'

He laughed softly. 'I know you did, my fiery Sienna,' he murmured. 'And I think that your expectations of costly gems are a little wide of the mark.' He put the box in her hand and closed her fingers around it, his black eyes washing over her. 'Please. Open it.'

Something in his manner made her obey him, her fingers trembling as she flicked open the catch to see a necklace lying against indigo velvet. But it was no ordinary necklace. The chain was as fine as a sliver of light and in the centre of it lay a tiny golden bird.

'H-Hashim?' she questioned shakily.

'Here.' He lifted it from the box and placed it into

the centre of her palm, where the fine chain lay coiled like an elegant snake, the small charm gleaming like the sun.

'What is it?'

'It is an eagle—a golden eagle. She flies on the flag of Qudamah and is the symbol of my country—for she represents freedom and power. This is the only time you will ever see her chained.'

Like him. The thought flew unbidden into her mind. Freedom and power and never to be chained. She studied it intently, focusing fiercely on the workmanship because at least that kept the tears at bay. 'It's...beautiful.'

'Shall I put it on for you?'

Sienna nodded, unable to speak for fear that she would blurt out words which could never be taken back. Words of love which would mortify him and make their parting even more painful.

He slid his hands around her neck, wanting so much to linger there—to raise the heavy weight of her hair so that he could kiss the soft nape and then turn her head to take her lips, coaxing their luscious warmth into eager response.

'I thought you were going to put it on?'

Her faintly bemused voice disrupted his troubled thoughts. 'So I was.' He clipped it in place. 'There.'

For a moment their eyes met, and the pain which smote at her heart made her feel dizzy and weak. Turning her head to look out of the window with the desperation of a drowning woman struggling towards the surface for light and air, Sienna saw with relief that they were at the end of her road.

'Well, here we are! Thank you, Hashim.' She leaned forward. The touch of her mouth against his was fleeting and the pain increased. 'Take very good care.'

He touched her fingertips to his lips and as she pushed open the car door said something in his native tongue to the driver, who got out and removed her one small bag from the boot.

The tinted window slid silently down and all she could see were glittering black eyes—the only thing which seemed truly alive in the tight mask of his face. She flashed him a smile, and then she turned away.

Somehow she made it inside without crying, but once there the tears began to pour down her cheeks without stopping. Kat was away and she was glad, because it gave her time to get over the worst, to recover on her own like a wounded animal.

There was no one to tell her to eat. No one to question why she couldn't sleep. No one to tell her that it was wrong to shed her tears and that there were plenty more fish in the sea. Maybe there were—but none like Hashim.

By the third day she had begun to feel a little better. Her heart was aching, but she knew that Hashim would hate it if she became one of those women who let their whole lives collapse around them because a love affair hadn't worked out.

She bathed and washed her hair, and was just pulling on a big black sweater which virtually came down to her knees when the doorbell rang. She wondered if it was Kat back, having forgotten her keys.

She opened the door, completely unprepared to see the batallion of photographers who were jostling for position, jerking back in alarm as the multiple flash from their array of cameras temporarily blinded her. Someone thrust a phallic-looking microphone under her chin.

'Miss Baker!' called a TV-trained voice. 'Sienna! Is the Sheikh of Qudamah aware that you used to be a topless model?'

CHAPTER TWELVE

THE startled doorstep photo made the first edition and the second—only it ran alongside a much larger photo. There was her sand-sprinkled and sultry image plastered over all the tabloids.

Even the serious broadsheets gave it house-room—justifying their usual no-breasts policy with weighty pieces on the changing morals of the Middle East. And a censored version of it was beamed into homes the length and breadth of the country as an add-on to an otherwise boring television news show.

'*And finally, the Sheikh of the fiercely traditional State of Qudamah is rumoured to be dating a British glamour model. Stunning brunette Sienna Baker…*'

Female leader-writers took up the case in their mid-week columns, asking righteously: *What would you do if* your *son brought a topless model home?*

Trapped inside the house, unable to go out without fear of being accosted, Sienna was sitting in the kitchen at the back of the house with the blinds drawn down when Kat came in and handed her the telephone with a look which said everything.

She pressed the phone to her ear. She wasn't aware she'd actually said anything, but she must have made some sort of sound because she heard his deep and silky voice.

'Sienna?'

She bit her lip. Closed her eyes. She wouldn't cry. She *wouldn't*. But the sound of his dear voice was almost more than she could bear. 'Yes, it's me.'

'Are you all right?'

'Ask me another. How about you?'

He ignored that. 'The press are still there?'

'Well, not so many of them. I think they got fed up because I refused to say anything.'

'Good. If you feed a story it only grows.'

'Oh, Hashim—how the hell did they get hold of it? How did they even find out about it?'

Hashim's mouth tightened into a grim and forbidding line. He suspected that someone in Qudamah must have informed the foreign press about a juicy piece of gossip in their Ruler's life. In the power-play that was his life Sienna's past had become a weapon. And he must protect her from the fall-out.

'These things have a habit of getting out,' he said slowly. 'That's the way the world works.'

He sounded almost weary, as if he had seen sides of the world she did not know—and of course he had. She couldn't imagine what it must be like to be a sheikh, but she was fairly sure that it would be very hard to trust people's motives towards you. 'Yes,' said quietly. 'I imagine so.'

The silence between them seemed huge. 'I am sending some people to look after you, Sienna. If I come myself it will only add fire to the story. Is there somewhere you can go?'

She was suddenly and acutely aware that this conversation was a purely practical one, and not personal at all. He didn't want to talk—not *really* talk—and besides, what was there left to say? This was damage limitation time.

She bit her lip. Where did she always turn when she wanted an escape route? Who would always accept her with open arms and no questions asked? Who wanted the best for her no matter what. 'My mother wants me to go to her.'

'Then go. Let me arrange it.'

'Hashim—you don't seem to understand!' she said frustratedly. 'I have existing contracts to fulfil. And the phone hasn't stopped ringing with work requests—I've never been so popular. I think it's the curiosity factor,' she added acidly. 'Having your party planned by a so-called "Glamour Model." But some of the calls are from journalists pretending to be clients. I'm certain of it.'

He felt the dark dagger of self-contempt as he remembered that he too had done just that. Pretended. Masqueraded. Finally got his way by seducing her— and now what had happened? Had she ever deserved this because of some rash youthful decision made with all the best intentions? 'I'm sorry,' he said quietly.

She shook her head as if he was in the room, hating to hear his apology—so stilted and formal—like one stranger talking to another. 'It isn't your fault, it's mine. I should never have done it in the first place—I just didn't realise it was going to come back and haunt me in such a big way.'

'But that is down to me. To your relationship with me.'

The most precious thing in her life. *Past tense*, she reminded herself. She sighed, wanting to lean on him yet knowing she shouldn't. And anyway, she couldn't—not really. He was at his Palace, thousands of miles away, and she was holed up in her tiny terraced house in Kennington. There were no arms to hold her, no heart to beat next to hers, no hand to stroke her hair.

'Can you get someone else to honour your existing contracts and ignore all the others?' he demanded.

'And who is going to pay my mortgage in the meantime?'

There was a moment's silence, and Hashim chose his words with fastidious care, knowing that he trod on very sensitive ground here. 'That is simple. You must let me help you, Sienna.'

She froze. 'What do you mean—*help* me?'

He could hear the bristly defensiveness which spiked her voice and, while he silently applauded her fierce pride, he knew that it would not and could not serve her well—not in circumstances such as these. 'Just hear me out without interruption. That is all I ask of you. Please, Sienna, it is vital,' he said softly.

'If I took care of your mortgage for you—would that not free you up to get away for a while?'

'I'm not letting you pay for me!' Her voice lowered. 'You must be able to see why I stand so firm on this issue.'

For a moment he had to control the instinctive lash of his tongue. Stubborn woman! Could she not see that he was only trying to help her?

Drawing on diplomatic reserves he had never had to call on before, he tried again. 'Sienna,' he said patiently. 'I admire your independence and your spirit, but this is not some showering of expensive baubles on a mistress—this is me trying to help you get out of a bad situation which is mostly of my doing. To make some kind of amends. Will you not let me do that for you? Would not all that has grown between us be completely worthless if you will not allow me to behave as any true friend would towards another?'

There was silence. How appalled he would be if he knew that her thoughts were not of indignation that he was trying to buy her out of something but instead had fixed upon a word which resonated cruelly round and round in her head. Who would ever have thought that the acknowledgement that he was her *friend* could have unwittingly caused so much heartache?

'Will you let me?' he said.

What choice did she have? To brazen it out in London, aware of the eyes which followed her? The curious glances? Women looking down their noses at her and men looking…? Well, she didn't even want to go *there*.

'In a few weeks all the fuss will have died down,' he continued smoothly. 'The news will have moved on. That's what happens.'

And, stupidly, that upset her even more—for once it had died down it really would be over. And wasn't there a part of her—ever while loathing all this fuss and attention—that was secretly glad because it had brought Hashim back into her life when she'd thought that he had gone for good?

'All right. I'll go to my mother's,' she said.

At the other end of the phone, Hashim closed his eyes with relief. Outside his private study the court was in uproar, and Abdul-Aziz was prowling round the palace like a starving tom-cat, but Hashim didn't care. She was safe. She would be safe—he had the resources to protect her.

'I will have a car sent immediately,' he said, glad now that he could rely on action, for this was something he always felt comfortable with. 'And bodyguards will be placed at the entrance to your mother's home.'

She opened her mouth to say that he didn't even know where her mother lived, but then shut it again. Of course he did. He knew everything—and if he didn't he could get someone to find out for him. Hashim could get anything he pleased.

'Thank you, Hashim,' she said.

'Don't thank me,' he said fiercely. 'Just stay strong.

Can you do that?' He nearly said *for me*—except that in the circumstances he knew he had no right to ask.

She allowed herself to picture him, and knew she would not crumble. 'As an ox,' she said huskily.

Hashim closed his eyes. 'Or an eagle,' he whispered.

'Goodbye,' she whispered back, and put the phone down before she began to cry. Because although the structure of her life had been torn apart it didn't even register on the pain-scale.

Nothing touched her and nothing could—other than the heartbreak of not being with the man she loved.

CHAPTER THIRTEEN

'DARLING, calm down, sit down, and drink that cup of tea before it gets cold!'

Sienna sniffed and smiled, and took a sip of the fragrant Earl Grey. How some things never changed!

'That's better,' said her mother approvingly, brushing some mud from the leg of her jodhpurs and dunking a digestive biscuit into her own tea.

'Mum, I'm so sorry—'

'Oh, fiddlesticks!' said her mother cheerfully. 'It's done my reputation no end of good locally—I'll never be asked to judge the prize cauliflower section at the village show again!' She sighed. 'I was getting rather bored with it, if the truth were known.'

'No, I'm serious.'

'And so am I, Sienna,' said her mother firmly. 'In my opinion you look rather lovely in those photos—and if you compare them to some of the nudes in our national galleries, why, they're positively tame! It's all a question of perception. I admit that when you first did it I was angry—but not for long. How could I be when the money you earned from it meant that I could have my operation? I thanked you then from the bottom of my heart and I still do.' She finished her biscuit and edged her fingers towards another.

'Better not. Now, what I really want to know is—what's this young sheikh of yours really like?'

This, in a way, was even harder than explaining that for the time being there were two hefty body-guards stationed at the front gate.

'He's not young, Mum,' said Sienna. 'He's thirty-five.'

'Oh, positively ancient!'

'And he isn't…' No, this, *this* was the hardest part. 'He isn't mine. Not any more. He never was, really.' She put her cup down and stared candidly at her mother. 'I just had a relationship with him,' she said defiantly.

'Well, thank heavens for that!' murmured her mother. 'I was beginning to wonder when you'd find yourself a boyfriend.'

'Mum!'

'Well, you never seemed really interested.'

There was a question in her mother's eyes, and for the first time in her life Sienna spoke to her not as a mother but as another woman. 'I went out with Hashim years ago—a couple of years after I did the photos, actually,' she said quietly. 'And he was a pretty hard act to follow.'

Her mother replied in kind. 'I'm not surprised,' she said softly. 'He looks absolutely gorgeous.'

'Well, he is—but he just happens to be a sheikh and there's no future in it. He comes from a fiercely traditional country and anyway—he doesn't love me.'

'Are you sure he doesn't?'

'Of course I'm sure!'

'He didn't have to go to all the trouble of arranging protection for you, did he? Or deliver that gorgeous hamper and massive bouquet of flowers for me.' She stared happily at the massed display of blooms which were currently making the sitting room look like a florist's shop.

How could her mother ever begin to understand that for a man of Hashim's untold wealth such gestures were mere drops in a limitless ocean? 'He feels guilty,' she said flatly. 'This would never have erupted if it hadn't been for his position. That's all.'

'Have it your own way, darling—if you want to be stubborn, then I can't stop you. Now.' Her mother beamed at her. 'Do you want to see if you can fit into your old jodhpurs and give me a hand in the stables? A bit of good old-fashioned fresh air and exercise is just what the doctor ordered. Then later I've asked Kirsty over for tea. Cara is *three* now. Can you believe it?' She smiled. 'It only seems a minute ago since you and Kirsty were toddling off to nursery together at the same age.'

Sienna smiled too, because the thought of seeing her old friend was strangely comforting. It was all too easy to let friendships slip—though time and distance played their part. Sometimes she wondered what would have happened if she'd taken Kirsty's path in life—stayed around and married a local farmer, then started producing a brood of children. Would that have guaranteed her personal happiness?

It wasn't that easy, she decided, as she struggled into her old riding clothes. It wasn't the place you chose or the job you ended up doing—it was all to do with the man you ended up falling in love with and the path that took you on.

And she had just had the misfortune to fall for someone who wasn't taking her anywhere.

But her mother was right—the fresh air and exercise *did* work their own kind of magic. Physically, at least. The aching in her heart needed the kind of remedy which never provided instant healing. It needed time.

She got up at first light and went down to the stables. She did all the mucky stuff and some of the fun stuff too—for there was nothing more rewarding than watching fearful children grow in confidence as they began to master the skill of riding. Life suddenly seemed very simple—and her busy London existence like something which had happened in a past life.

She had thought she would miss the networking and the hectic pace of making people's party dreams come true, but she didn't. She just wished that she had the power to fulfil her own personal dreams, but she didn't. Besides, you shouldn't rely on a man to make you happy, she told herself. Everyone knew that.

And Cara was a delight—homing in on Sienna straight away, her eyes wide when it was explained that Mummy and Sienna had been just the same age as her once upon a time!

She had a habit of sticking her little tongue out of the corner of her mouth when she was thinking.

'Can I play with Sienna, Mummy?' she asked one day.

Kirsty shot her a glance. 'Oh, Sienna's far too busy—'

'No,' said Sienna firmly. 'No, I'm not, and I want Cara to come and play. We could make cupcakes one day if you like?'

'With chocolate chips?'

'Yes, darling—I *love* chocolate chips—and we can use those little silver balls too, if you're very good.'

At least there was plenty to keep her occupied—leaving little time for wafting around the house missing her lover. But probably the hardest part of all was accepting that it really *was* over. Because in a way things seemed just the same. Their feelings hadn't changed and they normally had weeks in between seeing one another anyway.

If only they could have rowed—or stopped speaking entirely—then she might have found it easier to believe that it was over. Easier? Well, maybe not. That was asking too much. What's it going to take to forget him? she asked herself. An announcement that he's going to marry someone else, as one day you know he will?

Sienna was making more cakes with Cara one afternoon when her mother came rushing into the kitchen.

'One of the bodyguards has just knocked!' she babbled excitedly. 'There is a visitor on the way to see you!'

Sienna's heart missed a beat. She held the wooden spoon in the air as if it was a magic wand—and, oh, how she wished it was. She would wave it, and…

'Is it Hashim?' she breathed.

'Oh, darling, no—I'm afraid it isn't. It's a man called…' Her mother frowned as she concentrated on saying his name correctly. 'Abdul-Aziz.'

Sienna hoped her face did not betray her disappointment. 'Then you'd better show him in,' she said courteously.

Abdul-Aziz swept into her mother's low-beamed kitchen as if he owned the place. It had been a long time since Sienna had seen him, and in his way he was no less formidable—his eyes still looked like raisins which had been created in the Arctic and his mouth was set in such a way as to show he meant business.

But some of the hardness of his features had dissolved, and Sienna found herself wondering if that was down to the calming effects of married life. Or was she in danger of attributing her own wistfulness to other people?

Five years ago she had been utterly intimidated by him, but a lot had changed since then. For a start she had grown up—but, more importantly, she had shared something very special with Hashim. He had given her confidence and belief in herself as a woman—and nothing could take that away from her.

Abdul-Aziz's eyes narrowed as he saw her, and Sienna was aware that she could not have looked worse—old clothes, no make-up, covered in cake mix, with a tiny girl clinging onto her apron and demanding to know, 'Who's that cross man?'

'It's someone I know,' she whispered, and looked at her mother. 'Would you mind finishing the cakes with Cara while I take my visitor into the sitting room?'

Cara snuffled a bit, and her mother looked disappointed that she wasn't going to get a ringside seat to hear whatever the 'cross man' had to say, but Sienna felt strangely serene as she led Abdul-Aziz across the hall and into the chintzy room. The worst had already happened and Hashim was not with her. Nothing could touch her now.

She looked across the room at him, and she'd have been lying if she hadn't admitted deriving a little pleasure from the look of perplexity on Abdul-Aziz's face. Had he been expecting her to be lolling around in some over-the-top boudoir, wearing nothing but a pair of racy stockings and suspenders?

'Would you like tea, Mr Aziz?' she asked politely. 'I'm not quite sure how to address you.'

'You can call me Abdul,' he said grudgingly. 'And, no, I don't want tea. Thank you,' he added, as if he had just remembered something.

Like his manners, thought Sienna wryly—for he gave the distinct impression of a man who was struggling to contain himself.

'What can I do for you?' she murmured.

'That child.' He cocked his head in the direction of the door. 'She is your child?'

Sienna started to say of course not—but there was no 'of course' about it—not in his eyes. If she suddenly produced a spellbook and started chanting incantations she didn't think he'd bat an eyelid.

'No,' she answered quietly. 'She is the child of my schoolfriend.'

Now he was staring at the tiny golden eagle which dangled around her slender neck and which she never took off.

'And my Sheikh gave you this?' he demanded.

'I suspect you already know the answer to that one. Yes. He did.'

He tossed his head back like a stallion about to rear up. 'You must renounce him!' he declared dramatically. 'Unequivocally and immediately!'

Sienna stared at him. 'I beg your pardon?'

'You have not heard?' he demanded.

'I haven't got a clue what you're talking about.'

'He has not told you?'

This hurt. 'No.'

'Sheikh Hashim is planning to go on State television and make an announcement!'

'What kind of announcement?'

Abdul-Aziz's mouth tightened. 'He refuses to say…stubborn boy!…but I know in my heart what it will be.'

'You do? You're some kind of mind-reader, are you?'

'He is going to declare his love for you!' he hissed.

Sienna's laugh was genuine, but it was tinged with sadness. 'You'd never make money out of clairvoyancy, Abdul,' she said. 'It's over between me and Hashim—he's not in love with me.'

'He isn't?' His suspicious look cleared and was replaced by an expression of bright hope. 'You are certain of this?'

'Yes.'

'Then what is he plotting?' questioned Abdul-Aziz to himself thoughtfully.

'Don't you think you should come right out and ask him yourself?'

'I have. He would tell me nothing.'

'Then it's very *disloyal* of you to come sneaking over here behind his back, trying to find out things he obviously doesn't wish to tell you.'

He glared at her. 'While your loyalty to the Sheikh is admirable, I am not used to being spoken to in such a way, Miss Baker. Especially by a woman.'

'How come I'm not surprised?' Sienna murmured.

'Will you try to stop him?' he persisted.

'I wouldn't dream of it,' said Sienna calmly. 'And even if I wanted to, I couldn't. He is a man in charge of his own destiny.' She stared at him. 'As we all are.'

An odd, calculating light came into Abdul-Aziz's

strange, cold eyes. 'Yes, indeed we are,' he said. 'You are a strong woman, Miss Baker.'

Was she? At that moment she felt a mixture of strength and weakness, but her strength came from her unwavering love for Hashim. And so too, in a way, did her weakness. 'Thank you, Abdul.'

The cold eyes narrowed. Had they softened fractionally, or had she just imagined it? 'You have a message for him?'

Tell him I love him. Tell him I can't stop thinking about him. Tell him that if I really did have magical powers then I would use them all to protect and guard him from evil for the rest of his life.

'Just tell him Sienna says hello.'

'Hello?' he echoed faintly, and then nodded, giving a deep bow before leaving the room.

Sienna felt as if she was operating on some kind of autopilot as she continued with the ritual of decorating cupcakes with Cara. She realised that she was waiting for something, but was not quite sure how she knew—or what, indeed, she was waiting for.

But then her mobile phone rang, and she knew who it would be even before she saw 'Hashim' flashing on the screen. Her heart started beating fit to burst.

'Sienna?'

'Abdul has been to see me,' she blurted out.

'I know he has.'

'You didn't think to warn me?'

'Did you need me to?' he questioned coolly.

'He says you're going to broadcast to the nation.'

'Indeed I am.'

'He wanted me to try and stop you.'

'And are you?'

Sienna laughed. 'It would be like trying to stop the sun from rising if you had your heart set on something.'

Oh, how true her words. Hashim smiled. 'Good,' he murmured. 'I am glad that we understand one another.'

'Hashim…' Sienna hesitated. 'You aren't going to do anything *foolish*, are you?'

Well, that was all down to which way you looked at it. But that was not the answer she needed to hear right now. 'No, Sienna.' His voice sounded strangely controlled, but there was a hint of mockery underpinning it. 'If I send a jet for you then will you fly out to Qudamah?'

Her world spun. A jet? To Qudamah? 'Why?' she breathed.

There was a pause. 'My mother wishes to meet you.'

CHAPTER FOURTEEN

SIENNA'S first sight of Hashim's palace was against a backdrop of stars—like a distant castle in a fairy tale—and she touched her fingers to her lips in disbelief and a growing sense of wonder. As if this could not be happening. Not now, and not to her.

But it was.

She was summoned to a room all golden and sapphire-blue, but she was scarcely aware of the lavish and opulent décor for only one figure dominated her line of vision. As he always did. Tall and lean and proud—the beautiful-ugly face tense. His flowing white robes made him look like a stranger, but his eyes were oh-so-familiar. Burning into her like smouldering coals that heated her skin and warmed her heart.

He nodded when he saw her, as if she had just confirmed something in his mind, but Sienna was terribly aware of protocol and of the presence of his servants—even though they had their eyes averted. And so she simply nodded back—as if they were two commuters who passed each other on the train platform every morning.

With a curt, clipped statement in his native tongue he dismissed the servants, and after the room was emptied he stood staring at her for long, countless seconds.

'Now come to me,' he commanded.

She went like a woman willingly sleepwalking. Towards him. Summoned by her Sheikh. Into his arms. The place where she most wanted to be.

There was no kiss, just a fierce embrace which seemed to force all the breath out of her lungs. He clasped her against him and pressed his face to her scented hair. His words were muffled.

'You know that I love you, don't you, Sienna?'

Sienna pulled away and stared up at him, her eyes blinking rapidly, certain that she must have misheard him. 'Hashim?'

'Can't you feel it in the beating of my heart?' He placed her palm over his chest, where the rapid thundering of his life-blood made her eyes widen in dawning realisation. 'It is no good, Sienna—for I have tried. By the mountains and the rivers, I have tried! I have attempted the impossible and have failed. To forget you. To imagine life without you. And I cannot. *I will not.*'

'But *love*?' she whispered.

'Yes, love.' He smiled. 'More powerful than the eagle—a force as powerful as life itself—can you not feel it gathering strength, Sienna—as the bird itself does just before flight?'

He waited.

But Sienna felt tongue-tied and strangely humble— and scared too, in these imposing surroundings. A declaration she had longed for and never thought to hear—and now that it had been made she was shaken. It was as if dust had turned to gold before her eyes, and she was terrified that it would change back to dust again.

Yet he was right. She could feel the strength emanating from him—waves of it washing over her barely believing self. She touched her fingertips to the charm at her neck, as if it could give her the courage to say the words to him. Words she had once had tossed back in her face. Words she had grown inside her for so long, all the while trying to deny them.

'I love you too,' Hashim,' she said brokenly. 'I have done right from the very start, and it never changed—never dimmed—even when I prayed that it would.' She stared into the black eyes which had softened now. 'But you knew that, didn't you? You could read it in my eyes.'

'Yes.'

'And it doesn't actually *change* anything, does it? Not practically. You're still a sheikh and I'm still a—'

'No!' He cut her words off with brutal force. 'Do not say it! You are more and then much more—but you are not that! A youthful folly does not define a person for the rest of their lives!'

'But that is how I will be perceived.'

'And that,' he said grimly, '*that* is why I am making the broadcast. They are setting up cameras in the small Throne Room.' He tilted his head—handsome and irresistible. 'Will you come in with me?'

'What are you going to say?'

'Will you come in with me?' he repeated inexorably.

'Yes.'

'And I must ask you something else, Sienna—and this is important. The life you live in England is incompatible with mine. My home is here. My place is here—increasingly more so. Could you renounce much of the freedom you enjoy in England? Is your love for me strong enough to embrace my life here? For if you decide to, you must do so without reservation. There can be no trial period, no waiting to see whether or not you can adapt. It must be a leap of faith and nothing less. You must decide whether your love for me is strong enough to commit to me, and to commit for the rest of your life. When you marry me,' he finished deliberately, his gaze fixed firmly on her face.

'*Marry* you?' she echoed, genuinely shocked.

Wry amusement vied with outrage in his black eyes. 'You think that I would contemplate any alternative to marriage?' he demanded. 'That I should not want you as my wife? Assuming,' he added arrogantly, 'that you wish to be my wife? But if you do then you will be taking on more than most women do, and you must be certain in your heart that your destiny is beside me.'

Sienna licked her lips. She thought of the eagle which hung around her neck—powerful and fearless—the symbol of his country. This strange land

with a tongue that was foreign to her. A place so very
different from all that she had known—and yet it contained the only thing which was important to her.

Hashim.

Was she fearless enough in her love to grasp it
tightly and never let it go? To make her vows to him
and mean them? Never to leave his side? To promise
to be true, no matter what life threw in their path?
But wasn't that what *all* marriages were supposed to
mean?

'Oh, yes,' she whispered. 'Yes, yes, and a million
times yes.' There was an odd kind of lump in her
throat. 'But will your people accept me?'

'If they want me as their Ruler, then they will have
to.'

'Do you want to take that chance?'

'I can't not,' he said simply. But he knew that he
could never rule—nor would be fit to rule—if he allowed his people to prevent him from seizing his
heart's desire. Because any man who turned away
from one of life's greatest mysteries could never be
a complete man.

'But…' Sienna bit her lip, not wanting to destroy
the beautiful magic his words of love had created, but
knowing that she must not hide behind her fears, must
face them head-on—even if expressing them might
put paid to all her future happiness.

'But what, my beautiful Sienna?' he prompted
softly as he saw the hurt and the pain in her eyes.

'The photos.' It came out in a bitter sigh. 'What if

your people see that calendar—how on earth would they ever accept me then?'

'They shall not see it,' he breathed. 'Not now and not ever.'

He sounded so certain that she stared up at him in bewilderment. 'How can you be so sure?'

'Because I have bought up all the rights to those photos—they are now exclusively mine. No newspaper will ever publish them, the calendar shall never be reprinted, and the negatives have been destroyed. I have even made sure that they will never appear on the infernal internet,' he finished grimly.

She opened her mouth to ask how, but then changed her mind. When you were as rich and as powerful and as determined as Hashim, then Sienna supposed anything was possible. Instead, she gave a rather wobbly smile, needing something more than words or reassurance now. Something which she had missed so unbearably. She was aching to have him touch her again. 'Won't you please kiss me?' she whispered.

He felt a strange kick to his heart as he bent his face to hers. Was it a kind of weakness for a man to be so in thrall to one woman? 'You wish your Sheikh to go before the cameras in a state of arousal?' he murmured.

'Oh, Hashim—I never thought of that! I've got so much to learn. Maybe we'd better not...'

He gave a low, rumbling laugh. 'And you think that I have not been aroused since the moment you first walked in, my love? That I can look at you without wanting you? Then, yes, you still have much to learn! Now, come here.'

It was a brief kiss, fuelled by a sense of coming home rather than passion—though that was bubbling away beneath the surface as his lips brushed over hers.

'Now,' he said firmly, and, bending down, rang a small golden bell.

A stream of people began to appear. Men in flowing robes who bowed briefly to her and then deeper still to Hashim. And then they were walking along cool marble corridors towards the 'small' Throne Room—which seemed pretty vast to Sienna, but there again she hadn't had much experience of them.

She had been in TV studios before, but never when everyone had been behaving with such genuine deference towards the interviewee.

Hashim settled her in a chair at the back of the room and she watched while the camera lights lit up his face like the brightest sunshine. And then the red light flashed and the cameras began to roll, and suddenly he was speaking live to the nation.

She watched on the screen, so that she could read the English subtitles, and much of it she missed, because her heart was beating so fast with nerves and excitement and protectiveness.

But key phrases would stay in her mind and her heart for ever.

'I have been charged with the running of our coun-

try.' His face grew very serious at this point. *'An awesome responsibility which I have always embraced and cherished. But your Ruler must be allowed to fulfil his own personal destiny in order to best discharge his duties to his homeland.'*

He sent her the briefest of looks before continuing. *'In Qudamah, your Sheikh is permitted by law to have a harem of up to sixty women.'*

Sienna sat bolt upright. She hadn't known *that*!

'But I do not wish to have sixty women. I wish for only one, for I believe in monogamy.'

There was an unmistakable ripple in the room—as if he had just come out and declared that he had converted to cannibalism!

Now his eyes were on her, and they were very steady.

'For I have found my very own houri, and I intend to make her my wife.'

Later, Sienna would discover the significance of that particular word. A houri was a beautiful young woman but—far more crucially—she was a *virgin*. He was telling his people that he had found a bride who, although she might not at first appear so, was actually a suitable bride for their Sheikh.

She would also learn that Abdul-Aziz had travelled to England with the intention of attempting to bribe her with unimaginable riches to stay away from the Sheikh. But then he had seen her playing with Cara in the homespun tranquillity of her mother's house.

'I realised that I had never allowed myself to think beyond the stereotype of what I believed you to be,' he told her. 'And of course by then I realised that my Sheikh had grown to love you—and suddenly I could see why.'

And it didn't take long to realise that Hashim's mother wanted only her son's happiness.

For when it all came down to it palaces and different cultures counted for very little. In the end, the human spirit was the same the world over.

EPILOGUE

A DOLLOP of mashed banana landed in a slimy lump on the back of her hand and Sienna giggled as she wiped it away, looking up into the bemused black eyes of her husband as he surveyed the breakfast scene before him.

Hashim smiled. How his life had been transformed! Gone was the starchy formality and the slow glide of numerous servants who catered to his every whim. Instead, there sat his beautiful Sienna, with their gorgeous wriggling son on her lap.

'What a merry dance he leads you,' he observed ruefully.

'Ah, but what wonderful co-ordination he has,' cooed Sienna. 'Only eight months old, and he's practically feeding himself!'

'Indeed,' he murmured diplomatically, as another dollop of fruit was relayed across the linen table-cloth by the lively Prince Marzug.

Hashim had long given up trying to get Sienna to bring their son up in the conventional manner of royal princes, and she had resolutely refused to have child-care except when strictly necessary.

'No one can love a baby like his mother,' she had

told him firmly. 'Or his father,' she had added impishly.

And in that he could not argue with her—though he enjoyed trying. For Marzug had stolen his heart the moment he had made his first lusty bawl. There was so much love in Hashim's world now. His senses were raw and on fire with it. And Sienna had started it all. He looked at her.

Hard to believe as she sat in this scene of cosy domesticity, despite the grand dimensions of the room, that last night she had stunned the visiting French Ambassador at a reception given at the Palace in his honour. Hashim had watched with pride and love and lust as she had danced—slender and graceful as a flower swayed by the summer breeze. And alone afterwards, in the glorious privacy of their apartment, she had…she had… Hashim swallowed.

'Are you all right, darling?' Sienna questioned innocently, her words cutting in to a train of thought which was probably not advisable when he was due to inspect the Qudamah army in a little under an hour.

'Yes, my beauty,' he murmured, watching her pick up a cream sheet of paper. 'What are you reading now?'

Absently, Sienna dropped a kiss onto Marzug's curly black hair. 'Oh, just a request—asking if I will be patron of the new children's charity which is being set up in Nasim.'

'*Another* charity?' Hashim frowned. 'But you do enough already.'

'I know. But some of the work is extra-special, and...' She put the letter down on the table, out of Marzug's reach, and smiled at him. 'I'm just flattered to be asked,' she said simply.

And he understood. Perfectly.

Because it hadn't been all plain sailing to get to where she was today. Sienna had had to work hard to get the people of Qudamah to accept her. Some of them hadn't—certainly not straight away—but she had understood their doubts and fears about their beloved Sheikh marrying a woman from so far away, who knew little of their culture.

And there were some who had not finally thawed until she had produced the plump and bouncing olive-skinned infant Prince and fireworks had lit up the skies behind the Palace. Then they had finally taken her into their hearts.

The wedding itself had been a bit of a challenge, too—there had been a civil ceremony and then a religious one, after her conversion to Hashim's faith. She'd had to memorise all her vows in Qudamahesh and she had spent the night before the marriage saying them over and over again, until she was word perfect. Learning the ancient language was something she had immediately set about doing—and was even more of a challenge!

But she was young and bright and eager to learn. And she was in love. Just as she was loved. And that put everything in its proper perspective.

She had been a bag of nerves before her first meeting with Hashim's mother—for the Princess was deeply revered by all who knew her. But their shared love for one man had been enough to unite them in a harmony which had soon grown into genuine regard.

She was both a wise and a perceptive woman. She had allayed some of Sienna's fears—recounting the tale of one of Hashim's ancestors, who had married the daughter of his fiercest enemy despite much opposition. 'So, you see, there is nothing new under the sun, Sienna,' she had said softly. 'No matter where they live, nor what they do, people are the same; they never change. They fall in love and they fight for that love, and that is just how it should be.'

Sienna knew that what Hashim's mother had told her was important. Not to compare, no—but to realise that life was very precious and very short. Once, she had wondered when the present became the past, but now she realised that it was happening all the time. Their wedding was already in the past, and their life would whizz by as everyone warned it did. They just had to make the most of it.

She pushed the bowl of banana away and Hashim judged it safe enough to reach out and ruffle his son's hair. 'Will we swim together later?' she questioned eagerly. 'In the Palace pool? Just the three of us?'

'Yes, my love,' Hashim murmured indulgently, wondering what the fabled Special Guard of the army might say if they could see their Commander-in-Chief being such putty in his wife's hands! 'And later we will have dinner alone.' His eyes glinted. 'Since our diaries are free. And at some point we must discuss your mother's visit, and the gift of the stallion I intend to make to her.'

'Oh, Hashim, she's going to be over the moon.'

He took her hand, briefly rubbing the shiny gold wedding band with the pad of his thumb and then lifting her fingers to his lips, licking them provocatively. His eyes captured hers with sensual allure. 'Well, then,' he said lightly. 'That makes two of us, doesn't it?'

'Three of us, actually.' She smiled. 'Well, four if you count Marzug.'

'Always.'

Their eyes met and Sienna's breath caught in her throat. She wanted to hold that moment in her heart for ever.

She had to remember that it didn't last long—and to say the things that counted.

'I love you, Hashim.'

His eyes were tender. 'I love you too, sweet Sienna.'

And Sienna put the baby in his highchair and moved into her husband's arms, wrapping herself close enough to feel the powerful beating of his heart.

Introducing a brand-new miniseries

FOR Love OR MONEY

This is romance on the red carpet...

For Love or Money is the ultimate reading experience
for the reader who has a taste for tales of wealth and
celebrity and the accompanying gossip and scandal!

Look out for the special covers
on these upcoming titles:

Coming in September:

EXPOSED: THE SHEIKH'S MISTRESS
by *Sharon Kendrick* #2488

As the respected ruler of a desert kingdom, Sheikh Hashim
Al Aswad must marry a suitable bride of impeccable virtue.
He previously left Sienna Baker when her past was exposed—
he saw the photos to prove it! But what is the truth behind
Sienna's scandal? And with passion between them this hot
will he be able to walk away...?

Coming soon:

HIS ONE-NIGHT MISTRESS
by *Sandra Marton* #2494

SALE OR RETURN BRIDE
by *Sarah Morgan* #2500

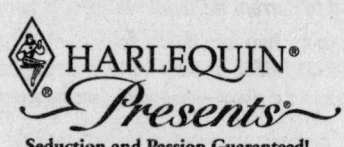

HARLEQUIN®
Presents

Seduction and Passion Guaranteed!

www.eHarlequin.com

HPTSM

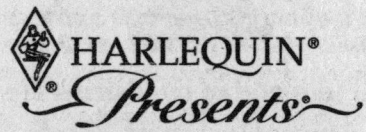

Coming Next Month

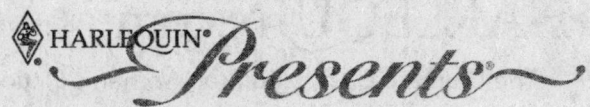

THE BEST HAS JUST GOTTEN BETTER!

#2493 THE BRAZILIAN'S BLACKMAILED BRIDE Michelle Reid
The Ramirez Brides

Anton Luis Scott-Lee is going to marry Cristina Marques. She rejected him years ago and his payback will be sweet: she will be at Luis's bidding—bought and paid for! But Luis will find that his bride can't or *won't* fulfill all of her wedding vows....

#2494 HIS ONE-NIGHT MISTRESS Sandra Field
For Love or Money

Lia knew that billionaire businessman Seth could destroy her glittering career. But he was so attractive that she succumbed to him—for one night! Eight years on, Lia's successful. When he sees Lia in the papers, Seth finds that he has a love child, and is determined to get her back!

#2495 EXPECTING THE PLAYBOY'S HEIR Penny Jordan
Jet-Set Wives

American billionaire Silas Carter has no plans for love—he wants a practical marriage. So he only proposes to beautiful Julia Fellowes as a ruse to get rid of her lecherous boss and to indulge in a hot affair—or that's what he lets her think!

#2496 A SCANDALOUS MARRIAGE Miranda Lee
Wives Wanted

Sydney entrepreneur Mike Stone has a month to get married—or he'll lose a business deal worth billions. Natalie Fairlane, owner of the *Wives Wanted* introduction agency, is appalled by his proposition! But the exorbitant fee Mike is offering for a temporary wife is *very* tempting...!

#2497 THE GREEK'S ULTIMATE REVENGE Julia James
The Greek Tycoons

Greek tycoon Nikos Kyriades wants revenge—and he's planned it. He'll treat Janine Fareham to a spectacular seduction, and he has two weeks on a sunny Greek island to do it. If Janine discovers she's a pawn in his game, Nikos knows she'll leave—but it's a risk he'll take to have her in his bed!

#2498 THE SPANIARD'S INCONVENIENT WIFE Kate Walker
The Alcolar Family

Ramon Dario desperately wants the Medrano company—but there is a condition: he must marry the notorious Estrella Medrano! Ramon will not be forced into marriage, but when he sees the gorgeous Estrella, he starts to change his mind....

HPCNM0905

Gil Addison Showed A Definite Talent For Stripping.

If he'd undressed any slower, Bailey would've ripped the shirt off. But she had asked for this. All she could do was watch in torment.

With her training, Bailey could bring most men down. But Gil...Gil was the real deal. His body rippled with muscle.

"Cat got your tongue?" he taunted.

Her legs shaking, she curled her arm around the bedpost. "Just admiring the view." She touched his chest. "I want to please you."

"You do, in every way. I love your strength, your integrity. The way you treat my son."

"He's lucky to have you."

His finger on her lips silenced her. "I spend all my time being Cade's father. Tonight...tonight I'm just a man. A man who wants you."

* * *

Beneath the Stetson
is a Texas Cattleman's Club: The Missing Mogul novel—
Love and scandal meet in Royal, Texas!

* * *

If you're on Twitter,
tell us what you think of Harlequin Desire!
#harlequindesire

Dear Reader,

I grew up in a family full of love and relatives. Imagining what it must feel like to have no roots is hard for me. My heroine, Bailey, reared in foster care, was the kind of kid who never took a step out of line, because she wanted to be loved and accepted. As an adult, she has built a wide circle of friends, but her job has become her life.

Loving means opening yourself up to the possibility of hurt. When Bailey meets a special little boy and his very sexy father, she must decide if falling in love with not one, but *two* Texas males is worth the risk of a broken heart.

I hope you are enjoying the Texas Cattleman's Club books, and I invite you to join me in April 2014 for the first installment of my new series, The Kavanaghs of Silver Glen.

As always, thanks for reading!

Janice Maynard

BENEATH
THE STETSON

—

JANICE MAYNARD

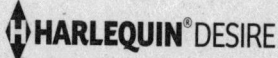 **HARLEQUIN**®DESIRE

Special thanks and acknowledgment to Janice Maynard for her contribution to the Texas Cattleman's Club: The Missing Mogul miniseries.

Recycling programs for this product may not exist in your area.

ISBN-13: 978-0-373-73289-0

BENEATH THE STETSON

Printed in U.S.A.

Books by Janice Maynard

Harlequin Desire

The Billionaire's Borrowed Baby #2109
*Into His Private Domain #2135
*A Touch of Persuasion #2146
*Impossible to Resist #2164
*The Maid's Daughter #2182
*All Grown Up #2206
*Taming the Lone Wolff #2236
*A Wolff at Heart #2260
A Billionaire for Christmas #2271
Beneath the Stetson #2276

Silhouette Desire

The Secret Child & the Cowboy CEO #2040

*The Men of Wolff Mountain

Other titles by this author available in ebook format.

JANICE MAYNARD

is a *USA TODAY* bestselling author who lives in beautiful east Tennessee with her husband. She holds a B.A. from Emory and Henry College and an M.A. from East Tennessee State University. In 2002 Janice left a fifteen-year career as an elementary school teacher to pursue writing full-time. Now her first love is creating sexy, character-driven, contemporary romance stories.

Janice loves to travel and enjoys using those experiences as settings for books. Hearing from readers is one of the best perks of the job! Visit her website, www.janicemaynard.com, and follow her on Facebook and Twitter.

For my wonderful Texas friends,
Karen, Rob, Elaine and Bob. Thank you for the fun,
the laughter and the "tall" tales of life in Texas.
I count you among my blessings!

One

Gil Addison didn't like Feds. Even when they came wrapped in pretty packages. Perhaps it was the trace of Comanche blood in his veins that kept an atavistic memory alive…all those years of government promises made and broken. Gil was a white man living in a white man's world, no doubt about it. Nothing much of his Native American heritage lingered except for his black hair, brown eyes and olive skin.

But the distrust remained.

He stood inside the house, hand on an edge of the curtain, and watched as a standard-issue dark sedan made its way down the long driveway. Technically, the woman for whom he waited wasn't a Fed. She was a state investigator. But she had been trained by Feds, and that was close enough.

"Who is it, Daddy?"

His four-year-old son, Cade, endlessly curious, wrapped

an arm around his father's leg. Gil glanced down at the boy, smiling in spite of his unsettled emotions. "A lady who wants to talk to me. Don't worry. It won't take long." He had promised Cade they would go riding today.

"Is she pretty?"

Gil raised an eyebrow. "Why would that matter?"

The child with the big, far-too-observant eyes grinned. "Well, if she is, you might want to date her and fall in love and then get married and—"

"This again?" Gil kept his hand over the boy's mouth in a mock insistence on changing the subject. He knelt and looked Cade in the eyes. "I have you. That's all I need." Single parenting was not for wimps. Sometimes it was the loneliest job in the world. And Gil wondered constantly if he was making irrevocable mistakes. He hugged his son before standing up again. "I think I've been letting you watch too much TV."

Cade pulled the curtains even farther aside and watched as the car rolled to a stop and parked. The car door opened and the woman stepped out. "She *is* pretty," Cade said, practically bouncing with the energy that never seemed to diminish.

Inwardly, Gil agreed with Cade's assessment, albeit reluctantly. Bailey Collins, despite the professional pantsuit that was as dark and unexceptional as her car, made an impression on a man. Only a few inches shy of Gil's six-one height, she carried herself with confidence. Wavy, shoulder-length brown hair glinted in the sun with red highlights. Her thick-lashed eyes were almost as dark as Gil's.

Though she was still too far away for Gil to witness those last two attributes, he had a good memory. Today was not his first encounter with Bailey Collins.

As she mounted his front steps, he opened the door, refusing to acknowledge that his heart beat faster than normal. The first time he met her, they had faced each other across a desk at Royal's police station. Even then he'd felt a potent mix of sexual hunger and resentment. But Bailey was on his turf now. He'd be calling the shots. She might think her credentials gave her power, but he was not prepared to accept them at face value.

Bailey caught her toe on the edge of the top step and stumbled, almost falling flat on her face. Fortunately, she regained her balance at the last second, because in the midst of her gyrations the door flew open, and a man she recognized all too well stood framed in the doorway.

Gil Addison.

Even as she acknowledged the jolt to her chest, she was taken aback by the presence of a second male. The man for whom she felt an unwelcome but visceral attraction was not alone. He held the hand of a small boy, most likely—according to Gil's dossier—his son. Even without written verification, she could have guessed the relationship. The young one was practically a carbon copy of his older counterpart.

The child broke free of his father's hold and stepped forward to beam at Bailey. "Welcome to the Straight Arrow," he said, holding out his hand with poignant maturity. His gap-toothed smile was infectious. "I'm Cade."

Bailey squatted, holding out her hand, as well, feeling the warmth of the small palm as it nestled briefly in hers. "Hello, Cade," she said. "I'm Bailey."

"Ms. Collins," Gil corrected with a slight frown. "I'm trying to teach him manners."

"It's not bad manners to use my first name if I offer the privilege," Bailey said evenly, rising to face the man who had already given her sleepless nights.

Cade looked back and forth between the two adults.

The thinly veiled antagonism between them was unfortunate, because Cade seemed first confused and then unhappy. The boy's chin wobbled. "I wanted my dad to like you," he whispered, staring up at Bailey with huge blue eyes that must have come from his mother.

Bailey's heart melted. "Your dad and I like each other just fine," she told Cade, daring Gil to disagree. "Sometimes grown-ups get frustrated about things, but that doesn't mean we're angry." Even as an adult of thirty-three, she remembered vague impressions of her parents arguing. Yelling. Saying wretched, bitter words that couldn't be unheard.

Bailey knew what it was like to be a child with no power to shape the course of events. It was because she *did* understand Cade's dismay, that she summoned an almost-genuine smile and aimed it in Gil's direction. "Thank you for seeing me today. If we can sit down for a few moments, I promise not to take up too much of your time."

With Cade standing squarely in between them, there was nothing for Gil to do but agree. He ruffled his son's hair, love for his child and wry capitulation in his gaze as he spoke. "Why don't you join us in the kitchen, Ms. Collins? Cade and I usually have lemonade and a snack right about now."

"You may as well call me Bailey, too," she muttered, not sure if he heard her or not. She followed the two of them back through the house to the historic but updated kitchen. Gil had taken over the property from his parents when they retired and settled in Austin. The senior Addisons had inherited the Straight Arrow from Gil's grandparents. The ranch, whose name ironically described its owner to a T, was an enormous operation.

Four years ago when Gil's wife committed suicide, Gil had hired an army of extra ranch hands and housekeepers, so he could be the primary caregiver for his toddler son. Bailey knew the facts of the situation because she had investigated the man …and admired him for his devotion. But that didn't make her any more forgiving of the way he had stonewalled her in their earlier interviews. Even though her file on Gil Addison was thorough and extensive, she was no closer to understanding the man himself.

Cade pulled out a chair for Bailey, sealing the deal. The kid was irresistible. Clearly Gil was not kidding when he mentioned teaching manners. Something about witnessing the boy's interaction with his father made Bailey's assessment of Gil shift and refocus. Surely a man who could be so caring and careful with a child was not all bad.

Bailey's own exposure to male parenting was more like a metaphorical slap up the side of the head. *Toe the line. Don't complain. Achieve. Be self-sufficient.* Even the most generous assessment of her father's motives left no room for seeing him as anything other than a bully and a tyrant—presumably the reason Bailey's mother had walked out, leaving her young daughter behind.

Bailey sat down somewhat self-consciously, and placed her cell phone on the table. While Gil busied himself retrieving glasses from the pine cabinets and slicing apples to go along with peanut butter, Cade grilled Bailey. "Do you have any good games on your phone?"

His hopeful expression made her grin. "A few."

"Angry Birds?"

"Yes. Are you any good at it?"

Cade shot a glance at his dad and lowered his voice. "He thinks that too much time with electronics will make me…um…" Clearly searching for the desired word, Cade trailed off, his brow furrowed.

"Brain dead." Gil set the glasses on the table and returned with the plate of apples. Taking a chair directly across from Bailey, he sat down and turned his son's hand over, palm up. The little fingers were grimy. "Go wash up, Cade. Ms. Collins and I will wait for you."

When Cade disappeared down the hall to the bathroom, Bailey smiled. "He's wonderful. And unexpectedly mature for a four-year-old."

"He'll be five soon. He didn't have too many opportunities to be around other children until I began bringing him to the daycare center at the club occasionally, so that accounts for the adult conversation. As much as I'll miss him, I think it will be good for him to start kindergarten this fall."

Bailey cocked her head. "I may have misjudged you, Gil Addison. I think you *do* have a heart."

"Don't confuse parental love for weakness, Ms. Collins. I won't be manipulated into helping you take down one of my friends."

The sudden attack startled her. Gil's classic features were set in grim lines, any trace of softness gone. "You really don't trust me at all, do you?" she asked, her voice husky with regret at this evidence of his animosity.

"I don't trust your kind," he clarified, his tone terse. "Alex Santiago was kidnapped, but now he's been found. Sooner or later he'll get his memory back and be able to tell us who took him. Why can't you people drop it and leave us here in Royal to clean up our own messes?"

Bailey glanced toward the hallway, realizing that Cade could return at any moment. "Surely you're not that naive," she said quietly. "Because Alex has no memory of what happened to him, trouble could strike again at any time. We have no choice but to track down his abductors. Surely you can see that."

"What I don't see is why you think anyone I know is responsible."

"Alex was well-liked in Royal, though obviously he had at least one enemy. *You* know a lot of people. Somewhere in the midst of all that I hope to find the truth. It's my job, Gil. And I'm good at it. All I need is your help."

Cade popped into the room, the front of his shirt damp from his ablutions. "I'm really hungry," he said. At a nod from his father, he scooped up two apple slices and started eating.

As Bailey watched, Gil offered her a piece and took one himself. His sharp white teeth bit into the fruit with a crunch. She tried to eat, but the food stuck in her throat. She needed Gil on her side. And she needed him to trust her. Perhaps that would require time.

Biting her lip, she put down her uneaten snack and tried the lemonade instead. As father and son chatted about mundane matters, she strove for composure. Usually it took a lot to rattle her. But for some reason, winning Gil's approval was important.

When his phone rang, he glanced at the number and grimaced. "Sorry, Ms. Collins. I need to take this in private. I won't be long."

Cade glanced up at his dad as Gil stood. "Don't worry, Daddy. I'll entertain her."

When Gil returned thirty minutes later, he felt a pinch of guilt for abandoning Bailey to his son's clutches. Not all women were good with children, and Bailey struck him as more of a focused career woman than a nurturer. When he crossed the threshold into the kitchen, he pulled up short. There at the table, right where he had left them, were Cade and Bailey. Only now, they were sitting side by side, their heads bent over Bailey's phone.

The lemonade glasses were empty, as was the plate that had held apples.

Bailey shook her head. "Remember the angles," she said. "Don't just fire it off willy-nilly."

When Gil's son gazed up at Bailey, Gil's heart fractured. Never had he seen a boy so starved for feminine attention. Despite Gil's best efforts at being a perfect parent, nothing could substitute for the love of a mother. If Gil were not careful, Cade would latch onto Bailey and create an embarrassing situation for all of them.

Gil cleared his throat. "Cade. If you'll give me half an hour to speak with Ms. Collins about some grown-up business, I promise you we'll leave for our ride immediately after that."

Cade never looked up from his game. "Sure, Dad. Let me just finish this one—"

Gil took the phone and handed it to Bailey. "You have permission to use the computer in my study. Now scram."

"Yes, sir." Cade gave Bailey a cheeky grin on his way out the door. "Will you say goodbye before you leave?"

Bailey rose to her feet and glanced at Gil.

Cade's father nodded. "I'll let you know when we're done."

In Cade's absence an uncomfortable silence reigned. The little boy's exuberant personality had served to soften the edges of Gil's aggressive displeasure.

Bailey hesitated, searching for a way to break the ice.

Gil did it for her. He held out an arm. "Since Cade is in my office, we might as well step onto the back porch. If that's okay with you," he added stiffly.

Bailey nodded. "Of course." The January weather was picture-perfect, and as was often the case during the winter, a bit erratic, as well. Last week Royal had endured storms and temperatures in the mid-fifties. Today the thermometer was forecast to hit eighty, almost a record.

As they stepped outside, Bailey had to smile. The

rienced a pang of regret for something that would never be. It had been a long time since she had met a man so appealing. But Gil didn't much like her, and her newest assignment was not going to improve matters.

With an inward sigh for her barren love life, she cut to the chase. "I need access to the membership files at the Texas Cattleman's Club."

"Absolutely not." He bowed up almost visibly.

Bailey leaned against the porch railing, her hands behind her. It was either that or fasten them around Gil's tanned neck and squeeze. The man was infuriating. "I have all the necessary warrants and paperwork," she said mildly. "But I'd prefer not to go in guns blazing. Why don't you be a gentleman for once and politely invite me to the club as your guest?"

The word he muttered made her wince. "I'm the *president* of the TCC," he pointed out…as if she didn't already know. His scowl was black. "People trust me with their secrets. How is it going to look if I turn all that over to an outsider?"

That last jab hurt, but Bailey held her ground. "You don't really have a choice…even if you do have a judge or two tucked away in your back pocket. These orders come down from on high. I'm going to comb through those files one way or another. You can either make my life miserable or you can cooperate. Your choice. But I *will* get the information I need."

Two

Gil ripped his hat from his head and ran a hand across his damp brow. It was January, damn it. No reason in the world the heat and humidity should be this bad.

Bailey, on the other hand, despite wearing an unflattering suit jacket, seemed cool and collected. She watched him warily, as if he were a dangerous rattlesnake about to bite.

What she didn't know was that he *had* fantasized about nibbling her…all the way from her delicate jawline to the vulnerable place where her throat disappeared inside that boring blouse. His body tightened. The woman probably had no idea that her no-nonsense clothing revved his engine. Instead of focusing on the government-employee quasi uniform, he imagined stripping it off her and baring that long, lean body to his gaze.

His sex thickened and lifted, making his jeans uncomfortably tight. With a silent curse, he stared out across the acres of land that belonged to him as far as the eye could see. Searching desperately for a diversion, he fell back on the universal topic of weather.

"Are you familiar with the Civil War general Philip Sheridan?" he asked, keeping his body half-turned to avoid embarrassing them both.

Bailey wrinkled her nose. "History wasn't my strong suit in school, but yes...I've heard of him."

"After the war, Sheridan was assigned to a post in south Texas. It's reported he said that if he owned Texas and hell, he would rent out Texas and live in hell."

"I'm surprised you would mention it. I thought it was heresy to insult the mother ship. All you native Texans are pretty arrogant."

"We have reason to be...despite the heat," he added ruefully, replacing his hat and wanting desperately to wrap this up before he pounced on her.

"So I'm to believe that everything in Texas is bigger and better?"

Shock immobilized him. Was Bailey flirting with him? Surely not. He glanced over his shoulder at her. As far as he could tell, nothing in her demeanor was the least bit sexual. Too bad. "Yes," he said curtly. "I thought you would know that, being from Dallas."

"I'm not *from* Dallas. My dad was in the army. We lived all over the world. Dallas is where I'm assigned at the moment."

"So where do you call home?"

Seconds passed. Two, maybe three. For a brief moment he saw bleak regret in her brown-eyed gaze. "Not anywhere, really."

Such rootlessness was hard for him to imagine. Texas was as much a part of his lifeblood as breathing. Sensing her unease with the topic, he turned to face her, at last

somewhat in control of himself. "Well," he said laconi-
cally, "at least if you weren't born here, you came as soon
as you could."

Bailey, arms wrapped around her waist, smiled. "I guess
you could say that."

He pursed his lips. "Apparently, I have no choice about
your interference. Is that what you're telling me?" The facts
of the matter still stuck in his craw.

"You've got it." Though seeing him admit defeat must
have pleased her, Bailey's expression remained neutral.

"Very well. Meet me at the club at ten in the morning.
I'll show you where to get started."

"I'm a highly trained computer specialist, Gil. I
shouldn't have to take up more than a week of your life."

Too bad. He glanced at his watch. "Come say goodbye to Cade."

In his office, he watched, perturbed, as once again his
son lit up at seeing their visitor.

Gil's son beamed. "I unlocked three more levels, Bailey."

She nodded. "Good for you."

Cade looked at his dad. "Are you gonna call her *Bailey?*"

"I suppose I will," Gil admitted. "She's going to be
around for a while."

Cade grinned charmingly. "That's good."

Gil pinched the boy's ear. "Behave, brat. I don't need
your help finding women."

Bailey's face turned crimson, affording Gil a definite
sense of satisfaction. It was fine by him if she felt uncomfortable. It was only fair. She was messing with his life
from stem to stern in all sorts of ways. Not the least of
which was his recalcitrant libido. The sooner she finished
what she had to do and left town, the better.

* * *

Bailey arrived at the Texas Cattleman's Club fifteen minutes early the following morning. A heat wave still held the area in an unseasonable grip. Though by no means reaching the brutal temperatures of July and August, the day was plenty warm. Which meant that the winter clothing Bailey had brought with her was stifling.

Deciding she could maintain a professional demeanor *without* her blazer, she stripped it off and laid it carefully in the backseat of the car. Rolling up the sleeves of her white silk blouse, she breathed a sigh of relief as she immediately felt cooler.

In all honesty, part of her warmth stemmed from the prospect of facing Gil Addison again. Gil was in the clear as far as the investigation went, but she was going to have to work with him to some extent in order to do her job. The fact that she was attracted to him complicated things.

As she approached the club, she assessed the physical features automatically. Built around 1910, the large, rambling, single-story building was constructed of dark wood and stone with a tall slate roof. For over a century, it had been an entirely male enclave. In the past couple of years, however, a handful of women had finally been admitted as official members. During her stay in Royal, Bailey had heard rumblings of discontent. Not everyone thought change was a good idea.

Despite her early arrival, Gil was waiting for her in the lobby. Guests were admitted only in the company of a member. She wondered if Gil felt he was betraying his position by bringing Bailey into the mix.

She greeted him quietly and looked around. High ceilings gave a sense of spaciousness even as dark floors and big leather-upholstered furniture created a cozy, masculine space. "Nice," she said. "Is Cade with you?"

Gil pointed to the room just to the left of the entryway. "The old billiards room has been converted into the new day care center. I promised Cade if he behaved nicely for a couple of hours, he could join us for lunch."

"I'd like that," she said. "Your son is a pretty awesome kid."

"I happen to think so." He shoved his hands in his back pockets. Today, perhaps in deference to his position as president, he wore a tweed blazer over a white dress shirt. He hadn't given up his jeans, however. Although Gil hadn't worn his hat inside his own home, apparently within the walls of the club, a Stetson was de rigueur.

It wasn't fair, Bailey thought desperately. How was she supposed to be businesslike when everything about him made her weak in the knees? Well, *almost* everything, she amended mentally. His arrogance was hard to take. She had come up against Gil's bullheadedness in her initial interview with him. Pushing for answers had been like a futile military assault against well-fortified defenses.

Gil was a man accustomed to steering his own course. Though she didn't pick up any vibes that he scoffed at the idea of a woman working in law enforcement, nevertheless she suspected he didn't like having to cooperate.

As they walked down the hall toward Gil's TCC office, she asked the question that she should have asked the day before. "Have you been to see Alex since he's been found?"

Gil pulled a key from his pocket and unlocked the solid oak door. Ushering Bailey inside, he nodded. "I did…but since he's lost his memory, the visit was rather pointless. He had no clue who I was."

"Were you close before he disappeared?"

"Close enough. Not bosom buddies, but we knew each other pretty well."

"You probably should go see him again when you have

a chance," she said. "You never know when a face or voice might jog something loose."

"I'll think about it...."

She placed her purse and briefcase on a low table. She and Gil were standing in what appeared to be an outer reception area. More masculine leather furniture outfitted this small space. Someone had added a stuffy arrangement of artificial flowers, perhaps hoping to soften the ambience. But with various examples of taxidermy staring down from overhead, it was hard to imagine any woman feeling at home here.

Apparently, the office itself was through the closed door a few steps away. "I don't want to snarl up your day," she said. "If you don't mind writing down the user name and password...and giving me a quick rundown of the program you use to input information, I should be able to work on my own."

Gil smiled, genuine amusement on his face. That expression alone was enough to shock her. But the momentary appearance of an honest-to-God dimple in his tanned cheek took her aback. "Did I say something funny?"

He stepped past her to open the other door. "See for yourself."

Expecting to discover the customary computer and printer equipment inside, she drew up short at the sight facing her. A dozen wooden file cabinets, four drawers high, lined the opposite wall. By the window, a deep bookshelf housed a collection of thick leather ledgers. Dust motes danced in a sunbeam that played across a patterned linoleum floor. A battered rolltop desk sat just to the left, its only adornment a brass placard that said President.

She held up her hands in defeat. "You can't be serious."

Gil leaned in the doorway, his relaxed posture in direct opposition to her own state of mind. "There's something you need to understand, Bailey. The Texas Cattleman's Club is an institution, certainly as much a part of Royal's history as the churches and the mercantile or the feed store and the saloon. Men have come here for decades to get away from wives and girlfriends…to play poker and make business deals. Anyone who walks through the door as a full member has money and influence."

"And your point?"

"Heritage and tradition are etched into the walls. The guys around here don't like change."

"Which is why the child care center drew so much controversy."

"Yes. That, and the inclusion of women. So it shouldn't come as any surprise to see how we keep records. The good old boys may have their iPads and their internet, but when it comes to the TCC, the old ways are the only ways. At least so far."

"So there's hope for modernization?"

"Maybe. But I can't force it on them. It has to be a gradual process. If I'm lucky, and if I can spin it the right way, they'll think it was their idea to begin with."

"And it won't hurt matters if a few of the old guard ride off into the sunset in the meantime."

"You said it, not me. The TCC was here before I was born, and it will be here long after I'm gone. I'm under no illusions that being president gives me any real power. It's more of an honorary title, if you want to know the truth."

"I'm sure they think a great deal of you."

His eyebrows lifted. "Why, Ms. Collins. Was that a compliment?"

The teasing grin caught her off guard. Apparently, dumping her in a dusty room full of nothing but file folders sweetened his mood. "I doubt you need compliments of *any* kind, Mr. Addison. In fact, I'm surprised your head isn't already too big for that clichéd cowboy hat."

"Don't insult my hat," he said solemnly, though his eyes were dancing. "Since I'm stuck with you for the foreseeable future, we might as well drop the formality, don't you think?"

"Does that mean you trust me now?"

"Not for a minute," he said promptly. "But I figure it's my job to keep an eye on you…Bailey."

The way he said those two syllables made her stomach curl with something that felt a lot like desire. But such an emotion was doomed to wither on the vine. Despite her unwilling host's humor, she was not deceived. Her presence at the TCC was tolerated at best.

For a man who was innocent of any wrongdoing, Gil seemed curiously suspicious of authority. Was there something in his past that made him so? What did he have to fear from Bailey? Nothing that she could see. So perhaps it was government interference in general he hated. Not a particularly uncommon attitude, especially in this neck of the woods. But she felt the sting of his disapproval nevertheless.

Maybe in time she could prove to him that she was more than an outsider meddling in his business. She liked to think they could get to a place where he regarded her as something more than a nuisance. In a tiny corner of her heart, she wondered what it would be like if she and Gil were on the same side. If no walls between them existed. If they could be just a man and a woman. Exploring the sweet lure of attraction.

"I suppose I'd better get started," she said, trying not to let him see the way her hands trembled and her breathing quickened at the thought of actually being on friendly terms with the sexy rancher.

"Start where?"

"Are you genuinely interested, or is that another suspicious question?"

He shrugged, straightening and running a hand across the back of his neck. "A little of both, I guess."

She nodded, deciding not to take offense at his honesty. "My plan is to pull all the files of the people I interviewed in the initial investigation. I'll comb through them and see if anything stands out."

"In other words, you're looking for a needle in a haystack."

"Despite what television and movies would have you believe, law enforcement is seldom glamorous."

"Why did you choose this career path?" he asked, his gaze reflecting genuine interest.

Bailey hesitated.

"Sorry," he said quickly. "None of my business."

"No. It's okay. I suppose I was debating how to answer that. As a teenager I would have told you I wanted to serve my country."

"And that's not true?"

"It *is* true, but I'm not the starry-eyed idealist I was back then. And I'm a little more self-aware, I think. I've come to understand that I do what I do because I wanted to make my father proud of me."

"I'm sure he must be."

She grimaced. "Not really. He wanted me to go into the military. He's a career army guy. But that never seemed like the right fit for me, so state law enforcement was my compromise. I thought he would come around eventually, but he hasn't."

"Parents can be shortsighted. Do you regret your choice?"

No one had ever asked her that. Her job was fulfilling

and she was good at it. But she wasn't sure it was going to be her life's work. "To be honest, I wanted to be a musician. I'm pretty good on the guitar and the piano. I took advantage of almost all my electives when I was in college to sign up for music courses."

Gil stared at her. Hard. As if trying to see inside her head. "You're an interesting person, Bailey Collins."

She might not be the most experienced woman on the planet, but she knew when a man wanted her. The look in Gil's eyes was unmistakable. There was enough fire and passion in his dark eyes to make her body go liquid with longing. She had felt the spark the first time they met and doggedly ignored it because he was a potential suspect.

But Gil was innocent, and the feelings were still there. If she encouraged his interest, things might get very intense during her time in Royal. The truth was, she was afraid that getting involved with someone who played a role in her investigation was unprofessional at best. Keeping a clear line between business and pleasure was not going to be easy.

She met his gaze reluctantly. "So are you, Gil. So are you."

He jerked when she said his name. As if her utterance of that single syllable shocked him. Now the frown returned in full force. "I have things to do," he said gruffly. "Are you all set?"

If she hadn't known better, she would have thought he was ready to beat a hasty retreat. "I'm fine," she said. "How long do I have before we meet Cade for lunch?"

"A couple of hours. He gets a snack at the center, so I made a reservation in the dining room for twelve-thirty. Does that work for you?"

"Of course. And will I be able to come back this afternoon and pick up where I left off?"

"Yes. Feel free to leave everything out. I'll lock the door when we go to eat, and no one will bother your papers."

"You're being very accommodating all of a sudden."

"I've been pretty rough on you," he admitted, his neutral gaze hard to read. "I know you're merely doing your job. I don't like it, but I suppose there's no point in shooting the messenger."

She took a step in his direction just as he did the same. Suddenly they were nose to nose in the small office. Her hands fluttered at her sides. "Thank you, Gil. Your cooperation makes my life a lot easier." She heard the huskiness in her voice and winced inwardly. Her eyes were level with his throat. They stood so close to each other she could see the hint of a dark beard on his firm, sculpted chin.

Without warning, Gil slid his hands beneath her hair, thumbs stroking her neck. He tipped her face up to his, their lips mere centimeters apart. His beautiful eyes teemed with turbulent emotion "You're going to be trouble, aren't you, Bailey Collins?"

"Why would you say that?" she asked, knowing full well what he meant but wanting to hear him admit that the attraction wasn't one-sided.

His lips brushed hers in a caress that could barely even be called a kiss. She leaned into him, wanting more.

But straight-arrow Gil Addison was a tough man. "Women and government are always trouble. When you put both in the same package, there's likely to be hell to pay."

Three

Bailey leaned against the desk for a full three minutes after Gil left the room, her legs like spaghetti. She had wanted to know if he had felt it, too, the heated connection between them. Now she had irrevocable proof. It was a wonder the tiny room full of aging paper hadn't gone up in flames on the spot.

Fanning her hot face with one hand, she reached for her briefcase and pulled out her laptop and portable scanner. It was one thing to contemplate seducing the steely-eyed rancher, but another entirely to realize that all he had to do was touch her and she melted.

She was here to do a job. Before she contemplated any hanky-panky, she needed to get her priorities in order. Fortunately, she had made a plan already, so even though her concentration was shot, she was able to follow through with her agenda.

The method of attack was fairly simple. Using a list

of interviews from her earliest days in Royal, she pulled file folders methodically, keeping them in alphabetical order. Though she hadn't anticipated the complication of not having anything digitized, she would cope. As long as she didn't do something stupid like knocking a pile of paper off the desk, she should be able to proceed with relative efficiency.

Thirty minutes later she had finished reading through three folders and had developed a throbbing tension headache. She banged her fist against her forehead. Not only was much of the information *not* typed or organized in any discernible fashion, but the handwritten portions were barely legible.

To call this mess *record-keeping* was generous. It was impossible to compare one file with the next, because every member's information was different. Other than an initial sheet that documented simple details such as name, address and date of initial membership, all the other pages were a hodgepodge of business deals, sporting records and family connections.

It took her another half hour, but she finally managed to come up with a spreadsheet that allowed her to input the pertinent items that might be of use in the investigation. Her stomach growled more than once. She hadn't eaten breakfast, too nervous about meeting Gil again to be very interested in food.

She glanced at her watch and sighed. The minutes crawled by. Perhaps she was bored with the job, or maybe she was looking forward to lunch with Gil and his precocious son. Her distraction didn't bode well for the days ahead....

Gil prowled the familiar halls of the club, pausing again and again to greet and chat with men he had known for years, many of them since he was a child at his father's side. He was comfortable within these walls, centered, content. The Texas Cattleman's Club had suffered a few growing pains lately, but it would survive and thrive.

Tradition and stability were important. Which was why Gil had passed the day-to-day running of his ranch over to other hands so he could concentrate on his son's well-being. One day, everything Gil owned would go to Cade. Cade would get married, settle down and hopefully have better luck in the romance department than his father had.

What really stuck in Gil's craw was the knowledge that the genesis of his unease sat not far away, her beautiful head bent over a stack of dull club papers, trying to find dirt on someone who might be Gil's friend. Perhaps the real problem wasn't that Gil didn't trust Bailey. Perhaps what bothered him the most was the notion that someone in Royal could have committed such a terrible crime.

Alex was back home, true. But a man with no memory was as vulnerable as a baby in the middle of a busy city street. How would Alex know if the perpetrators came at him again? How would anyone ever know what evil roamed the streets of Royal if Alex *never* remembered?

For years, Royal had been a great place to live, to raise a family. Occasionally the sheriff was forced to contend with cattle rustlers. And once in a while a two-bit drug dealer might try to set up shop. Of course, there were the usual domestic disturbances, or teenagers letting off steam on a Saturday night. But all in all, Royal was a pretty safe place.

At least it was until Alex Santiago had disappeared. The local and state authorities had crawled all over the town in the beginning. There were rumors of a potential drug war or maybe even bad blood between Alex and Chance McDaniel, who had appeared interested in the same woman.

But since that time, everyone Gil knew intimately had been marked off the suspect list.

Which was all well and good except for the fact that *still* no one knew who the kidnappers were.

Maybe Gil should be more helpful to Bailey. He wanted his town back to normal, and Bailey wanted to close her case. So perhaps it was in Gil's best interest to help her. The sooner she was finished, the sooner she would leave town and go back to Dallas. That would be the smartest thing that could happen.

Gil didn't need the complication of an uncomfortable sexual attraction that was not likely to go anywhere. Already, Gil's son liked Bailey. Which meant that soon Cade would be weaving scenarios where Bailey became his new mom. Gil had seen it happen before. The boy's unwavering fixation on finding a mother meant that Gil no longer dated in Royal.

Not that he ever had dated much. When his physical needs became too demanding, he either dealt with them via a cold shower, or he met up with an old female friend in another town who was as uninterested in a serious relationship as Gil was. Those encounters left him feeling empty and oddly restless. But Gil had yet to find a woman who came even close to what he thought his son needed.

Bailey was a career woman whose job involved a lot of travel. Though Bailey and Cade had clicked at their first meeting, Bailey didn't strike Gil as the nurturing type. Cade had lost so much. If and when Gil ever remarried, it would be to a woman with traditional values, a woman who believed in the importance of being a full-time parent.

Gil had played that role for a very long time. And never once regretted his decision. Cade's sweet spirit and outgoing personality were proof that Gil had at least done something right. But Cade would soon be going to school full time. As much as Gil would miss his son, he was looking forward to once again taking an active role in the management of the Straight Arrow.

What he and Cade needed was a down-to-earth woman, one who would supervise the domestic staff, plan meals for the housekeeper to carry out and organize social events… tasks Gil had no interest in at all.

That paragon of a woman was out there somewhere. Gil had to believe she was, because the prospect of spending his entire life as a single parent and a single man sounded very lonely indeed.

At ten after twelve, he gave up the pretense of being busy and headed back to his office. Bailey didn't appear to have moved at all since he left her two hours ago. She was surrounded by stacks of paper. Her fingers flew with impressive speed over the keys of her laptop computer.

She didn't even notice when he came in.

He cleared his throat. Bailey's head snapped up as she glared at him. "It wouldn't hurt you to knock," she said. "You scared me to death."

"It's *my* office," he responded mildly. "You're only visiting." He grabbed a ladder-back chair and turned it around, straddling the seat. Bailey was behind his desk, so he now faced her across the cluttered surface. Her thick russet hair was drawn back into a ponytail at the nape of her neck. Tendrils waved around her face. Her work must have been frustrating, because the vibe he was getting from her was definitely harried. "Problems, Bailey?"

Her eyes narrowed. "You *knew* how impossible this was going to be, didn't you?"

He lifted a shoulder. "I have the utmost faith in your capabilities." He paused. "Any luck?" He didn't really want to get involved in what he considered a breach of privacy for the members of the club, but at the same time, he didn't want to be blindsided with any surprises.

She gnawed her lip, her gaze flitting back to the computer screen. "It's a little early to tell. But I do have some questions about this man." She shoved a folder toward Gil. "According to his file, he's been cited three separate times for fighting on club property. Do you know if he had any kind of grudge against Alex Santiago?"

Gil glanced at the name on the tab and shook his head, grinning. "Just a good ole boy who gets rowdy when he's had one too many beers. We keep track of such incidents, just in case, but our policy is to prevent members from doing damage to themselves or anyone else. Someone usually takes the offender home and keeps his keys until the following day. I know this guy, Bailey. He didn't kidnap Alex."

The slight frown between her brows deepened. She handed him a second file. "And this one? He filed a formal complaint when the club hired a Hispanic chef. His letter includes a number of racial slurs."

Gil flipped open the folder and shook his head. "You're grasping at straws. There are bigots everywhere. But that doesn't mean this guy had any reason to kidnap Alex." He touched her hand briefly, surprising himself when he felt a *zing* of something from the simple contact. "Have you considered the possibility that you might be stirring up unnecessary trouble?"

"What do you mean?"

She was so earnest, so dedicated to her work. And clearly able to take care of herself. Even so, Gil felt a distinct urge to protect her. Her white silk blouse was thin, thin enough for Gil to notice the outline of a lacy bra. Despite her extensive training and her credentials, she seemed vulnerable and surprisingly feminine even taking into consideration her deliberately bland and professional clothing.

Bailey's soft skin, gently rounded breasts, and graceful hands reminded Gil that beneath the outer shell of efficiency, she was a woman. He met her brown-eyed gaze with a calm he didn't feel. Some way, somehow, he had to convince her to back off this investigation. The feeling in his gut could be called premonition…or simply common sense. But he trusted that feeling…always.

"What you're doing is dangerous, Bailey. If word gets out that you're poking around in the TCC records, whoever kidnapped Alex may get spooked and try to harm you."

She sighed and closed her computer. "Is this genuine concern, or are you trying to get rid of me?"

"All of the above?" He asked it jokingly, but he sobered rapidly. "Alex escaped and made his way back home. Which means somebody out there is really pissed off and may try again. There's a good chance Alex is still in danger. By involving yourself in his situation, you court the same trouble."

Her chin lifted. "I'm doing my job. No more, no less."

"And if your job could get you killed?"

"I'm a paper pusher, Gil."

"You're a pain in the butt," he groused, realizing he wasn't going to win this round. But hearing her say his name was a small victory, nevertheless. He stood and held out his hand. "I'm starving, and Cade will be, too. Let's go find him."

The club dining room was packed. Bailey looked around with interest as the hostess led them across the floor. In a far corner at a table for two sat Rory and Shannon Fentress, still basking in the glow of being newlyweds. It was rumored that Rory had his eye on the governor's mansion.

Like Bailey, Shannon was not much of a girlie girl. She owned and managed a working ranch and dressed accordingly when she was in town on business. Judging by the way Rory looked at his new wife, he liked her just the way she was.

Gil had reserved a table by the window because Cade liked to watch the horses outside. Though of course the TCC had a parking lot, it wasn't at all unusual for someone to ride up, tie his mount to the wooden railings out front, and saunter inside for a bite of lunch.

Cade was his usually bubbly self. "I'm glad you're eating lunch with us, Miss Bailey." His form of address was the compromise Gil had allowed in his insistence that his son learn manners.

Bailey smiled at him. "Me, too. Did you enjoy yourself this morning?"

Cade nodded, already filling his mouth with crackers.

Without saying a word, Gil removed the basket from his son's reach. "I think a lot of the members have been surprised at how nice it is to be able to drop off a son or daughter or even a grandchild and to know that the kids are close by, happy and safe."

"Do you think the trouble is over?"

"I do. I really do. I still hear grumbling, of course. Particularly from the old guard."

"You mean like him?" Bailey cocked her head unobtrusively, not letting Cade see. A few tables away sat Paul Windsor, a charter member of the TCC.

Gil grimaced. "Yeah. He's one of the worst. But even so, I doubt he'd ever actually do anything to cause problems for the center."

Bailey shuddered inwardly. She had interviewed Paul during her initial investigation, and the man had given her the creeps. Divorced four times, Windsor considered himself a ladies' man. During the course of her questioning, Bailey had discovered without a doubt that Windsor was perhaps the most overt and obnoxious chauvinist she had ever met. He made no secret of his disdain for Bailey.

"I feel sorry for Cara," she said, "having such an overbearing father." Bailey knew what that was like far too well.

"I'll admit…Windsor can be a jerk. But he wields a lot of influence around here, so it would be a plus to stay on his good side if you want to make any progress with your investigation. If he were to raise a stink, he could convince others that you shouldn't be here in the club."

"But I have a legal warrant."

"Yes. And ultimately that would prevail. In the interim, though, things could get ugly."

"Is my presence going to cause big problems for you, Gil?" The thought troubled her.

He laughed, his dark eyes warm and teasing. "I can handle trouble, Bailey. Don't worry about me."

Cade, tired of being ignored, piped up, a sly smile on his face. "Do you know how to cook, Miss Bailey?"

Bailey raised her eyebrows. "Where did that come from?"

Cade took a bite of the hot dog their server had delivered moments ago. Pausing to chew and swallow, he fixed her with the blue eyes that helped make him such a cute kid. "I dunno," he said, the picture of innocence. "Dad says when I'm getting to know someone, it's nice to ask them questions…but not too personal," he added hastily, glancing at his father with a guilty expression.

"That's good advice," Bailey said. "So, in answer to your question, yes…I'm a pretty good cook. I started learning when I was not much bigger than you."

Cade nodded solemnly, his milk mustache adding to his charm. "And do you like little kids?"

Suddenly, she understood what was happening. She was being interviewed for a job. As Cade's mommy. *Dear Lord.* Fortunately for her peace of mind, the rest of their meal arrived, and in the hubbub of drink refills and the server's chatter, the moment passed.

Bailey had looked forward to an intimate lunch with the two Addison men, but unfortunately, this was not the venue. Gil could barely eat his meal because of repeated interruptions from club members happy to see him. What Bailey suddenly understood was that Gil had sacrificed an enormous amount in choosing intentionally to be the caregiver for his son.

Over the course of almost five years, Gil was wealthy enough to have hired the best nannies in the world. He could have gone about his business, running the ranch, hanging out at the TCC, meeting women, perhaps marrying again. Instead, he had made his son a priority. Fortunately, his current role as TCC president was more of an honorary position than a demanding job.

The enthusiasm with which club members greeted him during one short lunch indicated both that Gil was extremely popular and well-liked, and that he likely was not able to be present at the club as often as many of his cohorts.

Cade bore the intrusion of one table guest after another with equanimity. Several of the men addressed him personally. For a child not yet old enough for school, his composure and patience were commendable.

Not many boys of Bailey's acquaintance would be able to tolerate an extended meal in public without raising a ruckus. She sneaked him a couple of extra French fries off her plate while Gil was otherwise occupied. "Is it always like this?" she asked.

Cade nodded. "Yep. Everybody likes my dad." The words were matter-of-fact, but Bailey heard the pride behind them.

"So," she whispered conspiratorially, "do you think we get dessert?"

Cade wrinkled his nose. "If I eat most of my salad." He stared dolefully at the small bowl, clearly not a fan of spinach mix.

"I remember once when I was about your age, my mother made me eat black-eyed peas that I didn't like. I broke out in a rash all over my whole body, and I never had to eat them again."

"Can you teach me how to do that?" Cade's eyes widened with fascination.

"Unfortunately, I think the rash happened because I was so upset. But you could always try using a red marker to put dots all over your skin. I'm kidding," she said hastily, suddenly visualizing an awful scenario where Gil realized Bailey had been giving his son tips on how to bypass healthy eating.

"I know that." Cade rolled his eyes. "You're funny, Miss Bailey."

Bailey had been called a lot of things in her life… responsible, hardworking, dedicated. But no one had ever called her funny. She kind of liked it. And she very much liked Gil's precious son.

Gil stood and touched Bailey's shoulder. "If you two would excuse me for a few moments, I need to speak to a gentleman at that table in the corner. I won't be long, I promise."

"Your food will get cold," Cade said.

"I bet the chef will warm it up for me. Love you, son. Back in a minute." Gil kissed the top of Cade's head and strode away.

Four

Bailey looked for signs that Cade was leery of being left with a virtual stranger, but quite the contrary. With his dad out of the picture, Cade was free to resume his interrogation. "What *kinds* of things do you like to cook?" he asked, returning to the original topic.

"Well, let's see…" Bailey folded her fancy napkin and laid it beside her plate. The meal had been amazing. Tender beef medallions, fluffy mashed potatoes and sautéed asparagus. A hearty meal that men would enjoy. Not a ladies' tearoom menu with tiny bowls of soup and miniature sandwiches.

She grinned as Cade poked halfheartedly at his spinach. "I love to bake," she said. "So I suppose I'm good at bread and pies and cakes."

Her companion's eyes rounded. "Birthday cakes, too?"

"I suppose."

"My birthday is comin' up real soon, Miss Bailey. Do you think you could make me a birthday cake?"

She hesitated, positive she was negotiating some kind of hidden minefield. "I'll bet your dad wants to surprise you with a special cake."

Cade shook his head. "Our housekeeper will make it. But her cakes are awful and Dad says we can't hurt her feelings."

Just like that, Bailey fell in love with Cade Addison. How many years had she come home from school on her birthday, hoping against hope that her father had remembered to stop by the corner grocery and pick up a store-bought cake.

But he never did. Not once.

By the time she was nine, Bailey had quit expecting cakes. Two years later, she quit thinking about her birthday at all. It was just another day.

"I tell you what, Cade," she said, wondering if she were making a huge mistake. "If I'm still here when your birthday rolls around, and if your father doesn't mind, then yes…I'd be happy to make you a cake."

Cade whooped out loud and then clapped a hand over his mouth when several people turned around with curious looks. "Sorry," he mumbled.

"It's okay. This room is noisy anyway. Eat your salad, and when your dad gets back, we'll order dessert."

Cade managed four bites with some theatrical gagging, but when Bailey didn't react, he finished it all. "Done," he said triumphantly.

She high-fived him. "Now that wasn't so bad, was it?"

"I guess. But I'd rather have ice cream."

"Who wouldn't?"

They laughed together. She marveled at the connection she felt with this small, motherless child. On impulse, she leaned forward, lowering her voice, though it was doubtful she'd be overheard in the midst of the loud conversations all around them. Texas cowboys had a tendency to get heated when they discussed politics and religion and the price of feed. There was a lot of testosterone in this room.

"I want to tell you something, Cade."

He looked up at her trustingly. "Okay."

"I know you want a mother, but you are a very lucky little boy, because your dad loves you more than anything in the world. Do you know that?"

He seemed surprised she would ask. "Well, yeah. He tells me all the time."

"Not all dads are like that." Her throat closed up as unexpected emotion stung her eyes.

Cade stared at her, mute, as if sensing her struggle. "Are you talking about *your* daddy, Miss Bailey?"

She nodded, trying to swallow the lump. "My mom ran away and left us when I was about your age. And she never came back. So it was just me and my dad. But he wasn't like your father. He was…" She trailed off, not sure what adjective to use that an almost-five-year-old would understand.

Elbows on table, chin in hand, Cade surveyed her solemnly. "He was mean?"

Out of the mouths of babes. "Well, he didn't hurt me, if that's what you're thinking. But he didn't care about me. Not like your dad cares about you. Be patient, Cade. One day your father will find a woman he loves and he'll marry her and you'll have that mother you want. But in the meantime, be a kid, okay? And not a matchmaker."

Gil halted suddenly, shock rendering him immobile. Bailey Collins had just given his son the kind of advice Cade needed to hear. And she had done it lovingly and in a way he could understand at his young age. Gil was torn between gratitude for her interference and compassion for the personal pain she had revealed.

He backed up a step or two and approached the table again, this time more loudly. "You were right, Cade. I bet my lunch is cold. Sorry it took me so long. You ready for dessert?"

Bailey flushed from her throat to her hairline, her expression mortified. "How long have you been standing there?" she asked.

He kept his expression neutral. "I just walked across the room, Bailey. Why?"

"No reason," she mumbled, taking a gulp from her water glass.

Gil noticed the exchange of glances between his son and Bailey, a conspiratorial look that was oddly unsettling. Gil was accustomed to being his son's sounding board, his protector, his go-to guy. To see the boy so quickly accept and relate to Bailey made Gil worry. Perhaps he should keep the two of them apart.

When Bailey returned to Dallas, inevitably leaving a heartbroken Cade behind, Gil would have to pick up the pieces. On the other hand, would it be fair to deprive Cade of a relationship that provided him enjoyment in the meantime? Again, the frustration of being a single parent gave Gil heartburn. He was not the kind of man to unburden himself to anyone and everyone.

He had friends. Lots of them. But raising Cade couldn't be left up to a committee vote. Gil had to decide what was best for his son.

Over ice cream and pound cake, Cade grilled his father. "Are you and Miss Bailey going to do this every day?"

Gil lifted an eyebrow, looking to Bailey to answer that one.

"A week…ten days. I'm working as fast as I can, but it's slow going."

Cade grinned widely. "I like the child care center. They have a computer station and about a jillion Lego blocks, and my friends miss me when I don't come."

Gil rubbed a smear of ice cream from his son's chin. "Well, in that case, I'll set up some meetings with the executive committee for the next few days and get some club business out of the way."

When the meal was over they dropped off Cade and headed back to Gil's office. Walking in, he noticed the faint, pleasing scent of Bailey's perfume lingering in the air, something light and flowery. The scene that transpired in the dining room had affected him deeply. It was hard to mistrust a woman who treated his son with so much gentleness and compassion.

"Do you need any help?" he asked abruptly, wishing he had a reason to stay.

Bailey glanced at him, her gaze guarded. "No. But thanks."

He leaned a hip against his desk. "What do you do for fun, Bailey Collins?"

"Fun?" The question appeared to confuse her.

"I'm assuming you've heard of the word."

"I have fun," she said, her tone defensive.

"When?"

Her mouth opened and closed. "I like to read."

"So do I. In bed. At night. But what do you do in your leisure time?" He shouldn't have mentioned the word *bed*. His libido rushed ahead in the conversation and visualized the two of them entwined on soft sheets.

Bailey shrugged. "I work long hours. But in the evenings I like to walk around my neighborhood. It's a close-knit, established community with sidewalks and people who sit on front porches. I have several older friends I check on from time to time."

"Sounds nice."

"It is."

"And is there a man in your life?" Well, he'd done it now. There was no way she could interpret his question as anything other than what it was. He was attracted to her. And he wanted to know if he'd be stepping on any toes were he to follow up on those feelings.

Bailey glanced at her watch. "I need to get back to work."

"Does that mean, 'Back off, Gil'?"

"What? No. Not at all. But I…"

He waited. Silently.

"You don't even like me," she said, her expression troubled.

"Correction. I *tried* not to like you. That first day in the police station when you were grilling me like a seasoned pro, I found you wildly appealing, despite my disgruntlement. And since I am a man who believes in laying all the cards on the table, I think you should know."

"What changed?"

"Dogs and children are very good judges of character. My son adores you already."

"But that makes you uncomfortable."

The sadness lurking in her brown eyes shamed him. "It does. I don't want him to get too attached to you."

"Because I'll be leaving soon."

"Yes."

"I suppose I can understand that."

"It has nothing to do with you personally. But Cade has this unfortunate tendency to latch onto any woman who walks into my life, no matter how briefly."

"Why haven't you married again?"

He hadn't expected the blunt question. It caught him off guard, and for a moment, grief, regret and disappointment flooded his stomach. He shoved the negative feelings away. "There aren't too many women these days happy to be stuck out on a ranch in the middle of nowhere."

"Oh, please," Bailey said, giving him a reproving look. "You're rich, handsome and successful. I'm sure some poor soul in Royal would apply for the job."

Her mock scolding erased the momentary sting of allowing the past to intrude. "But not you?"

"I have a job."

"One that could get you killed." The realities of her position still disturbed him. Alex needed to get his memory back in a hurry. Before somebody else got hurt. Gil hadn't meant to change the subject, even if he was genuinely worried about her. "May I be honest with you, Bailey?"

"Please do."

"As angry as I was with you when we first met, I felt a definite *something*. In the weeks you've been here, I haven't stopped thinking about that feeling and wondering if it was one-sided."

She paled and wrapped her arms around her waist, clearly shocked by his candor. "It wasn't one-sided," she said quietly.

Exultation flooded his veins, despite the tiny voice inside his head that said he was making a mistake. "Good to know." The three words were gruff, but it was hard to speak when arousal made his entire body tense with need. "There's more," he said.

A tiny smile appeared and disappeared. "I'm bracing myself."

He stood up, no longer able to feign relaxation. "It's not easy for a single man my age to live in a place like Royal and do something as prosaic as dating. When Cade was almost three, I tried it for the first time."

"And?"

"It was terrible. Everyone tried to give me sympathy and child-rearing advice, or they offered to bake me casseroles."

"Not altogether bad things."

"Of course not, but I wanted to forget for a while that I was a single dad. I wanted companionship and…"

"Sex."

He saw no judgment in her gaze, but his cheeks reddened nevertheless. "Yeah," he sighed. "It would be easier if I lived in a big, anonymous city, but here in Royal everything I do is fodder for the gossip mill. I value my privacy, and I don't think my personal life needs to be front-page news."

"But you don't want to spend a lot of time out of town because of Cade."

"Exactly."

"You've given up a lot for him."

Gil frowned. "I haven't given up anything. He's my son. And I love him."

Bailey crossed the tiny distance between them. Putting a hand on his chest, she looked up at him. "You're a very nice man, Gil Addison." Her smile warmed him to a sobering degree.

He moved restlessly, fighting the urge to grab her. "It's not about being nice, damn it. It's what a parent does."

Some of the light left her eyes. "Not all of them."

He wanted to tell her that he had heard what she said to Cade, that his heart broke for a little girl with no mother and a surly dad. But her confidences had to be freely given or not at all. He wouldn't embarrass her that way. "Cade is the best thing that has ever happened to me. His childhood will pass quickly enough. I don't want to miss out on anything."

She went up on tiptoes and pressed a soft kiss on his lips. "If you're asking me to spend some...*time*...with you while I'm here, then the answer is yes. I understand the rules. You don't have to worry. And I will do my best not to let Cade get attached to me."

He winced. "God, you make me sound like an ass."

Her expression was wry. "Not at all. You're simply a straight arrow of a guy who doesn't hide behind platitudes. I respect that."

He gave in to temptation and stroked his thumb over her cheekbone. "You have the softest skin," he muttered. Slowly, he cupped her face in his palms and tipped her mouth toward his. "Have I told you how much your ugly suits turn me on?"

Bailey melted into him. "My suits are not ugly. They're professional." Her tongue mated lazily with his, hardening his sex to the point of pain. Of all the dumb ideas he'd ever had, this one ranked right up near the top. The door wasn't locked. Though no one was likely to disturb them, their current behavior was risky at best.

He kissed his way down her throat, toying with the buttons on her silky top. Bailey's eyes were closed, her lips parted. More than anything he wanted to bend her over his desk and take her hard and fast. Lust wrapped his brain in a red haze. His hands trembled as he found his way past her blouse to her breasts covered in lace.

Each soft mound was a full, perfect weight in his hand. He squeezed gently, shuddering when Bailey's low moan went straight to his gut and stoked the fire. He was rapidly reaching the point of no return. The problem with long bouts of celibacy was that a man tended to go a little insane when the woman he wanted was in touching distance.

"Tell me to stop," he pleaded.

Her hands tore at the lapels of his jacket. He helped her remove it and tossed it aside. He was burning up from the inside out.

"Touch my skin," she pleaded.

How could he say no? Each delicate nipple furled tightly as he stroked her with reverence. He lifted her onto the desk. Now he could reach her with his mouth. Shoving aside the gossamer cups of her bra, he first licked her, then suckled her, growing more and more hungry with every second that passed.

Her hands tangled in his hair, pulling him closer. "Bailey. Bailey…" He didn't even know what he wanted to say.

"Gil," her voice was little more than a whisper.

He inhaled sharply, close to begging. "What?"

"I think we have to stop. I don't want to, but we're at the club."

"At the club?" He could barely make sense of the words. He needed to be inside her more than he needed to breathe.

She shoved him, her two hands braced on his shoulders. "Stop, Gil. Please."

At last her protest penetrated the fog that bound him. He staggered backward, wiping his mouth with the back of his hand. It hurt to look at her. He leaned against the file cabinet, burying his face in his arm. Agony ripped through him. He had caged the tiger that was his lust for too long, and now the animal was free.

Seconds passed. Minutes. He sucked in great lungfuls of air, desperately trying to regain control. Behind him he heard rustling sounds as Bailey adjusted her clothing.

When her hand touched his back, he jerked. "Don't," he groaned. "Not if you want me to leave."

"I don't want you to go," she said quietly. "But for now, you have to. I'm sorry."

He whirled around. "Sorry for what?"

Her eyes were huge and dark. "I didn't mean for this to happen."

"Neither did I. At least not right now." He had never been as torn as he was at this moment. Everything inside him insisted he lock the door and make her his. But he dared not. Not for her sake, and not with his son in the same building. "We'll talk…tonight…when Cade is in bed. I'll call you and we'll make plans."

Her gaze searched his. "I'd like that very much."

Five

Gil didn't call that night. Bailey took his silence stoically, though deep inside her, a little kernel of excitement shriveled. Clearly, Gil's second thoughts about getting involved had trumped his momentary sexual need. She could understand his reluctance. He was not free to follow every whim or passing fancy.

In the cold light of reason, he had probably weighed the risks and benefits of getting involved with her and decided it was too risky. It hurt that he hadn't bothered to call and tell her straight up that he had changed his mind, but perhaps he'd been busy with Cade.

As much as it pained her to admit it, Gil's about-face was probably for the best. Bailey had her own doubts. She'd never been a rule-breaker, and though it wasn't technically illegal or even unethical for her to have a personal relationship with Gil, it was at the very least unwise.

She needed to be able to rely on him as a source of information in her investigation. If he ended up in a position of having to defend one of his friends against her accusations, the situation could get ugly fast. No matter how much she responded to Gil physically, it was better for everyone if she ignored the needs of her body and her heart and focused on doing her job.

The following morning, she and Gil met at the club as they had the day before. Only this time, Gil still had Cade in tow. Not by word or expression did Gil evidence any memory of the heated interlude in his office the afternoon before. Bailey didn't know whether to be relieved or insulted, but she guessed he didn't want to give anything away in front of his son.

Cade bounced up and down in his father's grasp, finally breaking free long enough to wrap his arms around Bailey's thighs in an exuberant hug. "Hey, Miss Bailey," he said. "Are you going to eat lunch with us again?"

Bailey glanced at Gil. The slight negative shake of his head let her know the answer. "I'd love to, Cade, but today I'll probably just snack at my desk. I have a lot of work to do."

The disappointment in his big blue eyes filled her with guilt. "I understand." His body language imploded, leaving him long-faced and dejected.

Gil's jaw tightened. He removed a key from his pocket and handed it to Bailey. "I have a full schedule today," he said, the words terse. "Be sure to lock the door whenever you have to step out. I'll stop by before you go home and retrieve this."

"Thank you," she said, her words as stilted as his. As she watched, Gil turned on his heel and led his son toward the entrance to the child care center. Cade looked over his shoulder at Bailey just before they disappeared. She gave him a little wave and smiled, hoping to cheer him up. Truthfully, she liked the little boy, almost as much as she liked his taciturn father.

Feeling unsettled and confused, she made her way to the office and got to work. Today went a little faster, since she had at last decided how to comb through the files in a way that was more organized and less haphazard.

Here and there names popped out at her. Slowly, she began to build a list of men she would like to interview. She wondered if Gil would stonewall her when she suggested it. Every man she flagged had been interviewed in the initial investigation, but with Alex still in the dark, it was imperative that she not miss any links to motive or opportunity.

Her stomach growled loudly midday. Fortunately, she had an apple, a bottle of water and a granola bar in her tote bag. No one was allowed to eat in the club dining room unless he or she was the guest of a member. And since Gil had made it clear that he wasn't interested in sharing lunch with Bailey, she was on her own.

She could have taken a break and headed over to the Royal Diner. The food was good and the ambiance cheerful, but she wasn't in the mood to talk to anyone, much less defend her reasons for spending time at the club. Often, her job made her as popular as an IRS agent.

The day crawled by, but at five o'clock, she was satisfied with the amount of work she had accomplished. She had shut down her laptop and was straightening the various stacks of files she was using when, after a brief knock, someone opened the door.

It wasn't too difficult to guess the intruder's identity. Bailey was very proud of her calm, friendly smile. "Hello, Gil. I was just finishing up." She fished in her pocket. "Here's the key."

When he took it from her, their fingers touched. His

were warm and slightly calloused. She almost jerked her hand away in reaction, but instead, turned to scoop up her tote bag and purse. "See you tomorrow." If her voice had been any brighter, she could have powered a lightbulb.

Gil touched her, curling his hand around her forearm. "Stay," he muttered. "For a minute."

Her stomach quivered at the unmistakably intimate tone. But she wouldn't be so easily won over. "No."

"Please." His dark eyes were contrite.

"You didn't call me last night," she said evenly. "That was rude and uncalled-for."

He nodded. "I know. I'm sorry."

"Why didn't you?" She was genuinely curious in the midst of her pique. Gil was standing so close, she could see the tiny flecks of amber that gave light and depth to his night-dark irises.

He stroked her arm, almost absently, with one fingertip. "I couldn't decide what I wanted to say. You confuse me." His breath was warm on her cheek.

"Is that good or bad?" To hear that he was as conflicted as she was calmed some of her indignation. Today, he wore a simple button-down oxford shirt in lemon-yellow. The color suited him. As did the neatly creased dress slacks whose precision fit came only from hand-tailoring.

Bailey wished she had worn something more appealing than her usual workaday attire, but an investigative agent on the job had to be prepared for any eventuality. Occasionally, despite the clerical nature of her customary assignments, she had to chase down a bad guy or crouch in a grimy location to do surveillance.

Feminine vanity was useless in her line of work. Unless, like Sandra Bullock, she was ever called upon to pose in a beauty pageant, her chances for wearing seductive clothing on the job were slim.

Gil ignored her pointed question. But judging from the way he looked at her, the answer was definitely *good*. "Have dinner with me tonight," he said abruptly. "Cade is spending the evening with my cousin and his wife. I don't have to pick him up until nine. I'll take you to Claire's."

Claire's was an upscale restaurant with white linen tablecloths and real silver cutlery, definitely a special-occasion place. Bailey's heart beat faster at the implications. And because it did, she was determined not to let him see that his invitation rattled her. "As long as I pay for my own meal to avoid any ethical considerations. And besides, are you sure you want to be seen with me in public?" Her tart question was a fair one given his ambivalence.

He winced. "I deserve that. I'll admit that I still don't like what you're up to…a witch hunt that may bring down one of my friends. But I find that my scruples are far less compelling than the taste of your lips."

Pulling her close, he kissed her gently, lazily. Where yesterday had been frantic and laced with desperation, this contact was infinitely sweet, deeply tender, endlessly erotic. She linked her arms around his neck, sighing when he aligned their bodies perfectly.

As a teenager, she had hated being taller than many of the boys in her class, but now, her height gave her an advantage. She felt the press of his belt buckle against her belly, inhaled the spicy scent of his aftershave. Beneath her fingertips, his hair was silky and smooth.

He held her confidently, like a man who knew his way around a woman's body. Despite his professed lack of opportunity, his technique was not rusty at all. Against her breast, she felt the steady thud of his heartbeat. Perhaps it was a bit ragged, who could tell? She only knew that this moment had been weeks in the making.

"You're very persuasive," she whispered. When his teeth nipped the ticklish spot below her ear, she laid her cheek on his chest.

"Is that a yes?"

"I'll have to go home and change. I could meet you back here in an hour." She was staying at McDaniel's Acres. Though she had no time to indulge in the dude ranch activities offered, her single room in the spacious ranch house was comfortable and more private than a B and B.

Gil tugged her ponytail. "I'll pick you up."

"It's not necessary."

He stepped back and cupped her face in his big hands. Searching eyes met her reluctant gaze and held it. For one instant, she felt a connection that was more than physical. "Don't fight me on this, honey," he said. "No matter how we both might twist and squirm in the wind, we're caught in this together. Let's see where it leads us."

"It won't lead anywhere," she said flatly, not sure why she had to remind him of that.

His half smile was laced with self-derision. "But we might have fun along the way, right?"

She wasn't armed against the charm of a man whose masculinity was as potent as hundred-proof whiskey. He had made an indelible impression on her the first time they met, and nothing had changed in that regard. "I suppose I have to wonder if you'll stand me up," she muttered. "Considering I waited by the phone last night like a silly schoolgirl."

With his thumb, he traced the curve of her ear, a newly discovered erogenous zone. "I'll make it up to you." Suddenly, he was kissing her again. Any sweetness that had lingered on their lips was instantly vaporized by a shot of pure fire. She felt it from her breasts to her pelvis, a tingling, sizzling vein of sensation.

His arm was hard across her back, his erection thrusting urgently against her lower body. The unapologetic passion he offered her was persuasive. She wanted to melt into him, feeling incredibly alive yet, at the same time, fearful of losing herself.

She pulled away, though it required great resolve. "I'm going now," she said, the words hushed.

Gil stood, head bowed, and pressed the heels of his hands against his eyes. "I'll be there at six-thirty. Don't make me wait."

He shuddered when the door closed behind her. Bailey had no idea how tenuous his control was around her. Perhaps she imagined that her drab clothing could disguise the appeal of her body, but she was wrong. When he held her, he felt the strength and softness of her frame. Neither skinny nor overweight, she was the epitome of a healthy young woman. Her required training regimen kept her fit. He liked that. A lot.

And though it only made his physical discomfort worse, he couldn't help imagining all that energy and flexibility at his disposal in bed. God help him.

When he could leave the room without embarrassing himself, he locked the office and went in search of his son.

Thirty minutes later he dropped Cade off in town and raced back out to the ranch to change clothes. Taking Bailey out tonight would spark gossip, but for once, he didn't care. Perhaps if word got around that the two of them were an item, no one would look too closely at Bailey's reasons for spending time at the club.

As he drove out toward Chance McDaniel's thriving operation, he contemplated the fact that Chance was about the only person he could think of who might have an ax to grind with Alex Santiago. Both men had shown inter-

est in Cara Windsor, but it was Alex who had managed
to put an engagement ring on her finger. Since Alex and
Chance were very close friends, Chance might have seen
the other man's actions as a betrayal of their friendship.

Gil wasn't sure what impact Alex's disappearance and
subsequent memory loss had made on Alex's relationship
with Cara, but it couldn't be easy for a woman to be with
a man who didn't remember her.

As Gil pulled up in front of the impressive ranch house,
Chance waved at him from across the corral. It occurred
to him that Bailey must be seeing a lot of the handsome,
blond cowboy. The lick of jealousy he felt was disconcert-
ing. Chance was his friend. And since Bailey still had not
ruled out Chance as a suspect, Alex was relatively sure
that neither Bailey nor Chance would be inclined to get
chummy. With Bailey suspicious and Chance on the defensive, they would likely keep their distance.

Gil's unsettling thoughts were derailed when Bailey
stepped out onto the front porch. His first thought was
"Hot damn." She had worn her hair loose, and it rippled
around her shoulders in the evening breeze. Her gaze met
his directly, but with a hint of reserve. She still wasn't
sure of him.

The knowledge hurt. He'd been so busy with his self-
righteous indignation at being questioned, he hadn't paused
to consider how his truculence would affect Bailey.

He met her halfway up the stairs and held out his hand.
"You look beautiful," he said, wishing there was another
word for her vibrant appeal. The black knit, V-necked wrap
dress she wore emphasized her narrow waist and curvy
breasts. Cap sleeves revealed slender arms.

"Thank you."

Bailey's skirt ended several inches above her knees. For
the first time since they met, Gil got a glimpse of her legs.

The vision was enough to hog-tie his voice. He decided then and there that it was a crime for such beauty to be covered up by an ugly pantsuit. But on the other hand, at least her mode of dress meant other men weren't ogling her.

Gil considered himself an evolved, twenty-first-century kind of guy. Yet when it came to Bailey, he was finding himself strangled by impulses that were decidedly Neanderthal. He had no right to be possessive, no right at all. But he couldn't deny what he was feeling.

Conversation languished on the ride into town. By the time they were seated at Claire's and looking over the menu, though, he recovered enough to make small talk. "Have you eaten here before?" he asked.

Bailey shook her head with a grin. "No. These prices are a little bit above my per diem meal allowance. But I can splurge occasionally."

Gil chuckled. "I can recommend the salmon and the beef bourguignonne."

He barely noticed what he ate. Bailey was enchanting…sweetly serious about her job, and yet she possessed a dry sense of humor that took him off guard at times. He knew they were being watched by curious diners, most of whom knew him well. But he couldn't bring himself to care. It was the most enjoyable evening he had spent in a long, long time.

Over coffee and dessert, he decided he had to come clean about the secret he was holding. "Bailey…"

She smiled at him. "Yes?"

"I have a confession to make."

Some of the sparkle left her expression. "Oh?"

"I heard what you said to Cade. About your father."

Color flushed her cheeks and then faded away, leaving her pale. "I see."

"I'm sorry. I didn't want to embarrass you yesterday."

"But it's okay tonight?" The words had a bite to them.

He shrugged. "I need to have honesty between us. It's important to me. You don't have to explain, but I *am* sorry that your childhood was so difficult. I really appreciate what you said to Cade. It was very generous of you."

She crossed her arms, the posture unconsciously defensive. "I had food and shelter growing up. Lots of kids don't have that much."

"True. But love is important. Perhaps your father didn't know how to show you what was in his heart."

"I told myself that when I was a teenager. I took a psychology class in high school. Learned a little bit about how pain can make people turn inward. But it didn't really help to know the reason why. My father and I barely speak. A couple of awkward meals at the holidays. The obligatory birthday gifts. I tried for years to get him to open up to me, but he's a stone wall with no apparent desire to change."

"He's missing out," Gil said soberly.

Bailey exhaled and took a drink of water, her hand trembling visibly. "Thank you."

After a moment's awkward silence, she leaned forward and clasped her hands on the table. Her beautiful brown eyes were earnest. "If there's a possibility that you and I are going to become…*intimate*…I wonder if I may ask you a personal question."

"Of course."

"Does Cade remember his mother at all?"

He hesitated. This wasn't a road he had expected to go down. But since he had inadvertently overheard Bailey's extremely personal confession to Cade, it seemed only fair that Gil should reciprocate. "No," he said slowly. "She died before his first birthday. Took her own life." Even now, it hurt to say the words. And since Bailey had dossiers on half the people in town, she probably already knew that.

"Oh, Gil. I am so sorry." Bailey took one of his hands in her two smaller ones and held it tightly.

He squeezed her fingers, warmed by her genuine sympathy. "It was a long time ago. And to be honest, our marriage was doomed from the beginning, though I didn't realize it for a long time. My wife had severe emotional problems that she hid well."

"You don't have to explain," Bailey said, still holding his hand.

"It's okay. I want to tell you. It might help you understand why I'm so protective of Cade. When things started to go wrong in my marriage, I urged Sherrie to go with me to counseling. In the safety of that situation she was able to reveal that she had been abused as a young teenager. I found it almost impossible to believe at first, but her parents were part of a religious cult that 'married' young girls in the church to older men."

Bailey released him and sat back, her gaze stricken. "That's horrible."

"Yes. To her credit, Sherrie really did want a child, and she was so happy to be pregnant. But postpartum depression took a toll on her, and she was never able to recover."

"So you made Cade your priority."

"Don't paint me as noble," he said soberly. "There was more to it than that. My in-laws took me to court and tried to steal Cade away from me. Faced with the prospect of losing him, I realized how much I loved that little innocent baby."

"Thank God they didn't succeed."

"I went through a hellish eight months of court-ordered visits and psychological evaluations…"

She nibbled her lower lip, her eyes huge, her expression sober. "I'm beginning to see why you have a chip on your shoulder about government intervention."

"I suppose I do, but I came close to losing everything. My in-laws paid off a judge, and it nearly worked. Fortunately for me, I have a lot of friends in Royal and in the state at large. Powerful friends. In the end, justice prevailed, but it was a close call."

"I've admired you since I first came to Royal," Bailey said quietly. "Now, even more."

Six

Bailey was shaken by what she had heard. Imagining Gil without his son was a picture she didn't want to paint. The two of them were a tight family unit. Despite the absence of a female figure.

She had wondered from time to time if Gil were still in love with his dead wife…and if that was why he hadn't remarried. Apparently, the truth was more complex. He wanted to protect his son, and that included not letting Cade's little heart get broken time and again if his father indulged in short-lived relationships.

Bailey had to admire Gil's selflessness. But how long could a virile, healthy man suppress his sexual needs before he did something reckless? Like initiating an intimate relationship with a woman he barely knew…a woman just passing through.

Sitting across the table from him was like a romantic fantasy come to life. She seldom had opportunities for fine dining, and never with someone who looked like Gil. His expensive black suit showcased broad shoulders and a trim waist. A crisp white shirt and red tie completed the image of a successful businessman. Though he would have fit right in wearing tooled leather boots, he had chosen more traditional dress shoes for their date. She found that she missed his cowboy look, though this man was wildly appealing, as well.

But no matter how much she was drawn to him, the truth of their situation gave her pause. If she made unwise choices and things blew up in her face, she could face a formal reprimand from her boss, or even worse. She'd seen other colleagues terminated because they let their judgment be clouded by personal involvement on a case.

Beyond the professional implications, Bailey didn't want to be Gil's guilty pleasure. She didn't want to be filed under the category *secret dalliance* or *enjoyable mistake*. Not that he was hiding anything tonight. They were eating dinner in front of half the town, it seemed. But letting Cade know was another story.

Her suppositions were confirmed when Gil glanced at his watch and muttered in dismay. "It's almost time for me to pick up Cade," he said. "I didn't know it was so late. I'll run you home and come back to get him."

She and Gil had talked easily and at length, with a comfort that Bailey rarely found in relationships with the opposite sex. The time had flown by. Underlying all of the conversation was the unspoken subtext of what they both wanted.

"That's not necessary," she said. "Too much driving back and forth. Let me call Chance. I'm sure he won't mind sending one of the ranch hands into town to pick me up. Go get your son, Gil. Take him home to bed." The Straight Arrow and McDaniel's Acres, both south of town, were not that far apart. It made no sense for Gil to crisscross the county when the solution was simple.

Gil waved a hand for the checks and tucked both of their credit cards in the folio, frowning. "I invited you to dinner tonight. I'll take you home." He grimaced, clearly conflicted. "I suppose he's old enough to know that not every relationship ends in wedding bells. We might as well go get him together."

"I appreciate your chivalry," she said wryly. "But I don't need a grand gesture. I've already told you how I feel. You're a sexy, appealing man, and I find myself very attracted to you. That won't change simply because you have responsibilities."

The tightness in his jaw eased, and his expression lightened. "Thank you, Bailey." He stood and took her wrist to pull her to her feet. "But we'll go together."

Outside, the weather had taken a turn for the worse, or at least toward the more seasonable. Temperatures had dropped while they were eating, and now, wind-driven spritzes of raindrops dampened the air.

Bailey shivered, wishing she had remembered to bring a wrap. Gil shrugged out of his jacket and tucked it around her shoulders without asking. The fabric smelled like warm male. "Thank you," she said, drawing the lapels closer together.

The car was not far, so they made a run for it. Gil tucked her inside and ran around to the driver's seat. When they were both safely inside, they laughed, shaking water droplets from their hair. The windows fogged up almost immediately.

He didn't start the engine. Instead, he turned toward her and studied her intently. Her taut nipples pressed against the fabric of her dress, perhaps visible even through her thin bra. Not that Gil could see. But *she* knew.

"Do you need the heater?" he asked gruffly, his gaze dark and hungry.

She shook her head. "It's not that cold in the car."

Their stilted, prosaic conversation might have been funny if she hadn't been wound so tightly. Her skin hummed with the need to feel his touch. Fortunately for her, Gil must have been on the same page.

"Come here, Bailey." They were sitting in the front of his fancy, enormous truck. The wide bench seat presented all sorts of intriguing possibilities.

She scooted closer, barely noticing when his jacket slipped away. "Why?" she asked. "Do I need to warm you up?"

His lips quirked in what might have been a grin had he not been so focused on finding her mouth with his. "Any warmer," he groaned, "and I'll be in danger of getting arrested." He cupped the back of her neck in one big hand and used the other to anchor her chin. Lazily, with no apparent hurry, he kissed her. His lips were firm and warm and took without asking. He tasted faintly of coffee and whipped cream.

"Gil…" The word trailed off on a whimper when he released her chin and found her knee.

Slowly, he glided his palm up her thigh. His whole body jerked when he discovered the edge of her stocking and the tiny satin rosette that was her garter. "Sweet heaven," he groaned. "You little tease."

She nipped his chin with sharp teeth. "I spend a lot of time on the job," she murmured, loosening his tie and unbuttoning two buttons at his throat. "When I dress up, I like feminine lingerie."

His fingers played with the edge of the stocking, his hand warm and hard. "Promise me something," he groaned, the words like ground glass.

She felt him trembling and understood the power she wielded. Both exultant and abashed, she struggled to find footing in the quicksand at her feet. Was this right for her? For Gil? What were they doing?

"Promise you what?" she asked. More than anything she wanted to take his hand and push it higher. But they were in a public parking lot, and it was time to pick up Cade.

"Promise me you'll wear this the first time we're together." He caressed the bare skin around her garter with his fingertip. Everything inside her went hot and shaky. She felt reckless, and that was enough to slow her down. Bailey Collins was never reckless. Not in her job and not in her personal life.

Someone had to be strong in the midst of insanity. This time it had to be her. With great regret, she removed his hand and slid to her side of the vehicle as far as she could go. "Will there be a time like that?" she asked.

"God, I hope so," he said, banging his fist on the steering wheel. "Because if I don't have you soon, I can't be held responsible for what happens."

He was exaggerating. She knew that. But the desperation in his voice was real and unmistakable "Look at your watch," she pleaded. "We have to go."

That he obeyed her was no victory. She wanted to stay with him in the intimate confines of the truck cab. In fact, she would have stayed there all night if he had asked. Though she hadn't fooled around like that as a high school kid, the idea held a certain appeal to a woman whose love life had been barren of late.

On the brief drive to Gil's cousin's house, silence reigned. The swish of the windshield wipers was the only sound. At their destination, Gil parked by the curb and hopped out. Minutes later, he returned, carrying a sleeping Cade. At Gil's motion, she leaned across the seat and opened his door.

Gently, his face unreadable, he scooted Cade to the middle and belted him into his booster seat. The boy's body was limp. When he slumped in Bailey's direction, she put her left arm around him and held him close. He smelled like peanut butter and little-boy sweat.

Gil climbed in and stared at his son. "He's dead to the world."

"Just as well," Bailey said. "Maybe this will all seem like a dream to him."

"Thank you for understanding. Most women would be offended."

"Not me. You're a father first and foremost. I respect that. Cade is a very lucky boy." She kissed the top of the child's head. "Take me home, Gil."

Gil drove more slowly than usual, fully aware that he was distracted. Bailey's care and consideration for his son impacted Gil in ways he couldn't explain. His brain ran in circles, torn between imagining intimacy with Bailey one second and wondering how he could ever test a relationship with a woman without dragging his son into it.

At McDaniel's Acres he pulled to a stop in front of the ranch house and put the truck in Park. Bailey put a hand on his arm. "Don't get out. You can't leave him here alone."

Gil shook his head. "He's fine." He went around the truck and opened Bailey's door, holding her hand to help her out. Remembering what she was wearing beneath that demure black dress made him hard all over again. "Good night, Bailey." He slid his hands beneath her thick, silky hair and anchored her head for his kiss.

She leaned into him, her lips eager and soft, her breasts crushed against his chest. Though he knew her to be tough and capable, when he held her like this, he wanted to protect her at all costs. The danger inherent in her job was never far from his mind.

He wedged a thigh between her legs, pulling her hips against his, letting her feel the extent of his need. "I'm working on an idea," he said. "Will you trust me?"

She toyed with his belt buckle. "Of course." The breathless note in her voice told him all he needed to know. He wasn't in this alone.

"Tomorrow. At the club. I'll explain."

"Yes." She ran her hand over the late-day stubble on his chin. He opened his mouth and bit gently on one of her fingertips.

The erotic action was a big mistake. The rush of lust almost crippled him. Backing away from her the way he would an angry rattler, he put the body of the truck between them. It was good that his son was asleep in the cab of the truck. Otherwise, Gil just might have taken Bailey standing up.

His forehead broke out in a cold sweat thinking about it. "Sleep well," he said, knowing that he wouldn't.

Bailey walked halfway up the steps, then turned to look at him. "I had fun tonight." Her voice carried on the night breeze. "Good night, Gil."

He got into the truck and leaned his forehead against the steering wheel, his heart slugging in his chest as if he'd run a marathon. Something was going to have to change. And soon....

Bailey entered the house quietly, though since it was not yet ten, likely no one was asleep. Chance McDaniel stood in the lobby chatting with a couple of gray-headed ladies from Ohio. Bailey had met them when she first arrived. Learning to ride a horse was a big item on their bucket list, and Chance's patient staff was helping that dream come true.

The owner of the dude ranch excused himself when he saw her enter and crossed the floor. "Everything okay?"

Her face must have reflected some of her turmoil. She flushed. "Fine. No problem."

He lifted an eyebrow. "Was that Gil Addison's truck I saw out front?"

Her flush deepened. "It was. We had dinner together."

Chance's smile was more of a grimace. "I suppose that means at least one of us is no longer on your suspect list."

"A man is innocent until proven guilty," she said.

Chance shook his head, his gaze hooded. "Doesn't feel that way from where I'm standing."

Bailey headed for the stairs, wishing she had the luxury of becoming friends with Chance. Already, in the short time she had been around, she felt like he was a man who could be trusted. But hard evidence was composed of facts and not feelings. Until she could completely clear his name from the suspect list, she couldn't get too friendly. It was impossible to imagine Chance committing a kidnapping. But she knew better than most that some people hid unimaginable secrets. Chance didn't. She was almost positive. Hopefully, soon she could prove it.

Upstairs, she stripped out of the one nice dress she had brought with her to Royal and stared at her reflection in the mirror. The tiny undies and demibra that matched the garter belt were intensely feminine. Closing her eyes, she tried to imagine the look on Gil's face if he saw her like this. His raw passion elated her, made her feel special and wanted.

In the shower, she imagined Gil at her side, his face all planes and angles as he stared at her with male determination. His body was intensely masculine, strong and rugged. The juxtaposition of his tenderness with Cade and his ruthless pursuit of Bailey should have confused her, but in a way, it made perfect sense. He was a man of deep emotions, whether it be love for his son or hunger for the woman in his arms.

She wouldn't be the woman in his *life*, not long-term. But if the fates were kind, she would certainly enjoy exploring her sensual side with him until it was time for her to leave.

Sliding her soapy fingers over her slick breasts, she inhaled sharply as arousal pumped through her veins like thick honey. Her nipples were taut nubs, their ache an ever-present reminder that she was young and in need of a man's touch.

Dragging the washcloth between her legs, she winced as her body demanded attention. It didn't take more than a few languid strokes before she came with a low moan and rested her forehead against the tile as her heartbeat slowly returned to normal.

On shaky legs, she got out and dried off, already anticipating the following day. What did Gil have in mind? And how long would they have to wait?

She was almost asleep when the cell phone on the bedside table vibrated suddenly. Snatching it up, she glanced at the screen. Though she had only dialed it once before, she recognized Gil's number. "Hello."

"Bailey. I just looked at the clock. I'm sorry. Were you asleep?"

"Not quite." She shifted, sitting up against the headboard. "Is something wrong?"

The silence on the other end of the phone lengthened. "Define wrong."

"Is Cade okay?"

Gil's voice was hoarse. "He's fine. Never even woke up when I carried him to his bed."

"That's good."

"Yeah." The awkward conversation was going nowhere. "I wish our evening could have lasted longer," he said.

She knew exactly what he meant. "Me, too." Suddenly, something struck her. "Are *you* in bed?" she asked, not sure if she wanted to know or not.

"Yes. And wishing you were here beside me."

She swallowed hard. The man was nothing if not honest. "I need you to be sure, Gil. Things will be complicated, and I don't want you to resent me when this is all over."

"I wasn't very nice to you at first, was I? And you're not sure if I fully trust you."

She heard the regret in his voice. "You were entitled to your opinion. In your place, I might have been just as aggravated. It's never easy to be questioned about a crime. It makes innocent people jittery. I understand."

"I don't want you to think I'm taking advantage of you. I really like you, Bailey. In spite of your job."

She smiled, smoothing her free hand over the soft, faded pattern of the double wedding ring quilt on her bed. "I like you, too, Gil. In spite of your bullheadedness."

"Touché."

His chuckle warmed her. "I'm not having phone sex with you," she said firmly, yet willing to be persuaded.

"Trust me, Bailey, when we finally have sex, it's going to be a helluva lot more exciting than mere words. I'm going to let you turn my world upside down and then return the favor."

Her breath caught as her legs moved restlessly against the sheets. "You're awfully confident."

"It has nothing to do with confidence. You and I are two of a kind. We're loners. Who feel things deeply and have a strong sense of responsibility toward those who depend on us. I think that's why I felt something for you the first day we met. You're not only beautiful and sexy, but you care about things. About people. About a little boy who wants a mother...."

"You know I'm not applying for that job, right?"

"I know. But how do you feel about the boy's father?"

Bailey sucked in a breath. Perhaps it was easier to be honest when he wasn't staring at her face to face. "I want to spend time with you, Gil...in all sorts of ways...."

He said something short and sharp that she couldn't quite hear. And then his voice echoed over the connection more strongly. "Not all women are as honest as you," he said.

She smiled, knowing he couldn't see. "Have I shocked you?"

"Only in the best possible way." He paused. "Go to sleep, Bailey. I'll see you tomorrow."

"Tomorrow..."

She fell asleep thinking about all the possibilities tied up in that one wonderful word.

Seven

Bailey worked her way through one drawer after another, her pile of file folders growing along with her list of questions. She'd been at the club all day, and Gil had never once shown his face. When she had arrived at ten as usual that morning, the club receptionist met her and handed over a key, saying that Mr. Addison had been detained.

Bailey tried not to brood over hurt feelings, but her reaction to Gil's absence was beginning to make her question whether it was wise to get involved with him at all. She didn't want to analyze his every move for evidence of whether or not he really cared. Fear of making an embarrassing misstep in their relationship kept her on edge.

At a quarter to five she began packing up her things, prepared to go home and pore over the new information she had gleaned. Still, nothing and no one jumped out at her as a likely suspect. But there were a lot of club members who had connections to Alex, and Bailey was pretty sure that given the chance to talk to them she might be able to make progress with her case.

When Gil walked into the small office, again without announcing his presence beforehand, she sucked in a sharp breath, but otherwise managed to face him with a neutral expression. Her hands continued to move, tidying up the work space, but her body was rigid.

Gil didn't look any happier than she felt. "I had five phone calls today," he said abruptly. "All of them wondering why I've allowed a woman I'm dating to spend time at the club without me present."

She winced. "So they know what I'm doing?"

"Not specifically. It's my fault for giving the receptionist my key. She's a nice woman, but she can't keep her mouth shut."

"What did you tell them?"

"I thought about making up a story, but frankly, you're a state investigator. Everyone in town knows it. Sooner or later, people were going to put two and two together. It was one thing for you to be seen eating lunch with Cade and me at the club. But I should have thought through the implications of you being here on your own today."

"So you told them the truth."

He nodded his head. "I did. And I can't repeat most of what was said in return. People don't like knowing that their personal business is being opened up to an outsider, especially one with government connections."

"I'm sorry, Gil."

"It's not your fault." He shrugged, his expression rueful. "You're merely doing your job. I can handle a little heat, Bailey. It's you I'm worried about."

"I told you…I can take care of myself."

"Alex Santiago would have told me the same thing,

and look what happened to him. Some nutcase decided to kidnap him."

"There had to be a reason. Some connection we're not seeing."

"Yes. And because we can't point to the perpetrator yet, the danger is still very real. What if someone tries to dissuade you from probing any further?"

"I take precautions. That's one reason I'm not staying in town. Chance's place is as safe as anywhere I can think of. Too many people around for anyone to get to me unnoticed. Not to mention the fact that I can keep an eye on Chance."

Gil ran a hand across the back of his neck, his face a thundercloud. "He has nothing to hide, Bailey. I'll be damn glad when this is all over."

"Not me," she said quietly. "At least not entirely. Because that means I'll have to head home."

His jaw tightened as the truth of her words sank in. Whatever time the two of them shared was likely to be very brief. Her heart shied away from that knowledge. Leaving Royal was a reality she didn't want to contemplate. Especially not now that Gil had admitted he wanted her.

He frowned as he took her shoulders in his hands and squeezed gently. "*Please* be careful, Bailey."

She moved closer into his embrace, kissed his cheek, and sighed. "I'm always careful." For long seconds, they stood there quietly as something fragile and precious bloomed. To have the right to lean on him, even symbolically, was very sweet. His hard frame seemed to shelter hers, even though she was quite capable of caring for herself.

The pull of his masculinity called to a part of her she often kept out of sight. Being "girlie" was the last thing she needed in her line of work. But with Gil, she felt herself letting down barriers. Softening. Needing.

"Tell me," she said, idly running her fingers over his collarbone. "What is this idea you were working on?"

He set her at arm's length, his expression unreadable. "You want to interview club members—right?"

"Yes. Maybe half a dozen or more."

"The thing is, Bailey, I can't stop you from doing what you were sent here to do, but I also can't condone using the club for those interviews. The TCC is where guys come to get away from life. To chill out and kick back. They have a right to their privacy. But…"

"But what?"

"But I think it might go down better if we do it at my place. I'll contact whomever you tell me and invite them out to the Straight Arrow tomorrow night. I won't lie. I'll tell them flat out why they're coming. But I'll throw some steaks on the grill and open a case of beer, and hopefully, we can mitigate any negative backlash."

"You'd do that for me?" What he was suggesting made perfect sense. Neutral territory.

He kissed her nose. "It's not that big a deal. But, yes."

"What about Cade? Will he be there?"

"Actually…"

For the first time since she had known him, Gil looked uncomfortable.

"What? What are you not telling me?"

"I have friends in Midland with a little boy exactly Cade's age. They're planning a sleepover birthday for their son and they want Cade to come. I'm driving him up there in the morning."

She fidgeted, not sure if she was reading him correctly.

Gil's smile was crooked. "I hope you'll pack a bag and stay at the Straight Arrow with me once our guests are gone."

* * *

Twenty-four hours later, Bailey drove out the familiar road to Gil's sprawling ranch, wondering how she had gone from being a hardworking investigator to a woman contemplating a night with her lover in one dizzying swoop.

The juxtaposition of professional and personal in the upcoming evening made her skittish. It was important that she come across as businesslike and competent when she interviewed Gil's friends and acquaintances. If any of them got wind of what Gil had planned for later, her credibility would be shot.

But there was no real cause for alarm. Gil didn't want gossip any more than Bailey did. For his son's sake, if nothing else.

When she arrived, Gil greeted her at the door. Two high-end pickup trucks were already parked out front. "Come on in," he said. "I thought you could go ahead and get started before dinner. We'll set you up in the front parlor. It was always my mom's holy of holies, but I think it will give you the privacy you need."

As they traversed the narrow hallway to the back of the house, Gil suddenly dragged her to a halt and pushed her against the antique wallpaper for a hard, hungry kiss. "I missed you today," he muttered, his hips anchoring her to the unyielding surface.

She returned the kiss eagerly, inhaling the scent of starched cotton and well-oiled leather. Gil was dressed casually in jeans, cowboy boots and a white shirt with the sleeves rolled up. He radiated tough masculinity, and despite her advanced degrees and the level to which she had risen in her career, it was humbling and embarrassing to admit that she was definitely turned on by his macho swagger.

"I missed you, too," she said primly. "And I want you

to know how much I appreciate all you've done to set this up tonight."

He nibbled the side of her neck. "You can thank me later. There's a full moon tonight. The view from my bedroom window is spectacular."

The breath caught in her throat as he hit a particularly sensitive spot. "Promises, promises..." She swallowed back an embarrassing moan. "There are vehicles out front. I assume we're not alone?"

As a protest, it was weak.

Gil rested his forehead against hers, his thumbs brushing the thin cotton of her blouse where it glided over her breasts. "You make me want to forget everything. That's dangerous."

"Should I apologize?" Her arms linked around his neck, feeling his warmth, his solidness.

"Come on," he said gruffly. "Let's get this over with."

Gil had to hand it to Bailey. She knew how to be charming. Her manner with the men he had invited hit just the right note. Neither authoritative nor tentative, she invited the guests to speak with her in private one by one. And as each man returned from the parlor, no one seemed particularly bent out of shape by Bailey's informal interrogation.

Over dinner, Gil surveyed the assorted group of men. Only two on his list had begged off. Sheriff Nathan Battle, who was on duty, and Paul Windsor, who was out of town on a business trip.

The rest had varying degrees of history with Alex Santiago. Douglas Firestone, Ryan Grant, the twins—Josh and Sam Gordon, Zach Lassiter, and Beau Hacket. With the possible exception of Hacket, Gil liked and respected every man present. And even Hacket, despite his son's recent vandalism of the child care center at the club, hardly seemed the type to kidnap anybody.

Fortunately, the medium-rare steaks were a big hit, the beer held out, and Bailey had the good sense to excuse herself from the table before the party became rowdy. By the time the evening wound down around ten, Gil was fairly certain that none of his guests really remembered why they had come. Each one went home with his belly full and perhaps a forbidden cigar or two smoked on the way out.

Gil closed and locked the front door, leaning against it with a sigh. As male bonding went, the evening was a home run.

But all he could think about was getting Bailey naked.

He found her in the parlor, her laptop open, her head bent studiously over a legal pad of notes. "Did you get anything good?" he asked, sprawling in a chair that was more comfortable than it looked.

She glanced up at him, her teeth worrying her bottom lip. "I have no idea. They all claim to like Alex. Firestone does admit to arguing with him, but insists it was nothing significant. Hacket tried to schmooze me and pretend that he's a saint. But overall, I came up with nothing that I didn't already know or suspect."

He saw the frustration on her face. "I invited Chance, but he was reluctant to come."

"I know. He glares at me when he thinks I'm not looking." She rubbed her temples with her index fingers. "I've had plenty of opportunity to talk to him, and if he's the kind of man to commit a felony, I'll be very surprised."

"Men in love do strange things."

"Is he? In love, I mean? You know him better than I do."

"I don't know. He and Cara were very close. But once Alex came on the scene, she had eyes for nobody else."

"So with Alex gone, Chance might try to make his move?"

"Even if he does, it still doesn't mean he had anything to do with Alex's disappearance."

"True…"

She stood up and stretched her arms toward the ceiling. "Enough of this. I'm officially off the clock until tomorrow."

Gil linked his hands behind his head. "I like the sound of that."

Hands on hips, she stared at him.

"What?" he asked, raising an eyebrow.

"Will I seem hopelessly inexperienced if I tell you I'm nervous?"

He rolled to his feet and walked toward her, grinning when she backed up and nearly toppled an antique glass pitcher. "There's nothing to be nervous about."

"That's what you think. I'm having trouble with the shift from work to play."

He tucked her hair behind her ears, glad that she had left it loose tonight. "I can help with that." Scooping her into his arms, he ignored her squeak of protest. "We're alone at last. I thought they would never leave." Striding out of the room and up the stairs, he felt his heart beating faster and faster, though carrying his burden was no strain. "In case it matters," he said, nuzzling her ear, "you're the first woman I've ever invited for a sleepover."

Bailey clung to Gil's neck, mortified that he had picked her up. She was not a petite woman, yet he seemed completely at ease. In the midst of being flustered by his romantic gesture, she was also taken aback by the casual way he told her this night was special.

In the doorway to his bedroom, he paused. "Last chance to say no." His dark eyes held not a flicker of humor.

She ran her thumb along his chiseled jawline. "I don't want to say no. I need you, Gil. I want you. Even if this night is all we have."

His slight frown told her he didn't like that last bit, but she was trying to be practical. Cade couldn't be shuttled off to friends and neighbors all the time, and Gil didn't want to parade his love life in front of his son. Any way you looked at it, tonight's encounter was not likely to be repeated.

Gil strode toward the bed and set her on her feet. He held her hands, his expression unreadable. "I've watched you for weeks," he murmured. "And even when I told myself you were an officious pain in the ass, I knew in my heart that I wanted you."

"All I saw was the disapproval," she confessed. "It hurt that you thought so little of me. And you seemed angry all the time."

"A defense," he said simply. "I hoped you would leave and I could forget the way your hair shines with fire in the sunlight or the way your long legs carry you across a crowded street."

Bailey's heart fluttered. Poetry from the man who was pragmatic and straightforward. He didn't dress it up or spout it effusively, thus making the quiet, sincere words all the more powerful.

She swallowed. "I had no idea."

"You weren't supposed to. I've done my damnedest to stay away from you. But when you called me about access to the club, I knew I was a goner." His smile was lopsided. "A man can only have so much self-control, and you tested mine to the limit. Turns out, I'm not as strong as I thought."

"I wish I could tell you I'm sorry about that, but I'm not. I've had an embarrassing crush on you since we first met."

"Nice to know." He grinned, the flash of white teeth literally taking her breath away. Gil bore great responsibilities and had a serious streak a mile wide. But this man, this lighthearted, teasing man, looked younger and happier than she had ever seen him.

She tugged her hands free and punched him in the arm. "You have to know that every woman in town thinks you're a hottie."

His smile faded, replaced by a searing look in his deep brown eyes that made her toes curl. "The only woman whose opinion interests me is you, Bailey." He curled an arm around her waist and dragged her closer. "But I think I'm done talking."

Wild elation streaked through her veins. His arms were hard and strong, binding her without mercy. She kissed him recklessly, clumsily, as if somewhere a clock counted down the seconds they could be together. The air in the room was charged.

"Take off your boots," she demanded. Her fuddled brain knew the priceless antique quilt on Gil's bed shouldn't be damaged. He released her only long enough to obey, toeing off each one and facing her in his sock feet.

He should have looked more vulnerable, less of a threat. But somehow that wasn't the case. "Any other orders?" he asked, the words mild despite his hot, determined expression.

She nodded slowly. "Now the belt."

Like the boots, the belt was constructed of expensive hand-tooled leather. Gil unfastened the buckle and made a production of sliding the length of cowhide through each loop. When it was free, he coiled it and tossed it on a chair.

His jaw flexed. His chest rose and fell rapidly with each labored breath. "Whatever you want, Bailey."

The way he looked at her made her body go lax with arousal, even as her hands fisted helplessly at her sides. Her thighs pressed together. Where her body prepared for his, she was damp and ready. She had known sexual desire in the past, but never this writhing hunger that turned her insides into an ache that consumed her.

Paralyzed suddenly by the knowledge that she wasn't really a femme fatale, she fell silent.

Gil seemed to read her hesitation. "You were on a roll," he muttered. "Don't stop now."

Apparently her bent for bossiness entertained him. She shifted from one foot to the other, realizing suddenly that her clothes were far too tight, much too hot. "The shirt," she said. "Unbutton it slowly."

Eight

She had created a monster. Straitlaced Gil Addison showed a definite talent for stripping. If he had loosened his shirt buttons any more slowly, Bailey might have lost it and ripped the fabric apart with her two hands. But she had asked and he had answered, so all she could do was watch as he tormented her.

When the shirt hung open, he stopped. She hadn't requested that he take it off, and he was obeying the letter of the law. His silence rattled her. What was he thinking? The uncertainty dried up any further desire to script this encounter. Her momentary lead in the dance no longer appealed.

They were separated by a distance of only three or four feet. Close enough for her to see the shadow of late-day stubble on his chin. The evidence of his masculinity underlined the differences between them. Bailey knew how to use a weapon and could even bring most men down using her training in martial arts.

Many people would describe her as tough.

But Gil…Gil was the real deal. His sleek, long-limbed body rippled with muscle. His olive skin gleamed with health and vigor. He was a man capable of defending those he loved. At the peak of his physical strength and power.

Bailey's heart twisted. Hard. What would it be like to be loved by Gil Addison? Clearly, he had loved his dead wife once upon a time. And of course he loved his parents and his son. But to be a woman loved by a man like Gil… that would be an incredible thing. In the present context, though, that thought was a fantasy, one she might as well put out of her mind.

Tonight was about human need. Sex. That was all. She and Gil were drawn to each other, because they both spent too many nights alone. So during this brief moment in time, they were going to cling to each other and enjoy the pleasures of carnal excess.

Perhaps Gil was more intuitive than she realized, for he abandoned his sexy pose and stalked her, backing her up until her hips hit the bed. "You aren't saying much," he taunted. "Cat got your tongue?"

She curled an arm around the bedpost, clinging in hopes that her shaky legs wouldn't give out. "Just admiring the view." It wouldn't do to let him know how much seeing his beautiful body in the privacy of his bedroom rattled her.

He shrugged out of the shirt and let it fall. Taking her free hand, he placed it flat over his heart. "Feel what you do to me."

The rapid thud of his heartbeat was unmistakable. Without thinking, she rubbed gently, as though she could absorb his life force through her fingertips. Touching him was both intimate and arousing.

Gil groaned and closed his eyes. Was it possible that he was as turned on as she was? Experimentally, she scraped her thumbnail across one flat, brown nipple. Gil put his hand over hers, trapping it against his hot skin. "Don't poke the tiger, Bailey. I have plans for tonight, and they don't involve coming too soon like a callow teenager."

His blunt speaking made her cheeks flame. "I want to please you. I need to know what you like."

"You *do* please me, in every way. I love your strength and your integrity. And I love the way you treat my son."

"He's lucky to have a dad like you."

Gil caressed her cheek, his gaze hooded. "I spend much of my time being Cade's father. I know that role inside and out. Tonight…" He paused and she saw the muscles in his throat contract. "Tonight I'm just a man. A man who wants *you*."

She slipped her arms around his neck, appreciating the distinction, even if it wasn't wholly true. Gil could have any woman he wanted, but in a town like Royal, such a relationship would be tricky. Sleeping with Bailey was less complicated. She understood that.

Resting her head on his shoulder, she whispered the bare, honest truth. "I want you to make love to me Gil. More than I've ever wanted another man. Don't make us wait any longer."

Gil felt the sting of strong emotion in his throat and his eyes. Bailey Collins was the most fascinating, unconsciously sensual woman he had ever met. Now that she was here—in his bedroom, about to make a number of his more torrid fantasies come to life—all he could think about was how soon he was going to lose her.

He slammed the door on those images. Who and what he needed was right in front of him…literally. Bailey was warm and real and so very, very beautiful. Running his hands though her hair, he imagined what it was going to look like spread across his pillow. "In other circumstances, I might insist that anticipation is half of the pleasure. But tonight, I'm in no mood to delay anything at all." He unfolded her arms from around his neck. "My turn, lovely Bailey."

As her cheeks turned the color of a ripe tomato, he undressed her bit by bit, supporting her arm as she stepped out of her clothes. His surmise had been right on target. She wore naughty undies beneath, this time pale pink trimmed in mocha lace. The tiny bikini panties and matching bra were ultrafeminine, reminding him that despite the toughness she exhibited in her job, Bailey was all woman.

She seemed reluctant to dispense with the final layer that shielded her full nudity. So he matter-of-factly shucked his jeans and boxers and socks in a couple of quick moves. Bailey's eyes widened. The expression on her face was gratifying.

He was fully erect, and aching to possess her. But first he was going to have to coax her into relaxing. "I don't know what you're thinking," he complained. "Is that deer-in-the-headlights look you're giving me because you've changed your mind or because I'm going too fast?"

She licked her lips, arms crossed beneath her breasts. "Neither," she said quietly. "I'm enjoying the moment."

"Could you possibly enjoy the moment under the covers? I'm getting cold feet."

That made her giggle, and some of the rigidity left her posture. "I'm on board with that."

He tugged her close for a quick kiss and then turned back the covers on the large, wide bed. His sheets were soft white cotton, scented with sunshine. The housekeeper was a big fan of using a clothesline, and truth be told, Gil liked it. The smell made him think of being a kid.

When he helped Bailey crawl beneath the sheet and the quilt, however, childhood was the last thing on his mind.

His brain blanked for a moment, all his senses absorbing the novel and gratifying sensation of feeling Bailey's arms and legs tangle with his. She was soft, so soft. He held her tightly, burying his face in her hair.

"I've imagined this moment for weeks," he admitted, flattening his palm on her belly and teasing her navel with his pinkie. It would almost have been enough just to hold her. To revel in the knowledge that she had come to him of her own free will and *wanted* to share his bed.

Bailey kissed his chin, her hands roving across his pecs and his shoulders. "Does it measure up?"

He wedged a thigh between hers and groaned as his thick, almost painful shaft rubbed against her leg. "I'm not sure. I'm having trouble believing this is real. I don't want to wake up in a minute and find out I was dreaming."

Without warning, her hand closed around his erection. "I'm real," she said. "We're real. Here. Together."

When she began stroking him, his eyes closed involuntarily. He had been leaning over her on one elbow, but now he fell back on the bed, his hands fisting in the sheet. *Holy hell.* It wasn't the effects of extended abstinence making him insane. It was the way she touched him. Her gentle movements were exactly right.

The first sexual encounter between a man and a woman was supposed to be fraught with pitfalls, neither partner knowing the other's preferences. Bailey was putting paid to that idea. Everything she did was gut-level perfect. Now she was the one leaning over *him*, her silky hair falling around them as she kissed him softly. Kiss/stroke. Kiss/stroke. The sequence made him dizzy with lust.

His sex quivered every time her lips found his. He held the back of her neck to deepen the kiss and to make sure she didn't stop what she was doing. But soon, far too soon, he had to call a halt. Sucking in raw lungfuls of air, he shook his head, half-crazed with hunger. "Enough," he croaked. He hovered on a knife-edge of arousal.

As he predicted, the moon had found its way into his bedroom, the silver orb framed by his window. The drapes were open. Shafts of white light spilled over Bailey's face, giving her the look of an ice queen. But no ice queen ever emanated the kind of warmth that could save a man's life. Gil hadn't fully understood the depths of his loneliness until he brought Bailey to his home and to his bed.

He had told himself repeatedly over the past few years that being Cade's father was more important than anything. And it was. A sacred obligation. But Gil was neither a monk nor a saint, and in this instant he realized how sterile he had allowed his life to become.

Every cell in his body cried out at the indulgence of touching Bailey, of kissing her. Like flowers blooming wildly in the once-barren desert after a storm, he found himself drunk with pleasure. She rolled with him in the bed, laughing softly as they bumped noses.

"This is nice," she said, the voice more prim than her actions. "I never knew Gil-the-sex-maniac existed."

"You're not naked," he complained.

Sitting up, she reached behind her back and unfastened her bra, dropping it at the foot of the bed. Now, the moon painted two perfect breasts with a magical palette of light and shadow. Bailey dragged her hair over one shoulder, her head cocked as she tried to read his expression. He, unlike his partner, was cast in semi-gloom.

"Is this what you had in mind?"

"Getting there," he muttered. He slid his hand between her smooth thighs and stroked the center of her panties. The scent of her came to him, warm and heady. "These, too." Rising to his knees, he shoved the offending scrap of nylon down her hips.

Bailey lay back, arms above her head, and let him finish the job. The moon took her natural beauty and made it supernatural, as though a fairy or a sprite had come to him in a mirage. Touching her was the only way to prove she wouldn't fade away.

Kneeling between her legs, he leaned forward and mapped her body like a blind man, his caresses making her whimper and stir restlessly. Her face, her throat. Each lovely breast. The narrow span of her waist. The flare of her hips.

He stopped there, breathing hard. Running through the back of his mind was the knowledge that he was missing something very important, something key to this moment.

Bailey put a hand on his thigh. "Do you have condoms?" she asked softly.

He sensed that the question embarrassed her. "Yes." Leaving her momentarily was unthinkable, but he would never do something she would regret. After sheathing himself in latex, he went back to her, his hands shaking as he sprawled on his side.

She turned her head to look at him, her lips curved in a smile that made him want to drag her beneath him like a caveman. But his evolved side held sway…barely. Tonight was about more than his sexual starvation. It was about pleasing Bailey.

He parted her sex with gentle fingers and tested her readiness. Warmth and wetness met his touch. Inserting two fingers into her tight passage, he played with her until she began to beg.

"Now, Gil. Please. Now."

Surprisingly, her urgency enabled him to chain his own impatience. Though his arousal pulsed and throbbed like a raw, aching nerve, he found himself entranced with tormenting Bailey. Locating the tiny nub that was her nerve center, he rubbed softly, exulting when she cried out and arched her back as the climax rolled over her.

When she was limp and still, he began all over again.

Bailey didn't know what she had done in a previous life to deserve such a night of enchantment, but she wasn't about to complain. Her world had narrowed to the confines of Gil Addison's bed. Nothing beyond that perimeter mattered for the next few hours.

Her body sated with pleasure, she struggled to focus her fuzzy thought processes. She was aware that Gil watched her, hawk-like, his features masked in the semidarkness. His back was to the window, so while *he* could look his fill of her nakedness painted in lunar glow, she was less able to gauge his mood.

She lifted a hand and let it fall. "You've destroyed me," she said, the words slurred. Her orgasm had been intense, unprecedented. To realize that he could draw such a response from her was daunting. What if tonight's affair ruined her for other men?

When he touched her again, she flinched.

Laughing softly, he spread her legs and positioned the head of his sex at her core. "I want you to remember every second of this night," he said hoarsely. "Because I'm going to make love to you until neither of us can remember our names."

Bailey believed him implicitly. Heat radiated from his big body, warming her chilled skin. Now that her pulse had settled back to normal, the room was cool.

Gently he stroked her swollen folds with his shaft. She was so sensitized that the caress was almost too much. Incredibly, as he brushed her intimately, her body began to thrum again with the need for him, the urgency to have him inside her.

Suddenly, desperately, she wanted to turn on a light. She wanted to catch every moment of the insanity, to revel in every nuance of expression that crossed his face as he pleasured both of them.

Her breath caught when he cupped her bottom and canted her hips. "Now," he promised, the single syllable guttural. "Now, Bailey."

He was thick and hard. Her flesh yielded to his penetration slowly. On the heels of her earlier climax, this claiming was overwhelming. She shook her head from side to side, incredulous that such feelings were real. Nothing in her past had prepared her for Gil.

He held her tenderly as he took her with the confidence of a man who knew what he wanted. What she wanted. Kisses interspersed with raw lunges that took him all the way to the mouth of her womb. His arms quivered as he kept his weight from crushing her into the bed.

She wrapped her legs around his waist, feeling the power, the potency. Her fingernails dug into his shoulders, marking him as hers. She could fall in love with him so easily... For many weeks she had watched him from afar, seeing the respect people afforded him, witnessing the joy in his son's face, understanding the position and influence Gil wielded in the community.

Tonight, though, her feelings went far beyond admiration. Gil had taken her heart. Perhaps he didn't even know it. Perhaps it didn't even matter. For a stolen moment in time the only real measure was how they each gave and received pleasure.

She clung to him as he thrust wildly, his force shaking the bed. A tendril of heat curled in her lower abdomen, spread throughout her pelvis and burst into full flame as she pitched over a sharp edge in the midst of Gil's hoarse shout of completion.

* * *

They must have dozed in the aftermath. When she opened her eyes, the moon had shifted and was barely visible in the corner of the window. The room was quiet. Gil lay half on top of her, his face buried in the sheet. Despite the chill in the air, they were both sticky with sweat.

She eased to one side, wincing when he muttered in his sleep. Stealthily, she moved an inch at a time until she could free herself and slide from the bed. After using the bathroom and freshening up, she pondered the possibility of a hot shower. The lure was impossible to resist. A thick terrycloth robe hung on the back of the door, so she dropped it on the floor in arms' reach and turned on the water.

Soon, steam filled the roomy enclosure. Clearly, Gil had spent money on modernization at some point. Bailey applauded his choice. The bold turquoise and amber tiles reminded her of Spain's artistic influence in Texas architecture.

The water was hot and reviving, chasing the chill from her bones. She didn't bother with her hair, keeping it mostly dry. Though Gil had invited her to spend the night, she was already feeling anxious about "the morning after." Perhaps it would be better to say farewell and head on home very soon. Things that seemed perfectly natural and normal under the hypnotic effects of moonlight could develop into awkward realities in the cold light of day. She didn't want to spoil a perfect memory with an uncomfortable goodbye that left her feeling empty and lonelier than when she started.

Suddenly, the frosted-glass shower door opened and Gil's big body appeared in the opening. "Room for one more?"

Nine

Gil caught the play of emotions that skittered across his lover's face. Surprised pleasure. Shy embarrassment. Wary uncertainty.

She nodded. "Of course."

There was no *of course* about any of this. He and Bailey were breaking new ground, and he sensed that she had gotten cold feet in more ways than one. Giving her a moment to adjust to his presence, he took the soap and turned his back as he washed himself. His sex was hard and ready, but he wouldn't rush her. This was too important.

When he felt two hands on his back, rubbing his soap-slicked skin, he closed his eyes and smiled. "That feels good," he groaned, resting his head against the wall, feeling the hot, stinging spray pound his skin.

Bailey's arms encircled his waist from behind. He sucked in a sharp breath when he felt the press of her soft breasts on his back. "I was thinking about going home now," she said.

Gil jerked in shock and spun to face her, nearly depositing both of them on the slippery floor. He grabbed her upper arms to steady her. "What the hell are you talking about?"

Her eyes were huge. She shrugged helplessly. "You have employees and obligations. Tomorrow morning things will be different."

"Different, how?" His temper simmered.

"You know…weird."

He ran a finger down her nose and shook his head with a sigh. "Why do women have to be so complicated?" He turned off the water and pulled her into his arms, deliberately pressing his erection against the notch where her legs met.

"Life is complicated. *I'm* pretty simple."

He felt her shiver. "As much as I'd like to debate that last point, I think I need to warm you up. Put on my robe and I'll build a fire."

As they both dried off, he tried not to look at her, but it was like telling sailors not to gaze at sirens on the rocks. His gaze tracked her every graceful movement. The moment when she shrouded her nude form in his enveloping robe was a major disappointment.

The fireplace in his bedroom was original to the house and, like the other three scattered throughout his home, cost a fortune to insure. He rarely took the time to use this one, because many nights he was late coming to bed.

Now, though, he was glad of the ambience.

In his peripheral vision he was aware of Bailey climbing back into bed and huddling under the covers. In addition to growing up on a ranch, Gil had been a Boy Scout, so he soon had a roaring blaze that popped and crackled and began to fill the room with cozy warmth.

He rose from a squatting position and found her watching him, unmistakable arousal in her eyes. Her lips parted. Her breath came quickly. Men were rarely as modest as women, so it gave him not a second's pause to stride toward the bed, naked and determined. She couldn't hide what she was feeling. Not now.

When he scooted in beside her, she squawked as his cold feet made contact with her legs. He dragged her close, spooning her and kissing the nape of her neck. "I'm not letting you leave, Bailey. So get that out of your head. If you're worried about waking up tomorrow morning, perhaps I'll keep you up all night so it won't be an issue." He shuddered as he thought of the possibilities. "I don't have a problem with that."

She laughed softly, wriggling onto her side so she could face him. "You don't lack confidence, do you?" Reaching out, she ran her thumb over his bottom lip. Which seemed to Gil like an open invitation to nibble the tip of her finger. He sucked it into his mouth and felt the pull in his groin.

Breathing hard as he pulled back, he brushed aside the lapel of the robe she wore, baring her breasts. "It's not confidence if it's a fact. Every time I get near you, I get hard."

"Gil!"

He nuzzled her nose. "What, Bailey?"

She shook her head, surveying him with a slight smile. "I never knew you could be this way."

"I'm guessing you saw me as an uptight, judgmental, obstructive pain in the ass."

The smile broadened. "You said it, not me. But that's not all. I knew you were a gorgeous man and a loving father, so that balanced out your less stellar qualities."

"I'm sorry I made your job difficult."

"You're hardly the first. I'm rarely a popular person."

"I can't believe that. Criminals probably line up for the opportunity to be alone with you in a tiny interrogation room."

"You've been watching too many cop shows on television. I do a lot behind the scenes, but it's rarely glamorous."

He stroked her hair from her forehead, tucking it behind her ear. "I'm glad you're here tonight," he said, deadly serious.

Her gaze searched his. "Me, too."

This time, he was clearheaded, but no less hungry. He retrieved protection, rolled it on, and returned to her side. Slowly, wanting to draw out the moment, he moved over her and into her. Bailey lifted her hips and took him deep, her wide-eyed gaze holding mysteries he was unable to fathom. Did she feel the earth move? Was she already thinking about leaving him tomorrow?

The warm, tight clasp of her flesh on his made him woozy. He closed his eyes, concentrating on the lazy slide in and out. Bailey tried to urge him on with incoherent pleas. But he was set on a course that was as immovable and inexorable as the tides. What had started out as something of a one-night stand was shifting and changing. His brain shied away from the implications, even as he grappled with his need for her.

He had a son to consider. And a home in Royal. But the woman beneath him, her body soft and yet strong, had bewitched him. How could he go on with life as usual, knowing what he was giving up?

She was no happy homemaker in apron and pearls. Bailey was a competent career woman. Based in Dallas. Where she would have ample opportunities for advancement.

His body said with finality that the time for analysis

was over. His jaw tightened and his legs quivered as the urge to come struck furiously and without quarter. Dimly, he heard Bailey cry out as she found completion. His own climax was more of a tornado, snatching him up, ass over heels, and dropping him into a void of sated bliss so dark and deep he wanted to revel in it forever.

They stayed in bed this time, too exhausted to move. Bailey's head lay on his chest. One of her arms curled across his waist. He floated on a sea of contentment that was unprecedented. In that moment, he believed anything was possible.

Bailey stroked his chest idly, her fingers tracing the line of hair that ran from his collarbone to his groin. So mellow was he that her first quiet question didn't even cause him heartburn.

She sighed softly, her eyes shielded by long lashes. "Will you tell me more about your wife?"

He kissed her forehead. "Not much left to tell. We married young. She had serious emotional problems. Her parents were wackos who subjected her to an unimaginable adolescence."

"Does Cade ask about her?"

"He used to, from time to time. Now he's more interested in finding Mrs. Addison Number Two."

"Has he ever visited his maternal grandparents?"

Gil stiffened. "Not a chance in hell. My wife took an overdose of pills but lingered long enough to beg me not to ever let our son near her parents or their way of life. The custody case drew statewide attention. I think the cult—for lack of a better word—that my in-laws embraced began to worry that the government might take a closer look at them, so they moved the entire group over the border into Mexico."

"I'm so sorry, Gil. It must have been a nightmare for you."

"It was a long time ago."

She was quiet for a few minutes, and then she sat up in the bed. "If you have one more of those little packets, I think I'm in the mood to see the view from the top."

When Bailey awoke the next morning, the spot beside her was empty. In an instant, full recollection of what she had done rolled over her in a mix of exhilaration and panic. Raising up on her elbows, she saw a note on Gil's pillow written in dark scrawl on a scrap of paper:

Didn't want things to be "weird," so I'm giving you your space.

He had signed his name and added a crooked smiley face. She smiled, half-sorry he wasn't with her, but more than a little relieved to have a moment to compose herself. Lying in Gil's bed felt deliciously decadent. She was usually an early riser, eager to start the day. But for once, she allowed herself a few minutes to revel in the memories of last night.

Becoming Gil's lover had been eye-opening. Never had she dreamed that inside his no-nonsense exterior was a tiger ready to pounce. He had wooed her, coaxed her, seduced her. And she had been a willing participant every step of the way.

The scent of his skin still clung to her pillowcase. When her body reacted to the images that masculine fragrance evoked, she knew it was time to get up.

After a quick shower, she dried her hair and dressed in the clean clothes she had packed in her overnight case. She made the bed, repacked her things, and carried the bag with her downstairs to set it by the front door. Coming face-to-face with the housekeeper was a bit of a shock, but the older woman never batted an eyelash. She smiled kindly and offered to scramble some eggs or make whatever Bailey wanted for breakfast.

Settling for black coffee seemed the safest choice. Bailey's stomach fluttered with nerves. Even now, dressed and in control somewhat, the prospect of seeing Gil was nerve-racking. He was a contained man, a private man, and though he had opened up to her last night in a very intimate way, she did not delude herself into thinking that she knew him well. They hadn't been together long enough for that.

The housekeeper seemed flustered that Gil's guest wasn't interested in eating, so to keep the peace, Bailey accepted a plate of toast and carried it and her coffee out onto the back porch. The morning was chilly, but her blazer, the one at which Gil turned up his nose, was warm enough to warrant an alfresco meal.

It was a shock to find that her host had entertained the same idea. He sat on a cushioned wicker love seat, his phone and iPad on the glass-topped table beside him. When Bailey stepped out on the porch, he jumped to his feet. "Join me," he said, his smile warm.

She would rather have chosen the chair across from him, but that didn't seem to be an option. Her stomach tightened as she sat down at Gil's urging, hip to hip with the man who had wakened her twice during the night for lovemaking. Despite her best efforts, her cheeks reddened.

He rested an arm across the back of the seat, his fingers stroking her shoulder lightly. "Did you sleep well?" His voice was a low rumble, the words husky and intimate.

She set the plate of toast, uneaten, on the table, and gulped her coffee, not caring that it scalded her tongue. "Yes." Staring out across Gil's beautiful ranch, she pretended an intense interest in the view.

His fingers moved to her neck, just below her ear. "You're shy," he accused, humor in his tone.

The innocent caress turned her insides into a soft, yearning puddle of need, reminding her of the danger she faced. She was no more willing than any other woman to have her heart broken. "I'm thirty-three years old. I'm not shy."

"Then what is it? Look at me, Bailey."

She half turned, studying the face that had become dear to her. His chiseled good looks added up to so much more than a handsome man. His integrity, his decency, his willingness to do the right thing by his son...all those things touched her heart and made her love him.

Staring into his eyes, she tried not to let him see the revelation that had knocked her sideways. When had she first known the truth about her feelings? Only last night? Or had her regard for him grown almost imperceptibly in the weeks she had studied him in his element? Even during that first interview when he had been angry and borderline obstructive, she had been drawn to his masculinity, to his aura of command, and even to his arrogance.

Some men used their power and influence to ride roughshod over women and anyone they perceived as weak or inferior in any way. But Gil was different. He used his strength and capabilities to protect and support both his son and his wide circle of friends.

It hadn't escaped her notice that Gil was extremely popular in Royal. He was admired by women and respected by men. The truth was, in all her interviews, no one had ever spoken harshly or critically of Gil. He must have a few enemies or naysayers...most men in his position would. But if he did, she hadn't come across them yet.

Perhaps her mental "checkout" hadn't been as long as it seemed. Because Gil waited patiently, his dark-eyed gaze a little too perceptive for her comfort. She didn't want him to know the truth. She didn't want him to think she was angling for something permanent. She didn't want him to think she would be kind to his son to win points.

"I enjoyed last night," she said quietly, her mouth dry and her throat constricted. "But I do have a job I need to attend to. It's late. I have to get back to town."

He frowned. "That's it?"

"What do you mean?"

"You can just walk away after last night?"

Her fists clenched. "What do you want me to say, Gil? It was wonderful. But we both have responsibilities."

"I'm tired of being responsible," he said, the words flat. "What I want is to go back upstairs with you and close the door."

Her heart raced. The image he conjured was unbearably tempting. "So would I," she said. "But that's not really an option, and you know it. Please let me go, Gil."

Something vibrated in his big frame and flashed in his eyes. Anger. Desire. He jumped to his feet and paced. "I'd rather you stay away from the club for a few days. Until some of the gossip and complaints die down."

She nodded. "I was almost done, anyway."

He folded his arms across his chest, looking more combative than amorous. "So why do you need to work today?"

"You are a stubborn man."

He shrugged. "I know what I want."

"If you must know, I had planned to speak with Alex again. The doctors only allowed me a brief moment with him when he was found, and of course, he remembered nothing."

"You think that has changed?"

"No. But perhaps on his home turf I can pick up some small clue…anything we might have missed earlier."

The ring of a cell phone interrupted them. Bailey glanced at Gil's phone where it lay on the table. "It's the sheriff."

"I'd better take this. Nate doesn't call to chitchat."

Bailey listened unashamedly during the extremely brief conversation. When Gil hung up, she quizzed him. "Anything wrong?"

He nodded, sober-faced. "Alex was rushed to emergency during the middle of the night with an excruciating headache. And now there's some kind of uproar at the hospital. Nate asked me to get in touch with you and let you know."

Her mind raced. "Is Alex critical?"

"I'm not sure. Nate was in a rush and didn't take the time to explain. Do you think we should head over there?"

She nodded. "I certainly want to. Especially since Sheriff Battle was being mysterious. When do you have to pick up Cade?"

"Not until mid-afternoon. I'll drive you to the hospital."

"Thank you. But I'll take my own car. I don't know how long I'll be there. I don't want to be stranded when you leave."

He didn't like her choice. She could tell. But he didn't argue further. Instead, he pulled her to her feet, wrapped his arms around her and kissed her. Her arms circled his waist, feeling the heat of his body, the power, the ripple of muscle in his lower back.

His mouth was hungry, but gentle. They were essentially on display, though no one appeared to be close by at the moment. The broad light of day was far less protective of secrets, however, and far less private than a shadowy bedroom and a moonlit mattress.

She kissed him back, unable to resist. The way he held her conveyed so many things that hadn't been put into words. In his embrace, she felt not only desire, but also a tenderness that disarmed her.

His tongue teased the recesses of her mouth, making her knees wobble and her stomach tighten with pleasure. When she tasted him in return, he cursed quietly and set her away from him. The lines of his face were carved in frustration and thwarted need. "We're not done with this. Make no mistake."

Ten

Gil brooded on the way to the hospital, his hands wrapped around the steering wheel in a death grip. Only a short time ago he had awakened feeling jubilant and sexually sated and better than he had in a long, long time. A sleeping Bailey lay nude in his arms, her leg angled across his thighs, her hair a dark cinnamon cloud around her face.

He had held her close in the predawn darkness, deeply grateful for whatever path led her to him. She walked alone in life, it seemed. Halfway estranged from her father. No other close family. Though Gil admired her self-sufficiency, he wished she would not discount the possibility that her current assignment put her in danger.

The urge and desire to protect her was strong. As was the need to stake a claim somehow. That last bit didn't make sense. Bailey was not involved with anyone else sexually or otherwise. She might be staying at Chance's dude ranch, but Gil had no real worries on that score.

Even if Chance made a move on her, Bailey would never get involved with someone who might be key in her investigation.

But still the urge remained.

Gil knew that some bridge had been crossed last night. Over the years, particularly when Cade was too small to realize that his dad was gone overnight, Gil had spent an evening with an amenable woman and had his sexual needs fulfilled. It hadn't taken very long for him to realize that such encounters left a sour taste in his mouth.

Apparently, he wasn't cut out for casual sex.

As a young man, before he had fully understood the extent of his wife's emotional trauma, he'd had every reason to believe that he and Sherrie would spend a life together at the Straight Arrow, potentially filling the house with a number of children.

Once the truth came out, Sherrie withdrew, both physically and emotionally. Despite Gil's every effort, he had been unable to reach her. The loneliness of living in such a marriage hit hard, and had only increased tenfold after Sherrie's death.

Not even to himself had Gil admitted the great void in his life. It seemed ungrateful and almost wicked to complain when he had so many blessings. A happy, healthy son. A family property that generated a very comfortable lifestyle. A wide circle of friends.

But a man needed a woman in his bed at night. A woman by his side. A partner who would share dreams and sorrows and joy and troubles. Bailey seemed convinced that she was only passing through. And in truth, Gil had believed they had little basis for a long-term relationship. Their lives were so different.

But after last night…well…after last night, Gil was prepared to move heaven and earth to prove to her that she was wrong. He had no clear plan, no road map for avoiding the obstacles in their way. Nevertheless, he wasn't prepared to walk away from an experience and a woman who had made him rethink his monastic lifestyle.

A cynical person might point out that sexual euphoria was no basis for making serious life decisions. That simply because Gil had made love to Bailey Collins five times in one night didn't mean they were soul mates. That he was thinking with his male anatomy and not his brain.

Throughout history, sexual mistakes had brought down men with as much or more to lose than Gil. Sex often made fools of those who had the hubris to think they were invincible. Gil got it. He really did. But stubbornly, he believed his situation was different. That he and Bailey were different. They had connected last night with a fire and an intimacy that was as rare as it was stingingly real.

His thinking was muddled. There were things to be sorted out. And he felt as if he had a hangover, though he was stone-cold sober. But the future seemed brighter this morning. And for now, that was enough.

At the hospital, he parked and went to find Bailey. Royal Memorial was a modern, well-equipped facility outfitted with the latest in technology. Though Royal might not have the population of bigger towns and cities in Texas, there was plenty of money to go around, and the citizens had chipped in to endow various wings and such with generous gifts.

Bailey was waiting for him in the lobby. She had already checked with the information desk for the room number, so when Gil joined her, they headed for the bank of elevators.

"He's in a regular room," she said. "That's a good sign."

Gil kissed her cheek, hugging her briefly with one arm. They were alone in the elevator as they rode up. "I'm very proud of you, Bailey. Alex is a lucky man to have you on his side."

Her small smile was gratified. "Thank you. But until we bring this to a close, I won't be able to relax."

They got off on the third floor. A doctor was just coming out of Alex's room. Bailey flashed her badge and asked for an update.

The physician shook his head. "Not much to tell. We're running some tests, but the headache is most likely tied to the concussion. Not to mention the fact that Santiago is trying so hard to force himself to remember. I've cautioned him to back off. To rest. To give his brain time to heal. But patience isn't his strong suit."

Gil had known the doctor for many years. The man was, in fact, a longtime friend of Gil's parents. "Nate said there's some kind of commotion going on."

The doctor raised a bushy eyebrow, his expression slightly harried. "That's why we wanted to alert Ms. Collins. You might say there are some new developments in the case. And unfortunately, the sheriff was summoned away on an emergency."

Gil saw Bailey tense. "What kind of developments?" she asked.

"Mr. Santiago's father and sister have arrived from Mexico. The sheriff examined their credentials thoroughly before we allowed them to have access, though he has posted security guards, as you can see. Alex is awake and resting comfortably at the moment. We did give him something for pain, so he's a little groggy."

Gil put a hand at Bailey's back, following her into the room. By the window stood an imposing man with short, jet-black hair who bore a striking resemblance to the patient in the bed. The older man, probably in his mid-fifties, wore an expensive gold wristwatch and the kind of clothes that were made by a personal tailor. His brown eyes were not warm. Instead they had the flat, mud-like appearance of stagnant water.

Sitting in a chair by the bed was a striking young woman with long black hair. Her figure was curvaceous to say the least. A large, intricate necklace of thin gold filigree inset with deep burgundy rubies accentuated modestly revealed cleavage. The color of the stones was passionate. But their fire was not reflected in her face. She seemed exhausted.

"Who are you?" she asked, her voice deeply accented. "And why are you in my brother's room?"

Bailey stepped forward, hand extended. "I'm Bailey Collins, state investigator. I've been assigned to work the case involving Mr. Santiago's disappearance. And this is Gil Addison, president of the Texas Cattleman's Club."

The Latin beauty shook Bailey's hand briefly, her ample bosom confined in a jade silk dress. "Pardon my frankness, Ms. Collins, but from what Alex tells us about his ordeal, your progress in the case is, how do you say it… zippo. Nada."

Gil had to admire Bailey's self-control. She took the criticism without flinching. "I understand your frustration. But I can assure you that we are narrowing the field of suspects day by day. We *will* find out who did this." She paused. "I know the sheriff took a look at your identification, but I must ask to see it, as well. I'll need to scan it into our database as a precaution. I hope you understand that I can't merely take your word as to your connection with Alex."

The beautiful woman shot a look at the stranger by the window. "This is all his fault. Ask *him* about our IDs."

The older man ignored her.

Alex interrupted, his face etched in discomfort, his voice subdued. "Why would they lie?"

Gil watched in silence as Bailey eyed the visitors. After a brief hesitation, when Gil had the impression she was weighing her options, she offered her hand to the man, as well. "I'm pleased to meet you, Mr. Santiago."

The man's eyes flashed and he ignored her overture, forcing her to drop her arm. "Enough pretense," he hissed. "The IDs I showed the sheriff are fakes. My name is not Santiago. I am Rodrigo del Toro." His voice resonated with arrogance and pride and a thick Spanish accent. "This is my daughter, Gabriella, and the man in the bed is my son, Alejandro."

Gil tensed. "Alex lied to us?" Alex had never talked about his background, particularly not the fact that he had family in Mexico.

Alex, looking almost frail despite his fierce masculinity, winced. "It's damned hard to answer that since I can't remember a damn thing."

Gabriella slapped his hand despite the fact that it was attached to an IV. "Language, *mi hermano*."

"Sorry." Alex grimaced. "I don't know who you people are, and I don't know why everyone thinks I'm Alex Santiago." His face reddened. "I'm trying. Hell, I'm trying!" The monitor beeped as Alex's blood pressure spiked.

A nurse came running, her brows drawn together in a frown. "I must ask all of you to leave the room. Mr. Santiago needs to rest. There is a small conference room at the end of the corridor. Feel free to continue your conversation there."

Alex's father and sister each kissed him on the cheek with muttered apologies, and walked out. As Gil watched, Bailey approached the bed and laid a hand on Alex's shoulder. "It's not your job to figure this out," she said softly. "There are a host of people looking out for you, and many professionals working on your case. I need you to quit worrying about things and concentrate on getting well."

Alex's jaw tightened, his hands gripping the sheet at his hips. "I have no clue if that man and woman are related to me or not. I remember you asking me questions when I was found. Do you really not know who did this to me?"

"I don't. But I will. Let me do my job. And in the meantime, try not to push yourself to remember. Everything will sort itself out in the end."

Bailey approached the conference room with a sense of exhilaration. This new information had the potential to break her case wide open. Gil walked at her side, his quiet presence comforting.

Once seated at the small table, Bailey and Gil faced the del Toros. Neither of Alex's family members looked encouraging, though they did hand over their real driver's licenses and passports, albeit grudgingly. But Bailey had been stonewalled by the best, and she wasn't afraid of a little conflict. She pulled a small notebook and pen from her purse. Ordinarily, she would do an audio recording of an interview in addition to entering notes straight into her laptop. But she hadn't come prepared for that scenario, and even if she had, she doubted if the two people eyeing her with varying degrees of hostility would agree to going on the record at this point.

Before Bailey could pose a question, Gabriella leaned forward, her anger clear, though it was not perhaps directed at Bailey. "My father is to blame for this *horrible* situation. He sent Alex here as a spy. No wonder my brother was kidnapped."

Bailey turned to Rodrigo. "Is this true?"

The intimidating del Toro had ice in his gaze. She imagined that a man like him resented being cross-examined by a woman.

He leaned back in his chair, simulating calm, though his posture was rigid. "I assume that what I tell you is in confidence?"

She shook her head. "Not at all. If what you divulge to me is relevant to my investigation, I have to share salient points with other members of law enforcement. But you should realize…the more I know of the truth, the more quickly we can solve this case."

The scowl on his cold but handsome face darkened. "I sent my son to Royal to gather information about Windsor Energy. My company, Del Toro Oil, is interested in a corporate takeover."

For several long beats, silence reigned in the room. A quick glance at Gil told Bailey that he was as shocked as she was.

Gabriella's dark eyes shone with tears. Her voice quivered. "It was the most wicked idea. *Madre de Dios*, Father. Alex could have been killed."

Bailey fixed her attention on Gabriella's father, speaking sternly. She felt sympathy for the sobbing woman, but she also knew this was a chance she couldn't afford to miss. "Start from the beginning, Mr. del Toro. When was the last time you talked to your son?"

"From the accounts I have read in your newspapers, a couple of days before he disappeared. At the time, I did not know anything was wrong. We had agreed to be in contact only infrequently, because I wanted to keep a low profile."

"What did you talk about that day? Was it privileged information?"

His jaw tightened. "No. We argued. He told me that he had *una novia*, that he had proposed marriage to her."

"And you didn't approve?"

Del Toro pounded a fist on the metal table, once. But with enough force to make his daughter jump. "I am one of the richest men in Mexico, Ms. Collins. Alejandro is my only son. He is destined to marry someone of his class and background. Not the daughter of a man whose business I plan to grind into the dust."

"Charming," Bailey muttered. "So the woman of whom you speak is Cara Windsor?"

"Yes. She bewitched my son somehow. Alejandro has always honored and obeyed his father. Suddenly, he was shouting at me. Insisting that he could no longer carry out my plan, because he had to prove to this Cara person that his love for her was real. We have telenovelas in my country, Ms. Collins, somewhat akin to your soap operas. I have seen the overly romantic drivel that passes for true love. But the real world is not so easily manipulated. I expect loyalty and obedience from my son."

"How did your conversation end?" Bailey was chilled by the man's hauteur.

"He hung up on me. I did not know until almost a week later that he had disappeared."

"Why didn't you come forward immediately?"

"My son is resourceful. And I did not want to tip my hand. I assumed that he would show up eventually."

"And when he didn't?"

"I was packed and ready to hop on a plane when the news service indicated that Alex had been found."

"But without his memory."

"True. These things, however, are usually temporary. I had great hope that he would recall his purpose in coming to Texas and would carry on with the job at hand."

"And when it became clear that his amnesia was not going to clear up overnight?"

His jaw tightened. "I realized I had no choice but to come here and identify my son."

"When you walked into the room, did he show any signs of recognizing either one of you?"

Gabriella spoke up. She had been standing with her back to them, gazing out the window. She turned now, her cheeks streaked with moisture. "Alex knows nothing." Her voice was thick. "My beloved brother knows nothing."

The tears started again. Bailey's heart went out to the young woman. Though Bailey had no siblings of her own, she could only imagine what it must be like to have a loved one regard you as a stranger.

She tapped her pen on the pad, her brain whirling with questions. "Do you plan to stay here in Royal for any length of time?"

"I will not leave until my Alex is fully recovered." Gabriella's words were adamant. Her father appeared less sure.

"We will see what happens," he said.

"You may be very unpopular," Bailey pointed out. "Alex made many friends in his time here, but no one likes a mole."

"A mole?" he asked.

Though both del Toros spoke immaculate English, perhaps the slang did not translate. "An informant. A corporate spy."

Gabriella wrapped her arms around her waist, her lashes spiky. "We need additional security for my brother, Ms. Collins. Now that the truth has come out, he will have more enemies. And whoever kidnapped him will no doubt realize that he is an extremely valuable asset, a bargaining chip if you will. They may try again."

"That will be a problem," Bailey said. "My employers are chronically understaffed."

Del Toro glared at his daughter. "Money is no object. I will hire bodyguards for Alejandro. And perhaps investigators of my own."

Bailey was startled to see Gil stand up, his face a thundercloud. "Watch your step, del Toro," he said, the words low and vibrating with anger. "This woman has spent more hours than you can imagine trying to find out why your son was kidnapped and by whom. You *will* give her the respect she is due."

The older man bristled, but he looked at Bailey and waved a hand. "I meant no insult. I am sorry if I gave offense."

As apologies went, it was weak, but Bailey accepted it at face value. She was stunned by Gil's impassioned defense of her work. Stunned and deeply touched. But she didn't need Gil fighting her battles. To allow him to do so would make her look weak.

She stood, gathering her things. "My job and my reputation are very important to me. And I have given my all to this case, though it isn't necessary for Mr. Addison to point that out." She scowled at Gil before continuing to address Alex's presumed family. "I appreciate your cooperation, Mr. del Toro. Ms. del Toro. I will have someone return your identification papers in the next hour or two. I assume you both will be staying with Alex?"

"If he will have us." Gabriella managed a weak smile.

Her father rose to his feet, as well. "My family will be together. And all of my resources are at your disposal, Ms. Collins. The sooner my son's attackers are behind bars, the sooner we can return home."

Eleven

Gil took Bailey's elbow as they walked across the parking lot. "Well, that was a surprise."

She nodded, her face troubled. "I felt like I was making definite progress with the investigation up until today, but del Toro's revelations put things in a whole new light."

"Does this mean Chance is off the hook?"

"I know you don't want to think he had anything to do with Alex's kidnapping. But I learned a long time ago that a surprising number of seemingly nice, normal people are capable of committing terrible sins in the heat of the moment. Chance certainly had motive."

"Because Cara broke his heart? You don't know that."

"True. And he doesn't act like he has a broken heart. But he could be hiding both his feelings and his guilt."

"We'll have to agree to disagree on the subject of Chance McDaniel," Gil said as he backed her up against the truck, his hips pinning hers to the door. No one was anywhere around. He bent his head and kissed her, sliding a hand around the back of her neck. "I wanted to stay in bed with you this morning," he confessed, his heart pumping as arousal brought his erection to full throttle.

Bailey's brown-eyed gaze clung to his. "I appreciated the privacy *and* your note. It was awkward enough as it was running into your housekeeper. I felt like I had a scarlet *A* on my chest."

He frowned. "Surely she didn't say anything to embarrass you." The woman had worked for him almost a decade, but he'd fire her on the spot if she had been rude to Bailey.

"Oh, no. She was lovely. But since you told me you'd never had a woman stay over, I felt extremely conspicuous."

"My housekeeper is not paid to speculate about my private life."

"People are human, Gil. She's probably discreet, because you're a good employer, but I *know* she was curious. Anyone would be."

"Change of subject," he insisted, kissing the side of her neck. "Tell me how soon we can be alone again."

Her wince gave him warning of what was to come. "With this new evidence," she said, "I have to buckle down on the case. I'll be spending time interviewing Alex's father and sister, assuming their story pans out. And I have to take a look at all my old notes in light of this new evidence. I can't have any distractions. You understand, don't you?"

She looked up at him so beseechingly, he had no choice but to swallow his disappointment and give her the support she deserved.

"I understand," he said, kissing the top of her head. "But I don't have to like it."

Bailey stroked her thumb across his bottom lip, her

fingertips cool against his skin. "I'll make it up to you. I promise."

He backed away from her, reminding himself that he was a grown man capable of delayed gratification. "I'll hold you to that," he said gruffly.

Fortunately for Gil, he was a busy man with many responsibilities. Even so, the subsequent week and a half dragged by with agonizing slowness. He and Bailey talked on the phone every day. Often more than once. But it was a poor substitute for having her in his bed...for feeling her naked body pressed against his. Somehow, without him even noticing, Bailey had become indispensable to his happiness. Without her, the days seemed dull, even with the presence of his precious son.

It didn't help that Cade asked about her constantly. The boy was single-minded in his determination to see her again. Gil made vague promises, but in truth, he had no idea when Bailey would be back under his roof.

On day eleven, he took matters into his own hands. Tracking her down took most of the morning. He finally found her vehicle parked at the courthouse...and waited with admirable patience for her to exit the building. When she saw him, her expression changed, but he couldn't pinpoint the mix of emotions that danced across her face.

Walking to meet her when she descended the steps, he slung an arm around her shoulders and steered her in the direction of his truck. He had parked in an adjacent alley, taking advantage of the shade from a large building, a spot that had the added benefit of giving them a modicum of privacy. "When was the last time you had a day off?"

"That's your best pickup line?" she quipped, smiling at him with joy in her eyes.

"Answer the question." He hadn't known for sure that

she would be glad to see him. Witnessing her pleasure erased some of the misery of the past ten days.

Bailey toyed with the buttons on his shirt, her fingers warming his skin through the fabric. "I don't remember."

"That's what I thought. You need a break. I know for a fact that you've been working dawn to dusk."

"And what would I do with this free day?" She glanced at her watch. "Now that it's almost lunchtime?"

Gil was getting desperate. Making love to Bailey… repeatedly…had not slaked his hunger for her at all. If anything, he wanted her more, because now he knew what it was like to have her in his bed. The memories made him sweat. Not to mention the fact that he was, at the moment, hard and hurting.

Bailey made no effort to move. Obviously she was aware that his erection nudged eagerly at her lower abdomen. He shuddered, dangerously close to ripping open the door of the truck and shoving her on the front seat.

He cleared his throat. "Cade spent the night with my friends again. I have to pick him up. In Midland. At four." He was barely able to string words together. "Come with me."

Her head shake was instantaneous. "Your parental instincts were good…thinking you needed to protect your son. I don't want to do anything to hurt him."

"I was wrong. I'll be honest with him."

"And say what?"

"That I like you. A lot. And I like spending time with you. But that your job and your home are in Dallas."

"What are we doing here, Gil?"

In her eyes he saw a mixture of resignation and sadness. Both emotions hit him hard, because he was responsible for putting them there. He stroked her hair from her face, cupping her cheek in his right hand. "Let's not analyze it, Bailey. I'm a man. You're a woman. Let's take a drive on a beautiful sunny afternoon and worry about tomorrow later."

"That's a dangerously open-ended philosophy for a man like you. Or a woman like me, for that matter."

He made himself step backward. "I won't coerce you. But I hope you'll say yes."

She waited long enough for his gut to tighten. Finally, she nodded. "I suppose it couldn't hurt. But again, we both have a vehicle."

He groaned. "I'll pick you up at Chance's place in forty-five minutes. Change into something that will be comfortable for a picnic." The day was not as hot as it had been earlier in the week, but still wonderfully pleasant for January.

"Who supplies the food?"

"My invitation, my responsibility."

She went up on tiptoes and kissed him square on the mouth, ducking away before he could grab her. "There's that nasty word again...*responsibility*."

Gil swiped the back of his hand across his forehead. Bailey's kisses, even quick ones, were lethal. "Believe me, Bailey. Taking care of you and your needs is pure pleasure."

Bailey didn't have much time to dither over her wardrobe. But she did intend to prove to Gil that she wasn't all business all the time. He had used the word *comfortable*. Men, however, were clueless at times about what was appropriate. If Bailey and Gil were picking up Cade at the home of a family friend, there was a good chance Bailey would be meeting someone. And she didn't plan to do so in old jeans and a T-shirt.

The outfit she picked out was one that packed easily, but

was comfy and fashionable at the same time. The short-sleeved, burgundy knit shirtdress was striped with navy and ended several inches above her knees. She paired it with navy leggings trimmed at the ankle with lace. Black espadrilles matched the black headband she used to push back her unruly hair. When she looked in the mirror after changing clothes hastily, the woman staring back at her definitely looked in the mood to play hooky.

Throwing a few things into a black tote, she gave her hair one last brushing and a warning to behave. Gil had seen her plenty of times with her hair confined for work. But because today he wanted her to let down her hair and goof off, she decided to indulge him both literally and metaphorically. The only thing left was to grab up a black cashmere cardigan in case the weather turned colder later.

Gil was right on time. No surprise there. She walked down the wide front steps of the ranch house and tried not to bounce like a giddy teenage girl. The prospect of a few hours away from work—in the company of the man with whom she had shared such dizzying intimacy—made her happy. A profound emotion, but one that was at its core plain and simple.

He helped her into the front seat of the truck and went around to the driver's side. "There's a belt in the center," he said, his lips quirking in a mocking smile.

Bailey smoothed her skirt over her thighs and put her tote at her feet. "I'm fine right here," she said, staying well toward the passenger door. Midland was fifty miles away. Boundaries had to be observed if they planned to make it on time.

As they pulled out onto the highway, Gil shot her a look, his expression amused. "You look cute today, Collins. I like it."

She rummaged in her tote for a water bottle and took a

long drink. "As much as I appreciate the compliment, I do want to point out that you promised to feed me."

"Patience, woman. The hamper's behind us, filled with all sorts of goodies."

She peered over her shoulder at the small space behind. Cade's little booster seat occupied one corner…a large rattan picnic basket, the other. "And how long do I have to wait?"

"There's a spot about twenty miles down the road where Cade and I like to stop. The property actually belongs to me, but I've never done anything with it. A tiny wet-weather stream cuts in in half. I thought you might like to have lunch beneath a little copse of cottonwood trees."

"You do know it's January. And all the leaves are gone."

"Use your imagination. I have a quilt."

"And sunscreen?"

"I'll cover you with my body."

Her jaw dropped and her face flamed. She'd been holding her own until that last comment. Now she lapsed into silence, her blood pumping with excitement. Surely Gil was joking.

Without asking, she reached forward and turned on his satellite radio. Picking an upbeat contemporary channel, she hummed along, relieved to have something to fill the silence. At times like this she realized that Gil was a man with one thing on his mind.

The turnoff to Gil's property was unmarked, nothing more than a narrow, rutted side road. The big truck handled the terrain comfortably, though Bailey was jostled rather more than she expected. If not for the seat belt, she would have ended up in Gil's lap.

When he finally stopped, at least four or five miles down the road, he rolled down the windows and cut the engine. "This is it."

The scene was peaceful, though remote. No one would disturb them. If another vehicle did approach, they would hear it coming long before it arrived. Above, puffy white clouds scudded across a sky the color of a robin's egg. A light breeze stirred the occasional flurry of dried leaves. With no power lines to mark the landscape, it almost seemed as if they had been transported back in time.

Bailey pressed her knees together, her hands clasped in her lap. "Very pretty."

Gil slung an arm across the steering wheel and turned to face her. "You look like a scared rabbit."

Bailey lifted her chin. "You flatter yourself."

His lopsided smile reached inside her chest and squeezed her heart. "I won't apologize for wanting you, Bailey. You're a very desirable woman."

Her cheeks were hot enough to fry an egg. She wasn't accustomed to talking about sex so matter-of-factly. She had been raised by a father who never did a thing to acknowledge that his daughter might need some education about her body and other personal matters. Nor did he offer her books or anything else to guide her in the murky waters of boy-girl relationships.

She'd been forced to stumble along on her own.

But she had managed. Refusing to let Gil know she was feeling off-balance, she managed a genuine smile. "You promised me a picnic. Food first. Flirting later."

"You've got your priorities muddled," he grumbled. But he grinned as he unloaded their supplies.

Bailey hopped down from the truck and helped spread the quilt. Gil's housekeeper had managed to put together a mouthwatering array of food, especially given the short notice. Chicken salad, fruit salad, homemade bread and oatmeal raisin cookies made Bailey's mouth water.

She was astonished to see Gil unpack a padded container that held china plates, crystal flutes and real silverware. "Wow. I was expecting paper and plastic."

He poured her a glass of champagne. "I may be a little rusty when it comes to dating, but I think I remember a few of the finer points when trying to impress a woman."

She sipped the champagne, recognizing that the taste alone declared it to be ridiculously expensive. "We're not dating, Gil." She had information he wasn't going to like to hear. So there was no reason to play games. "But I appreciate the effort."

He ignored her insistence on clinging to reality, choosing instead to serve a plate and hand it to her. "Dig in. I don't want you passing out from hunger on my watch."

They ate in silence for several minutes. A comfortable silence that acknowledged the beauty of the day and their unspoken contentment in sharing a stolen moment in time. Bailey sat cross-legged, her plate in her lap, while Gil sprawled on his side, his big body ranged comfortably as he propped himself on an elbow and ate one-handed.

The food was good. But after a while, it sat like a stone in her stomach. She believed in the concept of carpe diem, she really did. But she was also a realist. For every wonderful minute she spent with Gil, there would be a corresponding experience of pain when this whatever-it-was came to an abrupt end.

It was foolish and self-destructive to ruin a lovely interlude with such maudlin thoughts. Life didn't have to be perfect to be enjoyable. Happiness came in snatches, sometimes almost unnoticed. She wouldn't ask of Gil more than he was able to give.

When they were done eating, she helped him pack everything back in its spot. They had barely spoken a dozen words during the meal. Gil stood and carried the hamper and the dish tote back to the truck. Bailey pulled her knees to her chest and encircled them with her arms. For one brief moment, she allowed herself to wonder what it would be like if Gil were hers. Permanently.

She already knew he was an incredible father and an intuitive lover. It wasn't a stretch to imagine him as a loving husband, as well. He had softened toward her, given more of himself than she had expected. Closing her eyes, she entertained the fantasy of a rosy future.

Gil sat down beside her, his hip inches from hers. "Whatever you're thinking about must not be too pleasant. You have a tiny frown between your eyebrows." He rubbed the spot with a fingertip. "This picnic was supposed to be fun."

Shaking off her weird mood, she laid her head on his shoulder. "It *is* fun," she said honestly. "I get so wrapped up in my work, I sometimes forget how nice it is to do nothing at all."

"You've given a lot of yourself to your career."

Was there a veiled criticism in those words, or was she being overly sensitive? "I suppose I've let my job act as a substitute for family. I do have many good friends, but we all work together, so that has a downside. I'm rarely able to leave my cases when I go home at the end of the day. Not like someone who works in a factory or a department store. I'm always thinking about the next step."

"You care deeply about things, Bailey. I like that about you."

She linked her fingers with his, resting their hands on his thigh. Today he wore dark dress pants with a light-weight cotton pullover sweater in a shade of blue that echoed the hue of the sky.

His words of praise made her uncomfortable. Perhaps because she had grown up without that kind of verbal support. But also because she was hiding something from Gil. News she had received only today.

"Did you bring me out here so we could have sex?" she asked, the words far more calm that the riotous emotions pinballing inside her.

He squeezed her hand, his thumb massaging her palm. "It might have crossed my mind."

This would be their last chance. She knew it, and she was pretty sure Gil knew it, too. Their lives were too complicated to carry on an affair, clandestine or otherwise. Especially in a place like Royal where even the walls had ears. Turning to face him, she cupped his neck in her hands and pulled him closer for a kiss. "I was hoping you would say that."

Her blunt statement sent shock skittering across his face before it was replaced by hunger and determination. He reached into his pocket and extracted a series of condom packets hooked together. "I wasn't making any assumptions, but it never hurts to be prepared."

"Don't tell me. You were an Eagle Scout."

"Guilty as charged." He unbuttoned the top two buttons of her dress. "I also learned how to unhook a girl's bra with one hand, but that wasn't a Scout badge. More of an extracurricular activity."

"You're not such a straight arrow after all, are you Mr. Addison? I'm seeing you in a whole new light."

He eased her down onto her back with her cooperation. The sun blinded her, so she was forced to close her eyes.

His lips caressed her ear as he whispered. "You have no idea."

Twelve

Gil studied Bailey's face...the creamy skin, feminine nose, stubborn chin. In the broad light of day, her hair caught every ray of sun and glowed red with fire. Her slightly parted lips were the color of pale pink roses. Beneath her soft dress, her chest rose and fell rapidly.

In his head, the clock was ticking. He'd called his friends and asked for an hour of grace. Cade was having a blast and wouldn't begrudge the later arrival time.

Selfishness. All selfishness. Because Gil couldn't bear to let her go. Not without one last chance to bury himself in the tight, hot clasp of her body. To hear her cry out when he sent her flying. To lie with her in the aftermath and count the beats of his heart.

She had kicked off her shoes when she sat pretzel-fashion to eat her lunch. Now he studied her narrow, highly arched feet, bemused that the sight of them made him wonder for the first time if he had such a fetish. Her small toenails were painted the same color as her lips.

A tiny smile curved her lips. "I have my eyes closed, so I can't be sure. But it seems as if you've lost your way."

He stood and pulled her to her feet. "Your skin is turning pink. Let me move the quilt." With trembling hands, he dragged it into the patch of shade cast by the truck. "That's better."

When he turned back around, Bailey had pulled her dress over her head and stood facing him clad only in a lacy black bra and the leggings that clung to her shapely limbs.

He put a fist to his chest. "Be still my heart."

"Not that I'm criticizing, but it seems like one of us needs to remember the clock."

"I don't have to be there 'til five. I called them."

Her eyebrows went up, her expression scandalized. "You asked your friends if you could be late so that you and I could fool around in the middle of nowhere?"

He shrugged, not the least bit repentant. "That's about it."

She threw herself across the small space separating them, forcing him to catch her by the waist and lift her against his chest. He staggered backward, but caught himself.

Laughing down at him, her eyes sparkling with an innocent joy he'd rarely seen compared to her serious side, she rested her hands on his shoulders. "I do like this naughty version of Gil Addison. Very much."

For that, she deserved a kiss. Slowly, he let her slide down his body...like the hero's maneuver in a romantic chick flick. Her breasts nestled against his chest, giving him a mouthwatering view that was more provocative than total nudity. When her feet touched the quilt, they were both breathless. He tunneled the fingers of one hand in her hair, grabbing a handful and pulling her close. "And I do like this bra."

She rested her cheek on his shoulder. "I'm waiting to see your fancy maneuver." Grabbing his left hand, she brought it to her lips. "Show me what you've got."

To his eternal embarrassment, it took him three tries to unfasten the bra clasp one-handed.

Bailey just laughed. "I think I'm glad you aren't any better than that. No woman likes to be part of a crowd."

He pulled her down to the quilt again, this time knowing that nothing was going to stand in his way. "You'll never be one of a crowd, honey." She didn't know how true that was, but now was not the time to convince her with words.

He knelt over her, dragging the belt from around his waist and tossing it aside. Thankful that he hadn't worn his boots today, he kicked off his shoes and socks and unfastened his trousers. His erection bobbed thick and ready, tenting the thin fabric of his boxers.

Bailey licked her lips. "This feels wicked," she murmured.

"What does?"

She waved a hand. "Doing it outside in broad daylight."

"All the better to see you with, my dear."

"So that makes you the Big Bad Wolf?"

He grinned, shucking the pants but leaving the boxers for now. His sweater was far too warm, so he dispensed with it, as well. Bailey's interested gaze studied him from head to toe and all points in between. Her unconcealed perusal aroused him even more, if that were possible.

"You could say that," he said calmly. "I do have an inclination to gobble you up. Lift your fanny, woman." He peeled her leggings down and off, exposing thighs and calves that were long and shapely. The black lace panties he revealed matched the bra that now lay nearby.

He shook his head, trying to dispel a rush of dizziness, possibly caused by all the blood that had traveled south.

Bailey bent one knee, placing her foot flat on the quilt. The new position was provocative to say the least. "You okay?"

He nodded, hands on his thighs. "I need a minute. Looking at you may give me a heart attack."

"Very funny."

"I'm not kidding," he insisted. "Have you seen yourself in a mirror? You're a knockout, Bailey."

"It's the champagne talking. I may have to drive to Midland. I think you're delusional."

Trapping her thighs between his, he straddled her waist. The rocky ground beneath the quilt was hell on his knees, but the pain was a good thing if it kept him from rushing the moment. "Don't argue with me. I'm always right."

"You like to think so."

"If I kiss you, will it shut you up?"

"Why don't you try it and see?"

He crouched over her, stroking her curves with hands that trembled. Though the afternoon was plenty warm, small nipples pebbled at his touch. Despite her saucy bravado, he detected a hint of shyness even now. Her eyelids fluttered shut as he played with her breasts.

Her hips moved restlessly. He recognized the signs and felt the same urgency. "I want to make love to you," he said, the words ragged and hoarse. He felt as if he could barely draw a breath.

As she lifted up on her elbows without warning, she brushed the underside of his erection. "Then we're both going to get what we want." Her smile was pure female mischief.

Wiggling her hips, she used one hand to remove her last tiny scrap of underwear. He stood and followed suit. Donning a condom, he dropped down beside her and splayed a hand on her belly. "You dazzle me," he said roughly, with perfect truth. When he had fallen in love with his wife-to-be, he had been no more than a callow young man, hardly aware of the pitfalls that could loom in a relationship.

His marriage, or rather its failure, had almost broken him. When Sherrie ended her life, Gil had drowned in pain and guilt. During Cade's brief lifetime, things had gradually improved, because Gil had willed it to be so. But he had been convinced deep down inside that he would never have another chance at love.

Yet without warning, Bailey Collins had burst into his life. First he had resented her. Then he had wanted her. And now…he could barely even describe to himself what it was that he was feeling.

Bailey smiled at him wistfully, her eyes dark, mysterious. Was she even a fraction as hungry as he was?

Her hand wrapped around his erection, moving gently up and down, her fingers circling the head of his shaft. "I will always be glad I came to Royal," she whispered. Her voice broke on the last word.

"Don't say that. Don't write an epitaph before we're done."

Her eyes glittered with moisture. "Time's running out, Gil. Come here and give us both what we need."

He obeyed blindly, because joining his body with hers was what he wanted more than his next breath. Touching her gently, he felt the slick heat that signaled her readiness. He thrust slowly, closing his eyes at the sensation of rightness. Somehow he had to make this new turn in his life work. Somehow…

The sun moved inexorably in the sky. Already the rays

burned his back, the patch of shade shrinking. Each of his senses was painfully heightened. Bailey's skin was soft and warm everywhere he touched. The sound of their breathing mingled and floated away on the breeze. He smelled the fragrance of her perfume and the scent of his own sweat.

He withdrew briefly, though it cost him. Lightly, he teased the tiny spot that gave her the most pleasure. Her back arched off the quilt and she cried out as she climaxed, her body beautiful in its sensual abandon.

Before the last ripple of her orgasm faded, he entered her again, this time with far less finesse. Wildly he took her, over and over, until he felt a scalding rush of heat that ripped through his gut and drew a harsh shout from his parched throat at the end as he came endlessly, his head buried in the curve of her neck.

Bailey peeked through half-closed lashes, eyeing the buzzard that circled far overhead. Had she and Gil been comatose that long? She lifted her hand and squinted at her watch. Almost four o'clock. By the time they put themselves to rights and finished the drive to Midland, Cade would be waiting on them.

She nudged her lover's shoulder. "Gil."

"Hmm?" He didn't stir.

"We have to go."

"I bought us an extra hour," he mumbled.

"We've used that and more. I'm serious. Move, Addison."

He levered himself up on one elbow and blinked. "Crankiness is not a nice trait in a woman," he said. "Maybe you could work on that."

His droll humor made her smile. "Duly noted."

He helped her to her feet and she leaned into him, relishing the intimate feel of skin-to-skin contact.

Gil pinched her bottom. "I'd kill for a shower."

"Yes, well…you're the one who opted for alfresco shenanigans."

"You're the only person I know who could use that word with a straight face." He kissed her nose.

"It's a perfectly good word."

"Do they teach you that in law enforcement training?" He lowered his voice. *"I've got a sixty-two fifty-one down at the Motel Six. Shenanigans without a license."*

She burst out laughing. "You are so full of it. Get dressed before someone comes to arrest us."

They were woefully unprepared for the aftermath of their romp. Fortunately, Gil remembered a container of wet wipes in the glove box. With the aid of those and the items in her purse, Bailey was able to restore her appearance to some semblance of dignity and decorum. Though she had left home looking perky and fresh, she was now definitely disheveled.

It didn't help that Gil kept trying to snitch her bra or tweak unprotected body parts. And that was not the only distraction standing in her way. Who could help noticing the breadth of his muscled shoulders or the fact that even now, he was semierect. As if his hunger had been only partially sated by their coupling.

But at last, they finally climbed back into the truck and headed out to the highway. When they made it onto even pavement, Gil shot her a look. "I have a favor to ask."

She pulled down the visor mirror and checked her reflection, wetting her finger to remove a tiny bit of something stuck to her eyebrow. "I'm pretty sure you used up all your markers back in Dry Gulch."

"I'm serious."

"Okay." She closed the mirror. "Tell me."

"I'm meeting up with a friend tomorrow morning and

helicoptering three counties over to check on some stud bulls we hope to buy. I use a high school girl in town to babysit Cade in the evenings whenever I need her. But it occurred to me that he would really enjoy spending part of the day with you. Chance has activities for children out at the ranch, doesn't he?"

"Yes. But you don't have to do this. I don't need a grand gesture to prove that you trust me with your son. It isn't necessary."

"So you don't want to hang out with him?"

She sighed. "Of course I do."

"Then what's the problem?"

Now seemed as good a time as any to share the news she had been sitting on since midday. "I talked to my boss when I went home to change clothes."

"You called him?" Gil's jaw was tight.

"No. He called me. Apparently as soon as we left the hospital, Rodrigo del Toro did some digging and went up the chain of command. He informed my boss that he would assume responsibility for the investigation since he had unlimited funds and Alex was safely back at home."

The word Gil said under his breath was harsh. "So that's it? The state drops the case without a resolution?"

"No, of course not. But del Toro doesn't like working with a woman, and he holds the purse strings right now, unfortunately. They'll send someone else to step in for me here in Royal. And besides, I'm needed back in Dallas to take over a new case."

"When?" It wasn't her imagination. He was pale beneath his tan.

She swallowed, feeling on the defensive and not sure why. "This coming Thursday. I have to wrap up all my notes and file a final report."

"I see."

The next few miles passed in uneasy silence. She didn't understand Gil's reaction. It was no secret that her assignment in Royal was temporary. Perhaps Gil was angry because Alex's kidnapper hadn't been apprehended.

"I don't think you have to worry about public safety," she said, after at least fifteen minutes had elapsed on the dashboard clock. "We're almost ninety percent sure that Alex was targeted specifically. This isn't some rogue criminal who poses a threat to the general population. And now that Mr. del Toro is here—with money to spare for security details—I think any real danger is minimal."

"For Alex's sake, I hope you're right." Even after her earnest reassurances, his shoulders were still rigid, his hands white-knuckled on the steering wheel.

She bit her lip. Confrontation had never been her strong suit. But in ten minutes or so, the talkative Cade would be joining them. Before that happened, Bailey wanted to clear the air.

"You seem upset," she said.

Gil's scowl was dark. When he took his eyes off the road for a brief moment to look at her directly, the turbulence in his gaze shocked her. "And you're not?"

"I don't understand."

With a jerk of the steering wheel and a flurry of gravel, he pulled off onto the side of the road and shoved the gearshift into Park. Turning to face her, he shocked her with the vehemence of his icy tone. "Maybe I can explain it in words that make sense to a by-the-book government type."

"That's not fair," she said, tears stinging her eyes.

"Too bad, because that's how I see it." He was furious, that much was clear. "Your boss summons you, and it doesn't bother you at all that you and I are in the middle of a—"

She punched him in the chest, halting the flow of heated

sarcasm. "I *know* what we're in the middle of," she cried. "But we both know the statistics on long-distance relationships."

His lips twisted, his expression bleak. "So we were merely scratching an itch?"

"Don't be crude." She was shaking. Wrapping her arms around her waist, she held on to a thread of composure. "When we were together before…and again today. It was wonderful."

"The sex, you mean." His eyes were flat, accusing.

"What do you want from me, Gil?"

The silence lengthened. "Nothing, Bailey. Nothing at all."

Thirteen

She didn't know what to do. Never in a million years had she expected this reaction to her announcement. Inside, she grieved for the moment she would have to say good-bye. Of *course* she was sad. The thought of leaving Gil was tearing her apart. But moaning about it wouldn't help.

He moved back out onto the highway, merging with the traffic and eating up the miles to Midland.

The hostile silence shredded her nerves. "Tell me about your friends," she said. Anything to pass the time until Cade would join them. With the little boy in the truck as a buffer, the trip home wouldn't be so bad. At the moment, however, her head was throbbing, and she needed a distraction sooner rather than later.

For several long seconds she thought Gil was going to ignore her request. But finally, he inhaled and exhaled, and some of the tension left him. "We all went to college together," he said. "Got married about the same time. Had a son about the same time. They were an incredible support to me after Sherrie was gone. Food. Companionship. Advice when I asked. A shoulder to cry on."

"I can't imagine you letting down your guard enough to admit you needed help." It was a true statement, but as soon as the words left her mouth she realized they came out sounding sarcastic. Fortunately, Gil didn't take offense.

"I was a mess," he said with raw honesty. "I was still adjusting to being a parent, and I was terrified I would do something wrong. Plus, the guilt about Sherrie was overwhelming."

"It wasn't your fault."

"Doesn't matter how true that is or how many times you tell yourself so, the burden is crushing when someone you love commits suicide. I felt like a complete failure."

Only hours ago she would have slid across the seat and put her arm around him. Now, she didn't feel as if she had the right. "I'm glad they were there for you."

"My parents were, too. They still lived in Royal back then."

Bailey stared out the window. She was under no illusions that her father would ever rush to her aid in a similar situation. The divide between them was much too large to cross.

Perhaps that was why she hadn't let Gil see the depth of her despair about leaving Royal…about leaving him. She had learned early on in life to pull herself up by her bootstraps and deal with hardships on her own. Self-sufficiency had been one of the few things of value her father gave her. That and the certainty that if she ever had a child of her own, she would wrap him or her in love that would never be doubted.

In the midst of her soul-searching, the truck rolled to a stop in front of an attractive two-story home in an upper-middle-class neighborhood. Bailey touched Gil's arm. "I'm going to stay here." He had already told her he didn't plan to linger.

Gil frowned. "Don't be ridiculous. Come meet my friends."

She shook her head. "They're an important part of your life. If I go in with you, they'll make assumptions. Let's not complicate things."

"Lord, you're stubborn."

"Go get Cade. I'll be fine."

He stalked away, clearly displeased. Her decision was the right one, though. If Gil showed up with a woman in tow, his friends would think something was going on. And it wasn't. She and Gil were having recreational sex. To fill a void in their lives.

Wanting more didn't make it so.

As Gil walked back to the truck with Cade, he ruffled his son's hair. "I have a surprise for you."

"What is it?" Cade looked tired and not quite as bouncy as usual. No doubt the boys had stayed up far too late.

"I brought a friend with me."

Gil opened the truck door and helped Cade climb into the back. The boy grinned hugely when he saw who sat in the passenger seat. "Hi, Miss Bailey. Wish I could sit up front with you."

She leaned over the seat and patted his knee. "We have to obey the law. Wouldn't want Sheriff Battle to arrest us."

Gil climbed in behind the wheel. "What is this obsession you have with being arrested?" he asked, the words barely audible.

Wincing, she remembered using the very same words only an hour before…when she and Gil had stood stark naked beneath the afternoon sun. She closed her eyes, still

able to see in her mind's eye the two of them tangled together on an old, dusty quilt.

Ignoring Gil's provocative mutter was her only option.
"I have an idea," she said. "Why don't I ride in the back
with Cade? That way he won't be all alone."

Cade squealed with delight even as his father's face
darkened with frustration. "If that's what you want."

Cade chattered nonstop three-fourths of the way back
to Royal, and then without warning fell sound asleep, his
little body slumping against Bailey's shoulder trustingly.

Her eyes met Gil's in the rearview mirror. "Poor thing
is exhausted."

"Well, I haven't slept much for the past ten days. And
you don't seem to be worried about me."

"Gil!"

"I'm not going to let you pretend nothing happened,
Bailey. Things are different now."

"How?"

Fortunately for her, the question stumped him. Either
that or he wasn't willing to talk about it in front of his
son. Her blunt question put an end to any conversation at
all. She leaned her head against the window and dozed,
enjoying the feel of Gil's son pressed up against her side.

It was getting dark when they made it out to McDaniel's Acres. Lights in the farmhouse created a welcoming
glow. Cade never stirred when Gil opened the passenger
door and helped Bailey climb out of the backseat.

When her feet hit the ground, he continued to hold her.
"We have to talk about this. But now is not the time."

Her heart swelled with hope and longing. Was he going
to tell her something important? Something that could
change her life forever? For the better?

She knew he was right about timing. Serious conversation required privacy. But when he bent his head and

kissed her so very gently, she wanted to blurt out the truth. *I love you, Gil.*

Any anger and frustration he felt had melted away or had been stuffed into a box marked Don't Spoil the Moment.

She strained against him, feeling the urgent hunger that was never far from the surface. He didn't try to hide his arousal. Knowing he needed and wanted her was almost enough. But not entirely.

Wrapping her arms around his neck, she tried to read a deeper meaning into his tenderness. Did he feel anything for her beyond simple lust?

At last he released her. Breathing harshly, he rubbed a thumb over her cheekbone. "Don't fret, sweetheart. Everything is going to be okay. I promise."

What did that mean? What was he planning?

Before she could press for answers, he was gone…the taillights of his truck shining red in the gathering darkness as he headed home with his young son.

She walked up the steps slowly. Would it matter if she asked her boss for one more week? Or would that simply prolong the pain of walking away from Gil?

It startled her to realize that Chance was sitting on the front porch swing. And he was not alone. Cara Windsor stood abruptly. To Bailey's trained eye and with the illumination from the porch light, it was easy to see that the beautiful blonde had been crying.

Before Bailey could do more than say a quick hello, the other woman dashed down the steps, got into her car and drove away.

Chance spread his arms across the back of the swing, his long legs outstretched. "Was that Gil I saw bringing you home?"

Her cheeks flamed. She and Gil had kissed on the far

side of the truck. Chance couldn't have seen much. But it was still embarrassing. "Yes. I rode with him to Midland to pick up Cade."

"Cute kid."

"Yes."

"I hope you haven't planted doubts in Gil's head about me."

What could she say to that? "Gil makes his own decisions. And he's very loyal to his friends."

"Yes, he is. But men can do irrational things when a woman is involved."

Here was her opportunity. She dropped her tote on the floor and leaned against a post. "Is that what you did, Chance? To be with Cara?"

The smile faded from his face. "Things aren't always what they seem, Bailey. To be honest, I had no idea I was still on your list."

"She's not wearing her engagement ring anymore, is she? I like you, Chance. But it's hard to overlook the fact that she's been hanging around here instead of helping her fiancé regain his memory. Is there anything you want to tell me?"

He stood in one fluid motion and faced her, topping her by several inches. His move could have been threatening. But in her gut she knew it wasn't. "You've already questioned me, Bailey. Twice, if I remember correctly. And I told you everything I know about Alex's disappearance. Which is pretty much zero."

"And was everything you told me about Cara the truth? Did you perhaps leave out some pertinent details?"

"I did not. There's nothing more to tell."

"That tête-à-tête I interrupted a few minutes ago didn't look like nothing. Why don't you tell me what you were talking about? Why was she crying? Was it because the man she thought she loved doesn't even know who she is? Is that it?"

He folded his arms across his chest, his expression grim. "Cara's business is her own. If you want answers, you'll have to ask her."

"She didn't look like she wanted to talk to me."

"Perhaps not."

"I'm not the bad guy in this equation. Unless of course you really are guilty. In which case, you're out of luck. Because I never give up until I solve a case." She winced inwardly, because technically, that wasn't true. Not this time. Thanks to her boss, she was not going to have the satisfaction of finishing *this* investigation.

"At the risk of looking guilty when I change the subject, I'd like to give you some advice."

"Okay. I'll bite. What is it?"

"Gil Addison is a hell of a nice guy. And he's had some rough knocks. He deserves to be happy more than most anyone I know."

"And this concerns me how?"

"Don't let your passion for the truth hurt him. If you're not serious about a relationship, then walk away."

She pondered Chance's pointed remarks as she climbed the staircase to the second floor where her room was located. Was she giving up too easily? Did Gil believe he and Bailey had a deeper connection than she was giving them credit for?

Tossing her tote and sweater on the bed, she pulled her phone from her pocket and saw that she had a text from the man who filled her thoughts so completely.

Is it possible for u to meet me at the club in the morning...11:00 a.m....so I can hand over my rambunctious son??

She frowned as she curled up on the window seat. Under the circumstances, she would rather not see Gil again until she'd had time to process her emotions. But she had made a promise, and she couldn't disappoint the child caught in the middle of an adult conflict.

No problem. 11 it is. What will he want for lunch?

Gil's reply was swift.

Anything that ends with ice cream.

She tapped the keys.

So the diner would be good?

Definitely.

Resisting the urge to ask him what he meant earlier when he said everything would be okay, she added one last note.

See you then…

She set the cell phone on the bedside table and began changing out of her dress and leggings. Moments later, the text alert dinged again. Curious, she glanced at the screen.

My bed looks empty without you…

Torn between caution and excitement, she debated answering. Perhaps he would think she was in the shower if she didn't respond.

A second *ding* heralded another message.

I know you're reading this. I can feel your anxiety all the way over here. Quit worrying.

Easy for him to say. Since she couldn't think of an appropriate answer, she stood there staring at the prompt...

What we have is more than good sex, and you know it.

Her lips curled in a reluctant smile. How long would he carry on a one-sided conversation?

It's going to be a long, uncomfortable night. Every time I close my eyes and think of you, sleep is the last thing on my mind...

Finally, bravely, she replied with what was in her heart.

I miss you, Gil...

This time the long silence was on his end.
After two full minutes, his answer came.

I miss you, too, sweetheart. Sleep well...

Gil plugged his phone into the charger and prowled his bedroom, pacing from one side to the other. He'd told Bailey the truth. Everywhere he looked he saw her. Naked, sprawled across his mattress. Laughing. Panting. Crying out when he made her come.

How could two incredible sexual encounters turn his entire world upside down? Before he had gotten to know this woman, he had learned to live with loneliness, with sexual deprivation. Hard work and dedication to his son's welfare had enabled him to forget—most of the time—

that he was a man in his prime, a man who had the same needs as any other man.

Now that the genie was out of the bottle, though, there was no way he could go back to the way things were. He stopped dead in the middle of the room, struck with the knowledge that he was falling in love with Bailey Collins already. His subconscious must have known long before now, because the intensity of what he was feeling didn't happen overnight.

He'd been so busy stonewalling her and arguing with her that it had taken him all this time to admit she was exactly the woman he wanted. She was tough and strong and not afraid to do what was right. She was gentle with his son and passionate in Gil's arms.

The fact that she wore boring suits with naughty undies enchanted him. Knowing that she was a positive, upbeat person in spite of her sterile upbringing only added to his admiration of her character.

He couldn't wait to see her again. Was the emotion he had seen in her eyes this afternoon more than simple hunger?

Was it possible that Bailey cared about him in return?

He considered himself a fairly intuitive person, though he'd be the first to admit that women were complex creatures. Was Bailey leaving because Gil had given her no reason to stay?

From her perspective, he'd done nothing concrete to say that he wanted her in his life permanently. It shamed him that she could believe he saw her as no more than a good time.

The fact that she had a job and a life in another city complicated things. Was there any point in trying the long-distance thing for a while? Gil couldn't walk away from the ranch that was his son's heritage and his family's roots.

Not to mention the fact that the Straight Arrow provided a considerable number of jobs.

But was it fair to ask Bailey to give up everything and Gil nothing? He had a lot of thinking to do and not much time to do it. With Bailey being summoned home on Thursday, he had less than a week to analyze his gut feelings and make a plan. And then there was Cade. Gil was pretty sure what Cade's reaction would be, but he needed to sit down with his son and tell him what was going on. That his father wanted to include Bailey in their family.

Imagining the three of them as a unit healed a lingering hurt in Gil's soul. A dream had been stolen from him tragically long ago. Now he had a chance to start over, to have the traditional family he had always envisioned.

As he showered and climbed into bed, he realized that he was far too wired to sleep. By this time tomorrow night, God willing, he and Bailey would have an understanding. Perhaps he could fly to Dallas with her when she went back and they could shop for a ring.

He would use any means in his power to make her happy. Everything was going to be perfect.

Fourteen

Bailey arrived in town fifteen minutes early. She was genuinely looking forward to spending the day with Cade, but even more than that, she wanted to see Gil. His mysterious promises had lit a tiny flame of hope deep inside her, hope that he felt the same connection, the same craving to make their relationship more than a passing fancy.

When Gil's familiar big truck pulled up at the club, he and Cade hopped out. The two males were dressed similarly, both wearing jeans and cowboy boots with light rain jackets. The skies were dull, and the forecast called for showers.

Gil's coat was black to match his hair. Cade's was bright blue and reflected his eyes.

The boy ran across the pavement. "Hi, Miss Bailey! I get to stay with you today."

She grinned, kneeling to hug him. "Yes, you do. And

I'm excited about that. I thought we'd start with lunch if that's okay with you."

"Yes, ma'am." Cade beamed.

Gil touched the child's shoulder. "Take my phone and sit on the bench over there for a minute, please. You can play that new game we bought. I need to talk to Bailey."

Cade did as he was told, leaving Bailey and Gil to face each other. She felt self-conscious about being seen by club members, given their location. When Gil smiled at her, though, all that faded away.

He reached out to touch her, but apparently thought better of it at the last minute, because he retracted his hand. "I want to kiss you, but I don't want to embarrass you," he said.

"It *is* a fairly public spot. Maybe later?"

"No maybe about it." His gaze roved her face, his eyes burning with hunger. "I didn't sleep worth a damn."

"Me either."

They stared at each other.

He raked a hand through his hair. "I want us to talk. Tonight. Serious stuff."

"Sounds scary, but okay."

"When you bring Cade home this afternoon, stay for dinner." He paused, a spark of devilment in his brown eyes. "And breakfast. You can stay in the guest room if it will make you feel better. But you should know that Cade sleeps like the dead."

"Won't it look odd if I bring a suitcase with me?"

"Throw a few things in a shopping bag. He won't pay any attention, I promise."

Joy bubbled in her chest. There was no mistaking his meaning. This was as good as a declaration. "In that case, I'd love to come."

He glanced at his watch. "I've got to get going. You'll

be okay with him? If he gets too rowdy, time-out usually works."

"Don't worry. We'll be fine."

Bailey held Cade's hand as his father backed out of a parking space and drove away with a wave. She glanced down at her charge. "You ready to eat?"

Cade nodded enthusiastically. "I'm starving."

The kid could put away a lot of food. After consuming a full-size hamburger and a mountain of ketchup-laden fries, he declared himself ready for dessert.

"What does your father allow you to have?"

"Two scoops of ice cream with chocolate sauce and one cherry."

"A man who knows his own mind."

Cade cocked his head. "What does that mean?"

She grinned. "It means you are definitely your father's son."

After a brief rain shower that left the air sticky and the ground damp, the skies began to clear. Out at McDaniel's Acres, Cade was in his element. He had grown up on a ranch, so much of the activity was familiar to him. But because Chance's place was geared toward tourists, there were extras to entertain a young boy. Pony rides, a miniature rodeo-themed playground, and best of all, a new litter of puppies out in the barn, just begging for someone to play with them.

Fortunately the little canines were old enough to be away from their mother some of the time. Cade sat entranced, holding two of the six in his lap. They were mixed breed, part hound and part terrier.

For a young child, Cade was remarkably patient. He stroked their ears and talked to them with such sweetness that Bailey was hard-pressed not to get teary-eyed. She'd never been allowed to have pets as a child. A moment like this was one she would have treasured.

Cade looked up at her. "Which one is your favorite?" he asked, very serious.

Bailey studied the pups carefully. "That one," she said. "The smallest one with the black patch on his ear."

"He looks like a pirate."

"I agree. If he belonged to me, I think I'd call him Captain Jack."

"Do you have any pets, Miss Bailey?"

She shook her head. "I have to travel a lot for my job, and it wouldn't be fair to leave an animal at home alone."

Cade looked up at her with his trademark grin. "Whenever you're at my house, I'll share my pets with you. I have two dogs and a hamster."

"That's a very nice offer."

"Dad told me before he left today that he asked you to come to dinner at our house tonight."

She gnawed her lip. "Yes." She wasn't sure she was ready for this conversation.

"Do you like him?"

It was ridiculous that she felt her cheeks warm. "Of course I do. Lots of people like your dad. He's a nice man."

Cade rolled his eyes, looking like one of the precocious kids from the Disney Channel. "Miss Bailey, you know what I mean. Do you want him to be your boyfriend?"

She squatted beside him, hands on her knees. "I thought we talked about this."

"I'm not asking for a new mom. I just want to know if you like him."

The kid should be a lawyer when he grew up. She studied his innocent face, his features so like his father's. "Some subjects are for grown-ups, Cade. It's not that I don't want to answer your question. But what you're asking me is a private thing. Between your dad and me. Do you understand?"

His sigh was theatrical. "I guess so." He rubbed the puppy's head, his eyes downcast. "He likes you."

Oh, crap. How dignified was it to pump a kid for information? But the temptation was too much. "How do you know?"

Cade's expression was earnest when he looked up at her. "I heard him singing in the shower this morning."

Bailey frowned. "So?"

"So my dad never sings in the shower."

"Maybe he was in a good mood."

"I told you. He doesn't sing in the shower."

Clearly, Cade's logic made perfect sense to him. But Bailey was befuddled. "I'll take your word for it," she said. Reminding herself that she was a mature adult, she derailed the provocative conversation. "Let's go back to the house. Chance's cook promised to fix a snack for you."

Cade stood up, a piece of hay stuck to his pink, round cheek. He tucked his small hand in hers as they walked back to the main house. "I like you, too, Miss Bailey. Thanks for babysitting me today."

An hour later, Bailey took Cade up to her room and washed his face and hands and removed the worst of the mud from his shoes. She couldn't return him to his father looking like a ragamuffin. "We'd better head out," she said. "If I'm late getting you home, I'll be on your dad's bad list."

Cade giggled. "Dad says people aren't bad. But sometimes they do bad things. Is that how you get on the list?"

She picked up his jacket and the small cowboy hat Chance had given him. "I suppose so. Your dad is a very wise man." And a darned good father. Cade's maturity and grounded personality didn't happen by accident. It was the result of unwavering love and the confidence he possessed that his father would always protect him.

Her car was warm from sitting in the sun. She cranked up the air and then made sure Cade was properly strapped into his booster seat in the back. His eyelids were drooping. He considered himself too old for a nap, but he had played hard today.

As the crow flew, the trip from Chance's ranch to Gil's wasn't all that far. But the only way to get from one to the other was to drive the several miles out to the highway, hang a right for another six or seven miles, and finally, traverse the long road out to Gil's house.

The whole trip took thirty minutes or so. Cade, bless his heart, was conked out before she even got to the main highway. Keeping the radio turned low, she hummed along to a favorite song, feeling her pulse race at the thought of being with Gil again.

Imagining what he wanted to talk about was tantalizing. But she kept her anticipation in check. It was a long time until Cade would be tucked in tonight. By the time she and Gil talked, it would be late. After that, would he expect intimacy? With his son asleep down the hall? Or would they go their separate ways?

She couldn't imagine that. Not after yesterday. Gil looked at her with such intensity in his gaze that she was under no illusions about what he was thinking. He was a virile man. A sexy, masculine alpha male. And he wanted *her*.

The knowledge was exciting. But she felt restless and nervous. The sting of continuous desire was a unique experience. She didn't know it was possible to feel such gut-level need and still be so uncertain about the future. Would tonight be a watershed moment? Or was she making too many assumptions?

Suddenly, seemingly out of nowhere, a car pulled out to pass her. She grimaced. Impatient drivers were the worst. In slow motion it seemed, she glanced in the rearview mirror to look at Cade and almost simultaneously realized that the vehicle beside her was not merely crowding her accidentally. The driver jerked his wheel sharply and sideswiped her, pushing her toward the side of the road.

Her training clicked into gear. She had to outrun them. But even as she stepped on the gas, she despaired. The car responded sluggishly, the front right tire hung up in the ditch. With shaking hands she grabbed her cell phone and texted 9-1-1 to Gil…and seconds later to Nate. Then, *dialing* 9-1-1, she dropped the phone on the front seat and left the call open.

Her heart in her stomach, she prayed that Cade would stay asleep. The thought of him being scared made her angry. When she determined that her car would go no farther, she put it in Park. Bitterly regretting that she had not brought her service weapon, she debated her options. If at all possible, she would not let whoever had disabled the vehicle get near Cade.

At the moment, there was no movement from the other car. It had stopped, as well.

She glanced at Cade. His thumb was in his mouth and he clutched the small plastic pony that was his favorite. But still he slept.

Adrenaline flooded her stomach with sickening force as the door of the other car swung open and a man exited the vehicle. He wore a ski mask. Walking rapidly, he closed the distance between them. Though his arm was not outstretched, he had a gun in his hand pointed at the ground.

"Get out of the car," he said loudly, standing several feet away, nothing but glass between them.

"What do you want? I have money." She reached for her purse. "Credit cards. Cash. Take it and leave me alone."

"Let me see both of your hands."

Her brain raced. Did he know she was trained law enforcement? Was this Alex's kidnapper? Slowly, wanting to draw his attention away from Cade, she held up her arms.

The man's posture was rigid. "Get out."

If she did as he asked, Cade would be completely helpless.

The man took two steps closer. "Now," he shouted. "Or I shoot the kid." He placed the muzzle of the weapon against the glass of the back window.

Bailey glanced desperately at the boy in her charge. "Cade," she whispered. Knowing she couldn't take a chance that the man was bluffing, she unlocked the door and stood up. The assailant charged her and struck the side of her head, and her world went black.

Gil flew down the street toward the sheriff's office. He'd been in the chopper, still a long way out from the airport when Bailey's text came through. His return call to her went straight to voice mail.

Parking his truck haphazardly, half on, half off the sidewalk, he jumped out and ran toward the building just as Nate pulled up in a squad car, sirens blazing. Gil stared at his friend, his heart pumping like a madman's. Before Nate could speak, Gil grabbed his arm. "What in the hell is going on? I got a 9-1-1 text from Bailey."

"Me, too."

"Damn." Fear like he had never known swept over Gil. It was a hell of a time to figure out that his love for Bailey was neither halfhearted nor theoretical.

The door to the building burst open and Nate's second in command ran to meet them. "A 9-1-1 call came in about forty-five minutes ago. From Ms. Collins. She left the connection engaged so we could listen in. As crazy as it sounds, it appears that someone tried to carjack her. We sent personnel out immediately."

Nate frowned. "Where?"

"We located her cell phone signal. She was about halfway between McDaniel's Acres and Mr. Addison's place."

Fury choked Gil. "Where in the hell were you, Nate?"

"On a domestic disturbance call north of town. Woman took a butcher knife to her husband. I got back as soon as I could."

The cell phone at the young man's hip crackled. He answered it, and the blood drained from his face. "I understand. Thank you."

Gil felt a great yawning void in his chest. "Tell me," he said hoarsely. "Tell me."

The twenty-something kid swallowed visibly. "They found the car. Ms. Collins was lying in the road…unconscious. Nasty blow to the head."

"And my son?"

The younger man was pale as milk. "He's gone, Mr. Addison. No sign of him."

Gil reeled mentally, though he kept himself upright by sheer strength of will. Everything seemed very far away, the street sounds muffled.

Nate took his shoulders and got in his face. "Steady, man. We're going to find him."

"He's only a baby." Gil had spent the past five years making sure his son was happy and healthy. "How could this happen?"

The deputy spoke up, his voice shaky. "We have a team going over the crime scene. They're very good."

Nate still held Gil's shoulders. "Why don't you go to the hospital and check on Bailey? I'll text or call you every half hour. We have a protocol, and we're going to be all over this. Trust me, Gil. I'll search for that boy as if he were my own son."

Gil wanted to argue. He wanted to get in his car and comb the county. But without a lead, he was stonewalled. "You have to find him. I can't lose my son. I can't lose my son."

Nate released him, but still frowned. "I'm not sure you should be driving."

Gil glanced at his car. "I'm fine," he said dully. "I'm fine. I want to go with you." Everything inside him screamed in agony. The woman he loved was hurt…badly. But Cade needed him. The cruel impossibility of helping them both sliced him to shreds.

Nate hesitated, obviously weighing the pros and cons of letting Gil ride shotgun. "It's boring work," he said. "We'll be there for a while."

"Doesn't matter. I might be able to help."

"Fine. Let's go."

Gil saw nothing of the familiar scenery as it flashed by his window. When Nate screeched to a halt in front of three other squad cars and a van, Gil saw Bailey's car. Bile rose in his throat, but he choked it back.

They got out, and he strode beside his friend, stopping only when he saw the unmistakable stain of blood on the ground. *God in heaven.*

Nate quizzed the detective in charge. "Tell me what you know."

A female officer, her eyes shadowed as she glanced at Gil, spoke calmly and concisely.

"The damage to the victim's car indicates that someone sideswiped her, forcing her off the road. We have de-cent tire tracks, as well as several shoeprints. Assailant was likely male.

"Any blood *inside* her car?"

"No."

Gil walked on shaky legs toward the vehicle and peered inside. "His booster seat is gone."

Nate followed him. "That's a good sign. Whoever took the boy means no harm."

Just then another officer climbed out of the mobile lab in the van and jogged up to them, his face red from exertion. "We found this, sir." He handed it to Nate. "It's a tracking device. No telling how long it's been on her car. We're trying to find the manufacturer."

Fifteen

Nate cursed as Gil's blood congealed. Gil squeezed the bridge of his nose, his fear mounting. "I told her that what she was doing put her in danger. She wouldn't listen."

Nate shook his head. "This may have nothing to do with Alex's disappearance."

But Gil could hear the uncertainty in the sheriff's voice. The timing was too much of a coincidence. Someone could have kidnapped Cade, knowing that the wealthy Alex Santiago would pay to ransom a child's life. And now that Gil knew the truth about Alex… Good Lord. If the attacker knew the truth, also, then he or she was aware that del Toro was one of the richest men in Mexico.

Gil cleared his throat. "A kidnapping for ransom would be a best-case scenario. If that's what happened, they won't hurt him." But Gil's innocent son would still be scared and alone. *Goddamn it*.

Nate pulled out his phone and dialed. "I'm calling the

hospital. If Bailey wakes up...*when* Bailey wakes up," he said more forcefully, "she may be able to give us a description of the car and the attacker. In the meantime, we'll put out an Amber Alert."

"But with no vehicle description and no way to tell who Cade is with, that will be pretty useless." Gil's fury was misplaced. Nate was trying to help. They all were.

Gil spun on his heel and strode down the road, away from the vehicles, away from the image of his son being dragged from the car, away from the sickening vision of Bailey lying in the dusty road.

When he had put several hundred yards between himself and the uniforms, he stopped, eyes scrunched closed against the piercing pain that threatened to explode his skull. *Dear God,* he prayed. *Protect them...please...* His brain was in such turmoil, those were the only words he could articulate. Over and over. *Protect them. Protect them.*

Nate followed him moments later. "I need to know what he was wearing."

Gil rattled off the requested information, trying not to think about how he had helped Cade get dressed only that morning, the little boy chattering excitedly about his day with Bailey.

Nate answered a call and listened intently. When he hung up, he touched Gil's arm in a brief gesture of reassurance. "Bailey's going to be okay. She has a severe concussion and required several stitches. It was a bad wound, but she's stable. The head nurse will call me when they have further news."

"I don't know what to do." The six words ripped his throat like sharp glass. His whole adult life he had been a man in control, the one to whom everyone else turned in a crisis. What kind of father stood by helplessly while his child faced God knew what evil?

"I think you should go to the hospital now. Call me with updates about Bailey, and I'll keep you apprised of our progress here. It's going to be critical that we find out what she knows."

Gil understood the sense of what Nate was saying. But he had the odd and terrible notion that he needed to stay right here. At the spot where his son was last alive and well. As if by some miracle, Cade might teleport back to Bailey's car and this whole thing would be a dream.

He nodded slowly, his hands fisted at his sides. The sense of helplessness was suffocating. But if he could not help his son in the short term, his only other option was to be with Bailey.

He had closed his mind to the possibility that she could have been killed. He couldn't process that thought in the midst of his son's disappearance. The brain could only handle so much trauma before it shut down. Bailey was fine. And she would understand his delay.

Leaving the crew on the scene to search for any last clues, Gil and Nate headed back into town. Gil got out of the squad car and stood on the sidewalk. It was a beautiful evening. All around them traffic bustled. People smiled and waved. The world went on.

But for Gil, time had stopped.

Nate hugged him. An unusual enough occurrence that Gil was both shocked and taken off guard by the other man's compassion.

Nate stepped back, preparing to go inside. "I'll keep you posted, and you do the same."

Gil nodded.

"Talk to someone at the hospital. You may be in shock. You won't do anyone any good if you collapse."

"I'm fine. Really." It was true. He was encased in ice now. Nothing could touch him. He had a plan and a mission. Watch over Bailey. Find out what she knew.

Leaving a concerned Nate staring after him, Gil strode to his truck, climbed in and started the ignition. For a moment, he couldn't remember which way he needed to go to find the hospital. Realizing that Nate still watched him, Gil took a deep breath and shifted into drive. He backed up, pulled into traffic, and rounded the corner.

Five minutes later, he pulled off into a narrow alley, put his head on the steering wheel and sobbed.

Had it been only a couple of weeks since Gil and Bailey had visited Alex? Kissing her in the parking lot seemed like a dream now…a bittersweet dream. Tonight was supposed to have been a threshold for them, a day of reckoning. Instead, anticipation had crumbled into sickening fear for his son.

Gil walked into the hospital, sparing only a fleeting thought to wonder if Alex had been discharged. Thinking about Santiago…or del Toro…or whatever his name was made Gil's anger rise again. It wasn't Alex's fault that Cade was gone. Gil knew that intellectually. But it was easier to shift his fury onto Alex than to admit that he had failed his son.

The waiting room was empty. Gil approached the pleasant-faced older woman volunteering at the information desk. "Bailey Collins. Can you tell me her room number?"

"Are you family?"

He ground his teeth. "She has no family in the area. I'm her friend."

"I'll need to check with the nurse…"

He gripped the edge of the desk, closing his eyes briefly and reaching for patience. "Ms. Collins and I are in a relationship. Do you understand what I mean? I have to know what's going on."

The lady in the pink smock flushed, her eyes wide. "I'm just following rules, sir. But I will take you at your word."

While Gil waited, the woman made a brief phone call, then hung up. She smiled hesitantly. "Ms. Collins is not in the room. She's having a CT scan and a couple of other tests as a precaution. As soon as she's back, they'll let me know."

Gil swallowed, feeling light-headed. "Thank you." Numb and filled with a black void of despair, he dropped into an uncomfortable chair on the far side of the room. A TV on the opposite wall, thankfully muted but with closed captioning on, played old reruns of *The Andy Griffith Show*. Opie was small in this episode, maybe Cade's age. He had broken his arm falling out of a tree, and Sheriff Andy was carrying him into the hospital.

Seeing the tears on Opie's face broke through Gil's calm, letting in a torrent of rage and terror. He dropped forward, head in his hands, elbows on his knees, and prayed.

An hour later, a doctor approached him. Gil leaped to his feet, swaying when spots danced in front of his eyes. He had skipped lunch knowing that the housekeeper was preparing a big spread for tonight's dinner with Bailey, hosted by Cade and himself.

It was after eight now.

The man stared at him with the same compassion Gil had seen in Nate's eyes. "Mr. Addison?"

"Yes."

"Your friend is back in the room resting."

"May I see her?"

"Only for a moment. She's had something to help her relax and sleep. We're monitoring the concussion."

"Are you aware of the situation?" Gil asked, his throat tight with a combination of frustration and dread.

The doctor nodded. "You need her to wake up. I get it. But you have to understand that her body needs rest and peace to heal. If she regains consciousness right now, she'll have to relive everything that happened, and she'll become agitated. At this critical juncture, I can't allow that. I'm sorry, Mr. Addison. Hopefully if her vital signs are good tomorrow, I can reconsider."

When the man departed, Gil pulled himself together and followed the directions back to the Bailey's room. Standing in the doorway, he felt his vision blur. Struggling to stand up straight, he moved toward the bed.

She lay still as death, her skin unnaturally pale. A large bandage covered an area that included her temple. An IV was secured in the hand that rested atop the sheet. Gil stared at that hand, remembering how it had caressed him.

Knowing Bailey, she would have done everything to save Cade. But it hadn't been enough. Bailey hadn't saved him, and neither had his father.

Emotion roiled in him, hot and deep. This was the woman to whom he wanted to propose marriage. By all rights he should be sitting at her elbow, promising to remain by her side.

But though every cell in his body wanted to hold her and comfort her, a sick guilt held him back. How could he think about loving Bailey when the only other person he loved with equal intensity was out there somewhere? Alone. Terrified.

A male nurse stepped in to check BP and temp and adjust the flow of medication. "She's doing as well as can be expected, sir. It was a nasty wound."

Gil leaned against the wall. No one told him she had cut her face. A neat line of stitches closed a gash on her forehead. She must have hit a rock or some other sharp object when she fell.

"Should I leave my number?" he asked, his lips numb as he formed the words. He felt as if he were outside his body observing.

The man nodded, moving about the bed with efficient, gentle motions. "Write it on the board, if you will. Someone will get in contact with you if there is any change. If you'll permit me to give you some advice, sir, I'd suggest you go home and get some rest. You look pretty bad. Visiting hours start at ten in the morning. There's nothing you can do for her now."

Gil didn't remember walking back to his truck, but he found himself behind the wheel. In some dim corner of his brain, he realized that he was impaired. Driving as slowly as a geriatric en route to Sunday church, he made his way home, determined not to hurt anyone else.

Though it was cold, he sat on the back porch to call Nate. But there was no news. The investigation was ongoing. They were doing everything they could to find Cade.

The housekeeper had gone home. She left instructions for heating dinner. Gil fixed a plate of chicken casserole and ate five or six bites. Moments later he was in the bathroom throwing up.

He couldn't walk upstairs. He couldn't look into his son's bedroom. He couldn't look at the bed where he and Bailey had made love with such happy abandon.

His soul in ashes, he stretched out on the sofa in the living room and slung an arm over his eyes.

Bailey didn't want to wake up. Somewhere just offstage, pain waited, deep and vicious. She clung to the drug-induced fog, well aware that the alternative was not something she wished to face.

Hours passed. Maybe weeks. She didn't know. She didn't care. Nothing could hurt her in this wonderful cocoon.

But eventually, her cowardice was challenged. Professional voices, sympathetic but demanding, insisted she accept reality. Swimming toward the surface, she noted the various aches and pains that held her down. The crushing throb in her skull was the worst.

She opened her eyes cautiously. The light was bright. Too bright. Turning her head slowly, she focused her eyes on the man sitting by her bed. Frowning, she tried to decipher what was wrong with the picture. "Nate?" she croaked.

The sheriff jumped to his feet, looking down at her with an indecipherable expression. "Let me get the nurse," he said.

"No, wait." She frowned. "Why are you here?"

He rubbed a hand over his chin. "I wanted to see how you're doing."

"Gil?" The omission of his name seemed ominous.

"He's on his way." The answer was too quick, too hearty.

She closed her eyes, sifting through the layers of memory. A hospital. Something had happened. Suddenly, the truth crashed down on her. A wail ripped from her throat. "Cade," she cried, her head pounding. "What happened to Cade?"

Nate went white, and suddenly the room was filled with medical personnel. Seconds later, the fog returned…

Gil and Nate stood at the foot of the bed. Bailey's doctor was there, as well. The older man's expression was grim. "We've backed off the sedative. You'll have to be quick.

This morning her BP skyrocketed when she realized what had happened."

"What if she can't help us?" It was Gil's worst fear. He had hung all his hopes on the fact that Bailey would be able to explain things when she woke up.

Nate shifted from foot to foot, his gaze watchful. "We'll work with what we have."

Slowly, almost imperceptibly, Bailey returned to consciousness. The first sign that she was at all aware of her surroundings was the frown that creased the space between her eyebrows.

The doctor looked at the monitor. "She's in pain. As soon as you have what you need, I'll give her more meds."

Gil shuddered. What they were about to do seemed little shy of torture. "You have to do it," he muttered to Nate. "I can't. I'll step over here where she won't see me."

Nate stared at him. "I understand."

As Gil watched, Bailey opened her eyes. Only for a few seconds. But in a moment, she tried again, this time focusing on Nate.

He spoke softly, reassuringly. "Hey, there, Bailey. Glad to see you're back with us."

Her lips trembled. "I'm so sorry."

Nate touched her hand. "Steady. I need to know if you can help me. Do you remember?"

Her expression destroyed Gil. He had never seen such agony on a woman's face.

"Yes," she whispered.

Nate nodded, his face calm, his eyes kind. "Someone ran you off the road and hit you on the head."

"Yes."

"Who was it?"

"I don't know. He wore a ski mask."

"Anyone else in the car?"

"I think so, but I'm not sure."

"And the vehicle?"

"A beige sedan…newer model. Maybe a Honda. The plate was dirty, but it was Mexican, I think. Had a 367 at the beginning."

"Anything else, honey?"

"It all happened so fast. They didn't want money. Cade was in the car asleep. I had to do something…" Tears welled in her eyes and spilled down her cheeks. "Oh, God." She sobbed aloud, groaning as her involuntary movements caused her discomfort.

Nate squeezed her hand. "Relax, Bailey. It's okay. You may remember something else later. Everything's going to be okay. I promise."

The doctor pushed something in the IV and Bailey's body visibly relaxed.

Nate exhaled. "Well, at least we have something. It's a start."

Gil shook his head, his heart sick. "It's damn little."

"Faith, Gil. Keep the faith."

Sixteen

The next time Bailey awoke, she knew exactly where she was and why. Gil sat beside her bed, his eyes closed, his face gray with exhaustion. She wet her dry, chapped lips. "May I have a drink, please?"

He roused instantly, poured water from an insulated pitcher, and stuck a straw in it. Holding it for her, he helped her take several sips. "You look a little better," he said.

"You don't have to stay with me. I know you have responsibilities at the ranch. And you need to help Nate look for…" Her throat hurt. She couldn't say the last word.

He shrugged. "They tell me civilians only get in the way."

She closed her eyes, processing what he wasn't saying. "You're angry with me."

"No." The answer was quick. "But I warned you that the investigation was dangerous."

His calm stoicism made her feel worse. Inside, he had

to be a mess. And all because he had entrusted Bailey with his son's care, and she had allowed him to be kidnapped.

"Is there any word about Cade?" She could barely voice the question. Because she knew the answer in her heart. Gil wouldn't be here if Cade had been found. He would be with his son.

Gil's expression was grim. "Not yet. Nate has brought in off-duty officers from other counties. I'm footing the bill for the extra help. They will find Cade."

"You sound so sure."

His gaze met hers square on, and for the first time, she saw the extent of his torment. "I can't allow room for doubt. I won't." His voice was raw.

Tears burned her eyes, but she blinked them away. "I never should have let myself get close to you or to Cade. We're all paying for my selfishness."

His scowl deepened. "We both made mistakes. Both lost sight of our primary goals. You had a job to do, and I had a son to protect. Have a son," he corrected swiftly, the words cracking.

A masculine voice in the hall caught her attention. It sounded like the sheriff. Gil stood up. "I'm going to grab a cup of coffee. I'll be right back." He pulled the door partway closed as he walked out.

The men conversed in low voices, obviously thinking Bailey could not hear them. But she was able to catch words here and there, enough to piece together what was being said.

They were arguing about possible theories. Judging from Nate's line of thought, he was still expecting a ransom note. She strained to listen. Gil was audibly upset, his voice growing louder.

Suddenly, the voices moved away and the hall was silent. Bailey shrank back in the bed, tears filling her eyes and spilling across her cheeks. Gil would never forgive her, even if and when Cade was found. Her actions had brought harm to Gil's family. One moment she'd been standing on the cusp of something wonderful, and now it was all gone.

The pain made it hard to breathe. She loved Gil Addison and his son. But she had lost them both. Shaking and cold, she punched the button to summon the nurse.

Moments later, the woman entered the room, her expression concerned. "Are you hurting? It's not time for medicine yet."

Bailey *was* hurting. Her dreams had shattered into a million pieces. Now was a heck of a time to learn that a heart truly could break.

She gripped a handful of the sheet, her breathing choppy. "Is it okay if I limit my visitors?"

The woman frowned. "Of course. Is there a problem?"

"I'm willing to see the sheriff. But no one else. Please."

The woman's eyes were kind. "Would you like me to ask the chaplain to come by?"

"No." Bailey's throat was so tight she could barely speak. "Thank you." She couldn't bear to look into Gil's eyes and see his anger and disappointment and fear. It was better to make a clean break.

"I'll make sure your wishes are noted at the nurse's station and on your door."

"Thank you."

The woman left. Bailey turned her head to stare out the window. The sun was shining brightly, in direct opposition to her bleak mood. How soon would she be able to travel? Her boss needed her back in Dallas, and Bailey wanted to go home. If there was more work to be done in Royal, she would ask to be reassigned. She couldn't come back here.

In her heart, though, she knew she would not be able to leave until she had the assurance that Cade was back in his father's arms…safe and happy. Thinking about the alternative was unbearable. Surely a ransom note would arrive soon. One victim with no memory, one child too young to plan an escape, and Bailey—who had been unconscious when the child was taken. It was an impossible situation.

Her brief burst of energy faded, leaving her drowsy and deeply sad. Cade had trusted her. Gil had trusted her. And she had failed them both. The knowledge haunted her.

She drifted into sleep, her dreams dark and threatening. Suddenly, she was back on the road between Chance's place and Gil's ranch…

She felt the cold slither of fear. The rapid beat of her heart. She stared at the man. He was tall. Maybe older. But the ski cap obscured everything important. Think, Bailey. Think. She focused on the car. It was ordinary. A figure sat in the passenger seat. Again, she saw Cade, sweet innocent Cade in the backseat. Then, something brutally hard hit her head. She crumpled, the ground coming up to meet her.

Bailey woke with a start even as the recollection of panic pushed adrenaline through her veins. The bland sterility of the hospital room was recognizable and reassuring. With shaking hands, she pushed the button to call the nurse.

Gil sat beside Nate in the squad car as they sped through town. "I don't understand. Why didn't she call *me?*" he asked

"Don't know." Nate slowed down for a stop sign, noted the empty side streets, and kept going. He had his lights flashing, but the sirens were off. At the hospital, they parked in a restricted zone. Both of them jogged toward the front of the hospital.

On Bailey's floor, a nurse with salt-and-pepper hair stopped them. "Hello, Sheriff. Mr. Addison."

Gil shifted from one foot to the other, impatient to hear what Bailey had to say. And to see for himself if she was improving. "We're here to see Bailey," he said, wanting to add, *Get out of my way, woman.*

"I'm sorry, sir. Ms. Collins has restricted her visitors."

Gil looked at her blankly. "What the hell does that mean?"

The nurse frowned at his language.

Nate touched his arm. "Take it easy." He addressed the woman calmly. "I had a message that Ms. Collins wanted to see me."

"She does. But Mr. Addison, I'm sorry. You can sit in the waiting room down the hall."

Gil felt his temper rise. He was on a short fuse from worry and lack of sleep. "I think there's been some kind of mistake," he said, injecting ice into his voice.

The woman didn't budge. "She was very clear. Only the sheriff."

Gil's eyebrows shot upward, incredulity in his exclamation. "I was here a few hours ago. What's this about?"

Nate gave him a glance. "Keep your mind on the goal, buddy. Let me go in and see what she has to say."

Relief washed over Bailey when she saw Nate's head poke around her door.

"You ready to see me?" he asked.

She nodded. "Pull up a chair."

When Nate made himself comfortable, Bailey managed a smile, though she hoped it didn't look as false at it felt to her. "I think I remembered something. It may amount to nothing. So don't get your hopes up. But then again, it might be a lead."

He leaned forward, elbows on his knees. "Tell me."

"I'm almost positive there *was* another person in the car that ran me off the road…a woman in the passenger seat. I remember seeing long hair. And today, something clicked. What if this has nothing to do with Alex? What if Gil's in-laws took the boy?"

Nate's gaze sharpened. "That's an angle we haven't considered."

"Were you in Royal when Gil's wife died?"

"Yes."

"So you remember that his wife's parents tried to get custody of Cade? And nearly succeeded?"

"True. But Gil hasn't heard from them in almost five years. I still think someone might have been sending you a signal to get out of Royal."

"You're probably right. But it won't hurt to check this out, will it?"

"I won't waste any time." He got to his feet, leaned down, and kissed her gently on the forehead. "Thank you. Now concentrate on getting better. That's an order."

"Yes, sir."

He stopped at the door and turned, his expression no longer as excited. "Why won't you see Gil?

"My reasons are private."

"You might want to cut him some slack. He's been through hell. Worried about you. Sick about Cade."

"I understand what's at stake here. But I'm not Gil's responsibility. He needs to focus on his son." She was proud of the even tenor of her voice and the calm expression on her face.

Nate shrugged. "I've seen the way he looks at you, Bailey. What's a man to do when the two people he cares most about are in harm's way at the same time?"

"I'm not upset with him, Nate, truly. Cade needs to come first. That's as it should be."

The sheriff looked as if he wanted to argue with her, but the clock was on her side. "You have a new lead to follow," she said. "Quit wasting time here."

"Can I let Gil come in to see you?"

She shook her head, her chest tight. "No, thank you. I'm going to take a nap. Please let me know when you have any news."

The door shut behind him, and finally she could release the tears that had been building.

If Gil had learned nothing else in this crisis, it was that he didn't like twiddling his thumbs. A man needed action to feel that he was making progress. *Hurry up and wait* was a special kind of torture.

One of the deputies brought him a cup of coffee. "There's a cot in the back room, Mr. Addison. It may be a while before we hear anything. Maybe you could sleep for an hour or so."

Gil managed a smile. "Thank you. I'm fine." He'd lost track of the number of hours he had been awake. Sleep had been nothing more than moments of lost consciousness every now and then. His eyes were gritty. His body ached. And a great yawning emptiness filled the space where his heart had been.

He had truly thought Bailey would be part of his life. But now he wasn't sure. Had she picked up on his ambivalence? His guilt over wanting her when Cade was missing? God, he felt as if he were being stretched on a rack. In dark moments when the fear for his son threatened to make him go mad, he escaped into his memories, seeing pictures of Bailey in his bed.

The images sustained him and gave him hope. But now

he had lost Bailey, too. If he had to, he would give his life for either one of them, his son or his lover. But what if he didn't get that chance? What if his life was reduced to nothing but emptiness? Would he ever recover?

Nate answered a phone call, his demeanor intense. He looked almost as tired as Gil. But a weary smile lit his face when he hung up. "They have the full license number. And the vehicle it's associated with belongs to your wife's parents. We've sent the information out statewide, and across the border, as well. It shouldn't be long now."

"Unless they've ditched the car and are hiding out."

"They must have been keeping tabs on you for a long time. When they realized you were getting close to Bailey, they started tracking her, as well. I'm betting they planned every possible scenario. A deserted road would have seemed like their golden opportunity."

Gil leaned against the wall, his body suddenly limp with fatigue. "Tell me we'll find him, Nate."

"We will," the other man replied, the two words allowing no room for doubt. "We will."

The next time Bailey awoke, the sky outside her window was dark, and Nate had returned.

She scanned his face. "Any news?"

He shook his head. "No. But we're cautiously optimistic. Your theory about the grandparents was right on target. What we *don't* know is whether they took Cade immediately across the border or if they've hidden out somewhere here in the states to avoid detection. The Mexican authorities are assisting every way they can."

"I see." It was a tiny comfort to know that she had been able to provide some help, after all. But it wasn't enough. The larger question loomed. Was Cade safe? Dear God, let it be so.

Nate yawned, and she glanced at the clock on the wall. "Please go home if you can," she said. "I'm feeling much better, and the night staff nurses are wonderful. I'd appreciate it if you would keep me updated."

He stood and stretched. "Of course."

"Thank you for all you've done."

He gave her a lopsided smile. "Gil is my friend. And you're a very nice woman. It's what we do here in Royal."

After he left, she pondered his words. It was true. She had seen it time and again since she had been assigned here. The community was tight-knit. And they would go out of their way for one of their own. What must it be like to have that kind of security? That depth of loyalty?

Her friends back in Dallas were all great people. But they were spread out across the city. Bailey didn't live with the kind of neighborly closeness that thrived here in Royal.

She was lucky that for the moment they were including her in the circle. It was a warm feeling. And one she wouldn't mind replicating.

The nurse came in to check her vital signs and also to give her a pain pill. Bailey had insisted on reducing the dosage. She didn't like being so drugged, and the throbbing in her head had subsided somewhat, at least enough that she could sleep. She punched her pillow into a more comfortable shape and tucked her hand under her cheek. When she turned out the light, she felt entirely alone.

Seventeen

Gil loitered at the end of the hallway until he was sure his presence would go unnoticed. Bailey's room was dark. He slipped inside and quietly pulled a chair close to the bed. Gently, he touched her head.

Stroking her hair lightly so as not to wake her, he whispered the words he had wanted to say long before now. "I love you, Bailey."

Though he had barely made a sound, she moved restlessly in the bed and opened her eyes. "Gil? How did you get in here?"

A tiny light on the panel above the bed was the only illumination in the room, but it was enough for him to see the wariness in her expression.

He shrugged, unrepentant. "I sneaked in when no one was looking." He took her hand. "How are you feeling?"

"Much better. I think they're going to release me in the morning."

"Why did you shut me out, sweetheart?

She withdrew visibly. "I want you to go." Her voice quivered.

"Please, honey. Tell me the truth."

Her big eyes were tragic. "I can't bear to see the look on your face. I know you blame me. And you have every right."

If he had ever felt more like scum in his life, he couldn't remember it. Shame made him drop his head, his forehead resting on her arm. She was so brave and so strong, and he had hurt her by not reassuring her from the outset that he didn't hold her responsible.

"Oh, Bailey. I don't deserve you. What a jackass I am, my love. I've been angry at the world and scared out of my mind and weaving on my feet with fatigue. But I should have realized you would feel this way. You're so very conscientious. I don't blame you. I would *never* blame you. I know you would protect Cade with your life."

She stroked his hair, a tentative, tender caress that was evidence of her generous spirit. "You're not just saying that to make me feel better?"

He sat up and stared at her sternly. "The kidnapping could have happened if he had been with me. Now stop worrying."

"I won't stop worrying until we have some good news."

"Is it good news to hear that I love you?"

She paled. "You're delirious."

"Not in the slightest. Tired, yes. And frightened for you and my son, yes. But completely in my right mind. I was all set to propose when things went south."

She stared at him, mute.

"I didn't think it would be such a shock," he said. "Surely you knew we were headed in this direction."

She shook her head. "No. I thought we were breaking up."

He grinned despite his exhaustion. "Well, think again. I want you in my life. I need you and Cade needs you."

"I don't think I can talk about this yet. It feels wrong."

He sobered. "I understand. But don't make me stay away from you. I can't bear that on top of everything else."

Her bottom lip quivered as she reached out to grip his hand with hers. "He's coming back to us. We have to believe that."

Gil's cell phone vibrated in his pocket, startling him. He answered it, his heart in his throat. Two minutes later, he hung up, his eyes damp. Inhaling a harsh breath, he leaned over and kissed Bailey...hard. "Nate's team has found Cade," he said, his voice gruff.

Her lips opened and closed. Tears trickled from her beautiful eyes. "He's okay?"

"Completely." He shuddered, swamped by a wave of relief so strong it made him dizzy. "My in-laws were hiding out with him in Del Rio, hoping to slip across the border into Mexico when the furor died down."

"Poor little man. He must be so confused."

"We'll make sure he sees a counselor. And we'll smother him with love." He nudged her hip. "Move over, gorgeous." He raised the head of the bed and leaned back against the pillows, gathering her in his right arm, tucking her against his chest. "Nate is driving him back to Royal early in the morning. I want you to be there with me at the Straight Arrow, Bailey, to welcome him home. If the doctor thinks you're well enough to be released."

She nestled into his embrace. "Oh, yes," she said. "I wouldn't miss it for the world."

Eight hours later, Bailey sat on Gil's front porch wrapped in a quilt, waiting for Nate's squad car to come into sight. When it did, she stood up, the tears flowing again. She hated feeling so weak and emotional, but her relief and joy were profound.

Gil put a hand on her shoulder. "Save your strength, honey. I'll bring him to you."

The car pulled to a stop at the foot of the steps, and a door flew open. "Daddy!" Cade ran toward his father, the two males meeting halfway in a boisterous hug that was beautiful to watch. Seeing Gil reunited with his son healed a deep crack in Bailey's heart. She may not have solved the case of Alex's kidnapping, but that failure paled in comparison to this victory.

Moments later she saw Gil whisper something in Cade's ear. The child looked up and saw Bailey. His mouth rounded in an *O* of surprise and his little face crumpled. "Miss Bailey," he wailed, running up the remainder of the steps. "You're okay." He threw himself at her, and Bailey winced as she tried to catch him without jarring her injury.

Hugging Cade tightly, she rested her cheek against his dark hair. "I'm pretty tough," she said. "And you were awfully brave."

Gil eased his son away. "We have to be careful with Miss Bailey, Cade. Her head is still getting well."

After that, Cade insisted on seeing her bandages, and of course, they all had to thank Nate profusely. It was almost an hour later before she was finally alone with Gil. Cade had run to his room to play with his toys. His father scooped Bailey into his arms and carried her up the stairs to his bedroom. She could hear the steady beat of his heart beneath her cheek.

"You smell good," she said, burrowing her nose in the crisply starched fabric of his white cotton shirt. In honor of Cade's homecoming, he had worn his best Stetson and his fanciest pair of cowboy boots.

Gil flipped back the quilt and the top sheet and laid her gently on the soft mattress. "Don't flirt with me," he begged. "I'm trying to remind myself that your recovery has a long way to go."

"I want to sleep with you tonight," she whispered.

A dark flush tinged his cheekbones. "Sleep only. I won't be responsible for putting you back in the hospital."

She tugged his hand. "Lie down beside me."

He kicked off his boots, removed his belt, and stretched out on his back, careful not to jostle her head. He closed his eyes and breathed deeply. "I feel so damn good, I may just float up to the ceiling."

Linking her fingers with his, she smiled up at the surface in question. "I'd miss you," she said.

After a long silence, he spoke again, this time with no humor at all in his voice. "I've been waiting to hear you say something very important, Bailey."

She froze, the words stuck in her throat. It was a huge commitment. Turning her life upside down. Giving up everything she knew. "You're asking if I love you?"

"Yes."

Why was it that she could face down an armed assailant without flinching, but taking this leap petrified her? She'd been on her own for a long time. Self-reliant. Depending on no one. Her emotionally unavailable father had taught her that.

But Gil Addison was an entirely different kind of parent. And an entirely different kind of man. He cared. And he wasn't afraid to show it.

The question was, could she be as brave? She turned on her side and put a hand on his chest, covering his heart. "I do care about you, Gil. How could I not?"

Her wording was not lost on him, because he grimaced.

"Thank God. For a while there, I thought you only wanted me for sex."

She laughed softly. "Well, that *is* a definite plus."

He lifted up on his elbow, head propped on his hand. His crooked smile was the kind of thing that made good girls get in trouble. "As flattering as that is to hear, I want more than your luscious body. I know we have problems to sort out, but we'll manage it. I love you, sweetheart, heart and soul and everything in between. I want to make a family with you and Cade. I realize you probably didn't bargain for getting hitched to a guy with a kid. But he's a pretty great kid, and he adores you."

"I adore *him,* but are you absolutely sure about this marriage idea?"

"One hundred percent. I know you're very good at your job, but maybe Nate could use you here in Royal. Alex still doesn't remember anything, and del Toro is throwing his weight around with no real success. Even in an unofficial capacity, your skills would be important. You'd be the one doing the sacrificing. I get that. And I know it's not fair. But the Straight Arrow is Cade's birthright."

Even though her head throbbed and she felt weak, her heart soared. "I wouldn't mind learning how to be Cade's mom. That would keep me plenty busy for a while."

"Is that a yes?" His hand toyed with the buttons on her blouse, his thumb brushing her nipple through the fabric.

A sweet trickle of arousal swam in her veins, making her light-headed and giddy. "All the single women in town will be gunning for me if I lasso Royal's most eligible bachelor," she teased.

"You can take them," he said. "I have faith in you."

She searched his face, wanting desperately to believe she had found her happy ending. "You won't change your mind? It might be the endorphins talking."

He nudged her to her back again and laid his head on her flat belly, his fingers stroking the center seam of her soft khaki pants. "I've never been more sure of anything in my life. Would you mind terribly if we made a few babies together?"

She smiled, though he couldn't see. "It might take a lot of effort on your part." His intimate touch made her shiver.

"I think I can handle it. But we have one more hurdle, Bailey. One glaring omission. When a man lays his heart on the line, it seems like he's entitled to a little sweet talk in return."

"I see."

"But only if you mean it." He sat up, one knee raised, and stared at her with some anxiety. "I know I'm pushing you…taking advantage of you in a vulnerable condition. But I…"

She put a hand over his mouth, her gaze intent. "I do love you, Gil Addison. For now and forever. Come here and kiss me."

As kisses went, it was a doozy. Deep and wet and hungry. They were both breathless when it ended, and a certain part of Gil's anatomy was hard as stone.

He stared down at her, dark eyes flashing. "How long until those stitches come out?"

"Seven more days, give or take."

"Can you plan a wedding in seven days?"

"People will think we *have* to get married," she said, daring to tease him when he was primed for action.

He lifted her hand to his lips, his handsome face solemn. "We *do* have to get married," he said softly. "Because I'm not willing to live another minute without you in my life and in my bed."

Bailey blinked, totally undone by the sight of this rough and tough cowboy baring his soul to her. "Then I believe my answer is yes, dear Gil. Because I feel the same way. There's just one more thing…"

One wicked eyebrow lifted. "Yes, my love?"

"On our wedding night, I want you to wear the Stetson to bed…"

And as it happens…he did.

* * * * *

TEXAS CATTLEMAN'S CLUB: THE MISSING
MOGUL
Don't miss a single story!

RUMOR HAS IT by Maureen Child
DEEP IN A TEXAN'S HEART by Sara Orwig
SOMETHING ABOUT THE BOSS... by Yvonne Lindsay
THE LONE STAR CINDERELLA by Maureen Child
TO TAME A COWBOY by Jules Bennett
IT HAPPENED ONE NIGHT by Kathie DeNosky
BENEATH THE STETSON by Janice Maynard
WHAT A RANCHER WANTS by Sarah M. Anderson
THE TEXAS RENEGADE RETURNS by Charlene Sands

COMING NEXT MONTH FROM

HARLEQUIN
Desire

Available February 4, 2014

#2281 HER TEXAN TO TAME
Lone Star Legacy • by Sara Orwig

The wide-open space of the Delaney's Texas ranch is the perfect place for chef Jessica to forget her past. But when the rugged ranch boss's flirtations become serious, the heat is undeniable!

#2282 WHAT A RANCHER WANTS
Texas Cattleman's Club: The Missing Mogul
by Sarah M. Anderson

Chance McDaniel knows what he wants when he sees it, and he wants Gabriella. But while this Texas rancher is skilled at seduction, he never expects the virginal Gabriella to capture his heart.

#2283 SNOWBOUND WITH A BILLIONAIRE
Billionaires and Babies • by Jules Bennett

Movie mogul Max Ford returns home, only to get snowed-in with his ex—and her baby! This time, Max will fight for the woman he lost—even as the truth tears them apart.

#2284 BACK IN HER HUSBAND'S BED
by Andrea Laurence

Nathan and his estranged wife, poker champion Annie, agree to play the happy couple to uncover cheating at his casino. But their bluff lands her back in her husband's bed—for good this time?

#2285 JUST ONE MORE NIGHT
The Pearl House • by Fiona Brand

Riveted by Elena's transformation from charming duckling into seriously sexy swan, Aussie Nick Messena wants one night with her. But soon Nick realizes one night will never be enough....

#2286 BOUND BY A CHILD
Baby Business • by Katherine Garbera

When their best friends leave them guardians of a baby girl, business rivals Allan and Jessi call a truce. But an unexpected attraction changes the terms of this merger.

YOU CAN FIND MORE INFORMATION ON UPCOMING HARLEQUIN® TITLES, FREE EXCERPTS AND MORE AT WWW.HARLEQUIN.COM.

HDCNM0114

REQUEST YOUR FREE BOOKS!
2 FREE NOVELS PLUS 2 FREE GIFTS!

◆ HARLEQUIN®

Desire

ALWAYS POWERFUL, PASSIONATE AND PROVOCATIVE

YES! Please send me 2 FREE Harlequin Desire® novels and my 2 FREE gifts (gifts are worth about $10). After receiving them, if I don't wish to receive any more books, I can return the shipping statement marked "cancel." If I don't cancel, I will receive 6 brand-new novels every month and be billed just $4.55 per book in the U.S. or $4.99 per book in Canada. That's a savings of at least 13% off the cover price! It's quite a bargain! Shipping and handling is just 50¢ per book in the U.S. and 75¢ per book in Canada.* I understand that accepting the 2 free books and gifts places me under no obligation to buy anything. I can always return a shipment and cancel at any time. Even if I never buy another book, the two free books and gifts are mine to keep forever.

225/326 HDN F4ZC

Name _____ (PLEASE PRINT) _____

Address _____ Apt. #

City _____ State/Prov. _____ Zip/Postal Code

Signature (if under 18, a parent or guardian must sign)

Mail to the **Harlequin® Reader Service:**
IN U.S.A.: P.O. Box 1867, Buffalo, NY 14240-1867
IN CANADA: P.O. Box 609, Fort Erie, Ontario L2A 5X3

Want to try two free books from another line?
Call 1-800-873-8635 or visit www.ReaderService.com.

* Terms and prices subject to change without notice. Prices do not include applicable taxes. Sales tax applicable in N.Y. Canadian residents will be charged applicable taxes. Offer not valid in Quebec. This offer is limited to one order per household. Not valid for current subscribers to Harlequin Desire books. All orders subject to credit approval. Credit or debit balances in a customer's account(s) may be offset by any other outstanding balance owed by or to the customer. Please allow 4 to 6 weeks for delivery. Offer available while quantities last.

Your Privacy—The Harlequin® Reader Service is committed to protecting your privacy. Our Privacy Policy is available online at www.ReaderService.com or upon request from the Harlequin Reader Service.

We make a portion of our mailing list available to reputable third parties that offer products we believe may interest you. If you prefer that we not exchange your name with third parties, or if you wish to clarify or modify your communication preferences, please visit us at www.ReaderService.com/consumerschoice or write to us at Harlequin Reader Service Preference Service, P.O. Box 9062, Buffalo, NY 14269. Include your complete name and address.

HD13R

Nate's brow furrowed, his eyes focused on her tightly clenched fist. "Put on the ring," he demanded softly.

Her heart skipped a beat in her chest. She'd sooner slip a noose over her head. That was how it felt, at least. Even back then. When she'd woken up the morning after the wedding with the platinum manacle clamped onto her, she'd popped a Xanax to stop the impending panic attack. She convinced herself that it would be okay, it was just the nerves of a new bride, but it didn't take long to realize she'd made a mistake.

Annie scrambled to find a reason not to put the ring on. She couldn't afford to start hyperventilating and give Nate the upper hand in any of this. Why did putting on a ring symbolic of nothing but a legally binding slip of paper bother her so much?

Nate frowned. He moved across the room with the stealthy grace of a panther, stopping just in front of her. Without speaking, he reached out and gripped her fist. One by one, he pried her fingers back and took the band from her.

She was no match for his firm grasp, especially when the surprising tingle of awareness traveled up her arm at his touch.

He held her left hand immobile, her heart pounding rapidly in her chest as the ring moved closer and closer.

"May I, Mrs. Reed?"

Her heart stopped altogether at the mention of her married name. Annie's breath caught in her throat as he pushed the band over her knuckle and nestled it snugly in place as he had at their wedding. His hot touch was in vast contrast to the icy cold metal against her skin. Although it fit perfectly, the ring seemed too tight. So did her shoes. On second thought, everything felt too tight. The room was too small. The air was too thin.

Annie's brain started swirling in the fog overtaking her mind. She started to tell Nate she needed to sit down, but it was too late.

Don't miss
BACK IN HER HUSBAND'S BED
by Andrea Laurence,
available February 2014 from
Harlequin® Desire wherever books are sold!

HARLEQUIN®

Desire

ALWAYS POWERFUL, PASSIONATE AND PROVOCATIVE.

Nothing ... nce his best friend
bet ... plodes into a
Texas-siz ... la del Toro, shows
up ... e his heart..

But will the web of deception her family has weaved ensnare
her yet again?

Look for **WHAT A RANCHER WANTS**
from Sarah M. Anderson next month
from Harlequin Desire!

Don't miss other scandalous titles from the
Texas Cattleman's Club miniseries, available now!

SOMETHING ABOUT THE BOSS
by Yvonne Lindsay

THE LONE STAR CINDERELLA
by Maureen Child

TO TAME A COWBOY
by Jules Bennett

IT HAPPENED ONE NIGHT
by Kathie DeNosky

BENEATH THE STETSON
by Janice Maynard

Available wherever books and ebooks are sold.

Powerful heroes…scandalous secrets…burning desires.